To Val, a friend who started as a reader. Thank you for all your encouragement and cheerleading. Hopefully, one day we will meet in person. Til then, stay safe and keep smiling. You brighten up the day.

GRACIE UNDER FIRE

WOMEN AND WAR 1

RACHEL WESSON

LONDONGATE PUBLISHING

CHAPTER 1
LONDON, 1936

The lights dimmed as Gracie Thompson settled comfortably into her seat, sucking on the toffee her twin brother Stan had bought her as a bribe for coming to see this film. She didn't like science fiction films but she'd flipped a coin and lost. If she'd won, they would have been about to watch the latest Charlie Chaplin film. He really made her laugh.

The heavy curtains drew open, the credits already rolling. The cinema filled with the sound of Christmas carols, and onscreen a family sat around a Christmas tree, the children opening their presents and playing with their new toys. Gracie listened as the male characters began talking about the possibility of war. With the outbreak of war in Spain, that's what all the men she knew did these days. She didn't have to waste money coming to the pictures to hear about fighting.

She glared at Stan sitting beside her but he just grinned back; she could see the white of his teeth through the cigarette smoke. He leaned closer. "Just relax, sis, you might enjoy it. Next time, I'll take you to a comedy, I promise." She couldn't be angry with him for long. He acted like a hard man when his football friends were around but inside he was as soft as a sponge cake. He was the joker of the family, always quick to laugh, making light of any difficult situation.

She glanced at him anxiously. Staring at the screen, his blue eyes were wide with delight, totally engrossed. She worried about her brother, especially with all the talk of war. Stan was a dreamer or – as their dad called him – a lover not a fighter. But he'd become obsessed with learning to fly recently and spent all his free time reading about the war in Spain. Funny, she didn't worry about their elder brother, Frank, who was already in the army. But Stan, he was different. She edged closer to him as a chill hit her neck; what if Stan had to go to war?

GRACIE HEADED into the lobby as soon as the lights came on, smoothing out the new dress her mam had made based on an outfit Mrs Simpson had worn. The fitted waist and slightly flared, mid-length pleated skirt suited her figure. Thanks to her mam's skills, she was dressed as well as any of the other ladies exiting into Leicester Square. Stan had to hurry to keep up with her.

"Did you see the way the pilot downed the bad guy?" he said as he joined her. "I wouldn't have given him a gun. They could've shot him in the back."

Gracie turned towards him and rolled her eyes. "Stan, you talk as if you were there."

"I felt like I was. It seemed so real, especially the bit about the—"

She threw her hands up in the air, then slapped him lightly on the arm. "I was sitting beside you. I don't need a rerun of the film. I can't believe I wasted my night off."

"Gracie … People are looking. I said I'm sorry. It wasn't a woman's film. But I had to see it and Alice is on nights. Now I know why everyone's talking about it. Can you imagine how it feels to fly?"

"You and your flying." Gracie threw Stan an irritated glance and tried to keep her hands by her side. Her mother said she spoke with her hands when she was excited or annoyed. "Thanks to you, I'll dream tonight about being bombed out of my home. Why do they make films like this, anyway?"

A man behind them spoke up. "Maybe to shock us out of complacency?"

Gracie crossed her arms and turned towards the broad-shouldered gentleman who had interrupted their chat. But her mouth went dry as she looked up into the clear blue eyes staring back at her. She couldn't say anything. She wanted to look away, but his fixed stare held her gaze. Her pulse throbbed wildly; she resisted the urge to put her hand to her neck. She was tall for a girl but he made her feel short.

"Charlie Power, what are you doing here?" Stan said as he shook the stranger's hand warmly.

"Same as you, although I didn't force my young lady to come with me," the man replied, nodding at Gracie.

"Nobody forced me. I wanted to see what everyone was talking about too," Gracie said, not sure why she'd lied. "Please excuse us." Overcome by the need to get away, Gracie pulled at her brother's arm. "Stan, we had best get home. The buses will be busy."

She turned for the exit, but Stan placed his hand on her arm, preventing her escape.

"But, Gracie, I thought we were going for

some chips first. Mam isn't expecting us for ages. Charlie, would you like to join us?"

Raising her eyebrow, Gracie said firmly, "I'm sure Mr Power has plans for the evening."

"No, I'm free and would love to join you, if I wouldn't be intruding. Stan, you haven't introduced us. Please excuse my friend's manners, Miss…?" He took a step towards her, holding out his hand. "Charles Power, but my friends call me Charlie."

He leaned in and her breath quickened. The smell of Brylcreem didn't mask his manly scent. For one crazy moment, she wanted him to hold her in his arms. She'd never had this reaction to any of Stan's friends. She turned and grabbed Stan's arm, afraid she'd fall.

He looked at her, eyebrows raised. "Gracie, you okay? You're awfully pale."

She pulled at the collar of her coat. "Stop fussing, Stan. I'm fine." What on earth had just happened? Almost afraid to look at the man and terrified to touch him in case he could feel her trembling, she quickly shook his hand. "Gracie Thompson."

"Thompson," he whispered. It was the only sound she heard, even in the noisy cinema lobby. Everything around them had faded. "You're Stan's sister?"

"Well, I'm hardly his mother." She knew she was being rude, but she couldn't help it. "Nice to meet you, Mr Power. I hope you enjoy the rest of your evening. Stan, I really want to go home now. I've a headache."

"Please take your sister home, Stan. It's getting late, and she seems out of sorts."

Gracie lifted her head and caught him smiling down at her. She resisted the urge to stamp her feet. He was laughing at her, and she only had herself to blame. She couldn't wait to get home; she wanted to curl up in bed and forget tonight had ever happened.

Stan grinned at his friend. "She's been acting odd all evening. Gracie's normally okay, but then that's girls for you. Are you free on Sunday? A couple of us are going to the game. Want to join us?"

"Are you going to the game, Miss Thompson?"

"No, I can't – I've to work on Sunday." Gracie met his gaze. "Nice to meet you, Mr Power. Please accept my apologies, but I must go. I don't feel well."

"I hope you feel better and I look forward to meeting you again, Miss Thompson. Soon." Charlie turned his attention to Stan. "The game sounds great. Will I meet you at the Hare and Hound?"

"See you there. Good night, Charlie."

GRACIE CLOSED the back door behind her, grateful for the warmth of the kitchen.

"Hello, love. How was the film?" Her mam hadn't lost her Irish accent despite living in London for over twenty years. She was sitting in the back room, a basket of shirts at her side, peering round the doorway to the kitchen to greet her.

"Awful, Mam. It was all about a war – all

bombs, guns and planes. I could kill Stan for making me go. He loved it. He's outside now telling the lads all about it."

Her mam shook her head. "It's all that Francis Brown's fault, him running off to fight in Spain, leaving his poor mother behind broken-hearted."

Gracie wished she'd kept her mouth shut about the film. The whole street had talked about Stan's mate running off to join the International Brigade to fight against the fascists.

"If Stan did something like that, I'd murder him myself," her mam muttered under her breath before forcing a smile. "I just put the kettle on, so why don't you sit down and I'll make a cuppa."

Gracie put her bag down on the kitchen table. "No, Mam, you finish turning that collar. I'll do the tea. Is Dad still at work?"

"No, Gracie. He's in – listening to the wireless." Her mam cocked her head in the direction of the front room.

Gracie knocked on the door to the front

room before entering. It was in darkness, and she was just about to turn and leave when she made out the figure of her father sitting there, alone in the dark.

"You all right, Dad?" She shivered; the room was cold. They only used it for special occasions, like Christmas or when the whole family was gathered for a birthday. "Would you like a cuppa?"

He didn't answer.

"Dad?" Worried, she went to him and gently touched his hand. He jumped.

"Sorry, love, I was miles away. What did you say?"

"I just wondered if you wanted a cuppa? Why are you sitting here in the dark? What do you have there?"

"Nothing, love."

She spotted the glint of metal and felt a chill at the back of her neck. It was bad enough spending the evening sitting through a war film without coming home to find her father with his medals. She gave herself a shake and decided to ask him about them.

"Let me see, Dad. You never talk about your medals. Mr Brownlow next door has his displayed on the mantelpiece. I think Mrs B. spends her life polishing them, they're so shiny."

"They're just pieces of tin. They mean nothing."

"That's not true, Dad. Mam said you got them for being brave."

Her dad shook his head. "I wasn't brave. I survived. Precious few of us did. They had to give out medals to someone."

She looked at him, hunched in his chair, then gently said, "Dad, why don't you talk about the war? Is it because of Uncle Percy?"

"Aye, your Uncle Percy and millions of others. Did you know someone had this daft idea to form regiments from local areas so the men would know who they were serving with? It's bad enough when a stranger dies, but when it's your mates…" Her father took a deep breath then continued in a shaky, husky voice. "I'll never forget the noise. I expected the sound of shooting, but when it's mixed in with artillery fire, grenades, bombs and the cries of men mortally wounded … grown men crying for their mothers – you can't imagine what it's like until you're standing in the middle of it. And the smell. We were warned about poison gas, but nobody mentioned the smell of the mud. It clung to your feet and anything else it came in contact with. We often had to fling ourselves onto the ground. Into that mud. On top of the countless bodies buried under our feet."

"Dad, stop, please." Gracie knelt at his feet. Although he looked down at her, she knew his eyes didn't see her.

"You learned early on not to look too closely at that mud."

He stopped talking, and his glassy eyes scared her more than his words had. She waited until he spoke again.

"They sent us in against machine guns. Rows and rows of men mown to the ground. Mates I'd had since birth blown to smithereens all around me. It's a wonder any of us survived. And now they want to start all over again."

"Maybe there won't be a war. Mr Baldwin signed that agreement with the other countries, not to intervene in Spain."

Her father looked at her properly then. "It's only a matter of time before another war breaks out, Gracie. Too much unfinished business from the last time. That Hitler isn't going to back down; just you wait, he'll have troops in Spain yet. It will be just like last time, only instead of cheering my older brother and my mates off to war, I've to send my boys. Be thankful you're a girl, Gracie. War is no place for women."

Seeing her father like this terrified Gracie. So downtrodden and despairing. She could have sworn she saw a hint of tears in his eyes. But that made little sense. Men like her father didn't cry, especially not in front of their daughters. For an instant, she wanted to be a little girl again, with her big brave father who would keep her safe forever. The world was changing, and Gracie wasn't sure she liked it.

Her dad gave her hand a squeeze, and she stood up and headed into the kitchen to make their supper. Cups of cocoa all round with cheese on toast. Cook had shown her how to grate the cheese to make it more delicate, though her dad preferred a thicker slice on his.

Her mam pulled up the chairs to the square table in the back room where they always ate. Stan came in just as Gracie set the food on the table.

She rolled her eyes. "Typical timing."

"Smells good, Gracie. Did you tell Mam about the film?"

"I did but let's not talk about it tonight, Stan." Gracie threw a pointed look at her father, hoping Stan would pick up on the hint. As they ate, Kenny sneaked down the stairs to steal a slice of toast. "Thought you and the girls were asleep," Gracie teased him as she ruffled his hair.

He ducked away. "Get off, Gracie. I'm older now, nearly a man, aren't I, Dad?"

To Gracie's relief, her dad smiled at his

youngest son. "That you are, son. Do you want some cocoa to go with the toast? Gracie, fetch another cup and some milk for the lad, will you please?"

Gracie caught her dad's eye and they exchanged a smile. With relief, she saw he was almost back to normal. If only all the world's problems could be fixed with a hot drink and a warm sandwich.

"Gracie, what time are you leaving in the morning? Will I wake you up?"

"Yes, Dad. I've to get back to the house before the ladies wake for breakfast." She was thankful her parents lived in Lewisham, not far from Belgrave Square. It meant she could stay overnight with her family on her days off so long as she was back to work in time for the breakfast service the following morning.

Gracie kissed her parents good night before climbing the stairs to share her sisters' bedroom. She got into bed, careful not to wake the younger girls.

As she closed her eyes, all she could think

of was Stan's friend, Charlie. Her cheeks flushed, remembering his eyes widening at her rudeness. Would they meet again? She'd have to remember to apologise, if he gave her a chance to.

CHAPTER 2
FRANCE, OCTOBER 1936

The dew glistened in the early morning wintery sunshine; it was chilly but at least the rain was holding off. In the distance, she could see the townspeople getting ready to start their day.

It wasn't fair. Life was going on just as it always had. But this was no ordinary morning. They should be here paying their respects. Hadn't they been mama's friends, neighbours and the people she'd worked for?

It was all *his* fault. Penny swore revenge as she stood at the side of her mother's grave, holding a single flower. After everything she'd been through, she deserved more. Mama hadn't asked for much: simply to lie beside the man she'd loved and lost all those years ago. But, even in death, there were those determined to keep them apart.

Monsieur Albert coughed nervously. He was standing a little behind her, holding his cap in his hands. Penny was grateful for his presence, even though she knew it was only the promise of some francs that was keeping him with her. As he picked up the shovel, she sighed and threw the rose into the gaping hole. But she couldn't bring herself to walk away.

I can't leave you here alone, Mama. I won't.

Penny knew she was fooling herself. There was nothing here for her now. She'd little money and had no idea where she was going. *He'd* made it clear that he expected her to fill her mother's place, so she had to leave.

Holding her back straight and head high, she dried her eyes, picked up her belongings and walked back through the village towards the station. Some of the people she passed stared at her, while others looked away.

It took all she had to keep walking and not crumple to the ground. But no one must see how much she was hurting. She must keep moving. Later, there would be time to grieve.

Just then, she realised someone was calling her, and turned to see Madame Bayard on her doorstep, gesturing for her to come into her home.

She loved Madame, who had always treated her as family. But Penny was deeply hurt that Madame hadn't turned out to pay her respects. Penny was torn between ignoring the other woman and needing to know why Madame had forsaken her mother.

"Come inside, my dear. Please, come inside." Madame Bayard waited until Penny had closed the door before continuing. "I'm so sorry I didn't come to the burial, but he warned me he'd cause more trouble for you if I did, my *petite chérie*. Sit down, now, and eat some breakfast."

Penny looked at the table. "I'm not hungry." But even as she said the words, the rumbling of her stomach gave her away.

"Penelope, my darling, you are angry. It is understandable, but there are things that you don't know. Listen to me first and then cast your judgement. Haven't I always been your friend? Come now, girl. Sit down here and drink some coffee. It will help with the shock." When Penny didn't take a seat, Madame pressed a cup of black coffee into her hands. "Drink. Your dear mama thought that this day may come, and she trusted me with something special. She didn't want him to get his hands on it."

The old lady moved to the fireplace and, removing a small brick from the wall, uncovered a hiding place. Reaching inside, she drew out what appeared to be a compact black satchel, and held it out towards Penny.

"This belonged to your father, God rest his soul. It contains some francs, your parents' marriage papers and those of your birth. You will also find the address of his family in

London. I bought you a ticket on the next train to Paris; from there you will catch the new night ferry to London."

Penny shook her head and took a step back. "I don't want it. They wanted nothing to do with Mama or me when she was alive, so why bother now?"

The old lady looked at her, and Penny could see pity and love in her eyes.

"*Ma petite*, you need them. They are your family. Where else are you to go? You cannot stay, much as I would love to offer you a home. I can't protect you from him. You are already in considerable danger – you must leave here today."

"Why did she have to leave me?" Penny mumbled as the old lady came towards her and gathered her in her arms.

Openly weeping, Madame replied, "She died trying to save you. She loved you so much, Penelope – always remember that. Now you must go. You must seek shelter and grow into the fine young woman your mama dreamed you would become. One day, you will be strong enough to find justice, but today is not that day. You saw what happened this morning. People are so afraid of him, they didn't go to your poor mama's burial. I had to stay here. I couldn't risk not being able to give you the bag." Madame Bayard shook her head, pressing her hand to her lips as her voice trembled. "If I were a man or my Bernard was still alive, this day would never have happened."

The old woman put her head on Penny's shoulder, her body shuddering as she tried to suppress her tears. Penny realised she wasn't the only one hurting.

"Please forgive me. I know you tried to help. You were Mama's greatest friend, mine too."

The lady pushed her back gently, her eyes widening with fear. "Penny, you must leave. Promise me you will go to London, find your father's family."

Penny clenched her teeth but Madame ignored her. "They are all you have now. You must go to them. Write to me when you get there." Madame took out a hanky, wiped her eyes and next time she spoke, her voice was stronger, more determined. "Every day I'll look for your letter, *ma chérie.*"

"Why don't you come with me?" Penny hated her begging tone but if she was truthful, the thought of leaving France was terrifying as well as heartbreaking. It would be easier if someone she knew was with her.

Madame shook her head sadly. "This is my home and I cannot leave Bernard or my sons. Who would lay flowers on their graves if I leave? No, my dear, this is your journey. Just remember that you will always have someone here who loves you and who will wait for your return. You are the grandchild I should have had. Now go, child. Please, before he comes for you."

Penny hugged her fiercely. "I swear I'll come back when I'm older. He'll regret ever touching Mama. I won't rest until I show the world what he really is."

Madame Bayard turned away, quickly

making a ham-and-cheese-filled baguette and wrapping it in paper. Shaking her head sadly, she handed the food to Penny. "Take this for the journey." She held onto Penny's hand, looking her in the eye. "Don't let Alain take more than he already has. Your best revenge is to be happy. Grow into a woman your mama would be proud to call her daughter. Remember, she loved you very much. She gave her life so you could be free."

Penny swallowed hard before taking the wallet and tucking it inside her blouse. After one last hug, she ran for the door, heading for the train station.

EXHAUSTED, Penny climbed down from the train coach. She'd only stopped looking over her shoulder when she left France. Alain hadn't been waiting for her at the train station in Souvigné but she couldn't relax until she was sure he didn't get on the night ferry. As the train pulled into platform two in London Victoria, she was glad she'd brushed her hair and changed her clothes before meeting the customs official.

He fingered her papers. "Not much luggage, miss. Why have you come to England?"

Grateful her mother had insisted she learn English, Penny hesitated; she didn't want to mention the Hamiltons by name. She didn't know how well known her uncle was, given that he was a lord. "I'm visiting my father's family for a short break." She smiled, crossing her fingers as she lied.

"Where do they live?"

"In London, sir, near Oxford Street."

"Enjoy your holiday, but mind how you cross the roads. We drive on the proper side of the road so be careful."

She nodded in acknowledgement. "Thank you so much."

Penny walked out of the station as if she knew where she was going. There were so many people and vehicles of all sorts and sizes. Everyone seemed in a hurry, some bumping into her rather than trying to avoid her. She grasped her bag closer, feeling a little lost.

"I saw you on the train, dear, are you all right or do you need help?"

Penny glanced at the woman wearing a beautiful suit and looking nothing like someone who had travelled all night. "I'm going to Belgrave Square to see family. It's near Oxford Street."

"I know exactly where it is. Come along, dear, we need to get the bus. It's a pity your family couldn't send someone to meet you." The woman tutted. Penny didn't admit her family didn't know she was coming.

As they boarded the bus together, the woman chatted away. "Wasn't the night ferry wonderful? I'm so glad the service started earlier this month as it's so easy to catch a train from Paris to London. Makes travelling much faster, don't you agree?"

Penny didn't have to answer. She'd have

concentrated on her surroundings but for the fact the woman never stopped talking.

"Oh, it is so good to be back, you know. I loved India but all the heat and the constant storms wear a body down. Been over there several years as a lady's maid but my young lady got married and is heading to Singapore. She wanted me to come along but I couldn't face being that much further away. Breathe in that air, doesn't it smell like home?"

Penny didn't want to appear rude but all she could smell was rotten eggs, petrol and unwashed bodies sharing the packed bus. She closed her eyes for a second, remembering the smell of her home. Her mother had used lavender to keep the house smelling fresh.

"You don't say much, do you? You have a lovely accent and your English is quite fluent. You should get more practice speaking it with your relatives. Right, here's my stop. You may as well get off here at Hyde Park too."

Penny didn't argue but followed the woman, thankful she was such a chatterbox as

it gave Penny no time to think about her
nerves.

THE WOMAN LEFT her at the corner of Hyde
Park with instructions to walk down
Grosvenor Crescent, telling her that from
there she'd find the square.

Penny was grateful to her for leaving her
alone with her thoughts. She sat in the square
near the statue of Christopher Columbus for a
while, trying to compose herself.

*I don't belong here. I should have stayed
in our cottage back in France.*

Her papa had grown up in these surroundings yet left it all to live with her mama.

She fancied she could hear her mama
whispering to her – *Come on, you can do this*
– but she knew it was only the wind moving
the leaves on the trees. She stood up, straightened her back and walked resolutely towards
the house.

The door opened soon after she knocked

and a man dressed very formally in what looked to Penny like evening wear said, "Be gone. The family do not give to beggars at the door. Now go, before I call the police."

She assumed from his uniform and his mention of *the family* that he must be the butler.

She made herself speak. "My name is Penelope Hamilton. Please tell Sir John that his niece is here." She ignored the look of surprise and disdain in the servant's eyes. "Give my uncle this; he should be able to identify it."

She handed over the picture of her father but kept the other items Madame Bayard had given her.

The butler glanced at the picture, his face revealing nothing. He motioned for her to come inside and told her to wait.

She tried to hide her fear, acting as if standing in the hallways of such magnificent houses was something she did every day. Her eyes took in all the details, from the plush carpets to the beautiful ceiling roses. The smell of beeswax polish and freshly cut flowers was intoxicating. She'd never seen such opulence, but could not let the servants guess that. *Papa left all this to live in the village with Mama.* He must have really loved her.

CHAPTER 3

Glancing out of the window of the guest bedroom, Gracie caught sight of a young beggar girl sitting in the square. How lonely she looked, slumped forward as if the weight of the world was on her shoulders. She watched the girl, aged about fourteen she reckoned, for a few seconds until the girl looked up. Gracie stepped back, afraid she'd be caught staring. Then she laughed. As if the beggar girl would report her to Lady Louise.

She turned away but from the corner of her eye, she saw the girl was making her way towards the house. Surely she wasn't going to call at the front door? Mr Perkins would have the police onto her in no time.

She went over to the doorway. From there, she heard the knock and Mr Perkins' steps as he walked sedately towards the front door, his shoes squeaking slightly on the tiled floor. Then the door was swung open wide, judging by the blast of cold air flowing up the stairs. She heard Mr Perkins knock and be admitted to the drawing room where the family were seated, waiting for supper to be announced. The butler asked Sir John to come to the hall.

Gracie crept out onto the landing and held her breath for a moment as she listened, as if that would help her hear the conversation. But she couldn't make out a word, and then the drawing room door opened again, presumably to let Sir John take his seat once more. Perkins didn't close the door fully behind Sir John. She assumed the girl had been sent on her way.

Loud voices coming from the drawing room proved she was mistaken. Lady Louise was shouting, "You can't be a Hamilton. Look at you."

Gracie moved closer to the stairs and leaned over the bannister.

A younger voice, foreign-sounding, echoed upstairs. "Yet you recognised my ring and your husband in my father's picture. My late papa was your husband's brother. That makes me your niece."

Gracie wished she could see who was speaking. It couldn't be the girl from the square, could it? She'd been too slight to face up to Lady Louise like that. Whoever it was spoke English but with a funny accent.

She bit back a grin as she heard Her Ladyship interrupt her daughter-in-law.

"Louise, be quiet. My dear girl, are you really my granddaughter? Come closer, let me see you."

Then Lady Louise's haughty tones rang out crystal clear again. "Why didn't your mother come with you? Please, Mother, don't indulge her."

"Mama is dead," the foreign voice said. "That is the only reason I'm here."

"Now listen to me, young lady. Nobody speaks to me like that."

Gracie imagined how Lady Louise must look, her eyes out on stalks at the idea of someone speaking back to her. She wished she could be in the room.

"Louise, that's enough. This young lady is a guest in *my* house." Her Ladyship's emphasis on the *my* made Gracie smile. There was a daily battle of wills between the old lady and her son's wife. The old woman usually won.

"Louise, my dear, please take a seat. Can't you tell the young girl is exhausted? She's probably hungry too, aren't you?" Gracie nodded approvingly as Sir John spoke; he could be relied on for thinking of others. "I shall call for Perkins to escort you to a suitable room. There, you should unpack and dress for dinner. We'll eat in an hour."

Gracie yelped under her breath. If Mr Perkins found her eavesdropping, there would be murder. Lifting her skirts, she grabbed her basket and ran down the backstairs, grateful she'd had a chance to straighten out the guest room. Miss Harriet had used it earlier in the evening and must have tried on and discarded every dress she owned. Gracie had hung some up in the wardrobe in the spare bedroom rather than return them to Harriet's room. They wouldn't be missed. It wasn't her fault she was still doing chores at this time of night. The house was too big for the number of staff. Sir John insisted Harriet and her mother share the services of one lady's maid, but Rose refused to help with any of the additional chores.

Gracie only stayed because of Cook's loyalty to Gracie's mother and the fact she'd given her a position at the age of fourteen without a reference. Still, that had been three years ago. Gracie reckoned she'd repaid the favour a few times by now.

She almost fell down the backstairs in her rush to get to the kitchen, where, as she burst in, the blast from the cooking range hit her in the face. She pushed the hair out of her eyes, back under her hat. "Cook, you will never guess!"

"What's got into you, my girl? You know better than to interrupt me when I'm about to serve."

"No, hold dinner for a bit."

"Hold dinner? *Hold* dinner?"

Cook glared at Gracie before the servants' bell distracted her. "What now? That's coming from the guest room. Nobody said anything to me about guests."

Cook looked at the dishes laid out on her table as if wondering which dish could stretch to cater for more people. To Gracie's mind, there was enough to feed the whole of London. What her father wouldn't give for meat as tender as the fillet heading to the dining room. Or a piece of whole salmon that would melt in your mouth. Cook was one of the best around and knew presentation of food mattered almost as much as the taste. To the gentry, anyway.

Gracie said, "That's what I was trying to

tell you. There's a young girl just arrived. You should see the state of her. She looks like a beggar, but she says she's Her Ladyship's granddaughter. She has just had a row with Lady Louise."

Cook stared at Gracie. "A beggar, the granddaughter of Her Ladyship? Of all the rubbish you have ever come out with, Grace Thompson, that takes the biscuit."

"Honest, Cook, she just turned up out of nowhere. I saw her across in the square. She looked ever so young and sad before she stood up and walked up to the front door. She's wearing some ring that Lady Louise recognised—"

"Hush, girl, I can't keep up with you talking so fast. You'd best go answer that bell."

With that, the cook turned back to her cooking, but Gracie heard her muttering, "Rings, beggars – what next?"

~

GRACIE RAN up the backstairs and careened straight into Mr Perkins.

"Oops. Sorry, Mr Perkins. I didn't see you there."

"That much is obvious, Thompson. What have I told you about running in the house? An obedient servant is always unseen, and you cannot be invisible if you are crashing into people. Now, see what you can do to turn our visitor into someone fit to sit down to dinner with Her Ladyship." He gestured towards the guest bedroom.

Out of habit, Gracie knocked at the door before entering, but there was no answer. As she went into the room, the young girl sitting on the bed didn't seem to notice her. On closer inspection, she wasn't dirty or bedraggled as she'd appeared from the window; though her clothes were ragged, they were clean, just different looking.

"Miss, my name's Thompson, and I'm here to help you dress." She noticed the glistening tears before the girl tried to brush them away. She looked younger close up, maybe not even fourteen. "Aw, miss, don't cry. We'll soon have you ready for dinner. Milady's bark is worse than her bite. Why don't you undress while I run your bath, and then we'll find you something to wear? I think one of Miss Harriet's old dresses in the wardrobe over there will fit you. Don't look so worried. Miss Harriet has so many. She won't miss one."

The girl undressed herself before she moved to the bathroom. Gracie's heart went out to her, sitting sobbing in the bath. She fought an urge to go in and give her a big cuddle. That wouldn't be appropriate if she was, as she claimed, Sir John's niece. What on earth was she doing here all alone? Had she really travelled from France by herself? Gracie was tempted to ask, but now was not the right time. Instead, she continued chatting to give the girl time to pull herself together.

"Here, let me help you wash your hair. It's a beautiful colour, almost purple it's so dark. And so long. Now, what's your name, miss?" asked Gracie, as she washed and dried her new charge before moving over to the wardrobe to select a dress.

"Penelope," the girl whispered. "But everyone calls me Penny."

Not people like me, Gracie thought. She rifled through the dresses until she came to the one, she thought would suit the girl best.

"Oh, look, Miss Penelope. This is just perfect."

She held up a rose silk dress, waiting for the girl's approval. Despite Penny's distress, her eyes widened with wonder as she stared at the silk gown.

"For me? *C'est magnifique* … I mean beautiful, but I cannot wear it."

"Yes, you can, and you will, miss. Your grandmother expects you to look like a lady of the house, and if you don't, it will be me who gets into trouble."

"But…"

"No buts. Now, get a move on or we'll both be in hot water with your grandmother."

Penny looked confused. "Hot water? She will want me to have another bath?"

Gracie laughed. "Oh, no, miss. That's just a saying. It means Her Ladyship will be angry if we don't get you downstairs. Now, put on this dress and then hold still while I do your hair."

Gracie worked all Penny's dark curls into a cascade of ringlets draping around her shoulders. The rose silk dress brought out her colouring, making her look older than when she first arrived.

Penny stood in front of the mirror. "I look like Mama," the girl whispered, as a tear rolled down her face.

"There, now, miss, you look beautiful. Hard to believe you are the same person. That colour suits you. Miss Harriet, she's your cousin, will burst a gut when she sees you in that outfit. She's so used to being the belle of the ball around here. You don't look a bit like her with those dark eyes and that hair. Altogether a prettier picture, although don't you go telling her I said that."

"Thompson – do I have to call you that?"

"Well, miss, people like you do. None of

the family ever calls us by our Christian names. But, well, my name is Gracie."

"Thank you, Gracie, for being so nice to me and for making me look like this."

"Oh, go on with you, Miss Penelope. It is easy to make someone who looks like you look good. There, now, don't you cry again. Your tears will ruin all my hard work." She softened her words with a smile.

Penny smiled back. "*Merci*, Gracie."

Gracie gathered that was the young lady's way of saying thanks. She was a nice girl, far too young and unsophisticated to have to deal with Lady Louise. Gracie crossed her fingers that she'd appeal to Her Ladyship. The old lady could fight off Lady Louise with both eyes closed.

"Come on now, Miss Penny, you can't keep Her Ladyship waiting any longer. When Master Hugo, your cousin, is home for dinner, he always goes to your grandma first to kiss her hand before he greets his parents. You should follow his example. It's a pity he's out tonight; he'd help smooth the waters – but let's just be thankful Miss Harriet is at dinner with friends."

"Until tonight, I did not even know what my uncle looks like."

"Oh, he's a lovely man, but only when Lady Louise isn't around. He may wear the trousers, but she's the boss. But this is Her Ladyship's house, and she isn't likely to let anyone forget that. She seems to delight in upsetting your Aunt Louise. But hark at me, I'm telling you all the secrets. My big mouth will be the undoing of me yet. Come on, off you go now. I'll come back to help you dress for bed."

Penny smiled shyly. "I am not a child, Gracie. I can go to bed on my own."

"That's as maybe, but I'll still be here. Just you wait and see."

AFTER TIDYING THE BEDROOM, Gracie returned to the kitchen and told Cook, "Poor girl, she's trying so hard to be brave."

Cook nodded. "Mr Perkins told me what she's told the family. I remember Mr James, that young lady's father. He looked ever so handsome going off to war in his uniform. He didn't want to go, you know. He mentioned becoming a conscientious objector once, but he wasn't a coward. He was such a gentle soul. You should have seen him with his animals. He used to look after all sorts, from birds to a wee fox that the milk cart ran over. He didn't believe in killing anything, let alone another human being." Cook sighed. "His father couldn't understand him and they had had a big falling out. They didn't speak to each other for years. It got worse when he met the French woman and let the family know he was staying in France. That devastated Her Ladyship. She'd always thought one day he'd come home, but that didn't happen."

"Poor Penny."

"Aye, poor wee mite, but I feel sorry for Her Ladyship, too. There's nothing worse than burying a child of your own. It's not natural." Cook sniffed and turned her back.

CHAPTER 4

Secretly, Penny was glad that Gracie was going to be there when she came back. As she made her way downstairs to dinner, she couldn't remember the last time she'd felt so nervous. She wished her mother was here with her. When Perkins announced her, he almost had to push her into the drawing room, where it was customary for the family to gather before sitting down for dinner.

Everyone was staring at her, and for an awful minute, Penny couldn't remember how to walk. She'd to conquer her impulse to run, not just out of the room, but out of the country. She remembered Gracie's advice, and walked over to her grandmother before curt-sying prettily and kissing her hand. The older lady's reaction confirmed that she'd acted correctly.

One of the two gentlemen present stood up. Penny's heart beat faster, as she looked again at the man who looked just like her papa, only older of course. Her mouth dry, she tried to say something, but found she couldn't. Her feet sank into the lush carpet, incapable of moving. To her relief, he came forward and greeted her warmly.

"Penelope, let's start again, shall we? I'm your uncle John. I'm so glad that you sought us out in your time of need. I'm just sorry that your dear mother could not come with you. My condolences on your loss."

The silence lingered before she found her voice.

"Thank you, Sir John."

"Uncle John will do just fine. You have already met my wife, Louise, so let me intro-duce you to her brother, Anthony."

The second gentleman came forward. "It

is lovely to meet you, my dear. I was a friend of your father's. We went to school together. He was a lovely chap and quite devoted to your mother. I only met her once, but she was enchanting. I see the apple hasn't fallen far from the tree."

"Please excuse me, but the apple and a tree? I'm sorry, I don't understand."

Penny's confused expression caused the other guests to laugh.

"It is a saying that means you have inherited your mother's beauty," Anthony said, with a bow.

Penny blushed, unused to being the subject of male admiration.

"Anthony, do you have to? She's but a child." Louise's sharp rebuke irritated Penny, who hated being called a child.

"Please forgive me, Miss Penelope. I've only recently returned from Ireland and have been trying to practice my newly found Irish charm. Now, let me take your arm and we shall go into dinner. I'm sure you must be hungry."

Penny smiled, before allowing Anthony to guide her into the dining room. Although it had been hours since she'd eaten a sandwich, Penny's mouth was so dry she felt unable to eat. Thankfully, her mother had taught her how to sit at a formal dinner, so she could pass herself off properly. She didn't make any mistakes with the cutlery or glasses, despite being extremely conscious that her new family was gazing at her. She felt like an exhibition at a circus.

Louise asked her questions, but one look from her grandmother and the subject was changed.

Her uncle John raised a glass and nodded to her. "I know you have only just arrived, my dear, but I do hope that you will consider staying with us. Our house is your home."

"Thank you very much, Sir— I mean, Uncle John. You are very gracious. I hope one day to return to live in France."

He nodded. "To live with your mother's family, perhaps?"

"No, Mama's family is all dead. I would like to return to live in Mama's house."

His wife's facial expression hinted at her disapproval. "On your own? That's ridiculous. That wouldn't be seemly."

Penny tried her best to remain civil, but rewarded her aunt with a disdainful look. "France is and always will be my home, madam," she spoke firmly. "I would like to be near my parents."

Sir John said, "Now, I don't think we really need to make plans for the future just yet. After all, Penelope has only just arrived, and I'm sure we would all welcome the chance to get to know each other properly. Harriet and Hugo have yet to meet their young cousin. Now, let's enjoy the lovely food Cook has prepared for us, shall we?"

Penny smiled gratefully at her uncle John and was slightly shocked when he winked back at her. He reminded her of Papa.

At the end of the meal, her grandmother led the ladies to another room, leaving the men to their brandy, cigars and talk of Germany, saying, "My newfound granddaughter looks rather tired. I think she should go to bed, don't you, Louise?"

Although presented as a question, it was obvious that the old lady didn't expect a reply. Louise rang for Perkins and asked the butler to take Penelope to her room.

Penny hesitated. She wanted to ask her grandmother why she'd deserted them in their hour of need, but did she want Aunt Louise to hear everything she had to say?

Her grandmother met her gaze. "We shall talk in the morning. Rest well, dear."

Penny nodded before she followed the silent butler out of the room.

CHAPTER 5

Gracie grabbed a quick supper while the family were eating. How she'd have loved to have been a fly on the wall of the dining room. Pity Miss Harriet wasn't in. There would be fireworks when those two met.

Rob Pike, the footman, walked into the kitchen. "Cor, you could cut the atmosphere in there with a knife. Her Ladyship seems to have taken a shine to the new arrival but Lady Louise, well that's another matter entirely."

Gracie swallowed a mouthful of Cook's delicious bread-and-butter pudding. "She's only fourteen; she looked much younger in her French clothes but in Miss Harriet's dress with her hair done up, she could pass for older."

Rob was about to say something when Mr Perkins' voice carried from his small office to the side of the kitchen.

"Pike, I'm sure you have duties to attend to rather than standing around gossiping like an old woman."

"Yes, Mr Perkins," Rob replied, his tone serious despite the wink he gave Gracie.

Gracie knew better than to risk Mr Perkins' wrath. The old butler lived in the last century, constantly talking about how life was much better back when Queen Mary was in charge. She stuffed the last of her supper into her mouth before heading back upstairs to wait for Penny's return, only just beating the young girl, who walked in seconds later.

"Ah, there you are, miss." Gracie welcomed Penny with a big smile. "How did you get on with dinner?"

Penny shrugged. "Aunt Louise wanted to ask me some questions, but my grandmamma stopped her."

Gracie giggled. "There's no love lost between those two. Milady doesn't like your aunt, and I don't think your aunt is overly fond of her, either. It is a good job that milady spends most of her time in the family estate in Suffolk."

"The family estate?" repeated Penny.

"Oh, yes, miss, her Ladyship lives on a big estate out in the countryside. She hates leaving her horses to come up to town. She only comes here if there's something important happening. Last night, Lady Louise hosted a dinner party for the prime minister. Her Ladyship wanted to quiz him over what's going to happen with the king and that awful woman, Mrs Simpson."

Gracie continued talking while undressing Penny and turning down the bed, before helping the girl in and tucking the covers around her.

"That woman will be the end of the king. What does she need another husband for? She's had two already. There are many women who never got to marry at all because of their men being killed in the Great War, and she thinks she can just pick up our king. The woman has no shame. You can't blame him, though. King or no king, he's just a man, and all men can have their head turned by a woman with a pretty face. Although, if you ask me, she isn't even that pretty. Do you think she's good-looking, miss?"

There was no answer to Gracie's question, as Penny had fallen asleep.

"You poor thing," whispered Gracie, as she turned out the light and softly crept out of the room.

GRACIE OPENED the curtains the next morning, waking Penny, who put her hands over her eyes in an attempt to hide from the light. It had been snowing overnight but the sun was out.

"I'm sorry, miss, but Her Ladyship has requested your presence in the drawing room. I was sent with your breakfast and told to help you dress." She glanced quickly at Penny, adding, "Don't look so worried. She likes to appear formidable, but she has a warm heart, unlike others I could mention."

"I'm not hungry, Gracie, and I can dress myself. I'm not an invalid." Penny smiled, getting out of bed and going over to her bag. She pulled out what was presumably her best dress from her travelling bag.

Gracie frowned, imagining the reception the dress would get from the ladies' downstairs.

"Oh, miss, you can't wear that. You can borrow a day dress from Miss Harriet. Her Ladyship is very particular about young ladies dressing properly. I'm afraid, miss, that your dress … Well, it makes you look like a servant."

Gracie went to the wardrobe and chose a light blue cotton dress and some shoes. "Her Ladyship will like these."

When Penny was dressed, Gracie styled her hair loose around her shoulders before escorting her to the drawing room.

"Thank you, Gracie." Penny gave her a grateful smile. "You have been so kind to me."

"You will be fine, miss," Gracie said before she knocked on the door. She opened it but Penny couldn't move. Gracie came behind her. "Go on in, miss."

WITH A SLIGHT PUSH FROM GRACIE, Penny found herself propelled into the middle of the room. She looked back as the door closed behind her, leaving her feeling trapped.

At first, Penny thought she was alone, but then she saw that her grandmother was sitting in a chair next to the window. She'd a woollen rug draped over her legs, despite the roaring fire in the fireplace. It was warm enough to be uncomfortable, yet the lady didn't look inconvenienced. Penny glanced around at the many shelves holding tonnes of books.

Her grandmother watched her for a moment and then said, "I always loved to read, and this is my favourite room in this old house. It's the warmest, and also the one least likely to be visited by other members of the family."

Penny glanced at the older woman, noting the scornful tone, but to her surprise she found her grandmother was smiling.

"Come over here, child. It is about time we got to know one another, is it not?"

"Yes, ma'am."

"It was evident last night that you don't remember me. Your father used to bring you to see me in Paris. You would have been about four or five. Your grandfather was working for a time in France, and we stayed at a hotel. Your father used to visit when my husband was at the office. We would have afternoon tea…"

Penny shook her head, sad that she could not remember. She noted that her grandmother looked disappointed.

"Perhaps it is best you do not recall those occasions. The last time you came to tea, my son and I argued horribly. That was the last time I saw your father. We were both stubborn and couldn't admit to being wrong. I was wrong not to accept your mother as his wife. But he was wrong, too. He could have waited and introduced her to the family. Perhaps, with time, we would have accepted their relationship. But we didn't get the chance to find out. Your parents moved from Paris shortly after that, and we lost all contact."

Despite the woman's advanced years and her sad tone, Penny knew she must speak up. She wasn't going to let her get away with anything.

"My mother tried to write to you at this address, but you never answered her letters. She even wrote to ask you to allow us to come and visit. She needed to leave our village, but you didn't answer. And now she's dead."

Her grandmother paled, her eyebrows raised as she listened. "I didn't receive any correspondence, but then, I'm rarely here. Once your father disappeared and my husband died, there was nothing left for me in London. At home, I have my horses. Do you have a horse, my dear? You should have. An animal will never betray or hurt you. Unlike humans. But why didn't your mother just come here, like you did? We wouldn't have turned her away. Not after all this time."

Penny ground her teeth as the heat of rage flushed through her body. She counted back from five, trying but failing to keep her anger in check. "How was she to know that? She wrote so many times and never received a reply. She didn't have enough money for us both to travel. She left a bag containing some money and personal possessions for me with a neighbour, a woman who was like a grandmother to me." Penny saw the old lady wince at her words, but she didn't care. This woman could have saved her wonderful mama but had ignored her cry for help.

"Penelope, please believe me. I never received any letters. I may not have condoned my son's actions, but I loved your father dearly. Do you really believe that I would have turned my back on his child?"

"I don't know what to believe any more. I didn't believe that they would prevent my mother from being buried beside my father. I never thought that our friends or neighbours would have missed her burial service. It wasn't my wish to come here, but it was important to my mother. She didn't want me to be on my own. But I don't care about being alone. I'm fourteen, and I've made it this far on my own. I'll leave today and get a job, and…" Penny wiped away her tears in frustration.

Her grandmamma held out her arms. "Oh, my poor child. I didn't know, I swear I didn't. Your mother's letters never reached me, although I suspect that they were delivered to this house."

Penny heard the anger in her voice. She swallowed hard, trying to stand her ground, but the sadness in the woman's eyes pierced her heart.

Her Ladyship threw aside the blanket and

stood up, moving toward Penny and drawing her down to sit on the sofa beside her.

"Of course, you're not alone. You are a member of our family. Stop all this nonsense about getting a job. Ladies in our family don't go out to work, especially when they are only fourteen. You have a lot to learn; we shall have to find you a governess and buy you a horse."

"But, ma'am, I can't stay here permanently. Aunt Louise doesn't like me."

"Leave Louise to me. This is my house, and I'll decide who lives here and who doesn't. I lost you once, Penelope, and I don't intend to let that happen again. Now tell me, child, about your father. Was he happy?"

Penny relaxed, softening at the memory of her dear papa. "Oh, yes, ma'am. He and my mother were always happy. He was hurt in the war and sometimes his back caused him pain, but he still smiled when my mother walked into the room. She was devastated when he got the flu. She called the doctor, but he only said that it was a miracle my father had not died of his wounds years previously. He said there was nothing that could be done, but my mother still didn't believe Papa was dying. She stayed up day and night nursing him, doing everything she could to break his fever. But he wasn't strong enough to fight the influenza. We buried him in a corner of the cemetery under an olive tree. Mama went to his grave almost every day. She enjoyed chatting to him. I think she'd have liked to have died with him, but she didn't want to leave me."

"What age were you when your papa died?"

Penelope looked in shock at the old lady. "You really don't know? Mama sent a telegram to the address Papa had given her. He died in June 1929; I was seven."

The old lady seemed to shrivel up in front of Penny. She immediately felt sorry for her and tried to soothe her feelings. "It's good he wanted to send a telegram, isn't it? He must have forgotten about your argument."

Her grandmother took her hand in hers, stroking it as she looked into her eyes.

"Oh, child, I hope he did. I loved James, even though he broke my heart when he refused to come home. But I'm glad he was happy. I used to wonder if he'd regretted his decision, but it sounds like he was very content with your mother. I wish now I had put aside my stupid pride and met her. Maybe then both of them would have come home, and you and I would have got to know each other all those years ago."

Penny didn't know what to say.

"Now, Penelope, let's start again. I'm your grandmother, and I want to be a real one." Although the old lady had emphasised the last phrase, Penny saw she was smiling.

"What shall you call me? Grandmother is a bit formal, isn't it? But then ma'am makes you sound like a servant and that won't do. You used to call me Meme, when you were little."

Penny swallowed the lump in her throat.

"Would you like to call me that now?"

Penny couldn't speak, so she nodded. Her grandmother squeezed Penny's fingers and then abruptly changed the subject.

"Now, what do you say to us going shopping? Your own wardrobe is rather inadequate, and you cannot keep borrowing Harriet's clothes. That young lady can sulk for England. Perkins can call us a cab, as I believe your uncle has the car. Afterwards, we'll go to tea at the Savoy."

Before Penny could reply, the door opened and a young lady she hadn't seen before came into the room.

"Morning, Grandmamma. Don't you look lovely? Are you going to introduce me to your guest, especially as she appears to be wearing my dress?"

Penny disliked her cousin, Harriet, on sight. She reminded Penny of a china doll her father had once bought for her in Paris, all blonde curls and perfect skin – but the doll's eyes had looked kinder. There wasn't an ounce of warmth in the blue eyes staring over at her.

"Harriet, try to be pleasant. This is your cousin, Penelope. She has had a long, and I dare say frightening, journey travelling here from her home in France."

Penny heard a knock on the door before it opened again, admitting Gracie with a tea tray. She smiled at the servant, who winked back after quickly checking nobody else could see her. Penny was tempted to laugh until she realised her cousin was speaking.

"France? I didn't know I had a cousin in France. That explains the lack of clothes. Your luggage must have got delayed. Are you from Paris? I love Parisian clothes. They are so stylish. We are about the same size, aren't we? I shall have such fun trying on your wardrobe. When do you think your bags will arrive? We'll have a great time getting to know one another. Once we see what your wardrobe is like, I'll tell Mama to book a shopping trip in Paris for all three of us. What do you say?" Harriet looked determinedly at Penny.

Their grandmother cut in, "Fiddlesticks,

you have more clothes upstairs than you could ever wear. Your mother spoils you rotten. Penelope doesn't want to go off gallivanting to Paris. She has only just arrived in London."

Harriet bristled. Penny clenched her hands by her sides and counted slowly to five before responding.

"I'm sorry, miss, but I didn't live in Paris. I've only been there twice. My home was in a small town called Souvigné. I lived there with my—"

"A village? You lived in a village? How awful. Next you will tell me that your parents had to work for a living." Harriet paused before adding, "They did, didn't they?"

"My father died when I was seven and my mother had no option but to work."

"Your mother worked? How dreadful."

Penny chose to deliberately misunderstand her cousin. "Yes, it was dreadful. Poor Mama had to work well into the night in order to provide us with shelter and food to eat. I helped her when I could, but she insisted that

I concentrate on my studies. She wanted me to have a proper education. She's – *pardon*, was – an amazing woman, and I miss her every day. Now, if you will excuse me, Meme, I would like to return to my room."

"Just one minute, Penelope. I want to make something quite clear. You are Harriet's equal, so will address her by her Christian name and not 'miss'. When addressing Louise or John, call them Aunt or Uncle, as is fitting for a young lady of your age. This is your home and you are a member of the family." The old lady fixed a glare on Harriet. "It is your duty to make sure your younger cousin settles into her home comfortably. Make sure I do not hear that you have done anything different. Thompson, please stop pretending that you are doing anything other than eavesdropping and take Miss Penelope back to her room. I doubt she has yet had a chance to familiarise herself with the layout of the house. We are going shopping this afternoon after luncheon. Tell Perkins to call us a cab for two o'clock."

The old lady turned and looked straight at Penny. "We shall have lots of fun together, just the two of us. There is no need for Harriet to come. She has everything she needs."

Penny nearly giggled at the look on Harriet's face, but thankfully was distracted by Gracie addressing the old lady.

"Yes, Your Ladyship. Come on now, Miss Penelope. We need to get ready for your outing."

Harriet bent down to kiss her grandmother on the cheek before saying, "Wait for me, please, Penelope."

She followed Gracie and Penny out of the room. As soon as the door to the drawing room had closed, Harriet turned on Penny with fire in her eyes. "Listen to me now, you country bumpkin. This is my home, and that is my grandmother. I don't have any intention of sharing any of this with you. I'll make your life a misery until you are begging to go back to that hovel you shared with your wretched mother."

Penny couldn't speak. After they had

watched Harriet storm off, Gracie said, "Don't take too much notice of her, Miss."

"Gracie, please stop calling me 'miss'. My name is Penny and in France I was the same as you. I don't belong to this..." Penny waved her hands around. "... life. And as for my cousin, I've looked after sows with better manners."

Gracie giggled, before putting a hand over her mouth.

Penny grinned. "Come on, I don't want you getting in trouble if I'm late."

CHAPTER 6

Penny bit her lip, trying to think of what else to write to Madame Bayard. She didn't have long before Miss Long, her governess, would be down for lessons. In addition to learning languages, she had to be trained in the art of etiquette. As if she needed to know how to greet an earl correctly or what outfits were suitable at different occasions.

Penny hated being stuck in the house learning how to become a lady. She longed for the days in France where she'd run around with the other village children, free as a bird. She lived for the moments when she could escape to the kitchen. Cook and Gracie were her type of people, not women like her aunt and her cousin, who refused to lift a finger to help themselves. Imagine ringing a bell to have someone help you dress. She turned back to her letter.

I hope you are keeping well, and I'm sorry it has taken me so long to write to you. As you can see, I've arrived safe and sound in London. I've met my father's family, although some I wish I didn't have to live with! Meme – my grandmother – took me shopping last week, so I could buy paper and stamps to write to you. We had a great day.

Meme took me to so many shops and bought me lots of clothes. My favourite shop was Selfridges. You should see the building. It is enormous.

When we went into the shop, some staff recognised Meme. They took us to a suite on one of the floors and then teams of young ladies arrived with dresses, hats, gloves, underwear and everything else you could think of. Meme let me pick some dresses, but really she chose most of the things. I tried to protest that it was too much, but she said my French clothes were not suitable for wearing at the house and, anyway, she wanted to spoil me after missing out on so many years.

I've made a new friend, too. Her name is Gracie Thompson, and she works as a maid for Aunt Louise. She's beautiful, with long blonde hair and blue eyes. She comes from a place called Lewisham. She has to live in the house and sleeps upstairs in the servants' quarters. I really like her. She's the nicest person I've met here, and she's only a few years older than I'm.

Meme is nice, too, once you get to know her. I can see why Mama said nothing bad about her. At first, I was afraid of her, but now I understand her better. She has a big heart and is always kind to me. She's taking me to see her other house and her horses next month. She loves her horses and was thrilled to learn that Papa had taught me to ride when I was younger. She has promised me that not only will I get to practise my horse riding but she'll give me my own horse.

I spend most of my time in the house where I've a governess. I may not go to school with other children. Aunt Louise believes I need a lot of help in becoming a lady. I think she secretly believes I'm a lost cause but won't admit it. I don't like Aunt Louise much, as she's always finding fault, but Uncle John seems a good man. He is a barrister but works for the government.

I've two cousins: Harriet, seventeen, and Hugo, nineteen. Hugo is abroad travelling. I hope he's nicer than Harriet, although that wouldn't be hard. I can't do anything to please her. She's so mean. She has plenty of male admirers who are always coming to the house, but I can't understand what they see in her. I guess they can't see past the blonde curls. I heard someone say that she looked like Shirley Temple. Maybe there's some resemblance in looks, but not in temperament. Gracie tells me to ignore Harriet, but she gets me into trouble with Aunt Louise all the time, so it's difficult. She's mean to the servants, it is not just me. All she cares about is how she looks and whether her clothes are the latest and the best. She throws away more outfits than the whole of Souvigné's female population would buy in a year. I hope she gets married soon and moves out.

The house is enormous. There are six bedrooms and bathrooms. It is so different from the house I shared with Mama. I miss her so much. I hope that you can lay flowers on her grave and that he hasn't mistreated you for helping me.

I'm sorry for being angry on our last day together. I know now that you were trying to do your best. Please write back to me.

Your petite fille,
Penelope

CHAPTER 7
APRIL 1937

Gracie sat polishing some silver as Penny read out her letter from her French friend, a lady old enough to be her grandmother. In the six months since her arrival, Penny hadn't settled to the role of being a lady. She was still a misfit, despite Miss Long and Lady Louise's best efforts. After bristling at first, Cook had got used to the newest member of the household perching at her kitchen table. So long as Lady Louise didn't find out, Penny was welcome. Cook even let her help with certain tasks, like decorating the different dishes for the upstairs meals. Her Ladyship knew about Penny's clandestine visits and encouraged them, knowing her granddaughter was like a fish out of water. Lady Louise would have put a stop to it, but thankfully she was much too busy shopping and socialising to care what happened when she wasn't home.

Gracie looked up from her work as Penny stayed silent. "So what does she say? You're frowning."

"She says I'm to be kind to my grandmother as she has buried her husband and her son."

Cook nodded approvingly. "She's a lovely lady, your grandmother. That's enough reason to be kind, I should think." She huffed as she beat the egg yolks for hollandaise sauce.

Penny continued, "She also said to be kind to Harriet, as it must be a shock to share her life with a stranger."

Cook rolled her eyes. "Your friend has never met Miss Harriet. If she did, she might have a different point of view."

Gracie hid a smile. Cook had been determined not to agree with any of the French woman's comments, telling Gracie loudly that

Her Ladyship should stop Penny from contacting people from her past.

"What did she say about you not catching flies with vinegar? Do you eat flies and snails in France?" Gracie pulled a face at the thought of a French meal.

Penny burst out laughing. "Of course we don't eat flies. I told you before, snails are wonderful when cooked properly. One day when you come to France, try them. You will love them."

Gracie didn't look too convinced. Cook made a tutting noise, muttering about snails and frogs' legs as she put her sauce to one side.

"Madame means that I won't make friends with Harriet if I'm mean to her. Poor Madame, she wants everyone to like each other and be happy all the time."

"As Cook says, it's easy for her to be like that. She doesn't have to live with Miss Harriet. Perhaps you could convince Her Ladyship to send Harriet to Madame Bayard for a few weeks. You could say it would be to help her French. After all, Lady Louise did say that she needs all the help she can get, as she sounds like a peasant."

Cook said, "Gracie Thompson, be quiet. It wouldn't do any good for anyone to hear you repeating Lady Louise's remarks." But the girls both giggled at the thought of Harriet living in France, eating snails and not having any servants. "Go on, the pair of you. Gracie, do something with Miss Penelope's hair. Her Ladyship may be less formal than Lady Louise, but she'll have kittens if Miss Penelope comes down to dinner with that bird's nest."

Gracie hurriedly finished the polishing and went to wash her hands. Penny waited until Gracie was ready and the two of them ran up the backstairs to Penny's bedroom. There, Penny continued to read the letter aloud to Gracie. Her face screwed up as she spoke about a man called Alain.

"She doesn't like that man she's referring to. What did he do to deserve such hatred?"

Gracie wondered, as she brushed out Penny's hair.

Penny opened her mouth to speak, but didn't say anything. She looked into the mirror and then up at Gracie. "Alain killed Mama," she whispered.

Gracie froze, her thoughts scrambling to understand what Penny had just said. "I thought your mama died of the flu. What do you mean he killed her?" She pulled herself to the edge of the bed, sitting up straight. She stared at Penny but her friend's eyes were glazed, caught up in the dreadful memories. She ached to take Penny's hand but was scared to interrupt her.

"He owned the house we lived in. Papa had taken a loan on the property from him some years previously, and we were behind with our payments. Mama tried her best, but without the income from the farm, she just couldn't get the money together to pay what we owed. He threatened to throw us out. She wrote to Papa's family, but heard nothing back."

Gracie couldn't hold her tongue or her tears. Her hands shook as she whispered, "Oh, your poor mama. Didn't she have any family herself?"

Penny fixed her gaze on Gracie. "No, her father and brothers had died in the war and my grandmother soon afterwards. Some friends in the village tried to help, but that man had a lot of power and people were afraid of him. Eventually…" Penny's voice faltered as she stood up and backed away from Gracie, turning to look out the window. Gracie was about to stand up to hug her but something stopped her.

Penny spoke so low, Gracie had to strain to hear. "Mama had no choice but to give Alain what he wanted. She was so ashamed, but she couldn't see any other way."

What did Penny mean, give him what he wanted? She said her mama had nothing … Gracie's eyes widened; she couldn't stop her gasp as the horror of the situation dawned on her.

Penny turned to meet her gaze, her shoulders pushed back as if expecting Gracie to judge her or her mother harshly. Penny flexed her fingers at her sides, but otherwise stood still. "He was cruel and often hurt her. She regularly had a black eye or bruises, although she tried to cover them up. He was content for a time, but then he began looking at me."

"No. No. Please don't tell me he…"

Penny carried on as if Gracie hadn't interrupted. "He made me feel funny, and I said to Mama that he was scaring me. The night I told Mama, she tried to kill him. But she failed, and instead she ended up dying. He said she'd stabbed herself, but we, Madame Bayard and I, knew the truth. Mama would never have left me alone."

Gracie's heart beat so fast it made her dizzy; she pushed down the urge to be sick. Poor Penny, and her mother. She'd died saving Penny. No wonder her friend looked so confused and down at times. Gracie reached out and pulled Penny to sit on the bed beside her. She rubbed her chilled hands as she said, "Oh, my God, it's no surprise you have nightmares. Did you not go to the police?"

Penny shook her head. "There was no point. He was too powerful. When the priest was told Mama had killed herself, he refused to allow her to be buried with my father. The priest said that what Mama had done was against the teachings of the church, so she'd to be buried on her own. That is why I hate him so much. Not only did he kill her, but he stopped her from being with Papa."

Gracie held Penny as she sobbed, her whole body shuddering. She rubbed Penny's back as she bit back her rage that any young girl had to go through something so horrific, and alone. Her anger conveyed itself in her tone when she eventually asked, "Do Meme and your uncle John know anything about this?"

Penny shook her head vehemently as she sprang to her feet and turned, her eyes blazing. "No, and they never can. Although, I would love to see Aunt Louise's face if she found out. She thinks the worst thing I can do to ruin her family is to become a nurse. If only she knew. If I take forever, I'll make him pay for what he did to my family."

IN THE LIBRARY, Penny turned the pages of the newspaper coverage of the Spanish conflict. Protests were building, and pressure was increasing on the British government to take in child refugees from the Basque region. Tears filled her eyes as she read the accounts of the ordeals they had experienced.

The door opened, admitting her grandmother. "Penelope, darling, why are you crying? Did you have bad news from France?"

Penny shook her head, pointing to the paper. "The reports from Spain are horrible. I feel so useless. I wish I could be like Hugo. He is out there, isn't he? Aunt Louise said he was away on business but I heard the servants gossiping. I wish I was a boy. I don't want to be a lady, sitting around all day doing nothing."

Meme's eyes lit up with amusement as Penny faltered, realising what she'd said. "Sorry, I mean…"

Meme patted Penny's hand. "I know what you mean. You are too restless for the life your aunt deems appropriate for you. We've been unfair to you, my darling, expecting you to shake off your early years and become something you aren't. Tell me, what would you like to do?"

Penny looked into her grandmother's eyes, as words failed her. What *did* she want to do?

"I mean, apart from going back to France. You have to see that is not an option," her grandmother said as she squeezed her hand. "At least, not while you are so young. There must be something you could do in the meantime. Would you like to come to Suffolk to my house? You might find there is more to keep you busy there."

"You are so gracious to me. But I want to be useful, Meme. I read the papers and want to help. I can't just sit here and do nothing while children suffer."

Meme gasped, her hand tightening around Penny's. "You can't mean to run away to Spain. It's one thing for Hemingway and others to go, but that is no place for a young woman."

Penny smiled. "No, Meme. I'm not that reckless. But there has to be something I could do. To help in some way. I said to Aunt Louise I would like to train to become a nurse when I'm old enough, but she won't hear of it. Why?"

Meme smiled but there was sadness in her eyes as if she was remembering an old hurt. "Your aunt has her reasons. It's not often I agree with my daughter-in-law, but in this case I can understand her reaction."

Penny blew her hair out of her face. "I can't. If war comes, we'll need more nurses. Why can't I be one of them?" Her grandmother didn't respond, so she changed tactic, mellowing her tone. "Please, Meme, explain why it is wrong."

"It isn't wrong, just too painful for your aunt."

Confused, Penny opened her mouth but closed it again as her grandmother continued. "You remind me so much of Louise's sister, Vivienne. She acted like a caged lion too, rebelling against the traditions of our time. Her mother despaired of her but Louise loved her sister."

"What did she do?" Curiosity was eating Penny alive. Aunt Louise was so straight-laced, so concerned with appearance and status.

"Vivienne was a suffragette and got herself into lots of trouble. You can imagine most women of our class didn't get involved with the marches and public protests. Many supported the cause in private but were too concerned about their reputations to do anything." Meme sighed. Penny waited to hear more, her foot tapping silently with impatience as the old lady took her time to speak again. "Vivienne didn't care what people thought of her. She was always involved in one cause after another. She spent hours working in the hospitals with the poor. Her parents despaired of her but nothing they did worked. She became more militant and spent some time in Holloway too. In fact, I think that was what killed her in the end."

"Holloway? What's that?"

"A prison."

Penny couldn't help it; her mouth fell open. Louise's sister had been in prison.

"She was arrested for protesting for the rights of women. England was gearing up for war, but Vivienne and her friends were fighting their own war at home. They wanted equality for all women."

Penny had heard a little about the suffragettes and their fight on the streets of London.

"What happened to her?"

"She died in France, nursing at the front. Her body was weak after the forced feeding she endured in prison. She worked long hours in abysmal conditions and I believe it all caught up with her." Meme's voice faltered, her eyes closing as if she were in pain.

Penny let the old lady dwell on her memories as she processed what she'd been told.

"Vivienne was my goddaughter and I feel I should have done more. Tried harder to understand her."

Torn between curiosity and wanting to stop Meme feeling sad, nosiness won.

"But doesn't she believe her sister was brave? A hero to volunteer to go and help…"

"Louise never understood Vivienne. She hated the attention it brought on her family, the negative articles in the press. She's adamant the germs she encountered nursing killed Vivienne. Since her death, Louise has done all she can to become the perfect hostess, the most ladylike, the best wife. She'd die rather than let anyone undermine her social position again. No matter what you do, Penelope, your aunt will never agree to having a nurse under her roof."

Penny stood and paced the floor. "She's my aunt by marriage. Not my guardian. How can she dictate my future?" Penny took a deep breath; it wouldn't do to fall out with Meme. She turned to face her grandmother. "Sorry, Meme. I just get so frustrated. I've never sat so much in my whole life."

Meme smiled as she patted the seat beside her. "As you grow older, you will learn you must accept other people's faults."

Penny raised her eyebrows as she sat down, making Meme laugh.

"Yes, you wicked child, I know I don't practise what I preach. I've no patience with Louise and her snobbery. But she's part of my family, your uncle's choice of partner, and I learnt the hard way not to fight my sons' choices in life."

Penny knew that Meme was referencing her own parents.

"Still, she's your elder and she deserves some respect. Try to understand her a little. At some level, she loved Vivienne even if she refuses to admit it to herself."

Penny didn't want to argue.

Meme patted her hand. "I know you are

strong-willed and if I don't find you something to do, goodness knows what choice you will make. I've a friend, Kitty, who is involved with several different projects, including the evacuation of children from Spain. I'll speak to her, see if she has a position for you, Penelope."

"Kitty?"

"Duchess of Atholl to give her, her proper title. You may have read about her travels. I believe she's currently in Spain."

Penny's stomach turned over with excitement; she'd read about the duchess. She gaped at Meme, despite knowing it was rude. "You are her friend."

Meme stood. "Penny, I know it is difficult for you, living in this new world. It is why I turned a blind eye to your friendship with Thompson. She has a good head on her shoulders and will look out for you. But you must make an effort to fit into our world too. Louise has a lot of plans for Harriet to make a good marriage and she doesn't want a hint of scandal to hit the family."

Penny bristled. What did they think she'd do, dress up as a man and head to Spain? She turned to see Meme staring right at her as if she could read her mind.

"With you, my darling, just about anything is possible. Just try to curb your impulses a little. In time, the divide between the worlds we came from will diminish but until then humour your aunt Louise a little. At least while I'm in town. I am too old to deal with constant arguments."

"I'll try, Meme."

"Good girl. Now I've a letter to write, and I believe Miss Long is looking for you."

CHAPTER 8
MAY 1937

Gracie gasped as she hit her head on the window frame after hearing the bedroom door open behind her. It was her own fault, hanging her neck out to see the decorations.

"Gracie, why is everyone so excited?"

Gracie turned towards Penny, rubbing her head. "It's the coronation of King George VI on Wednesday. That's what those flags are for, the ones hanging on all the streets. People will come from all over the country to see the new king and queen go by in their carriage, to spot their crowns."

"Oh, that!" Penny lay down on her bed and opened her book, sprawled across the bed in what her aunt would consider a most undignified fashion.

"This is going to be the biggest party London – the entire country – has seen in years and that's all you can say? Don't they do things like this in France?"

"We got rid of kings, queens and all that nonsense in the revolution. We celebrate our freedom on Bastille Day; it is in Ju ... What's the matter? What did I say?"

Gracie caught hold of herself, trying to temper her indignation with the knowledge Penny wasn't British. "You can't go round speaking about the king and queen like that. They're our rulers, so you should have more respect." Gracie moved to the window to watch the men set up the flag display on the railings in the square. "Not that the king wants to be king, though. It should have been his big brother's day. Would have been too if it weren't for that American woman."

Penny jumped from the bed, holding her hands above her head in mock surrender. "I'm sorry. I meant nothing personal. I'm sure he's a nice man and all that. I just don't think that people who live in palaces are in touch with those who live like—"

"Like you do … in a fabulous house like this, with maids like me to cater to your every … Ouch." Penny's aim was spot on as the pillow hit Gracie's head, sending feathers everywhere.

"Shush, Gracie, you know we're the same, you and me. You are my friend, not my maid."

"Don't say that too loud, Lady Louise won't like to hear it."

Penny pouted. "She doesn't like most of what I've to say. She won't hear me anyway. She's too busy fussing about her new dress for tomorrow's dinner and her attendance at the abbey. Although she's complaining she isn't seated near the front where all her friends are. But Uncle John said they were lucky not to be sitting outside with all the royalty coming from overseas."

Picking up the feathers and shoving them back into the pillowcase, Gracie didn't respond. She couldn't imagine actually being in the abbey. What an honour that would be.

"Are you going to listen to it on the BBC?" Penny asked.

"No, we're going to see it. Stan, Alice and me. We've got plans to camp overnight so we have a good view. I got a half day tomorrow and Wednesday off."

"Your parents said yes?"

Gracie's face flushed. "Not exactly." A quiver rippled through her stomach, remembering the argument at home when her father heard of her plans to sleep on the pavement. It was the only way to secure a good spot, but you would think she'd said she was running away with a foreign prince.

"Dad said no but Mam told him it was a once-in-a-lifetime opportunity. Dad insisted Stan come with us. Alice and me would have been fine on our own but now Stan will be there too, and I'll be a gooseberry."

Penny's eyes gleamed, a hint of a smile hovering on her lips.

Gracie looked at her suspiciously. "What?"

"Why don't I come with you? To keep you company. Then Stan and Alice can be together."

Gracie frowned and bit her lip, crossing her arms against her chest. "I don't think that's a good idea. What would Sir John say?" Torn between hurting Penny's feelings and losing her job, Gracie hoped Penny would decide not to come.

"He wouldn't need to know."

Gracie blew the hair out of her eyes. "One look at you and everyone would know. Your sort don't sleep out on the street, not even for a king's coronation."

Penny looked irritated. "That's the problem with this country. What do you mean by my sort? We're all the same."

Gracie opened her mouth but closed it again. Despite having lived in the house for months now, Penny still refused to behave according to the norms of society. But then it wasn't her fault; she didn't behave like Miss

Harriet and nobody held her to the same standard. There was no way Miss Harriet would be seen sitting at Cook's table. She doubted the young lady could boil water, never mind cook like Penny did. Even Lady Louise seemed to accept, albeit reluctantly, that Penny would never fit into blue-blood society.

"Nobody will miss me. I can borrow some of your clothes, can't I? Then I'll look just like any other London girl." Penny squealed with excitement. "This is going to be such fun. Wait until I write and tell Madame all about it."

Gracie rolled her eyes and left the room.

GRACIE SIGHED as they walked down to the Marble Arch Corner House to meet Stan and Alice. She should have known that once Penny got an idea into her head, she wouldn't take no for an answer. If Sir John or Lady Louise found out, Gracie would be looking for a new job. Not that that was a bad idea. She knew she could earn more money working in a store or even as a Nippy in a Lyons teashop. But it would mean leaving Cook in the lurch and she'd miss Penny, not to mention she'd need a reference.

In contrast, Penny couldn't stop smiling. She was acting like a child at a birthday party.

"Gracie, stop looking so sad. You said this was a party. Look around you – everyone's smiling. It's like the entire world stopped to celebrate. Maybe France should have a king and queen after all." Penny chattered on, the words spilling out of her mouth one after another, her accent growing thicker as she spoke. She put her hand on Gracie's elbow. "Stop worrying about Uncle John. I'll tell him it was all my fault; I ordered you to take me. I'm your mistress, after all." Penny giggled as Gracie put her tongue out at her.

Gracie couldn't stay angry for long, not when the entire street was in a party mood. Strangers were smiling and hugging each other, talking about what a great king George would make – not like his brother. And then there was Elizabeth, his wife. She was a proper lady, a British one from sterling stock. She was raising the two young princesses to be lovely young ladies too.

A woman nearby said, "Mark my words, the new royal family will bring us all the luck in the world. Such a beauty, our new queen. Has a lovely smile, don't she?" The woman didn't seem to be addressing her comments to anyone in particular. Gracie and Penny exchanged a smile before Gracie spotted her brother's girlfriend.

"Alice, we're here!" Gracie yelled, waving at the petite brown-haired girl looking around her self-consciously. Her face lit up with a look of relief when she saw Gracie, and she came over to join them.

"I'll murder that brother of yours. He knows I don't like standing outside the shops waiting. Someone might mistake me for one of those … Oh, hello." Alice, her face turning crimson, cut herself short when she spotted Penny.

Gracie introduced them. "Alice, this is Penny. Alice is studying to be a nurse and has the patience of a saint. She needs it to be walking out with my twin."

Alice bent her legs in a sort of curtsy, making Penny blush.

Gracie poked Alice in the side. "Alice, Penny is one of us today. She doesn't want anyone knowing who she is."

"Of course, Your Ladyship…" Alice simpered, and Gracie and Penny laughed.

Penny leaned towards Alice confidingly. "According to my aunt, I'm no lady. I'm Gracie's friend and it's lovely to meet you. I've heard a lot about you and of course your young man. And I'm so keen to hear about your studies – I'd love to be training to become a nurse too…" Penny's warmth melted Alice's wariness, and soon they were chatting as if they had known each other for years.

"They've decorated every back street from here to Lewisham with coloured flags of all shapes and sizes. Mum told me we should have stayed with her as they're having a party, but it wouldn't be the same," Alice whispered. "I was lucky to get time off. Everyone wanted to see the king and queen on the balcony at Buckingham Palace. They say the two young princesses will be there too, wearing real gold crowns. Imagine that, and they're only youngsters." Alice looked around them. "Where is Stan?"

"He's never on time. He'll be late for his own funeral." Gracie turned to look around her, scanning the faces in the crowd. "Speak of the devil, here he comes."

"Ladies! Aren't I a lucky man, escorting three beautiful women across town this evening." Stan grabbed Alice and kissed her, leaving her spluttering and protesting as he turned his attention to Penny. Gracie swiftly moved, putting herself between her twin and her friend. Penny might think of herself as one of them, but she was still a member of the nobility. "Stan, behave yourself. Penny isn't used to your antics."

"I can speak for myself, Gracie," Penny

cut in. "Nice to meet you, Stan. We were just discussing you."

Stan nodded, "All good, I hope. Right now, let's get a move on. Some people have been here for a week. Good job I've a mate who kept us a good place. Will be a bit of a tight squeeze, but I won't mind." Stan grinned as he took Alice's arm. "Follow me. Gracie, don't lose your friend in the crowds."

Gracie tucked her arm into Penny's and followed her brother, wondering if Charlie Power was the friend Stan had arranged to meet. Her mouth grew dry at the thought of seeing him again, spending the day in his company. She'd been disappointed Stan hadn't taken her hint to invite Charlie to their home on one of her days off. But if anything, her twin seemed to plan his visits when Gracie was working. *Maybe Charlie had found me too rude that evening at the cinema and didn't want to see me again.* She clamped down on those thoughts; this was a day to enjoy, not to waste worrying about a man.

All around them people were spreading

out blankets, opening Thermos flasks and getting food out of bags, while children sat munching ham sandwiches, their eyes wide with excitement. Gracie's smile slipped a little when Stan's mate turned out to be Brian Dodds, his football friend. Brian was pleasant and not bad looking but he wasn't Charlie. Brian had the foresight to bring a large ground sheet to provide some shelter from the rain. Alice and Gracie set out the blankets while Penny divided out the sandwiches. Cook had given Gracie some Marmite ones, despite knowing she hated Marmite, making the girls suspect she knew that Penny, who loved Marmite with everything, would be accompanying them.

The party atmosphere was intoxicating, and it was exciting to camp out overnight among the crowds. Nobody seemed to care when the heavens opened in the morning. Rain or not, they were there to celebrate their new king and queen.

CHAPTER 9

"Miss Penny, Her Ladyship wants to see you in the drawing room, dressed properly for your outing." Grace walked through the bedroom door as she spoke.

Penny studied her reflection in the bedroom mirror. "Do you think I look serious and grown-up?"

Gracie walked around her, eyes raking her up and down.

Losing patience, Penny said, "Gracie…"

"Now, ladies who want to look after children shouldn't be quick to lose their serenity." Gracie couldn't say any more as she was laughing at Penny's reaction.

"You!" Penny stuck out her tongue.

Gracie wagged her finger. "That's certainly not the behaviour required of a lady."

Gracie could mimic Aunt Louise's voice perfectly and the two of them dissolved into giggles. They didn't realise they were being so loud until Harriet burst in.

"For goodness' sake, what is going on in here? Some of us are trying to sleep." Harriet rubbed a hand across her forehead. "Where are you off to?"

"Shopping," Penny answered just as Gracie said, "Visiting, Miss Harriet."

Harriet stared at them incredulously. Penny could see Gracie was biting her lip trying to restrain another bout of giggling. Harriet gave them both a dirty look before turning on her heel and marching out of the bedroom.

"You'd best get downstairs before we both land in hot water. Go on, you look lovely as always. Those children are lucky to have you."

"You really think so?"

Gracie picked up some discarded clothing from the floor. "Of course. What other volunteer will be able to whistle and run just like a boy!"

With that, Gracie withdrew, leaving Penny staring at herself. She didn't want to let her grandmother down. She hoped the duchess agreed to take her on.

SHE KNOCKED on the drawing-room door and was relieved to see both her aunt and grandmother appraise her appearance without comment. She'd passed the first hurdle.

"Louise, I'm taking Penelope out this afternoon. We have an appointment."

"But I had…"

Penny hid a smile as Meme gave Louise a look.

Louise swallowed before adding, "Yes, Mother. Enjoy yourselves, and Penelope, please remember your lessons. Don't embarrass your grandmother in public. Also make sure she keeps warm; the air still carries a chill, despite it being the end of May."

Penny had to turn her face away for fear she'd laugh aloud as Meme's eyes widened at the veiled insult. Meme was hardly frail and weak for her age; she was only in her sixties, not an ancient crone like Louise suggested.

Meme insisted on taking a cab rather than use Louise's driver. They arrived at a large building with the Salvation Army banner overhead.

"I didn't know the duchess was involved with the Salvation Army."

"She isn't, at least not that I know of. But she asked me to meet with the lady in charge. This is one orphanage the children will be sent to. Mrs Appleton is the lady you have to impress, Penelope. She won't care about your lineage going back to Henry VIII or anything else that matters to your aunt. Mrs Appleton wants volunteers who won't turn pale and faint when faced with lice, fleas and other nasties these children may carry. She expects her volunteers to be brave, courteous and caring." Meme's voice softened. "All qualities you have in abundance. Now stop looking like a scared cat and be yourself."

Meme took the hand offered by the cab driver to get out of the car. Penny followed suit as her grandmother climbed the steps up to the door. On ringing the bell, they were admitted to a large hallway. It was painted in fairly drab colours, the brown walls almost merging with the brown tiles on the floor. Electric lights provided a poor stream of light compared to the beautiful crisp May day outside. Penny pulled her coat closer, the chill in the air seeping into her bones. This wasn't what she'd expected. She peeped at Meme but she didn't appear to notice their surroundings.

A rotund woman with tight curled hair under her uniform cap waited for them in the room they were shown to. She stood up to greet them, offering both a firm handshake.

"Thank you for coming, Your Ladyship and Miss Penelope. Kitty forwarded me your letter. She has remained in Spain to sort out some last-minute details." Mrs Appleton turned her gaze on Penny, scrutinising her from top to toe. It took everything Penny had to remain seated and not squirm under the examination.

"May I speak frankly?" Mrs Appleton addressed Meme, who nodded. "I admit to being rather curious about your reasons for volunteering. Your grandson's beliefs are causing some talk."

"Penelope is not Hugo."

"No, of course not, but..." Mrs Appleton pursed her lips for a second before taking a sip of water from the glass on her desk. "How can I put this delicately?"

Meme's tone would give anyone frostbite. "Just say what you have to say. Please."

Penny didn't realise she was biting her lip, the air of tension rising in the room. What had Hugo got to do with her volunteering? She sensed the fury building in Meme even though she looked so calm and collected.

"Your Ladyship, my intention is not to insult you or your family but you have to understand my caution. These children have been through so much already and I don't wish to expose them to any potential harm."

Penny's temper flared. "I want to help the children, not harm them. I had to leave my home in France so have some understanding of what they are going through. I don't speak any Basque, only a little Spanish, but I'm good at learning. I've plenty of time on my hands and, given my family position, am lucky I don't have to work to earn my living. Please, Mrs Appleton, until last October I'd never met my cousin. Even now we have seen each other a couple of times. I'm not sure what he has done to warrant your concern but believe me, he has never discussed anything more important than the dinner menu with me."

If anything, Mrs Appleton looked amused by her outburst but Meme sat even straighter.

"It appears you have been misinformed, Mrs Appleton. My grandson is a fine young man. The rumours surrounding his beliefs are just that. Since when did the Salvation Army listen to gossip?"

Mrs Appleton's nostrils flared slightly and her lips drew into a fine line. "I don't consider being photographed in the company of known Nazis to be gossip, Your Ladyship. These children are the innocent victims of the same type of people your grandson likes to associate with. You should understand, perhaps even share my concern."

Penny glanced from one woman to the other, trying to temper her anger. This was her decision, she was volunteering – not Hugo or her grandmother.

Meme broke the silence. "Many people including our royal family have associated with the same people. Surely you wouldn't bring that up should the young princess Elizabeth offer her services?"

Mrs Appleton's face turned crimson.

"I thought not. You have the recommendation from the Duchess of Atholl. I assume you consider her a suitable referee. When can my granddaughter start?"

"Next Monday." Mrs Appleton stood up in dismissal. "I hope you will be an asset to our organisation, Miss Hamilton, but believe me, no matter what your background, should you voice unfavourable views or behave in a manner not appropriate to your role, we will not hesitate to terminate your service."

"Thank you for your time, Mrs Appleton. I'm sure you will find no fault with my granddaughter. Good day."

Meme sailed out of the room, leaving Penny to send a glance of apology at the woman before following. She'd got the job and she knew she should feel exhilarated but instead she was confused by the conversation. What had Hugo done?

Meme stayed silent the whole way back to Belgrave Square. Only when they were inside the house, out of earshot of the cab driver, could Penny ask her to explain.

Meme sighed and indicated Penny join her in the library. Gracie arrived with fresh coffee for Penny and tea for Her Ladyship but, despite the curiosity apparent on her face, she didn't probe. She gave Penny a questioning look at the obvious tension but left without a word. Penny waited for her grandmother to speak, but when the silence grew uncomfortable, she had to break it.

"Meme, I'm sorry the meeting was so upsetting for you. Maybe I shouldn't take the position?"

"Don't you dare back out of it now. You are your own person and that woman had no right to drag Hugo into this."

"What has Hugo done?"

Meme sighed, putting the untouched cup of tea back on the tray. She folded her hands in her lap. Were they shaking? Penny's heart beat faster.

"Hugo spends a lot of time in Germany with friends he met in university. Some of those are now members of the Nazi Party."

Penny gasped but her grandmother ignored her.

"The papers have been quick to pick up on his associations and of course the gossips are having a field day. But…" Meme speared

Penny with a glance. "I know my grandson and things are not what they appear. There has to be a reason why he's behaving like he does."

Penny hesitated. She didn't want to say anything to hurt her grandmother. "I've heard him mention his friendship with the Duke of Westminster and Lord…"

"Hardly friends. They all go to the same clubs. It's nonsense, and that woman had no right to bring it up. You show her what we Hamiltons are made of, Penelope."

Despite wanting to discuss Hugo more, Penny heeded the dismissal. Meme's voice was faltering and she'd lost her usual confident bearing. She couldn't hide her concern about her grandson. "Yes, Meme."

GRACIE ARRIVED LATER that evening to help Penny dress for dinner. Though Penny always dressed herself, it gave them time to chat.

"Did the appointment not go well?" Gracie asked.

Penny stared at Gracie as her friend shifted from one foot to the other, obviously uncomfortable. "What? Why are you staring at me?"

"What do the servants say about Hugo?"

Gracie flushed and wouldn't meet her eyes. "Nothing for you to worry about."

Penny snapped, "Gracie. Stop treating me like a child."

Gracie flinched. "Don't speak to me like Miss Harriet does." Gracie swallowed before mumbling, "They don't like the fact that he's always travelling to Germany and seems to prefer reading their newspapers. Did you hear someone talking? Was it Rob Pike? You don't want to listen to any of them, Penny. Sure, what do they know?"

"The woman today didn't want me to volunteer. She seemed to think Hugo was a Nazi."

"No! She never? He's a nice man, not that I know him well. Your uncle would kill him, never mind Her Ladyship. What did your grandmother say?'

"She bullied the woman into giving me the job. I don't know, Gracie, maybe I shouldn't take it. I don't belong here, really. I should go back to France."

"That's ridiculous. You got yourself over here from France all by yourself. Are you going to let some stupid gossip stop you from doing what you want? That's not the Penny I know." Gracie softened her tone. "Come on now. You've fought your aunt every step of the way to get this job. After what you told me about those children, they need people like you. You go and show that woman and everyone else you are your own person. It doesn't matter what folks say about Master Hugo or anyone else. He's not volunteering, is he?"

Penny gave Gracie a hug. "Thank you."

"For what?"

"For being my friend. You're right. I'll show them."

CHAPTER 10

On her way back from an errand that had taken her to Oxford Street, Gracie stood for a second in the square watching the workmen remove all the banners and flags. She could still see Queen Elizabeth's face as she looked her way. Even though the Mall had been crowded, Gracie was convinced the queen had looked straight at her, those cornflower-blue eyes almost the same colour as…

A slammed door broke her concentration.

She saw Penny race out the front door of the house. She tried to call out to her as she ran toward the road, but Penny didn't hear her. Instead she kept running, crossing the road but looking in the wrong direction. She didn't see the delivery truck coming but froze when the driver hooted his horn, his brakes squealing.

Gracie dropped her parcels and ran – her first instinct to save her friend. She pushed Penny out of the way just in time, the wheels of the car grazing her legs slightly as the motion sent both girls flying onto the pavement.

Stunned, Gracie lay where she was for a couple of seconds.

She heard a man's voice say, "Miss, are you all right? I swear I didn't have a chance. I never even saw her until she was stood in front of me." The driver moved his hat from one hand to the other, his face wracked with guilt. Gracie lifted her head, but the world started spinning so she'd to put it down again. She glanced toward Penny, who lay unmoving on the pavement. "Penny?"

"Don't you worry about her, love, you stay still."

Gracie heard Sir John and Lady Louise in

the background, the latter shrieking like a flower seller from Covent Garden. Gracie reached out for the man's hand and tried to sit up, desperate to find out if Penny was all right. She saw Sir John pick Penny up in his arms and carry her into the house, brushing aside all offers of help from Mr Perkins. Rob ran toward Gracie, his hand holding her elbow as he helped her up and guided her towards the front steps. She murmured and pointed towards the back steps – Lady Louise would kill her if she didn't use the servants' entrance – but Rob insisted. She concentrated on putting one foot in front of the other as the world spun around her.

When they reached the kitchen, she was beyond grateful to sit down, Rob helping her into a chair at the table.

Cook clutched at her throat, the look of terror on her face contrasting with the harshness of her tone. "Oh my world, Gracie Thompson, but you almost got killed. What did you run in front of the lorry for?"

Gracie pushed her trembling hands together and ignored the question, instead asking, "Penny – is she all right?"

Mr Perkins arrived just in time to answer. "Sir John wants to speak to you, Thompson. Make yourself presentable now. Hurry."

Cook turned on the butler, taking her anger out on him. "You leave her be. The poor child's had a right scare. Sir John can wait a few minutes."

"He certainly can." Sir John's voice carried into the kitchen ahead of the man himself.

Cook's face turned scarlet. "Sorry, Sir John, I didn't mean no disrespect."

"None taken, Cook. You're quite right. I should have made my intentions clearer to Perkins. I want young Thompson – Gracie, isn't it? – to see a doctor to make sure she has suffered no injuries. The driver said she was dizzy, but he didn't think she hit her head."

Gracie said in a trembling voice, "I'm fine, Sir John. But what about Pen – I mean, Miss Penelope?" She cursed silently at her slip.

"She'll be just fine. She has a few bruises and perhaps a broken arm. You saved her life today. She must have forgotten she was in England and looked the wrong way when she ran into the road. She wants to thank you herself but my wife won't let her leave the couch until the doctor has been." Sir John held out his hand to Gracie. "We owe you a great debt. Perkins will see that a car takes you home to your parents once the doctor is happy with you. You could stay here but I imagine you'd like to see your mother."

"Yes please, sir, thank you."

"Take a week off, paid." Sir John turned his attention back to Cook. "Perhaps while the doctor sees the young ladies, you could put together something for Gracie to take back to her family?"

Cook dipped a curtsy. "Yes, of course."

"Thank you." He turned to leave but seemed to remember something. "Oh, can someone get the smelling salts for my wife? She's had an attack of the vapours."

And then he was gone, with Perkins following in his wake.

Cook let out a long breath. "Imagine the master himself coming down to my kitchen to check on you…" Cook mumbled as she put her hand on Gracie's shoulder. "That was a good deed you did today, my girl."

Shaking, Gracie tried to stand up but gave up when her legs threatened to fail her and sat back heavily in the chair. "Cook, I left the parcels on the road."

"Rob's been and fetched them. Not that they are much use, the bags all burst, but there's always more where they came from. So long as you are all right, Gracie. Wouldn't want to face your mam if you weren't."

Gracie put a hand to her head, which was now throbbing with a headache. "Why was Miss Penny so upset? She looked like she was crying as she ran across the street."

"She was. You missed the big fuss. Lady Louise found out about the young lady staying out overnight to see the coronation."

Gracie blew her hair out of her eyes and

fought tears of frustration; after all her years of hard work, this would be the end of her job. Would she even get a reference?

"She didn't tell Madam she was with you," Cook whispered. "Miss Harriet told her she was but Miss Penny insisted she was with some French friends the family didn't know. She protected you, so don't you breathe a word about it."

"No, Cook." Gracie didn't think she could speak about much at all. Her head was thumping too hard.

GRACIE COULDN'T WAIT to get back to work after a couple of days of her mam fussing over her. She loved her mother but she hated staying in bed or sitting around like an invalid. She was fine, apart from the dizzy spells over the first couple of days. The doctor said she must have hit her head without realising it and had what he called a mild concussion.

But her mother was concerned about her low mood. "Are you still worried about the young lady? I thought you said it was only a broken arm."

"It's not her injuries, Mam. She's just got a job volunteering, helping those poor children who escaped from Spain, but the people there don't trust her because of gossip about Master Hugo."

Her mother rolled her eyes. "People shouldn't believe everything they read in the papers."

"I'm worried she's unhappy and not thinking straight. She's talking about going back to France, saying she hasn't any friends and doesn't belong here…" Gracie brushed a tear from her eye, but not quickly enough, as her mam came over and gave her a hug.

"You've a soft heart, Gracie. Young Penny will be fine; she's made of strong stuff. She has to be, to have come over here from France all by herself and her not much older than my Kenny."

Gracie didn't argue. There was a world of

difference between her tree-climbing younger brother and Penny.

"Mam, I think I'll go back to work to-morrow evening. Go up early so I can catch up with Cook."

"And Miss Penny?"

Gracie nodded.

"Just promise me something, love. Don't you forget she comes from a different world to us. She belongs in the big house with the fancy clothes, and she has opportunities we can only dream about. I don't want to see you getting hurt when she finds friends in her own social standing."

"Mam! Penny was poorer than us when she was in France, she told me so. Anyway, we don't have money but we're good people, aren't we?"

Her dad coughed as he put his cigarette out. "Course we are; your mam isn't saying we aren't. She's just telling you how the real world works. She's worried about that soft heart of yours as she's got one the same."

Gracie grinned as her dad planted a big

sloppy kiss on his wife's cheek, making her turn scarlet and mutter, "You put me down at once. The children are looking."

"And what's wrong with them seeing their parents are still in love?"

Gracie walked out of the room, heading upstairs to pack. When she got married, she hoped she'd be as happy as her parents were.

CHAPTER 11
MARCH 1938

"Gracie, your brother Stan is at the back door. Cook says you must come and speak to him or he'll be arrested for loitering." Rob Pike's voice carried up the backstairs. The butler must be out or he'd have given Pike a clip around the ear for shouting.

Gracie's heart beat faster; what did Stan want? He knew better than to come and see her at work. Couldn't he have waited till her day off on Thursday?

Penny came out of her room and followed Gracie down the backstairs. "I'm sure everything is fine, Gracie. Maybe he got engaged to Alice?"

Gracie pushed her hair behind her ear, nodded to Cook and stepped out through the servants' entrance. Stan greeted her by sweeping her off her feet and swinging her around.

"Put me down, Stan, this minute. What if someone sees?"

"Who cares? I got the best news ever and had to come and tell you."

"Alice said yes?" Gracie stared at her brother's face. It was a long time since she'd seen him so excited.

"Alice?" He looked confused for a second before his ears turned red and he looked away.

"What is it then?" Gracie, impatient to get back inside, didn't want Perkins to catch her out here.

"I got accepted. I'm going to fly. The boss signed me off for two months. I'm off to Scotland, somewhere called Perth. Imagine, Gracie, yours truly is going to be flying. For real."

She couldn't find her voice. He was going

away to Scotland to learn how to fly. What would their parents think?

"Gracie, say something. Isn't it great news?"

"What did Mam and Dad say?"

"Don't know yet. Haven't told them; you were the first one. I thought you'd be excited for me. You knew all about my dream but…" His voice tailed off, the disappointment on his face making him look like a young child. "I guess I should have gone straight home. Seems stupid to think a girl would understand." He turned to walk away, his shoulders stooped like an old man's.

"Stan, come back here. Of course it's fantastic news. I know it's your dream. I'm just shocked. I thought it was expensive to learn how to fly. Can you afford it?" She whispered the last bit.

"Now I can. Someone decided men like me can have a chance too. Charlie got in of course as he's been to grammar school. He put in a good word for me and got the boss to write a reference. The new guvnor said they wanted men from all backgrounds and by my taking my classes at night, it showed them I could handle the commitment. I've got to spend two months up in this Perth place and then I've to build up my hours either after work or at the weekends. Whenever I get time."

"Alice will love that. She says she doesn't see much of you at the moment."

"Alice has her dream with her nursing. It's not my fault she works such long hours. She'll understand. I'd best get back home to tell the parents."

Gracie couldn't stop the tremble of fear. If Charlie knew how to fly, when war broke out, he'd be gone.

She hugged him, her hands holding him so tight, he protested. "I'm really thrilled for you, Stan." She released him and brushed the tears from her eyes. "You'd better pack some warm clothes; I heard it's bitter cold up in Scotland."

"I will, I'll take those socks you got me

for Christmas. Can you believe it, Gracie. Me a pilot."

"Good luck, Stan. Be careful. Wish Charlie good luck for me too." She didn't meet his gaze, not wanting him to guess how much she wanted to meet Charlie again.

"I'll tell him you were asking for him."

"No! You needn't do that. I just think it's nice of him to look out for you. That's all."

He kissed her on the cheek and with a wink he was gone, almost running down the street, reminding her of their youngest brother, Kenny.

She turned to go back into the house. Cook stirred something in a bowl and Penny tried to look fascinated by the contents but Gracie knew both of them were dying to know what had prompted the visit.

"Everyone at home is fine. Stan is joining the Royal Air Force volunteer reserve and has to go to Scotland."

"Scotland?" Cook queried at the same time as Penny clapped.

"Yes, Cook, for two months to do lots of flying and learn stuff."

"Gracie, you should be pleased. You told me how much Stan wanted to fly. He's getting his dream."

"I know, Penny, but ... well, it can only mean that the government thinks we're heading to war, doesn't it? Why else would they offer to train blokes who can't afford to learn how to fly?"

Both Cook and Penny stared at her but Gracie needed to be alone. She picked up a bucket and some soap. "Miss Harriet's bath looks like coal miners used it."

PENNY DIDN'T HAVE time to discuss Stan's news. She was due at the children's home. Mrs Appleton had proved a hard taskmaster and for a while Penny thought she'd never do anything right. But despite the put-downs and the cutting remarks, she kept going back. Week after week. Whatever else she was, nobody could say she was afraid of hard work.

"Miss Hamilton, is that you?"

"Yes, Mrs Appleton." Penny wiped her hands in her skirt, pushing some stray hairs back off her eyes. What had she not done this time?

"Come in and sit down, won't you?"

Surprised at the cordial tone, Penny pushed the door open and took a seat at the desk. She hadn't been in the office since the day Meme had brought her for the interview. Nothing had changed; if anything, it seemed even duller than before.

Mrs Appleton sat with her hands clasped on the table. She stared, not speaking, until Penny shifted in her chair. Was she waiting for Penny to speak first? *No. She's not going to bully me any more.* Penny stayed silent but held the woman's gaze.

"I'm delighted, and I've to confess rather surprised, by your conduct, Miss Hamilton. You are an asset to the orphanage. I feel somewhat ashamed for judging you so harshly when you came to visit us with your grandmother."

Penny opened her mouth but didn't say anything as Mrs Appleton held up her hand as if to stop her interrupting.

"You have worked harder than most of our volunteers. I've had excellent reports from everyone. They all say you give the same attention to the poorest child as you do to those blessed with, shall we say, more obvious gifts. Most of the time it is our prettiest or most intelligent orphans who gain the attention."

Penny didn't know whether she was expected to agree. She stayed silent.

"I wanted to apologise for my attitude to you and your family. I was wrong to judge you, even more so to assume you would be found lacking."

"Please don't apologise, Mrs Appleton. You gave me a chance to prove I'm more than a decorative ornament." Penny glanced at the woman to see her smile at the description. "My aunt believes I should sit around all day and be graceful. I much prefer letting my hair down and playing with the children. I've learnt so much from being here. Please don't tell me you want me to leave?"

Penny's heart was beating so loudly, she thought the woman could hear it.

"Leave? Of course not. I just wanted you to know I'm grateful for your efforts. You can stop working so hard now. You don't want to overdo things."

"I like going home tired. It's a good excuse to get out of my aunt's social gatherings."

Mrs Appleton smiled, a gentle smile which lit up her face, making her appear younger. "Miss Hamilton, Penny if I may, you should remember there are more ways to help than to spend time with our children. Your position in society offers you other opportunities. We're always short of funds so perhaps you could highlight the plight of our children when you attend these soirees?"

Penny grinned. She could just imagine her

aunt's face if Penny started begging her aristocratic friends for money.

"I've to send some volunteers on a first aid course. I'd like you to take it. You're not afraid of blood, I take it?"

Penny clenched her hands together, despite wanting to dance on the spot. If she was trained in first aid, the hospitals were sure to accept her as a nurse.

"Not a bit, thankfully. Can't afford to be afraid of blood when growing up on a farm." Penny covered her mouth; she couldn't believe she'd let her secret out. Aunt Louise would be furious.

To her surprise, Mrs Appleton laughed. "I thought there was more to you than met the eye, Mademoiselle Hamilton."

CHAPTER 12
MARCH 1938

Gracie was enjoying spending Saturday afternoon at home. Cook had given her a few hours off, as Sir John and Lady Louise had gone to visit friends for the weekend with Penny and Harriet, taking Perkins with them. Cook took advantage of the butler's absence.

"Gracie, I know it's your day off, love, but can you give me a hand with this?" her mam said. "Stan brought that nice Charlie Power home with him. Daft lad never gave me any notice. Still, it's so nice he's back after two months in that Scottish place. I missed him. I want to bake a sponge, maybe a seed cake as well."

Gracie's pulse raced; Charlie was here? She hadn't seen him since that night in Leicester Square yet had never forgotten her reaction to him.

"Where is he?" She wanted to ask her mam if he'd asked after her, but that would sound silly. As far as her mam was concerned, Charlie and she were strangers. And they were.

"Your dad took them off to see his allotment. Him and his vegetables. I swear he loves those marrows more than he does me. He pays them more attention." Gracie heard her mam chatting but it was like she was speaking at her through a window or something. She sounded distant while the noise of Gracie's pulse beating took over her head. Was Charlie single these days? Would she still be attracted to him? Should she apologise for being rude that time or just pretend it never happened?

"Gracie, are you listening to me?"

"Sorry, Mam, I was miles away. What did you say?"

"I was asking what's happening up at the house, Gracie? How is the young lady?"

"Mam, she's been keeping busy at the children's home but I know she's still unhappy. She doesn't feel she's doing enough. She's always listening to the news on the radio and reading the papers. She's convinced that Hitler is going to cause a war now that he's marched into Austria."

"What's a young lady like her doing worrying about what happens in other countries?"

"She's been working with those children from Guernica. You know the place the Germans bombed? She thinks our government is too trusting of Hitler."

Her mam pursed her lips. "I reckon she might be right. I've given up listening to the wireless or reading the papers. But your dad feels it's only a matter of time. Says there was too much bad feeling after the last war."

Her mam beat the eggs, flour and sugar into a batter before pouring it into the cake tin and sliding it into the oven. Then she started on the seed cake, her husband's favourite.

"Penny still wants to become a nurse, only the family won't let her."

Her mother looked shocked, and tutted. "I would have thought with all the talk of war, they would be glad she wants to do her bit."

"Lady Louise doesn't think it is fitting, as Penny could be expected to look after male patients. Miss Harriet wouldn't dream of being near a hospital. Both of them ignore Penny most of the time and leave her alone. In fact, the only time Harriet seems to speak to her is to make fun of her. God love whoever that young lady ends up marrying, as she'll make his life miserable." Gracie chopped the vegetables, using the knife as an outlet for her frustration. Her mam put a hand on her arm, before taking the knife out of her hand.

"Let me do them. It isn't the veggies' fault your friend isn't happy. From what you've told us, Miss Harriet is a spoilt young madam. I won't disagree with you there. I wonder if she's jealous of the attention young Penny is getting, particularly from Her Ladyship. What about Master Hugo?"

Gracie ran the water into the bowl to wash the pans her mam had finished with. She liked Master Hugo but was he the Nazi sympathiser the other staff said he was? She couldn't reconcile a kind man being associated with Hitler.

Her mam made a noise, reminding Gracie she was waiting for an answer.

"He's never there. He has so many friends he spends his time visiting their houses. He goes abroad a lot, too. I heard Her Ladyship say he was spending a lot of time in Germany." She hesitated, waiting to see what her mam's reaction was.

Her mam shook her head, pushing her hair back behind her ear. "He won't want to be doing that much longer, not with all the talk of war. He can't be friendly with the enemy. People won't like it."

They won't like him reading German newspapers or speaking the language either.

"If he lived in a house like ours, the coppers would be having words with him."

Gracie shrugged. "Nobody will say anything to him, though, will they, Mam? It's one rule for the rich and another one for the rest of us. It's always been that way." She let the pans fall into the water, causing it to splash both of them. Her mam opened her mouth but whatever she was going to say was taken over by a giggle. Gracie laughed too. Sometimes you needed a break from the serious side of life.

They worked in silence for a while, each occupied with their own thoughts. After putting the vegetables on to steam, Gracie's mam went out the back to put the vegetable peelings on the side for her husband's compost heap. She came back inside, a thoughtful expression on her face.

"Maybe things will change, Gracie. Sometimes I think it would be better if women ruled countries. They wouldn't be rushing into stupid fights."

Gracie filled the kettle and put it to boil

on the stove. "Don't let Dad hear you saying that. You know what he thinks about women and politics."

Gracie's mam raised her eyebrows, her eyes dancing with amusement.

"He may be right. What woman would have time for politics with a family to keep fed and clothed? Best get the food on the table, lass, or we'll have a riot on our hands."

"Can the girls set the table, Mam? I just want to go and get changed. These clothes stink of boiling cabbage."

Her mam cocked her head to one side but didn't argue. Gracie ran before her scarlet face gave her mam ideas. She quickly washed in cold water from the bowl on the dresser in the girls' bedroom before putting on a different day dress. She knew the pink chiffon material suited her colouring better than the navy one she'd worn home from work. She brushed her hair and at the last minute added a touch of rouge to her lips. Her father would kill her if she used any more make-up. Then she heard voices. Stan's, her dad's … and his.

Her knees turned to jelly and her heartbeat quickened.

She walked down the stairs just as her mam called her name. Despite the now-crowded back room, she only saw him. He was staring at her. The electricity between them crackled once more. His lips parted as he held her gaze. She walked towards him, seeing the flush spread on his neck. He felt something too.

"Gracie, you're here. Are you going on a date? You're all dressed up."

Gracie shut her eyes, wishing her twin would shut up.

"You leave her alone, Stan. Nice to see someone making an effort for once. Gracie, thanks for trying on the dress, it's lovely. I won't have to make any adjustments."

Gracie flashed her mam a look of gratitude for covering for her. Her mam winked back before turning her attention to the food on the table.

THE FAMILY SAT down to the meal and started eating once Gracie's dad had said the prayer.

Gracie couldn't look at Charlie. She pushed the food around her plate, her appetite having fled as her stomach turned cartwheels. She caught a disapproving look from her dad – he hated food being wasted – and quickly said, "Mam, this meal is delicious. You are the best cook ever."

"You'd best not let Cook hear you say that, or your life in the big house won't be worth living."

"Cook won't mind. After all, she taught you when you worked for the Hamiltons."

"Yes, she did, and looked out for me and all. She was only a few years older than me, but she'd been in service a long time before I started. You must take back some cake for her, Gracie."

"I will, if there's any left. Stan hasn't lost his appetite."

The others laughed as Stan wiped the crumbs from his face.

"Mam, can I go now? I'm taking Alice to

see a film."

"You should bring Alice home to see us, lad. It's been ages since we set eyes on the poor girl. Anyone would think you're ashamed of us."

Stan coloured but said nothing.

"He's worried you'll start talking about weddings, Mam." Kenny, now twelve years old, got a cuff around the ear for his cheek. "Ow, what did you do that for? I heard you and Dad talking about it one night…"

"That's enough, Kenneth."

Gracie felt for her younger brother; when their dad used their full names you knew you were in trouble. But he shouldn't have embarrassed Stan. She could tell her twin was desperate to leave; he hated any talk of weddings or being tied down. He'd asked Gracie to have a word with Alice to stop her talking about her bottom drawer. Despite loving her brother to bits, she'd refused. If Alice wanted to dream about getting married, who was Gracie to stop her? And if Stan wasn't serious about the young nurse, he should stop walking out with her. There was no room for dishonesty between couples.

"What are you going to see, Stan?"

"Don't know yet. Alice's turn to choose. Right, I'm off. Want to walk with me, Charlie?"

Gracie stared at her plate as if her life depended on it. She hoped he'd say no but she couldn't ask him to stay. Not in front of her parents; they wouldn't like her being forward.

"Charlie will stay and have some more cake and another cup of tea. Won't you?" Gracie's mother didn't wait for an answer but rose to put on the kettle. "Go on, Stan, don't be late. Give her our love."

Stan rose and pushed his chair in before grabbing his coat. "Thanks, Mam, you're the best. See you later, Charlie."

The front door banged as Stan headed off. Gracie stood to clear the table and take the dishes to the kitchen, making room for fresh tea. Charlie stood too, and took a step nearer to help. She was so conscious of him by her side, her hands shook. He rescued the plates, taking them out of her hands before she sent them crashing to the floor.

"Let me bring these out to the kitchen. Least I can do after such a fine meal."

She blushed, berating herself. It wasn't a declaration of love, just an offer of help. She looked everywhere but at him, feeling his eyes on her.

"You've lovely manners, Charlie Power, could teach my boys a thing or two." Gracie's mam sent her youngest a look but Kenny remained oblivious. They all sat back down and had more tea and Charlie accepted the last slice of seed cake. Gracie nearly got a fit of the giggles at the look on her dad's face when he realised his favourite had been given away but she damped it down.

Charlie stood up, his eyes flickering to Gracie, smiling as she blushed at being caught looking at him. He turned to her mother. "It's getting late and I should be going. Thank you for a wonderful meal, Mrs Thompson."

"It's a pleasure, Charlie. I was lucky that

there was a sale today at the market. Gracie's dad grew the vegetables down on his allotment." She beamed at her husband across the table. "I hope you will come again. Do you know your way back to the station?"

"I think I'll find it."

"Gracie, why don't you walk Charlie down to the station while I start on the tidying up? We don't want him being late back because he got lost."

Charlie grinned, sending a wink towards Gracie. "That's kind of you, Mrs Thompson. I hope you don't mind, Gracie."

Gracie's hands flew up in the air but before she could protest he knew the way, her mother answered. "She doesn't mind a bit."

Gracie gave her mam a look. Could she have made her matchmaking any more obvious? "I'll just grab my coat."

AFTER SAYING THEIR GOODBYES, they headed out into the street. Charlie's height meant

Gracie only reached to his shoulder. He was walking very close, so near in fact that their hands could touch by accident if she held hers out slightly. He smelt good too, a mixture of Brylcreem and aftershave. She didn't know many boys who wore perfume; it took her mother's nagging to get Stan to use soap. At least it had until he met Alice.

Her heart thumped as Charlie slowed his pace, his eyes meeting hers.

"I'm glad your mother suggested you walk me to the station." He'd a posh voice, not like hers. Then she remembered he hadn't gone to the same school as her brothers but to the grammar school.

"I'm surprised she thought you wouldn't find your way. After all, you've played enough football around here." She kicked herself for the catty reply. What was she doing? He was being friendly and she sounded like a witch. But instead of annoying him, her tone seemed to amuse him. He gave up all pretence of walking, standing nearer to her.

Charlie's blue eyes challenged hers. "You

could've said that I would know my way in the dark, but you didn't. I hope that means you might like me a little."

Her cheeks flushed. It was as if he'd read her mind, but before she could say anything, he continued, "Would you like to go for a walk sometime? I could meet you in Hyde Park and we could go for tea?"

Yes! She'd love to. But instead, she heard herself say, "I don't know when I would be free."

"Come on, Gracie, admit it. You would like to come out with me. After all, who wouldn't want to be seen with this specimen?"

With that, he did a turn on the street, his arms outstretched.

Gracie burst out laughing. "You are completely mad."

"Not yet, but if you don't say yes, I can't comment on the harm the rejection will have on my mental state."

She giggled as her nerves disappeared.

She liked him, a lot. He seemed to share the feeling.

"Okay, you win. Thanks. I get a half-day on a Wednesday when I finish at two o'clock."

His nose was almost touching hers as he stared down at her. She'd have a crick in her neck at this rate but she didn't care. Was he going to kiss her? Her hands grew clammy as her heart beat faster and faster. Then he moved slightly back. "Great. You work near Hyde Park, don't you? I'll meet you at the main gate at three o'clock if that suits you?"

Gracie nodded, not trusting herself to speak.

"Now, you'd best get off home. It was great to see you again – and in a much better mood than last time."

He grinned and Gracie couldn't help smiling back. It felt wonderful to be asked out. She went back into the house, humming. Her mam looked up and smiled at her eldest daughter before getting back to the dishes.

CHAPTER 13

"Well, how did your weekend go?" Penny asked Gracie, who was hanging up some dresses in Harriet's room. "I wish you could've come with us. It was so boring at Uncle John's friend's house. The girls could only talk about clothes. Harriet made sure they all knew I was her poor French cousin. I'd to put up with them all making fun of my accent."

"I'm sure it wasn't that bad, Penny." Gracie looked over at Penny lying on her cousin's bed.

"Oh, it was. Wait, why do you look so happy?" Penny sat up and looked at her friend. "Your weekend was obviously much better than mine."

"It was fantastic. Cook let me go home for dinner on Saturday."

"And what happened? You have a strange dewy look in your eyes."

Gracie fidgeted, fingering the material of the dress she was hanging up. "Penny, I've met someone who I think could be very special."

"What? You were only gone for the afternoon!"

"Stan brought this friend of his back for dinner. We met almost eighteen months ago at the pictures. I'd gone with Stan and was annoyed with him because the film was horrible. Charlie overheard our conversation and asked a question. I was going to tell him he was rude for intruding on a private chat, but when I looked at him I couldn't talk. He was so gorgeous, I couldn't take my eyes off him." Gracie walked over and sat on the bed beside Penny. "My mouth went so dry, I thought I would have a coughing fit. His name is Charlie. He's a volunteer pilot in the RAF and he's really nice. I walked with him halfway to the train station and we could talk. He is really easy to chat to and oh, so nice to look at." Gracie trailed off, realising she sounded silly.

Penny clapped her hands. "He sounds perfect. When are you seeing him again?"

"He said he'd take me out for tea next Wednesday. I'm meeting him at three o'clock at the main gate to Hyde Park."

Penny's face fell. "That doesn't sound very romantic. Afternoon tea? In France, he'd take you for dinner."

"We're not in France, though, are we?"

Penny shrugged her shoulders in that Gallic way of hers. But her smile was soon back as she leaned in and whispered, "Have you kissed him yet? What was it like? I'm dying to know what it feels like. It looks so romantic in films."

Gracie smiled. For all Penny's insistence on being grown up, she was still a child.

"Kissed him? I should think not. What

type of girl do you think I'm? My dad would kill both of us. Now, off you go, let me get back to my work."

Relieved to be alone with her thoughts, Gracie continued her work. What would it be like when he kissed her? She'd never kissed a boy. She hoped she'd know what to do. It didn't look that hard in films. But she doubted that actresses suffered from butterflies the way she did whenever she thought of him.

It seemed like years to Gracie before Wednesday finally arrived. She felt sick, her stomach turning over. She couldn't eat, and more than once over the last few days had decided she wasn't going.

Even so, once her work was finished, she headed up to her attic room to get dressed, telling herself to be calm.

She took off her uniform and had a quick wash using a flannel and a bowl of boiling water, shivering with the cold. She'd just put her underclothes back on when there was a knock at the door and Penny came in carrying something.

"Good, you haven't got dressed yet. I bought you a surprise." Penny held up a pretty, light blue blouse and cream skirt. The blouse had little cream flowers embroidered over the bodice. Gracie was speechless.

"Don't you like it? Meme helped me choose it. We thought it would be perfect for afternoon tea with Charlie."

Gracie gasped in disbelief. "You told your grandmother I was going out with a boy?"

Penny giggled. "Meme thought it was wonderful. She's a real romantic at heart. You know she reads Georgette Heyer novels all the time. Anyway, do you like the outfit?"

Gracie played for time, washing her hands again before picking up the blouse and skirt. How would she look Her Ladyship in the face again? "They're beautiful. Thank you, Penny." She was lucky her mam made her lovely clothes, but this outfit was special. She fingered the material; the blouse was silk, not cotton. She'd seen nothing so lovely before, and gratitude to her friend filled her heart.

"Go on, try them on. I want to see if they look as good as I think they will."

Gracie grinned before putting on the skirt, her fingers faltering at the buttons. Her hands shook with excitement.

After tying her hair up in a bun and applying the slightest touch of lipstick, Gracie turned to Penny. "What do you think?"

"You look gorgeous. He can't help but fall in love with you now."

Gracie's face fell as her insides turned over again. She put her hand on her stomach. "Oh, don't. I'm not even sure I want to meet him."

"That's just nerves. Off you go or you will be late." Penny smiled as Gracie took a deep breath and stole one final glance at herself in the mirror.

GRACIE HURRIED across the square and over to Cumberland Gate. She looked around but couldn't see Charlie.

Lowering her head, she walked around for a while, not wanting people to know she was waiting for someone. She looked up at the carriage gates, trying to imagine what life had been like for the ladies who travelled in carriages. She knew servants like her weren't always well treated, but at least they were free to marry whom they wished. The ladies of the house had little say in whom their parents picked as husband material.

Gracie kicked at a pebble, wondering why she was thinking about weddings and husbands. He hadn't turned up. Maybe he'd changed his mind about wanting to see her.

"Gracie, wait please," came a shout from nearby.

Gracie turned to see Charlie waving at her from across the street. His face was flushed, as if he'd been running. Some loose strands of hair fell across her face. Impatiently, she pushed them out of the way.

"I'm so sorry. I got caught up at work." He leaned forward to kiss her on the cheek, but she moved away quickly, leaving him kissing the air between them. "I hoped you'd wait."

"I was late myself. I thought I'd missed you," Gracie lied.

"Oh, that's a relief. I was worried you would be mad at me again." He smiled, causing a shiver to run through her. "May I take your hand? I thought we could take a walk first before we go to Lyons Corner House?"

Gracie shuffled her feet, her hands tightly by her side. She avoided meeting his eyes. Struck by unfamiliar shyness, she forced herself to let him take her arm and they walked through the park. It only took a few minutes for her to relax and start enjoying herself. Charlie kept her amused, telling her funny stories about himself.

Time flew by and soon she was standing outside Lyons without remembering the walk. She glanced inside as the waitresses moved swiftly, carrying trays laden with dishes and cutlery above the customers' heads. She was amazed at the way they didn't walk but glided across the floor. How graceful they looked in their black and stark white uniforms, each wearing a similar monogrammed hat and medium-heeled shiny black shoes. Cook would approve of this place. There was nothing she hated more than dusty shoes and slovenly appearances.

They waited for a seater to direct them to one of the many tables covered in white table-cloths. A band was playing. Gracie looked around at the finely dressed ladies. She fingered the blouse at her neck, thankful for her new clothes. "It's lovely here, isn't it?"

"Yes. You are easily the most beautiful woman in this room." Charlie helped her out of her coat and pulled the chair out for her to take a seat. When they were both comfortable, he moved to take Gracie's hand in his across the table. "I know we have only spoken a few times, but I feel like I've known you for years. I'm so glad you agreed to come out with me today. And so sorry I was late."

"It couldn't be helped. I was busy day-dreaming about what life was like for the people who used to use carriages and drive through those enormous gates." Too late she realised what she'd said and blushed.

"So you weren't late."

Gracie's cheeks grew hotter. "Only a little," she fibbed.

She smiled shyly, glad of the interruption caused by the arrival of their afternoon tea.

THEY ENJOYED THEIR TEA, chatting easily and watching the other people in the restaurant. Afterwards, Charlie walked Gracie back to Belgrave Square.

She stood at the servants' entrance, not wanting the day to end, and trying desperately to think of something interesting to say to prolong it. She glanced at him under her eye-lashes, wishing he'd talk. When the silence continued, she held out her hand. "Thank you very much for a lovely afternoon."

Charlie ignored her hand and leant in to kiss her lightly on the cheek. "I hope it's the first of many," he whispered, and gave her a smile before walking away.

She stood, her hand touching the spot on her cheek until he disappeared from sight. Thank goodness he hadn't looked back; she was behaving like a love-struck fool. Giving herself a good shake, she skipped down the steps ready to face Cook's interrogation.

CHAPTER 14
LONDON, DECEMBER 1938

Gracie knocked at her front door, Charlie hopping from one foot to the other behind her. His nerves were showing, despite the fact he'd come to the house many times before – as Stan's friend.

"I wish they would just give me a key; it's not like I live here now," Gracie whispered.

"You have to be twenty-one for that to happen. Mum is the same with me," Charlie whispered back before the front door opened.

"Hello, Dad," Gracie said, giving her dad a kiss.

Taking her and Charlie's coats, she hung them on the hooks behind the door, almost falling over the pile of gas masks as she did so. There was nowhere to store the boxes, and they had been warned to keep them handy just in case. It was yet another sign war was expected, despite Chamberlain's words.

"Hello, Mr Thompson, Mrs Thompson. Thank you for inviting me to your home again," Charlie said, nodding to her dad.

"Come into the back room and sit down, lad. We can have a chat while the girls get the tea on."

Gracie winked at Charlie as he left the room, and she went to help her mother in the kitchen. Through the open door, she listened in on the conversation, thankful her dad had turned off the wireless that now took pride of place on the back wall cabinet.

She peered round the doorway and saw her father take a seat in the chair near the wireless, leaving Charlie to perch awkwardly on the edge of the settee.

Mr Thompson spoke first. "So, you work in an office during the week, but fly at the weekends?"

"Well, yes, sir, I'm in the reserves just like Stan."

"What sort of planes do you fly?"

"Hurricanes, sir."

"Dangerous job, but I gather you love it."

"Yes, sir. I love to fly. I just wish I could do it all the time. I'm not too keen on the office job. I hate being indoors all day."

"I couldn't face working inside all day long, either. You should get yourself an allotment."

Gracie peeked into the room; poor Charlie's face was white. He caught Gracie looking and they exchanged a smile. When would he have time to grow vegetables? If he wasn't working or flying, he was meeting Gracie. She ducked out of sight again to help her mam.

"So, what are your intentions towards my daughter? I gather you two have been out a few times."

"I like Gracie and hope to keep seeing her. It's early days, but I see a future for us together." When his comment was met with silence,

Charlie hastened to add, "With your approval, of course."

"Make sure you treat her well, young man, or you will have me to answer to."

Gracie and her mam chose that moment to come into the room. Charlie let out his breath as he jumped up to take the tray from Mrs Thompson.

"Did you enjoy the film?" Gracie's mam asked.

"Yes, Mrs Thompson, although not as much as Gracie did. I think it was more for the ladies."

"I would love to see it, but I've yet to persuade Gracie's dad to take me. Would you like some sponge cake with your tea?"

"Yes, please, Mrs Thompson. That would be lovely."

"I've some seed cake if you prefer."

"No, the sponge cake is fine, thank you."

"I suppose your mam worries about you flying? I know I'm worried sick about Stan being so far up in the sky in one of those contraptions."

Gracie sat down beside Charlie, giving his hand a squeeze as she did so. He smiled at her before replying to her mother.

"Stan's an expert pilot. As for Mother, well, she not keen on it, Mrs Thompson, but I'm not sure it's the flying that bothers her. She'd prefer I'd more time to spend with her. Working all week and flying at the weekends doesn't leave me with much spare time. I only get to see her for a few hours, and being on her own, she finds that difficult."

"Do you not have any brothers or sisters, then?"

"Mam, stop asking so many questions. Give Charlie a chance to eat his cake," said Gracie.

"Gracie, your mother has a right to know more about me." Charlie smiled at Mrs Thompson before continuing, "I've a sister, Meredith, but, well, she's married and has a family of her own. She and my mother don't see eye to eye."

Gracie's mother nodded. "That can happen between mams and daughters. Thankfully we don't have that problem, do we, Gracie?"

"Not likely. They never stop talking, this pair," Gracie's dad added.

Her mam handed Charlie a slice of cake. "Gracie said your dad died in the last war. We were sorry to hear that."

"He died shortly after the war from the effects of the gas. At the end, it was a release, as he was suffering."

Gracie's mam nodded and said, "War brings misery to everyone, yet here we're facing another one. The last one was supposed to be the one to end all wars. I don't know why we can't just keep our heads down and let other countries fight their own battles."

Gracie glanced at her father and saw from his expression that his temper was rising – he hated them talking about another war – but her mam carried on regardless.

"I'm sure many agree with you, Mrs Thompson, but then we can't stand back and let evil men like Hitler just do as they please. That's not the British way."

"Aye, I know, but I didn't have three boys so I could lose them to a war. It was bad enough last time round, waiting for Gracie's dad to come home."

Gracie's dad spoke up. "Well, I came home and so will the boys. Now, hurry, woman, and pour my tea before I die from thirst."

GRACIE COULDN'T STOP SMILING as she returned to the big house. Despite her father's warning about his intentions, Charlie wasn't behaving any different. She wished she had Christmas Day off to spend with him but she had to work. As she climbed the backstairs, she heard someone sobbing. It sounded like Penny.

She hurried to her friend's room, knocking on the door before pushing it open. Penny was sprawled across her bed, her puffy face and eyes testament to how long she'd been crying.

"What is it? What's the matter?"

"Gracie, you've no idea. You wouldn't believe what I've seen and heard. The things the children told us, you couldn't make it up. I've never heard anything like the stories…" Penny couldn't speak any more, her sobs threatening to choke her.

Gracie poured her a glass of water. "Penny, drink this. Now breathe and breathe again. Shall I ring for your aunt or uncle? Maybe you need some brandy?"

Penny shook her head. She sat up slowly as if every movement hurt.

"Gracie, you should have seen them, some no more than babies, all on the run for their lives."

Thinking Penny was being overly dramatic, Gracie reached over to check her forehead for signs of a fever. Penny pushed her hand away. "I'm not ill; sick with horror, maybe, but I don't have a fever."

"Who were these children? Where were their parents?"

"Dead most likely." At Gracie's sharp gasp, Penny turned her eyes towards her. "Sorry, I didn't mean to shock you. Only it's true, these children are the Jewish survivors of Kristallnacht. The Night of the Broken Glass. You know, we heard about it on the wireless."

"Yes, but that was men being rounded up. No one said anything about kids."

"No Jew is safe in Germany or Austria now. Nowhere in Europe if Hitler's plans come to pass. Not all the children are Jewish; some are the children of those who spoke out about Hitler and have now disappeared or been imprisoned or are in the mortuary."

Sometimes Penny's direct translation from French into English meant she was more forthright than most English speakers but this time Gracie believed her friend was in shock. She moved closer, taking the top blanket from the bed and wrapping it around Penny's shoulders.

"Don't cry, Penny. You can't do anything more than you are doing. You should try to rest. Tomorrow may be better."

"How? There are thousands of children over there and only so many places here for them. The government doesn't want them, nobody does. How can people not save the kids?"

"Hush now. Getting in a state isn't going to help anyone. Tomorrow you can talk to Sir John about things. But for now, you should have a wash and get changed and try to sleep."

CHAPTER 15

Gracie glanced at the heavy brocade curtains now gracing the library windows, as she finished her polishing. All the talk of the war had sent people scurrying to the local stores to buy up heavy curtains, black paint, brown paper and drawing pins. There was constant talk on the wireless about what the blackout would be like if the time came. A glimmer of light could guide the enemy to bomb London.

"Gracie, what has that poor table done to you? By the time you're finished polishing, it will have a hole in the middle of it."

Gracie looked up at the sound of Penny's voice. Her friend looked tired, with dirt marks on her cheeks. She was wearing the uniform she'd adopted for her volunteer work. Lady Louise had deemed a dark-coloured skirt with a pastel-coloured blouse suitable for working with the Women's Voluntary Service, or WVS as it was better known. Lady Louise seemed to believe Penny had given up working with *foreigners*.

She put the cloth down and threw her hands in the air. "I'm just sick of all the war talk, aren't you? People are either talking about Franco in Spain or what Germany is doing to the Jewish people or those lot in Czechoslovakia. I don't even know where some of these places are, yet they are all I hear about."

"And for good reason," Penny replied. "You've heard the children's stories. How their parents were treated on the streets, how the Nazis behaved on Kristallnacht. We have to do everything we can to stop Hitler and his friends, Gracie, or you and I might be doing a goose-step down Oxford Street."

Despite the grim subject, Gracie had to

smile at the thought. Penny smiled back then turned serious again.

"I don't think anyone is taking enough notice of Hitler and his plans. France certainly isn't. My people seem to think that just because they beat the Germans last time around, they can beat them this time."

Harriet's haughty voice preceded her into the library. "They didn't beat anyone last time. The English won the war while the French all mutinied. Didn't you learn any history at your school?"

Penny turned on her cousin. "More than you did. The Americans and British helped the French win but they fought on the ground in my country. My papa died because of the war. Most of my friends in France lost at least one family member. So we know more about wars than you will ever know."

Harriet flicked her hair back from her face, casting a disdainful glance in Penny's direction. "Perhaps, darling cousin, you should return home and tutor the French men with your knowledge."

Gracie couldn't take any more; she pushed the polish tin off the side of the table. The tin clattering on the marble fireplace was enough to distract them. They both looked at her.

She gave an innocent shrug. "Sorry, miss, it slipped right out of my hand."

Harriet glared at her. "What are you doing in here, Thompson? Rose has left and I can't be expected to do my own hair. Why are you doing scullery work?"

Because your mother hasn't employed anyone else. Much as she was tempted to tell the girl the truth, Gracie just bobbed as she was expected to, and apologised.

"Sorry, Miss Harriet, but it needed doing and there was no one else available. Would you like me to come and dress your hair now?"

"No, it will have to do, otherwise I will be late. Peter is taking me for early luncheon. You can clean up my room; it's in a dreadful state and very cold. Why Father believes we shouldn't have a fire in our bedrooms is beyond me."

She swept out of the room.

Penny's nostrils flared as she glared at her cousin's retreating back. "Fires in her bedroom indeed. Why can't she pick up her own dresses? You aren't her skivvy, Gracie. You have enough to do, running around doing everyone else's jobs."

"You can't speak like that, Penny. Your aunt will have a fit."

Penny's head dropped to one side. "Like what?"

"When you first came here, you said I will, I will not, I did not. Just like the family does. But now you talk like me."

"I spend more time with you. It is better I sound more English for when I get a job. Stop changing the subject, why are you working so hard?"

Gracie shrugged. "Your aunt can't replace the staff – not with the higher wages other places are offering. Now that the men are all joining up, women can earn more in other jobs."

Penny's face fell. "Does that mean you will find another job?"

"No, you daft goose. If I got another job, who would keep you out of trouble?"

"Do you really mean that? Or are you just saying it?"

Gracie hesitated, not sure if she wanted to put her dream into words.

"Tell me the truth. Are you thinking of leaving?"

"Not really. At least not immediately. But I thought, if we do go to war, with Charlie being in the RAF, I might join the women's air force. Not that they will allow us to fly but they're looking for girls to join up."

"Oh, will you really?" Penny's face lit up like a candle on a Christmas tree. "I'd love to do that too if I can't get into nursing school." Then her face fell. "But they won't let me, will they? I can just hear Aunt Louise now. *You are too young, too foreign, too impetuous, too…*"

"Too busy to stand around here chatting. I promised Cook I'd help with dinner. Her hands hurt if she keeps them in water too long so I volunteered to peel the potatoes and whatever other vegetables she wants."

"I'll go and help Cook; you go see to my cousin's room. I'd hang her dresses up but the temptation offered by her nail scissors may prove too much for me."

Gracie burst out laughing as Penny raced off to the kitchen. Her friend might be seventeen now but she still ran everywhere.

CHAPTER 16
FEBRUARY 1939

Sweating from carrying the heavy pan of water to the sink, Gracie tipped it over. It was filthy but at least the tiles of the kitchen floor now shone to Cook's satisfaction. She'd forgotten how hard it was labouring in the kitchen but the staff shortage had worsened. Now it was only Gracie, Cook and Mr Perkins left. Rob Pike had surprised everyone by joining the army, and the other girls had gone to work for better wages in the factories.

Massaging the muscles in her shoulders, Gracie wondered again if she shouldn't resign. She'd earn more money for fewer hours and be able to live at home with her parents.

But that would leave Cook high and dry, and she'd always been very good to her.

A knock at the back door broke into her thoughts.

Cook called out, "Get that for me, Gracie, will you? I'm trying to sort out the shopping list for later."

Gracie dried her hands and, pushing the hair behind her ear, opened the door. She nearly squealed with delight at seeing Charlie until she took in the expression on his face. He looked serious.

"Charlie, what are you doing here? Is there something wrong?"

"Nothing wrong, Gracie, I just had to see you. Come up here and walk with me for a few minutes. I don't want to hang around the servants' entrance. Anyone could interrupt us."

Gracie looked around her nervously. "I only saw you on Saturday, and I can't skive off work now. Her Ladyship already looks like she's sucking a lemon. I'm going to be in the doghouse for weeks at this rate."

Charlie put his hand on her arm, slightly tugging her sleeve.

"It's important, Gracie. You can explain to your mistress when you get back." The imploring tone in his voice together with the strange expression in his eyes made her say yes. Was he excited or upset? She couldn't really tell.

She glanced over her shoulder, wondering if she should risk getting caught. It must be important for him to come up here when she was working. Then she laughed at herself. Hadn't she just been thinking she should find a new job? She grabbed her coat from the hook beside the door, calling out, "Cook, I'll be back in five minutes." She shut the door before Cook had a chance to answer.

They walked to the little park in the centre of the square. Once inside the gate, under the shelter of the trees, he took her in his arms and kissed her.

As he pulled away again he looked her deep in the eyes, and said, "I'm sorry, Gracie, but I couldn't wait until the weekend. I got my papers. They've posted me to Tangmere."

Shocked, she tried to breathe but her breath seemed to have disappeared. She saw the excitement in his eyes withering away as the silence grew between them.

He said, "Aren't you going to say anything? This is it. I'm going to fly for real. No more losing my eyesight staring at rows of numbers."

He grabbed Gracie and swung her around. It was only when she was standing once more that he seemed to notice her tears.

"Where?" she whispered.

"It's an RAF base in a village in West Sussex. I'm joining 43 Squadron for six months' regular service as I've built up so many flying hours." He was obviously trying to be gentle but he couldn't keep the excitement from his voice. He was dying to fly, desperate to get away from London. From her.

"When do you go?"

"Next weekend. I've to give Mr Saunders a week's notice as he's been so good to me. I can't wait. We'll be practising dogfights, air-to-air firing and everything."

"Sounds so exciting!"

"Don't be sarcastic, Gracie. You know how much I love flying. This is the chance of a lifetime."

She pulled away from him. "You can be so stupid." She raised her hands before she knew what she was doing, but caught herself just in time. She saw the flash of anger in his eyes at her insult but she was too annoyed to stop. "You sound like a little boy going off on a pleasure trip. They're teaching you how to fight. For God's sake, Charlie, if there's a war, you could die."

"I know I can't expect a woman to understand, Gracie."

She glared, and his expression softened. "This is everything I've ever dreamed of. Don't ruin it for me, please." He put his arm around her, feeling her shaking as he pulled her close to his chest. "Gracie, I have to go."

She wanted to hit his chest and scream, *No you don't.* But it wouldn't be any use. If

she asked him to choose between her or flying, she didn't know what his answer would
be. It wasn't something she was ready to take
a risk on.

"I know. But I don't have to like it." Her
tears made her voice sound different.

She pushed against him, wanting to be
free.

"I didn't say I wouldn't miss you, but I've
to go, Gracie." She heard the panic in his
voice. "The six months will pass really
quickly. I'm bound to get leave and I'll
write."

She looked into his eyes, seeing the storm
of his emotions. He wanted her, but he
wanted to fly too.

"I love you, Gracie Thompson."

"I love you too, Charlie, more than you
will ever know." She sniffed before saying,
"Please write as often as you can. I guess I
won't see you for weeks now."

"I don't know when I'll get leave, but I'll
write. Now, I've to get back." He hugged her

to him. "Darling, please dry your tears and give me another kiss. Be proud of me."

She kissed him. "I'm proud of you," she mumbled, before turning away and running back to the house.

CHAPTER 17

Belgrave Square, London, March 1939

Dear Madame,

I hope this letter finds you well. We're still in London, as Meme hasn't yet recovered from a fall and has to see the doctors on Harley Street. She's feeling better, but annoyed with the doctor, who says she should take more care of herself now that she's getting old.

It has been an exciting week here. My cousin, Harriet, was presented to our new king and queen. She wore white from head to toe. That's what most debutantes wear when being introduced to the court. Gracie and I gasped when we saw the jewels Harriet wore. We were too scared to try them on ourselves in case they would break. Meme laughed at that, telling us diamonds were the hardest stones. They glittered so much they looked like sparkling lights in Harriet's hair and on her ears and neck. Aunt Louise had to have a new dress as well. I don't think she was very keen on people knowing she had a daughter of eighteen, but she looked amazing. She wore some stunning jewellery, too.

I wasn't presented, of course, but I did sneak into the party Aunt Louise held afterwards to have a look at some guests. They all looked incredible, but there was this one girl who stood out from the crowd, possibly because she wasn't wearing white like the other debutantes, but a more flattering coral-coloured dress. It had a beautiful long train sewn with tiny pearls that shimmered as the light caught them. She wore the obligatory three white ostrich feathers in her hair, but had fastened them onto a mother-of-pearl pin to match her dress.

She was easily the most beautiful debutante there, not only because she was stunning-looking but also because she was brave. I mean, it must take bravery not to bow to the pressure to wear white when being presented. Aunt Louise was horrified and said the girl's mother should have insisted on her wearing the proper clothes, but I think she made the right choice. Meme thought so, too. Who wants to have to look like everyone else?

I would have loved to meet the coral girl, as I nicknamed her, but when I asked Harriet who she was, she wouldn't tell me. I don't know why, but Gracie said she thought it might be because the coral girl was the belle of the ball. Maybe Gracie is right, as usual.

Uncle John says it is only a matter of time before the war begins. He doesn't believe that Hitler is going to stay quiet. I'm still trying to persuade Aunt Louise to allow me to become a nurse, but I'm not getting very far. It is so *unfair. She believes I'm working with the Women's Voluntary Service. I do some hours with them but I spend more time at the orphanage dealing with German and Austrian refugees. They have so little. Mrs Appleton sent me on a first aid course so at least I'm not sitting around looking pretty useless.*

What will happen to you if there's a war? I asked Meme if you could come and live with us, and she said you could and would be very welcome. She said you could stay in her house in Suffolk or in the London house. I think you would prefer the Suffolk house, as I don't think you would like Aunt Louise or Harriet.

Please say you will come? I can send you some money for the trip, as Meme gives me an allowance every month. I've nothing to spend it on, so have quite a bit saved in the bank. You can have all of it. Please think about it?

With all my love,
Your petite fille,
Penelope

As she read over her letter, Penny wondered where the girl in the coral dress was now. She bet the girl wasn't begging and pleading to be allowed to join the services. From the library where she was reading, Penny heard raised voices. That sounded like her aunt. Muttering, she put her letter back in the envelope and opened the door just in time to hear her name being called from the drawing room. She took a few steps towards the drawing room but hesitated, instead putting her ear to the door to hear better.

"Penelope, come down here at once. Where is that useless girl?" Louise demanded of her husband.

"Leave her be, Louise. She has done nothing wrong."

"Not done anything wrong! I've had yet another letter acknowledging her application to become a nurse. A nurse? In our family? Whatever is she thinking?"

Penny almost groaned; she'd asked the hospital to address the letter to Her Ladyship care of the house in Suffolk but they'd obviously sent the letter here and Louise had opened it. She braced herself for the fight that lay ahead.

She brushed her hands down her skirt, patted her hair into place and, with a quick glance in the hall mirror, turned to open the door, just in time to hear her uncle speak up on her behalf.

"She probably doesn't realise what nursing involves. Try to be nice, my dear. Penny isn't doing this to annoy you, but because she's bored."

She flashed her uncle a smile of thanks before addressing her aunt. "Yes, Aunt Louise?"

"Penelope, how many times do I have to tell you that young ladies never run, but walk sedately and knock before entering a room?"

"Sorry, Aunt Louise."

But her aunt didn't stop to acknowledge her apology. "If I have told you once, I have told you a thousand times, no niece of mine is going to be a nurse. I will not tell you again, Penelope. You are not to apply for any more nursing positions. And stop shortening your words, you sound common. Do you hear me?"

"Yes, Aunt Louise," Penny said, watching as her aunt crossed the room and the door closed behind her back.

Her uncle turned to her, a sympathetic expression in his eyes. "Your aunt is rather exhausted at the moment, Penelope. She has a lot on her mind with this talk of war. She's rather concerned that Hugo will volunteer into the forces. Although, I have to say I cannot see him heading off to war. He doesn't like to get dirty."

Uncle John smiled at her before looking back down at his newspaper. The wireless was on in the background and Penny became aware that the man on the radio was reading the news. Penny moved to turn up the volume as she glanced at her uncle, who'd let the newspaper slide onto the floor. They both listened in shocked silence as the newsreader announced that Hitler had just reneged on the Munich Agreement and had swallowed up what was left of Czecho-slovakia.

"Uncle John, don't you think it is amazing that while Harriet was being presented to the queen, the Nazis were marching down the streets of Czechoslovakia? I know that Hitler had already taken the Sudetenland, but now it looks like he wants the whole of the country. I mean, our lives are going on as normal while the Czechs now have to live under Hitler."

"Hm?"

Her uncle didn't answer, but Penny knew he wasn't being intentionally rude. He was genuinely concerned about what was happening in Europe and felt that the government was not treating it seriously. She knew he hated Chamberlain, as he believed that he was making the situation worse by giving Hitler the impression that nobody cared what he did next.

Penny looked fondly at her uncle. He may be distracted and busy, but he'd always been kind to her. She wasn't often alone with him and quickly decided that this was her best chance to get him on her side. "Uncle, can you please have a word with Aunt Louise for me?"

Her uncle looked away from the wireless to face her. "We have been through this, Penelope. You are too young to get involved."

"Too young! How can you say that? There are boys younger than I'm getting ready to fight, should the war start."

"They are boys. That is different." He bent to pick the newspaper up from the floor.

"But why, Uncle? All right, so I can't fight, but I can still do something. I'm bored sitting at home all day long, and anyway it isn't good for Aunt Louise."

Her uncle tried but failed to look anything but amused.

"Why, pray tell, is it not good for Louise to have you at home?"

"Uncle John, you know that I annoy her. I can't seem to do anything right, and my presence only serves to increase her irritation. She'd be much happier if I was away from the house all day, being useful. Like a nurse would be…"

"Penelope, there may not be many opinions I share with your aunt, but this is one of them. Nursing is not a proper profession for a young lady."

"But I'm not a young lady. Aunt Louise is constantly telling me I'm a country peasant." Penny regretted saying that as soon as the words came out of her mouth. She quickly looked at her uncle, trying to gauge how angry he was. In amazement, she watched him struggle not to smile at her.

"Well, you don't look or sound like a peasant to me, but I still don't want you nursing. Sorry, Penelope, but you won't change my mind. Your father wouldn't have liked it either. Now leave me to read my paper in peace. There's a good girl."

Penny wanted to swear in frustration, and would have if only she knew any swear words. She was going to become a nurse whether or not they liked it. She'd already made enquiries, but at the moment she couldn't find a hospital willing to take her on. She was too young, too inexperienced despite her work with the Basque children under the care of the Salvation Army. But she was going to find a way somehow.

CHAPTER 18

"Gracie, pet, could you run a duster over the library and clear out the ashtrays. Open a few windows too, the place stinks of cigars. I don't know why the master can't smoke cigarettes like everyone else."

Gracie didn't bother to argue that cigarettes stank too. Cook was clearly in a mood again. She asked gently, "Did you have another letter from your nephew, Cook?"

The copper pot Cook had been holding clattered onto the table and Cook put both hands on her hips. "I did, the little sod. Guess what Dicky's done now? Only joined up in the navy. What did he have to go and do that for? Never had no one in our family go to sea. But he says he wants to see the world. He can't even swim, the little blighter."

Despite her furious words, Cook's eyes swam with unshed tears. Gracie handed her a hanky, pulling the woman down onto a seat.

"I'll get you a cup of tea."

"Tea! It's more than that I need. I swear to you, Gracie, what has the world come to? Wasn't last time enough for everyone? Dicky never got to know his father, killed at Wipers he was. But now, look at him, can't wait to join up. My poor sister doesn't know whether she's coming or going."

Gracie placed a steaming pot of tea on the table with some of Cook's own biscuits. "Families all over the country are dealing with the same. Frank told Mam, Stan had the right idea joining the RAF when he did. Those that join up now should get their pick of the services. He said once war comes, the powers that be will just shove them where they're needed. Maybe young Dicky is just thinking he'd prefer the sea to going into the army like his dad?"

Cook raised her eyes to meet Gracie's. "You think so? The daft blighter might think it's safer."

"I don't know, Cook. I just hope the war never starts and all this digging up Hyde Park and building shelters and having sandbags everywhere is just a waste of time. Try not to worry yourself too much." Gracie straightened up. "I'd best get on."

"That's another thing. It isn't right you running here, there and everywhere. You were promoted long ago. You shouldn't be cleaning or fetching."

"Someone's got to do it. Now have your tea."

Gracie didn't mind working in the library. She loved reading, and dusting the books gave her a chance to see if there were any that caught her eye. Sir John was good about that; he encouraged his staff to borrow whatever they wanted to read, no matter how old or valuable the books were.

She emptied the ashtrays, her nose wrinkling at the smell. Drawing the curtains helped bring the light in, and she lifted the sash to let some air in. The fresh air was sharp but a welcome change to the tobacco scent. Humming as she worked, she didn't notice the young master in the room until he cleared his throat. She hadn't heard he was back. He'd been away travelling in Germany and Austria for the last year. Blushing, she stammered, "Sorry, sir, I didn't mean to interrupt you. I didn't think there was anyone in here. Would you prefer if I came back later?" What was he doing sitting so low down in the chair in the dark?

"Don't worry, I'm going out anyway. You are Thompson, aren't you? What's your first name?"

"Um, Gracie, sir." Despite her best efforts, she sounded flustered. And why wouldn't she? He'd always been good-looking but had matured in the last year. He looked like some sort of Greek god with his blond hair and piercing blue eyes. He'd a nice smile too, his eyes crinkled at the side of his face. Oh heavens above, she was staring at him. "Sir?"

"Gracie, could you do me a favour? Can you please look out for my cousin? I know my request is unusual given you are a servant and she's the niece of a viscount but, given her upbringing, I imagine she's more comfortable with your class."

Gracie swallowed hard in a bid not to react to his throwaway remarks. He might look nice but he lost all attraction at that point. He didn't notice her reaction and continued talking.

"She has had an awful time of it lately. I'm afraid Mother gave her a roasting last night when the question of her training to become a nurse came up. I gather she has mentioned this before. She has yet to learn that once Mother makes her mind up, we can do nothing to change it. Being all alone is probably making her feel a bit under the weather. It would be nice if she could have a friend. There's little point in asking my dear, darling sister to do anything but look out for herself.

I've to go away again, so I won't be here to look out for anyone."

"Well, of course, sir." Gracie decided to speak the truth. "We're friends already, actually, but please don't tell anyone. I don't think Lady Louise would approve."

"Yes, dear Mama. She does rather live in the last century, don't you think? She forgets that poor Papa is rather stuck for funds. The death duties from his father and brother almost wiped out the whole estate. Thankfully, the property in Suffolk was in Grandmamma's name so it couldn't be forcibly sold."

Gracie remained silent. It wasn't her place to comment on the financial affairs of the family. If he thought the Hamiltons were poor, he should take a walk down to Mile End and see real poverty.

"There is a war coming that will change everything, but I think she prefers not to think about it."

"I think we all prefer not to think about it, sir."

"What? Oh, yes, of course."

"Sorry, sir, I didn't mean to be rude. My mam always says I should engage my brain before opening my mouth."

To her surprise, he smiled.

"Don't worry, Gracie, I didn't even notice. The war brings out many opinions. You probably have brothers, don't you?"

"Yes, sir, and they have already signed up. Stan is in the RAF. He works out at Northolt, training as a pilot, and Frank is in the army."

She couldn't help but look at Hugo directly in the face, wondering what part he'd play in the coming war. She got the impression he seemed to dash from one party to another. She doubted his social life would give him time to fight any war. But she told herself she was being unkind. She barely knew him and was just judging him on other people's opinions.

As if sensing her thoughts, he stood up.

"Right. I had best be off. My dear mother has arranged another social evening in Claridge's with the intention of finding me a bride. It's so tiresome." As if remembering who he was talking to, he stopped to light a cigarette. Throwing the match into the ashtray on the table but missing, he said, "Thank you, Thompson. I mean, Gracie."

Gracie picked up the newspaper he'd been reading when she came in, noticing as she did so that it was in a foreign language.

"Your paper, sir."

"Thank you."

He smiled again, and despite herself, she couldn't help but see the attraction he held for the ladies he visited. She wondered why Master Hugo was reading a paper with foreign words on it. And why was he being so nice?

LATER THAT EVENING, Gracie was reminded of the comment Hugo had made.

Cook said, "Gracie, can you see to Lady Louise tonight?"

"Yes, Cook." Gracie was thankful Lady Louise had chosen to entertain her guests at a hotel rather than at home. They were too short-staffed to cater for guests. Maybe her boss was becoming more practical after all.

Gracie went to Her Ladyship's bedroom to help her undress. Louise was talking to her husband and didn't stop as Gracie entered; she didn't appear to even notice that Gracie was in the room.

"But why does he have to go away all the time? How am I going to make a suitable match if he's never around?"

Gracie, careful not to show she was listening, hid a smile. So Master Hugo had been right; his mother was trying to marry him off.

Sir John sighed. "Leave him be, Louise. He is only young, and it is time for him to meet some women that you wouldn't consider suitable. It's part of a young man's journey to adulthood. Max will look out for him. We are good friends." Sir John's voice sounded tired.

"You mean you were."

"No, Louise, I mean *we are*."

Gracie jumped as the master raised his voice. He must have noticed as he seemed to collect himself, continuing in a more polite tone. "Max doesn't agree with Hitler's notions any more than I do."

Gracie brushed Louise's hair, trying to tease it into a proper chignon. She wasn't as practised as Rose. Louise winced a few times but her ire was directed at her husband.

"How can you know that? Time and experience changes people. You haven't seen Max in years, not since he came over back in 1937, and from what I recall you had some heated discussions."

Looking in the mirror, Gracie saw Sir John roll his eyes behind his wife's back.

"We enjoyed a lively debate as gentlemen. We didn't fall out, and I don't expect that to change. Hugo loves going to see Max's family, and he always gets a warm welcome. I imagine he goes out on the town with Max's son, Hans. They are of a similar age."

Louise, forgetting Gracie was just finishing her hairdo, twisted in the chair to face her husband. "But do Hugo's friends all have to be German? There are plenty of young men of his own age in England. They could have a beneficial influence on him. He doesn't appear to be rushing into any of the services when most of his contemporaries are already in uniform. I do not want our friends commenting on his frequent trips abroad. Not now."

"Our friends won't even notice. Well, not unless you bring it to their attention."

Louise laughed, but it wasn't a cheerful sound. Gracie put her hands on her mistress's head, gently persuading her to look straight ahead so she could finish up. She didn't like listening in to other people's conversations and it made her uncomfortable they seemed to have forgotten she was even there. What was Sir John doing in his wife's dressing room anyway? Couldn't he go downstairs and have a drink while waiting in the drawing room?

"Not notice? Have you not heard the questions? People want to know what service he's going into or what he's going to do once he's finished with college." Louise looked in the mirror and caught Gracie's eye for the first time, appearing surprised to see her. "Gracie, what are you doing here? Where is Rose? You know I prefer her to dress my hair."

Gracie hesitated; had the mistress forgotten Rose had left for a better-paid job in the factory? "Sorry, ma'am, there's only me left. Well, aside from Cook and Mr Perkins."

Louise sniffed, recoiled slightly from Gracie's touch. "I suppose you will be up and off leaving us in a lurch too."

Gracie wanted to tell her to do her own hair. Instead she whispered, "No, ma'am."

"Louise, stop blaming young Gracie. She's proved her loyalty by staying with us for so long. About Hugo, can you not tell people he's studying abroad? That will help excuse his trips, if what your friends think concerns you so much."

"My friends? They are your friends, too. You don't want to have to face questions at the office about your son and his love affair with the Germans, now do you?"

"Oh, my dear, I think you are making a lot

more of this than you need to. You know Hugo went up to Oxford and met Hans while he was there. We even entertained him for dinner, and if you remember, you thought he was a delight. I don't understand why you have an issue with Hugo going to stay with Max's family now."

"I don't have an issue with him staying with the family, but I'm not sure that Hans is the attraction. He has a beautiful sister, from what I recall."

"Hugo has never mentioned the sister."

"Yes, well, he won't tell his parents about his love affairs, will he? But a mother has an instinct for these things, and I believe there is a girl behind all these trips abroad. I can't see why you are not concerned. But then, unless it involves the office, you don't really care, do you?" snapped Louise.

"That's not fair, Louise. Now, please, let's not argue…" he cast a glance at Gracie and lowered his voice "… especially in front of the servants. Thank you, Gracie, but you can go now. I'm sure my wife can manage by herself now."

Gracie left the room, closing the door gently behind her. She couldn't help thinking about the conversation she'd overheard. So, it had been a German newspaper he was reading in the library, and there might even be a girl over there. That was a good thing. Being in love with a German girl wasn't the same as admiring Hitler, now was it? She knew what being in love was like and had some sympathy for Hugo. But she was glad that her brothers had more sense than to fall for a foreign girl at a time like this.

CHAPTER 19

Excitement or nerves. Penny couldn't tell what was causing the butterflies in her stomach. It was Gracie's nineteenth birthday and she'd invited Penny to her party. Now she'd be able to put a face to the names Gracie had mentioned over the years; she'd meet Nell, Gracie's mama and Kenny, Helen and the youngest girl, Mary. Would they like her? She'd bought them some sweets to help break the ice.

She stopped on the way to stare at her reflection in a shop window. Was she dressed properly? She'd chosen her clothes carefully, selecting a floral summer dress with a pretty, deep pink cardigan in case the weather turned chilly. She'd picked up a similar cardigan for Gracie's birthday present but in baby pink to suit Gracie's blonde colouring.

Cook had helped her put together a small food package as a contribution to the party. Penny wished Cook was coming with her, but she'd been firm. "You stand on your own two feet, Miss Penny. You travelled here from France on your own. Gracie's mam, Nell Thompson, is a real lady. I should know as I worked with her. Now go on and have a good time." Cook shooed her out of the kitchen.

It was quite an adventure to get a bus from Hyde Park to Lewisham. When she arrived, she had a fit of the giggles. Her uncle's chauffeur would have turned his nose up at the thought of driving "his" car through these packed streets filled with house after house, some in better condition than others.

Tons of scruffy-looking children were playing outside, enjoying the sunshine. She looked for number ninety-seven and soon found it, in the middle of a row of similar houses. Penny bit back her nerves as she walked to the front door, the step scrubbed clean and the door fittings all sparkling in the sunlight.

She knocked, her hand shaking. A buxom woman, a large smile on her face but an anxious look in eyes similar to Gracie's, opened the door.

"You must be Miss Penelope. Welcome to our home. It's not what you're used to—"

"Thank you, Mrs Thompson," Penny interrupted. "Your home is lovely."

"My name's Nell. Come in." Nell opened a door to what Penny assumed was "the good room" from the description Gracie had given her. It was empty, but she could hear people chatting and children playing, coming from the rear of the house.

"Sit down, please, Miss Penelope, and I'll find Gracie for you."

"Penny is my name and as Gracie must have told you, I grew up in a smaller house in France. Please don't treat me like my Aunt Louise. I'm here as Gracie's friend. Cook gave me some baked goods for the party; where will I put them?"

"I'll take those, thank you."

Penny gripped the box, wanting Gracie's mother to treat her as a normal person and not as part of the nobility. "Mrs Thompson, Nell, please. Let me carry it through and help. I want to be part of the party. I feel like I know you already."

Nell smiled and ushered Penny back out into the hall and indicated she walk through to the back room and kitchen. "Be careful what you wish for, Miss— I mean, Penny. My lot are completely barmy."

Penny giggled and put the box on the counter in the kitchen. Mrs Thompson introduced her to the rest of the family, and soon she was helping Gracie and the other girls make tea and sandwiches. The men, including the younger ones in uniform, were chatting, as always, about when the war would start.

Gracie's younger sisters insisted on bringing Penny out to see the Anderson shelter their dad had built. Mary held her hand out to Penny. "I'm six. Do I've to bow to you?"

Penny bent down to the child's level. "Why would you do that?"

"'Cause Mam said you're a real lady and you live in a big house and you have everything you want."

Helen, the older and quieter of the two, grabbed Mary's hand. "Hush up, Mary. Don't be rude."

"Helen, Mary, please just pretend I'm one of your friends."

"You're a grown-up. They don't know how to play." With that, Mary turned and walked ahead. Helen turned scarlet but stayed silent. They made their way through the beds of different vegetables growing in the back garden, which was about thirty yards long.

"It's for us to sleep in, but only when Dad says we can. Come inside and see," Helen explained as they came to the shelter. "Mam made little cushions to make it nicer inside. We can't wait to sleep here in the garden. It will be fun."

Penny tried to hide her fear of being underground from the little ones. She looked at the shelter dubiously. She couldn't understand how two curved walls of corrugated steel sunk three feet into the earth would save you from a bomb, but she kept her opinions to herself. Holding their hands, she allowed the little girls to drag her inside.

Overwhelmed by the smell of damp and feeling claustrophobic, she couldn't wait until she got back outside into the fresh air. She hoped that she'd never have to shelter in one of these things.

Helen turned to Penny, her eyes wide with curiosity. "Do you have one of these in your garden, miss?"

"No, sweetheart, we have a cellar in the house, so we use that instead."

Mary, picking at her nose with one finger, asked, "What's a cellar?"

"It's a gigantic room underneath the kitchen where Cook stores some food and other things."

Mary stopped picking, staring at Penny.

"If we go to visit you, can you show us the cellar?"

"Yes, sweetie, I will."

Penny saw Mrs Thompson coming towards them.

"Leave Miss Penelope be, girls, and off you go to play. Sorry about that, love, but they have heard so much about you from our Gracie."

"It's fine, Nell, but please call me Penny. The only person who calls me Penelope is my Aunt Louise." Penny looked at the children playing in the grass. "I enjoyed chatting with them, although I have to admit I could've done without the visit to the shelter."

Penny was immediately sorry she'd said anything, as Gracie's mother paled in front of her.

"It's pure madness to think that we're even thinking about having to use one of those things. Gracie's dad insisted. He rarely puts his foot down, but when he does, I listen. I can't bear to think of my kids having to go through a war. The last one was bad enough."

"I'm so sorry. I shouldn't have said anything."

"No, lass, it's me who should apologise. I just get so mad thinking about the fact that war is coming and there's nothing we can do about it. But let's not ruin today by talking about it. We're here to have fun. Now, off you go and mix with the young ones while I sort out some more food."

"Please, let me help you."

She chatted to Nell as together they cut more sandwiches and made fresh pots of tea. She went out to pass plates of food amongst the guests who had now spread into the garden.

On her way back into the house, Penny met Mr Thompson.

"Hello, Miss Penelope. Are you enjoying the party?"

"It's Penny, please, and yes, Mr Thompson. Thank you for inviting me to your home."

"Well, I guess it's not what you're used to, but we're lucky." He looked pensive before continuing, "Given what's to come, we should make this a birthday to remember. Hope you're good at dancing, girl!"

He smiled over at Penny before heading back to his friends.

Looking around, she was relieved to see Gracie coming towards her. "So, there you are. Why are you hiding out here? All the young men are out the front."

Penny smiled at Gracie. "I was just talking to your father. He's nice."

"Course he is. Where do you think I got it from? So, what do you think of my Charlie then?"

Teasing, Penny responded, "Who?"

Gracie gave Penny a playful pat on the arm. "You know right well. Have you met him yet? What do you think? He is gorgeous, isn't he?"

"Your dad pointed him out to me; he looks nice, but I haven't spoken to him. Now, come on, let's get back to the others. Someone will accuse me of monopolising the birthday girl."

THE PARTY WAS GREAT FUN, with a constant stream of neighbours and friends popping in to wish Gracie the best. Nell had baked a Victoria sponge cake, which she'd iced with her daughter's name and age. The party soon spread out to the road where the younger ones danced to the music coming from the wireless.

Stan had brought a few of his friends from the air force. The uniformed lads were happy to ask the local girls to dance. Penny watched Gracie dancing with Charlie, making Gracie look small and rather fragile as he towered over her. She smiled as she imagined Gracie's reaction to being called fragile, although at the moment her friend wasn't aware of anything but Charlie. You could light a fire from the sparks flying between the two of them yet they weren't kissing or behaving inappropriately. Charlie looked at Gracie as if the whole world spun around her. Penny sighed, any worries that the boy her friend had fallen in love with didn't feel the same falling away. She stood watching until they stopped dancing, Gracie pointing her out as they both walked in her direction.

Charlie smiled at her. "How do you do, Miss Penelope?"

Gracie laughed out loud. "Call her Penny – she gets all huffy if you call her Penelope. Penny, darling, could you look after Charlie for a while, as I need to go help Mam out for a bit."

Penny looked at the young man in front of her, who she guessed was feeling as awkward as she was. He opened his mouth a couple of times but seemed at a loss as to how to speak to her. She'd need to speak first.

"I'm not sure that you're the one Gracie believes needs looking after. I rather think she means me. So, how do you like flying?"

His eyes lit up with excitement and he spoke so fast he struggled to get all his words out.

"It's amazing. In the last six months, I've had to take navigation and signal classes and we've been learning how to march, salute and shoot. How many pilots need to know how to march? It's not exactly part of the job description." He shrugged as he seemed to realise he'd spoken without catching breath. "But I shouldn't complain. We spend most of our time flying."

Penny encouraged him to keep speaking, saying the first thing on her mind.

"I believe some of my cousin's friends joined the Auxiliary Air Force."

"Oh, they are the toffs. Oops, sorry, miss. I mean, Penny." His ears turned red as he blushed. "What I meant to say is that's where the officers go, but only those that wanted to join up part-time. Most have transferred into the RAF now, what with the need for more pilots and everything."

For the hundredth time, she wished she lived in a home like Gracie and people just spoke to her like a person. This class divide was so annoying and so stupid. Especially as she'd grown up poorer than any of the people living in this area.

She tried to keep calm. It wasn't Charlie's fault; it was the system, one her cousin Harriet and aunt did everything in their power to maintain.

"Yes, Gracie told me the RAF was short of pilots when she explained how you were in for six months." Penny thought it was sweet how Charlie went bright red at the mention of Gracie's name.

"Gracie spoke to you about me?"

Penny smiled. "Yes. A few times. She's a bit worried you will meet a girl in the town near your base."

"Oh, no, miss, there's only one girl for me. That's never going to change." He pulled at his collar, perhaps nervous or embarrassed at having shown his feelings. "Now, please excuse me, but I've some mates here from the RAF, and they don't know anyone else. I hope you enjoy the rest of the party."

Penny couldn't remember the last time she had so much fun and was sorry when the time came to leave. Stan and his girlfriend, Alice, dropped Penny back home. Alice had to be back at the nurses' home at the Royal Brompton.

Penny tossed and turned in bed that night. Her ribs hurt as she lay breathing. She hated to admit it but she was envious of Gracie's large family. Mr Thompson was, from Gracie's account, strict with his kids, but his love for his family was clear. Little Mary and Helen were adorable. How she wished she had siblings of her own.

A tear trickled down her cheek, as she clung to the last memory of her parents together. They'd all gone for a picnic by a stream. Papa, standing proud over the fish he'd caught. Her mama cooking them over a small open fire, exchanging secret smiles with her husband. Penny squeezed her eyes shut to try to stop the tears. The Thompsons might have little money, but they were far richer than her relations in Belgrave Square.

CHAPTER 20
JULY 1939

My petit fille,

Merci beaucoup to you and your meme *for the invitation, but alas, I must decline. France is my home, and I cannot leave now. I know you are concerned, my* petite chérie, *but please don't worry about this old lady. I'm happy here with my husband and my son. Who would look after their graves and that of your dear mama if I was to move to England?*

I really enjoyed reading about your cousin's presentation. It sounds like a wonderful affair. Will you be presented to the king and queen too, or do you have to be born in Britain to be a true debutante? Although if you were, I can see a big argument between you and your aunt regarding the colour of your dress. You always were a very high-spirited young lady and were never one to follow the crowd.

To be honest, I'm fed up with the talk of war. Spain's war is finally over and now everyone is talking about a war in Europe. You cannot buy a petit pain *without someone having an opinion on it. Will the Germans invade Poland? Can Hitler be stopped? Will he invade France?*

If you ask me, my darling, I don't think that Mr Hitler will be happy until we're all speaking German and walking the funny walk of his soldiers. But please don't worry about me. What would anyone want with one old woman?

I hate to tell you, but he arrived home from Spain and was greeted like a hero. Unfortunately, my prayers that he'd meet a Spanish bullet came to nothing. Perhaps God has a different and, hopefully, more painful death in mind for that devil.

I'm not going to waste any more ink talking about him. Please take care of yourself, my darling, and please continue writing. Receiving your letters always brightens up my day.

With much love always,
Dominique

PENNY WAS glad that Gracie's presence prevented her from sinking into melancholy. She loved getting Madame's letters, but they made her feel so homesick and concerned about what was going on back at home. One day she knew she'd go back to Souvigné, and then he'd be sorry ... And Madame's views on the war made her feel even more worried about what was coming.

"Penny? You're away with the fairies." Gracie rose from the library fireplace she'd just cleaned out. She sneezed.

"Sorry, Gracie. Did you ask me something?" Penny looked up from the couch as she put Madame's letter back in the envelope.

She'd learned the hard way not to leave correspondence lying around as Harriet would only read the letter and then tease her about the contents. The less her cousin knew about her life in France, the better as far as she was concerned.

"You seem tired … you're spending a lot of time at the orphanage."

"The children need people like me who understand what it is like to leave home. Alone. Those on the Kindertransport know they are lucky, they are safe. The older ones, those in their teens, also know their parents are in danger. Some of their fathers have already died on Kristallnacht or in Dachau and the other concentration camps. I can't help comparing their reality with mine. If I stay here, I just sit around all day until Aunt Louise drags me off to some social occasion."

Gracie smiled but Penny didn't feel like smiling. She was angry and frustrated but most of all exhausted. When she did get to bed, she couldn't sleep, thinking about the tales of horror the children had told her.

Hitler's goons were arresting anyone who spoke out against him. They had the German children, the so-called Aryans, joining the Hitler Youth and were encouraging those kids to spy on their parents. Everyone lived in fear of an outfit known as the Gestapo. She wished she didn't know all she did but more than that she wished she knew what to do with the knowledge. She couldn't just ignore it.

Gracie's voice interrupted her thoughts.

"Do you think Mr Chamberlain will avoid war? Even at this late stage?"

"I don't know, Gracie. Hitler seems intent on taking over whatever countries he considers German. The British government must see that he's a madman who needs to stop. We may know more after the dinner tonight, although I'm sure Aunt Louise will make us ladies withdraw before allowing the men to discuss the war. She…"

Penny stopped and stared into the mirror, looking at her friend's face. She'd only just noticed her puffy eyes and her unusual silence. Gracie was chatty at the best of times, and after a day at home, usually she never stopped talking. She'd barely said a word. "What's wrong, Gracie? Did something happen at home?"

"Oh, no, everyone's okay. Well, sort of. But my mam and dad were having words and they never do that. At least not in front of us kids. Some neighbours called in to listen to the wireless. They were all talking about when the war will start. When, not if. My dad rarely talks about what happened in the last war apart from saying he was lucky to survive. But we know things were bad, because he gets this look on his face whenever people talk about Hitler and another war. I just can't bear the thought of anything happening to Stan, Frank or Charlie. And, of course, there are the little ones. They say they will have to go away, but Mam won't let them go. She doesn't want them living with strangers. I've never seen my dad angry with my mam before. He keeps saying that if war starts, the kids have to go. They won't be safe in Lewisham."

Penny thought of the little ones at the orphanage and felt sorry for Gracie's mother.

"Maybe they won't have to evacuate?"

"I don't know. My dad lost some of his family in the bombings in the last war. Sarah, that's my mam's eldest sister, lost her fiancé. He was home on leave visiting his family. Now, it looks like it is going to start all over again." Gracie's voice trembled.

Penny turned to give her friend a hug. "Gracie, please don't cry. Mr Chamberlain may find a way out of this yet. Nobody wants another war…" She rubbed Gracie's arm and tried to think how she could help. "I've got it. Why don't we ask Meme if she'll take the children at her estate? It's far enough out of London to be away from the bombings, and the children wouldn't be going to strangers. I'm sure Meme will say yes."

"Oh, Penny, that would be wonderful."

"The kids can even help. I know Uncle John has mentioned a few times that he worries about how Meme will cope if the men from the estate join up. Maybe your younger brother can help the older staff. Your mother and father could even visit them to make sure they were okay. Let's talk to Meme first before you mention it to your family."

Gracie beamed. "Thanks, Penny."

PENNY WAS pensive entering the drawing room. She'd have preferred to skip dinner, but with Harriet and Hugo out, Aunt Louise had made it clear that she expected Penny to be present and behave like a lady. Sir James and Lady Dunn and Lord Beaverbrook were the guests. With Lord Beaverbrook being a widower, Penny was to be his dinner companion. Penny decided that the path of least resistance would serve her best. She'd do her utmost to be well behaved by her aunt's standards.

However, as the meal went on she found it hard to keep quiet during the dinner conversation. It was widely known that Lord Beaverbrook supported Chamberlain in his attempts to avoid war. His newspaper, the *Daily Express*, had used the heading, "There Will be No War". Penny couldn't resist asking him if he really thought that war could be avoided.

Lord Beaverbrook eased his considerable bulk in the chair, his expression a mixture of disdain and condescension.

"Now, Miss Penelope, a pretty young thing like you shouldn't concern yourself with the talk of war. You should be thinking of dresses, dancing and all the young admirers a person of your beauty will attract. My son, Max, is a flying officer in the RAF. He and his friends would be delighted to escort you anywhere you wish to go."

Despite her aunt's glares, Penny was not to be dissuaded. She was not some socialite like her cousin.

"But, sir, don't you think that Hitler is dangerous and should be stopped? Your newspaper could do more to help, to tell the ordinary public what the Nazis have done already." She saw his eyes narrow at her criticism but continued none the less. "The things he's doing to the people of his own country aren't right. How can we stand back and—"

He frowned as he interrupted. "Now, my dear, we don't know anything for certain about what Mr Hitler is doing. Of course, there are all sorts of rumours but none of us know what the real situation is. We cannot rush into another war based on some gossip or rumours. We have to tread very carefully. Mr Hitler has powerful friends. The Russians have no problem with him and are likely to support him if we did attack. You are too young to remember, but your uncle and aunt know exactly what the cost of war is and why we want to prevent another one."

He moved to pat her hand but hit the table instead as Penny lost control.

"I know the cost of war, sir," she retorted. His teeth clenched as his facial muscles tightened but she didn't care. She didn't dare look at the other diners. "My father died as a result of his war wounds, and his death caused the death of my mother." Penny's face burned with fury.

Her aunt spoke sharply. "Penelope, that is enough. Apologise at once to Lord Beaverbrook." Aunt Louise turned to her guest. "Please excuse my young niece; she has yet to learn the meaning of table manners."

Penny couldn't sit silently while her aunt spoke for her. "I apologise, Lord Beaverbrook, I didn't mean any offence. I'm just tired of being treated like a little girl. I'm worried not just about whether there will be a war but if there is, what will happen to my friends in France? I work with children who have been sent over here by their parents. These kids arrive with nothing, yet their families feel they are safer here than in Germany or elsewhere. At least here they won't be beaten to death or shot."

Lady Dunn cried out and Aunt Louise rose but had to sit down again immediately.

"Penelope, that is *enough*. We have plenty to worry about without you spreading unpleasant rumours. Go to your room now; I will deal with you later."

Uncle John glowered at his niece before turning to the butler. "Perkins, please bring the ladies some brandy."

"Yes, Sir John."

Penny appealed to her uncle. "But Uncle John, it's true. The other children have similar stories. They can't all be making them up, can they? Why aren't the papers reporting the truth?"

"Your room now, Penelope."

Penny rose from the table, knocking over her chair in her haste to leave. "I'm sorry…" she mumbled, before fleeing to her bedroom.

GRACIE WAS at the room waiting for her. "Oh, Penny, what have you done now? Mr Perkins said that dinner was a disaster."

Penny almost ripped her gown in her haste to discard it. She knew she'd behaved badly but why couldn't they see the truth? It was staring them in the face. Hitler wasn't going to be satisfied for long.

"I didn't mean to upset anyone, Gracie, but they were all talking about pointless stuff and I wanted to know why the papers weren't taking things more seriously. I mean, I know they are saying that the country is on the way to war and it appears that nothing can be done to stop the fighting."

Gracie came to her aid, helping her with the hooks and eyes at the back of the gown. She eased her out of it and then hung the dress on a hanger.

"I shall sponge it down in the morning." Gracie examined the dress but Penny knew she was just using it as a distraction. With Charlie and Stan both training, Gracie dreaded the outbreak of war more than most.

"Dad was just saying the other day that everywhere you went people were talking about Hitler and wondering what he'd do next. Dad thinks it is bad news that the Russians are going to be Hitler's ally. They have promised food to the Germans if our navy lads block their ports."

Penny wondered how Britain as an island would feed its people with the Russians and German navy patrolling the seas, but she didn't mention it.

"Yes, I read that, too, but the papers print nothing about what's happening to the Jews or other German people that Hitler doesn't like. They should interview the children arriving on the Kindertransport. They would give them the actual picture of what's happening inside Germany and what's likely to happen anywhere else that Hitler and his armies go."

Penny pulled her hair out of its pins.

"But what can we do, Penny? Or what did you want the dinner guests to do?" Gracie asked.

Penny understood she wasn't playing devil's advocate but really wanted to know. Penny wasn't sure she knew the answers – only that Hitler and his friends had to be stopped.

"They are powerful people. They could make Hitler stop the deportations or summary executions. If the Nazis can treat their own people like that, what are they going to do to the citizens of the countries they invade?"

Gracie shuddered before shaking her head.

"Come on, Penny, be reasonable. Do you think Hitler will stop just because Chamberlain asks him to?"

"But they could do more to help the children. How many are being left behind to live through awful experiences because their parents cannot afford to send them on the trains or aren't around any more to look after them? I can't just sit here and do nothing. I have to do something. What if Hitler goes into France? He could attack Madame Bayard or the children of the village while I sit here eating fancy dinners. I can't do it, Gracie. I won't do it. It's not fair. If I was a boy, I could go back to France and fight…" Penny threw herself on the bed, burying her head in the pillow to smother her tears.

"Aw, Penny, you're just overtired. The past few days in the orphanage have had more of an impact on you than any of us realised. Cry it out now. Mam always says that a good cry can do wonders."

CHAPTER 21

Excited and thankful that Cook and Penny had helped her get the weekend off, Gracie got ready to meet Charlie. He was on leave and they were going to Richmond Park for a walk. He'd promised to buy her afternoon tea. Gracie didn't care about the food. She'd eat paper if it meant she could spend time with Charlie.

Penny had given her some dresses, which Gracie's mother altered to fit. Her fingers stroked the jersey day dress she'd chosen today.

"Penny, are you sure I look okay?"

The light blue dress accented her thin

waist and fell in soft pleats to just below her knees. The bodice was plain, cut tight across the breast. She wore her grandmother's small gold cross necklace. Instead of wearing her hair pinned up as she usually did, Penny had helped her to style it so it fell in soft golden waves curling under at her shoulder.

"Okay?" Penny sighed. "You look beautiful."

Gracie flushed with pleasure. She hoped Charlie thought the same.

"Here, wear my wrap and get going. At this rate, you will be late." Penny almost pushed Gracie out of the door.

On impulse, Gracie kissed Penny's cheek. "Thanks." She hurried out, crossed to Hyde Park Tube station and headed to Richmond where Charlie would be waiting.

She spotted him on the platform as the train pulled into the station. He looked so handsome. She smoothed down the fabric of the dress before stepping out onto the platform. He came towards her, kissing her on the cheek before taking her hand.

"You look amazing. A beautiful dress for my gorgeous girl."

Caught up with happiness, she couldn't reply but squeezed his hand. Leaving the station behind, they walked past the parade of shops towards the park.

"It is so beautiful up here, isn't it? You could almost forget that everyone is talking about going to war," Gracie said, looking around her.

"Only if you were deaf and blind so you didn't see the uniforms or hear the troops practising. Not to mention the sandbags and the trenches being dug over there." Charlie laughed at the look his comment produced on Gracie's face.

"Oh, you. I'm trying to be cheerful today."

Charlie hugged her and kissed her thoroughly.

"Charlie, stop. It's the middle of the afternoon. Someone may see."

"Let them. I want to kiss my girl."

Gracie laughed, but then stopped as

Charlie was staring at her. Before she knew what was happening, he'd got down on one knee.

"Gracie Thompson, would you do me the honour of becoming my wife?"

"Your wife? Oh…" Her tongue got so tangled she couldn't say anything. She felt dizzy, and had a sudden mad urge to race around telling everyone how much she loved him. Her legs shook, but she didn't move.

"Is that a yes?" Charlie said, looking anxious.

Gracie could only stare as her ability to speak had failed. She tried to talk, but the words wouldn't come out.

"Come on, Gracie, darling, my knee is killing me and everyone is staring at us."

"Yes. Oh, yes." She rubbed her stomach to quell the butterflies.

Holding her hand, he got to his feet before swinging her into a big hug. "Did you all hear that? The most beautiful girl in England just said yes!" Then he put Gracie down and said to her earnestly, "I've to speak to your father, so don't go telling anyone yet. I don't want to get on the wrong side of your parents, not when they are going to be my mum and dad soon enough."

Gracie glowed with happiness. "Let's ask them now."

"Don't you think I should see your father alone?"

"Mam and I'll go and make the tea. That should give you enough time."

Charlie grinned. "Is this the way our married life is going to be, Mrs Power? You giving me orders?"

"Yes, and you'd best get used to it. Now, I order you to kiss me again."

"Yes, ma'am."

Gracie squealed as Charlie twirled her around before kissing her. Hand in hand, they ran to catch the train to Lewisham.

HER MAM and dad were sitting down listening to the wireless when Gracie and Charlie burst through the door.

"Don't tell me the Germans have invaded?" joked her dad.

Gracie caught her mam's eye. "Mam, can you come upstairs with me? I need your help with something."

"Just let me make Charlie a cup of tea…"

"Mam, I need you upstairs; we'll make him one soon. Come on. Charlie isn't ready for tea."

Charlie shook his head. Gracie guessed he wished he'd stopped for a swift pint, but the smell of drink wouldn't impress her parents.

"Come on, Mam," Gracie pleaded.

Her mam shot a knowing look at her dad before following Gracie out of the door.

They were longer than she'd expected before her dad called them both back to the room. Charlie looked miserable.

"Gracie, I'm sorry, but my answer is no," said her dad.

"What?" Gracie stared at her father.

"You and Charlie have only been walking out for a year. It's not long enough. Marriage is a serious business, and I don't believe you're ready for it yet."

"Dad, I love Charlie."

"Yes, I know you think you do, but you haven't had many boyfriends and…"

"I don't want many boyfriends. I just want Charlie. Mam didn't have lots of boyfriends, did she?"

"Don't take that tone with me, young lady." Her dad looked angry.

"Gracie, calm down. Your father has a right to worry about his daughters." Charlie looked directly at Gracie's dad before continuing, "Mr Thompson, I hope that you will reconsider in time. Nothing will change the way I feel about your daughter."

"I'm sure you're sincere in your belief, Charlie, but war changes everything. I'll agree to you getting engaged on Gracie's next birthday. All going well, you can set a date for her twenty-first. How does that sound?"

"Get engaged in May and wait a whole year to marry? How do you think it sounds?" asked Gracie incredulously.

Charlie put his arm around Gracie's shoulders and said, "What Gracie is trying to say is that sounds great. Thank you. Now, if you will excuse me, I'd best go home and collect my kit. I'm due back at training tomorrow, so I don't want to be late." He shook hands with both Gracie's parents. "Now, Gracie, darling, please stop glaring at me and see me to the train."

Mrs Thompson gave the young couple their coats before seeing them to the door.

"Thank you for understanding, Charlie. We both hope we'll see you again soon. Gracie, we'll talk when you come back."

"Yes, Mam." Gracie banged the door behind her.

She stormed off down the street, leaving Charlie to follow her. Gracie couldn't say anything. She thought Charlie had gone mad. Why hadn't he tried to persuade her mam and dad?

He caught her hand just as they got to the street corner and pulled her into a darkened doorway. He drew her closer to him, tilting her head, forcing her to look up at him. "Gracie, before you blow your top, I want you to know that I'm just as disappointed as you are."

"You have a funny way of showing it!" Gracie fumed.

"Oh, my darling. I want to marry you now. I want to carry you to a private room and shut the world outside." A funny sensation gripped her stomach. She moved closer to him. He caressed her waist before saying, "We have to abide by the rules. You don't want your parents to forbid us to see one another, do you?"

"They wouldn't do that."

"They might. But if we show them we're serious about each other, they may change their minds." Sliding his hand further around her waist, he drew her into a backstreet, taking her into his arms. "Come on, darling." She looked into his eyes. "Don't waste what little time we have left by quarrelling. Kiss me."

"Oh, but..." His lips silenced her argument. They kissed for a while. With a groan, he pulled away from her but kept hold of her hand.

"We'd best go to the train station."

"Kiss me again, please." Gracie stood on her tiptoes, willing him to hold her close once more. She didn't want these new feelings to stop.

"Darling, you will get us both arrested." Smiling, he stroked the side of her cheek. "Let's go."

He guided her out to the main street. Hand in hand, they reached the station. With a quick peck on the cheek, he was gone.

WHEN GRACIE GOT HOME, her dad had gone out. Her mam was knitting in the back room. Gracie took a seat, picking up a ball of wool, passing it from one hand to another. The ticking from the clock was the only sound in the room. When it was evident her mam wasn't going to start the conversation, Gracie pleaded, "Can you not change his mind, Mam?"

Her mam looked at her intently. "No, and anyway, if I could, I wouldn't. Young ones today think they are the only ones that ever fell in love. Your dad went off to war when we were courting, and my parents wouldn't hear about us getting married until he came back. I'm not saying it was easy – it wasn't – but they felt it was the right thing to do. I was lucky your dad was one of the good ones, and he loved me enough to wait for me. Now, there were times when temptation was hard to ignore."

"Oh, Mam, don't."

Her mam put the knitting down and took Gracie's hand in hers. "Yes, I know you don't want to hear it, but we were in love, too. Besides being in love with me, your dad respected me. He'd not take the chance of ruining my reputation and not being around to come back and fix it."

"Charlie respects me, Mam."

But her mam continued talking as if she hadn't heard her.

"Other girls I knew weren't as lucky. Their men pressured them into getting married, or worse, jumping the gun. They left them pregnant and alone with no ring on their finger. Others married men they barely knew and didn't recognise when they came back from the war. Marriage is for life, and some of those women have been miserable since."

"We won't be miserable, Mam. I love Charlie and he loves me. We'll be ever so happy, you wait and see."

"Gracie, you haven't lived a life of your own yet. We don't want you to rush into something that ruins your future."

"Marrying Charlie would improve my life, Mam."

"I know you think that now and, of course, we hope it's true. We like Charlie and think you're well suited, but you are young and war changes people. Our generation never wanted our children to see half of what we experienced in the last war. I can't bear the thought of your brothers leaving to go overseas. I'm proud of them and glad they are doing their bit, but that's not to say I want them to go."

Gracie knew her mam was getting distracted and wanted to bring her attention back to the matter in hand.

"But, Mam, you have just said it. People die in wars. My Charlie could die and I would have nothing left to remember him by."

"Oh, Gracie, I know that, but it isn't a good enough reason for rushing into marriage. If, God forbid, Charlie dies, you will have your memories. Now, don't start thinking like that." She squeezed her daughter's hand. "Both of you will survive and will enjoy a long and happy life together. Your dad has agreed to you getting engaged on your twentieth birthday and married on your twenty-first. Should war come, it may not last long."

Gracie could see her mother didn't believe that, but was trying to comfort her. She jerked her hand away.

"We could run away together."

"Now, stop it. You argue that you want us to treat you like an adult and then you make a childish threat. Never let your dad hear you threatening to run off. If he thought that Charlie Power would agree, that would be the last you would see of your young man." She softened her tone. "Come on, love. You have found a good man who loves you as much as you love him. Take your time to enjoy getting to know one another."

Gracie sat at the kitchen table, shoulders slumped. Her mother reached over to push Gracie's hair back from her eyes.

"Love isn't enough to keep a marriage going. Although, believe me, it helps." She rubbed her daughter's hand. "Anyway, you need some time to get your bottom drawer ready. A fine wife you would be if you have nothing to put in your new home. Start as you mean to go on, my girl, and remember it is up to you to keep things as they should be. Men get carried away so we women have to keep our heads. After all, it is we that pay the heavier price."

"What do you mean by that, Mam?"

Her mother wouldn't meet her eyes. Her face flushed; even her ears were pink. Gracie watched as her mam stood up, moving to the stove.

"Forget about it. I've said enough already. Now let me get back to work. Your dad will be in soon and I haven't got his dinner started yet. What will he think?"

Gracie knew it was pointless trying to get her mam on her side. Her parents had discussed it and made up their minds. Well, they could think what they liked. Nobody was going to stop her marrying Charlie.

Gracie ran upstairs to the girls' bedroom, thankful her sisters were outside playing with their friends. She buried her head in the pillow. Her mam always said a good cry was a great way to get on top of things. Gracie wasn't sure if it would help, but she couldn't stop the tears from flowing now, even if she'd wanted to.

CHAPTER 22

Penny was trying to decide between the deep blue wrap-around skirt and the rose-coloured jersey dress. She held both up against herself, reviewing her reflection in the full-length mirror, then stopped abruptly, shaking her head. What was she doing? The kids wouldn't care what she wore.

There was a quick tap on the bedroom door before it was flung open.

"Oh, Penny – they said no." Gracie flung herself on the bed, sobbing, for once not caring if she smeared the pristine white bed sheets.

"Who said no, and to what?" Penny went

over and knelt on the deep red carpet, rubbing her friend's back.

"To Charlie and me getting married. When I met Charlie at Richmond, he proposed. I said yes, of course, but then we had to talk to Mam and Dad."

"He asked you to marry him? Wow, that's fantastic, Gracie. I'm so happy for you."

Gracie sat up straight but looked down at her hands. She rubbed the space on her ring finger. "Well, don't be. Charlie asked my dad, but he said no. I thought I could talk him round. I've always been able to in the past, but this time it was no good. He is dead set against us getting married. Says we're too young and that there's a war coming and that couples shouldn't rush into things and … and…" The tears ran down her face. She wiped them away, but they kept on coming.

Penny got up and went over to the vanity table to get a hanky. She handed it to Gracie.

"Oh, Gracie, I'm so sorry, but maybe he's right."

Gracie glared at her through her tears.

"Now, don't go looking at me like that. But you're young, and marriage – that's serious."

"We are serious."

Penny wasn't sure how to respond. She turned away, concentrating on the rose-patterned wallpaper. She didn't want to upset her friend, and she knew she was too young to have any understanding of how Gracie felt, but she agreed with Gracie's parents. This was a strange time, when everything around them was changing. She imagined it would be easy to get carried away with being in love.

Hearing her friend sobbing, she said soothingly, "Come on, calm down and tell me what they said. Have they stopped you seeing each other completely?"

"No. In fact, they agreed to us getting engaged on my twentieth birthday, then married after my twenty-first." Gracie blew her nose on the hanky. "Charlie is going to be flying missions. What if he has an accident or finds another girl?"

"Well, if he finds another girl, you will be

relieved that your parents were sensible and didn't agree to you getting married." Penny's patience finally wore out. "Come on, Gracie, you have to count your blessings. Everyone knows war is just around the corner. Your parents have agreed to you getting married, just not yet. If you love Charlie as much as I think you do, you can wait to get engaged. And we can all pray that the war is over before your twenty-first comes so you can have the day you always dreamed of."

"I suppose you're right, but I want to marry him now."

"You are a lucky girl, Gracie Thompson, surrounded by family who love you and a young man who would go to hell and back to be by your side. Although, seeing that ugly frown on your face, he may prefer to stay away. Come on, you are always trying to cheer me up when I'm glum. You need to take some of your own medicine."

Gracie's half-hearted shrug told Penny she knew her parents and friend were only doing what they thought was best.

Penny dressed, allowing Gracie some time to get the emotions out. She brushed out her hair before pinning it up out of the way. The sheer number of kids at the orphanage meant nits were a constant hazard.

"Dry those tears and stop feeling sorry for yourself," Penny continued, but in a softer tone. "If you love Charlie as much as you say you do, have some faith in him and your love for each other."

Gracie turned away from her gaze, but not before Penny saw the blush pink her cheeks.

"I had a letter from Meme which will cheer you up. She said your whole family is welcome to go down to the estate, your dad too as there are plenty of jobs on the estate now all the men are joining up."

Disappointed Gracie didn't seem happy at the news, Penny said, "Least you could do is smile. You said your mother was desperate not to send the children to strangers."

"Sorry, Penny, it's wonderful news. Of course it is. Please thank Her Ladyship. Mam will be so relieved." Look sheepish, Gracie met Penny's eyes. "I've been rather selfish, haven't I? Talk of war is affecting everyone and look at me moaning."

Penny kissed her on the cheek. "I've to go now. I promised Matron that I would play with the children this afternoon. Do you want to come with me?"

"Not today, but thanks, Penny."

Penny set off for the orphanage, hoping her friend would be okay. Unlike the children she was going to see, Gracie had a future full of love to look forward to. The children who travelled to London on the Kindertransport trains and boats didn't know when they would see their families again, if ever. Penny wished she could get close to Hitler; she'd punch him on the nose for hurting those around her.

CHAPTER 23
AUGUST 1939

"Power, Thompson, you're wanted in the office."

"Been a naughty boy, have you, Power, or did you get him into trouble, Thompson?" laughed one of the lads in the canteen.

Charlie and Stan ignored him and made their way to the office.

"Any idea what this is about, Charlie?"

"No, Stan. I guess we'll find out soon enough."

They reached the office and waited for their commander, sitting at his desk completing some paperwork, to acknowledge them. While waiting, Charlie looked around the room, his gaze drawn to the medals on display. The old man was a flyer in the last war. His respect for his commander increased.

The officer handed the papers to a secretary and looked at Stan and Charlie. "Sorry about that. It was urgent."

"Yes, sir." The boys saluted.

"The 501 County of Gloucester Squadron, Auxiliary Air Force, is looking for volunteers. I'm putting both your names forward. They need pilots with actual flying experience. I take it you two are happy to go?"

"Yes, sir."

"Did you know that some of those playboys only have five hours' flying experience? They have a nerve calling themselves pilots. They consider themselves above us as they have the money to pay for lessons, but we'll soon teach them a thing or two. Any questions?"

"When do we leave, sir?" asked Stan.

"You get a week's leave and then you have to report to Filton, Bristol. I've given you both exemplary recommendations. Don't let me down. Good luck, men."

"We won't, sir," they chorused.

Their commander shook both their hands. "One more thing, lads, the 501 is a mobile squadron. Use your week's leave to say goodbye to your girls, as you'll probably be posted overseas."

"Yes, sir. Thank you, sir."

The boys saluted and walked out of the office.

As soon as they were out of earshot, Stan turned to Charlie and said, "This is it, Charlie. This is what we've been waiting for. I can't wait to tell Alice."

Charlie looked at his young friend. "I hope Alice is a bit more forgiving than your sister. Gracie will not be happy about an overseas posting."

"Ah, she'll get over it. Gracie knows we have a job to do. Everyone knows that war is going to break out any day now."

CHARLIE MET Gracie at Hyde Park, on the second day of his leave. He was late, and he watched her pacing up and down for a while before walking over to her. She turned towards him, arms folded across her chest and eyes blazing. She'd just happened to be at home when Stan had arrived yesterday full of the news he was off overseas. She'd left her mam crying at the news, having to get back to work.

"Is it true? Did you volunteer to go overseas?"

"I wouldn't say volunteer…"

"Stan said you did. Are you saying my twin's a liar?"

"Calm down, Gracie. Our commanding officer volunteered our services. It wasn't as if we could turn him down."

"But you would have done it anyway, wouldn't you?"

"Yes, Gracie. War is going to break out any day now, and I want to do my bit. I'm an excellent pilot and have tons of experience. I want to go."

"And get killed." He put his arms around her, but she pushed him away, hitting him in the chest. "This isn't some game, you know. You could die. You both could."

"What do you want me to do? Sit at home and wait for the Germans to come knocking at the door?" His jaw clenched as he tried to control his anger. Then he gathered his wits and adopted a soothing tone. "Gracie, darling. I love you and I don't want to leave you, but I've to do this. It's what I trained for. Nobody wants war, but we all have to do our bit. Your father fought in the last war and you've always been proud of him."

"I'm proud of him, but he survived. You mightn't," she whispered, her voice quivering with suppressed emotion. "I'm scared, Charlie."

He took her hands, pulling her close to him. "Come here, my darling girl. I love you. Look at me. I can't promise that nothing bad is going to happen, but I'll be careful." He kissed her gently on the forehead. "Now give us a smile. I've an entire week off before I go, and I want to enjoy it."

He stared into her eyes before kissing her again. Her lips were tender beneath his. He moved her body closer, kissing her deeply, then he pulled away, not wanting to take advantage of her heightened emotional state.

He squeezed her hands then reached up and brushed a tear from her cheek, saying tenderly, "Do you have time for tea?" She nodded. "Great. Let's go to the Corner House and see if we can get a table."

He wanted to be with her, but it was safer if they chose a public venue.

THE DAYS FLEW BY, and soon it was time to head for Bristol. Gracie couldn't get any more time off so Charlie went up to the big house to see her. Cook gave Gracie a few minutes to say goodbye.

"You'll keep your promise to be careful,

won't you?" Gracie's eyes shimmered with unshed tears.

Charlie cleared his throat. "I promise."

He kissed her hard on the lips, savouring her scent. He turned to go.

"Charlie, wait. I want you to have this." She struggled to get the words out.

He looked at her hand and saw a small cross and chain.

"That's the necklace your grandma gave you, Gracie. You never take it off." His scratchy throat made him sound hoarse.

"I want you to wear it. To keep you safe and to…" Gracie's voice broke.

Charlie hugged her close, taking a deep breath. "Don't cry. Please. I love you, Gracie Thompson." He gave her a last hug and, biting his lip, he left without looking back.

CHAPTER 24
SEPTEMBER 1939

"Gracie, where are you?"

Penny ran down the backstairs into the kitchen, almost bumping into Gracie, who'd heard her calling her.

"Stop shouting, Miss Penny. Your aunt will have a fit. What's the matter?"

"Come quick. Mr Lidell from the BBC said Mr Chamberlain is making an announcement in two minutes. Oh, Gracie, I think this is it."

The two girls ran back up the stairs and into the drawing room, skidding to a stop. It seemed as if everyone, staff and family alike, was gathered around the wireless. Everyone stared at the box as if, if they looked hard enough, they could see Mr Chamberlain himself, instead of just hearing his pained and anxious voice.

'This morning, the British Ambassador in Berlin handed the German government a final note, stating that unless we heard from them – by eleven o'clock – that they were prepared at once to withdraw their troops from Poland and a state of war would exist between us.'

Penny's lips were trembling and, feeling faint, she grabbed Gracie's hand. The prime minister continued.

'I've to tell you now that no such undertaking has been received and that, consequently, this country is at war with Germany.'

Penny watched her uncle blink rapidly, small beads of sweat visible on his upper lip. He walked over to the wireless and turned it off.

"I suggest that we all take a moment to join in the Lord's Prayer, although we have been expecting this news for some weeks now. I think I speak for us all when I say we hoped it would not come to this."

Instead of closing her eyes in prayer, Penny glanced around the room. Cook and Mr Perkins stood with their shoulders hunched and elbows pressed into their sides. They seemed to shrink in size right in front of her. She thought she saw Mr Perkins's eyes glistening with unshed tears. Penny was struggling to breathe; her heart, although beating, seemed to go very slowly. Her uncle's voice grew more distant. She could see his lips moving but couldn't make out the words.

"Penny, are you okay? Sit down. Do you want some water?" asked Gracie.

"I'm fine. Don't you think it's cold in here? My hands are frozen." Penny looked around the room once more and saw that Cook was crying openly now. She wanted to speak to Uncle John, but he appeared to be giving the butler some instructions. She turned back to Gracie, but then Sir John cleared his throat rather noisily, causing everyone to look at him. Such was his pose, Penny thought he was going to march around the room.

"Now, ladies and gentlemen, we have a troublesome time ahead of us. One thing is certain. We'll win this war. We all have a part to play and it is our duty to stand firm and prevent the enemy from darkening our shores."

Her heart was beating hard, and she felt like cheering. She put her shoulders back, made eye contact with her uncle, who smiled at her proudly.

"Tomorrow we'll all know what they expect from us. Today, I would suggest that those of you who have family living nearby take some time with them. The rest of us will share a meal together. We are in this for the long haul and as British subjects, we'll prevail. Now, Mr Perkins, perhaps you would ensure everyone has a glass in their hands."

"Yes, sir."

The butler moved quickly around the

room. As soon as everyone had a drink, her uncle raised the toast.

"Long live the king."

"Long live the king," chorused the room.

Gracie whispered to Penny, "I would love to see my mam. Do you want to come with me? We could tell her about the offer of the kids going to the estate."

Penny nodded. "Let's go now so we don't have to come back in the dark. I don't fancy finding our way in the blackout."

IT DIDN'T TAKE TOO long to get to Gracie's home, where they found her mam taping up the windowpanes.

"The air-raid warden called around yesterday to check the blackout curtains, and he said we should do this just in case a bomb drops close by."

Penny looked out of the window. It was such a beautiful day that it was hard to believe that they were now at war. Barrage balloons floated over the London skyline, and almost everyone they'd seen on the way there wore a uniform. It was still difficult to imagine what lay ahead of them. Penny said a quick prayer, asking God to keep everyone she knew safe.

"Mam, have you heard from Frank?" Gracie asked.

"He was on leave last week but has now re-joined his unit. He thinks they will be one of the first shipped out. It makes sense as they are properly trained soldiers. I called over to see June and Molly yesterday. June has decided to go down to stay with her parents on the farm." Gracie's mam sighed. "I'll miss her and, of course, little Molly but it will be safer."

"June won't enjoy giving up her home, though. She loves that house." Gracie got on well with her sister-in-law and didn't like the fact her niece would be so far away.

"At least they will be with their own family. I went to the local school on Friday. You should have seen all the children carrying their gas masks and a carrier bag. Each child labelled, just like a package you would send in the post. Their parents didn't even know where they were going."

"Aw, Mam, that sounds dreadful."

"The poor little mites looked scared. I spoke to one teacher going with them. She said some kids had little else but a change of underclothes and some sandwiches in their bags. I tell you, Gracie, I just couldn't put Kenny, Mary or Helen in the line. I grabbed their hands and ran back home before anyone could stop us."

Penny watched Gracie's mam pacing the kitchen floor. She didn't seem able to sit still. As soon as she sat, she got up again. She bent to pick up a toy from the floor and sat clutching it to her chest.

"I can't give up my kids to strangers. I won't."

"Mam, please don't cry. It will be okay. Penny asked her grandmother if the kids can stay on her estate and she said yes. There's room for you to go and all, if you want to."

"I can't leave your dad; how would he manage for his meals and washing? He's joined up too, as part of the ARP team." Nell must have seen the confused looks on the girls' faces. "The air raid precautions team – although your dad is part of the light rescue division. They will give first aid to those rescued from bombed-out buildings. They said he couldn't join the heavy rescue team due to his bad back." Nell put her hand to her mouth, horror filling her eyes. She stood again. "What have we come to when my husband is training to rescue people and my children are being sent to strangers."

"Mam, stop talking, take a deep breath." Gracie pushed her into the chair. "Listen to what Penny said: the children can go to the Hamilton estate."

Nell looked from one girl to the other. "Are you sure? Your dad put his foot down last night. He said I'd to be brave, and anyway the authorities would force me to let the kids leave. He said I was to tell the school tomorrow that the kids could go."

She dabbed her eyes with a corner of the apron she was wearing. A slow smile lit up her face. She jumped out of the chair.

"But now I don't have to. I'll have to check with Dad but I'm sure he'll agree. Oh, Penny, that's wonderful. Thank you." She gave Penny a warm hug before hugging her daughter.

"Easy on, Mam. You will do me an injury. You'd better get the children's clothes washed and packed. Dad will prefer them going to a place we know, not strangers. You don't have much time, as you said the government wants the children gone this week. Don't forget to pack their gas masks. They may need to wear them when they take their turn cleaning out the cowshed," said Gracie.

"Don't mind me, girls. Now, sit down and have a bite to eat before you head back to the house. A strong cup of tea will do us all good."

"If the talk of rationing in the papers is true, we'll have to get used to doing without tea and other stuff."

"Let's not worry about that for today. We can just sit here and enjoy the—"

Before her mother could continue her sentence, a loud wailing noise broke out.

"What's that?"

Gracie grabbed her mam's arm. "Quick, Mam, we need to get down to the Anderson. That's the air-raid siren. Blimey, they can't be bombing us already, can they?" Gracie looked at Penny.

Penny shrugged, but Gracie's mam said, "We're not standing around here waiting to find out. Get out in that shelter now, you two. I'm just going to grab the kids – they're playing upstairs."

THE ENTIRE FAMILY trekked out to the shelter and waited anxiously, but it turned out to be a false alarm.

Gracie's mam let out a long breath and said, "Thank goodness that's over."

Penny said, "Yes, Mrs Thompson, but

we'd best get back to the house. I don't want Meme to worry about us."

As they made their way up the garden to the house, Mrs Thompson said to Penny, "Please thank your grandmother for me. I don't think I would have slept again if I'd to give my kids to strangers."

CHAPTER 25

Penny volunteered to take Gracie's sisters and brother down to the family estate. Aunt Louise insisted she couldn't spare Gracie, although Gracie muttered that she'd soon have to if her maid left to join the services.

Kenny was excited about the trip. His parents drummed into him that, being the oldest, he was responsible for making sure Helen and Mary behaved. They didn't want the Thompson children causing any problems at the estate.

Cook kindly packed a picnic, and this helped to soothe the girls' tears at leaving their parents behind. Mr Thompson carried Mary on his shoulders as far as they were allowed and then all six of them stood on the platform, steam hissing from the trains not quite managing to cover the sound of people crying.

Penny stood back to allow the family to say goodbye. She saw Kenny bite his lip, trying to be brave. He shook his father's hand but Mr Thompson pulled him into a cuddle. Penny turned away to wipe the tears from her eyes. It wouldn't do anyone any good if she turned into a quivering wreck.

Mrs Thompson said, "Mind you do what Penny tells you. Don't be cheeky, Kenny. And you girls, you help out at that new place. And wash your teeth before you go to bed at night and in the mornings. Don't want anyone saying I got dirty children."

"Yes, Mam. No, Mam," the children chorused. They seemed torn between the excitement of going on a train and leaving their parents behind.

"Mam, will you write to us?" Helen held

Mary's hand so tightly, Penny could see her white knuckles.

"Course I will, you daft dope," Nell said, giving her daughter a kiss. "I'll write all the time. And so will your brothers and Gracie. You'll be sick of letters."

"If the bombs come, promise you will take Crystal to the shelter with you?"

Who was Crystal? Penny wondered.

"Mary Thompson, you know that darn cat will do just what she likes. She never took no notice of your mother and she isn't about to start now. Cats have nine lives so don't you be worried."

Penny said, "Meme has cats and dogs and horses at her house, Mary. She'll need your help to look after them."

Mary pouted, turning accusing eyes on Penny. "Me look after a horse? I can't. I'm too little."

Kenny elbowed his sister out of the way. "I'm not. I can't wait."

The whistle blew once more and the doors

to the train started slamming. The guard called out for them to get on board.

"Come on, children, we have to go."

"Bye, Mam, Dad." One by one they gave their parents a quick hug before racing each other onto the train. Penny turned to the Thompsons. "I'll stay with them until they are settled. They will be fine. I promise."

"You're a good lass, young Penny. Thank you." Mr Thompson put his arm around his wife. "Come on, Nell. Stiff upper lip and all that. The kids don't need to see you crying a river of tears."

Nell sniffed and blew her nose loudly before putting a smile on her face and waving.

Penny hurried to make sure the children were seated. She pointed out the different animals they could see from the train windows and was quietly amused at their reactions to seeing live cows and sheep. It was a longer journey than normal with the train having to stop several times. By the time they reached the right station, the children were all fast asleep.

MEME WAS WAITING to greet them at the station, surprising Penny by driving her own car.

"Don't tell your aunt and uncle. John despairs of me driving although I've driven for years. I guess I won't get much chance with the war. Petrol is bound to be rationed." Meme turned her attention to the three children. The girls had each taken one of Kenny's hands, holding on for dear life as they all stared at Meme.

"So you are Gracie's brother and sisters. I've heard so much about you. Kenneth, I believe you are here to work."

Penny hid a smile as Kenny stood straighter.

"I hope you are all very happy here. We are delighted to have you, and you must treat the house as your home. It's been empty for far too long. You can each have your own room." Meme hesitated, seeing Mary pale at this suggestion, her knuckles whitening on the hand holding her brother. "Or perhaps share if you prefer."

Penny ushered the children into the car, packing their bags in the boot. "They're exhausted, Meme."

"Cook is waiting with some soup and sandwiches and cocoa for everyone. I'm so glad you came, Penelope, I've missed you." Meme reached out a hand to stroke Penny's cheek before switching her focus back on the road.

"You live here? It's like a castle." Kenny's remark made Penny smile; she'd had a similar reaction when she first saw the old estate house. "Is this all yours?"

"Yes, child. You can explore the grounds tomorrow."

Kenny grinned, staring around him. His sisters were asleep either side of him, waking briefly to drink some cocoa before letting Penny take them up to bed. She left Meme chatting to Kenny, or to be more accurate answering the boy's questions about what type of animals they had.

P<small>ENNY KEPT</small> a close watch over the children once they'd arrived at the estate. After only a few days of settling in, Kenny quickly began to adapt to his new surroundings.

He thrived on the outdoor life, taking to farming as if he'd been born to it. Initially, Penny had been worried that he might get in the way. One day she went out to check what he was up to.

"Look at me, Miss Penny. Ralph says I can help with the milking in the morning if I clean this lot up."

Penny stifled a laugh as she looked down at Kenny. "Good job your mother can't see or smell you now, Kenny."

Penny turned to Ralph. "Are you sure he's not in the way? Meme told me you were very short of staff so you mustn't let the children interfere with your work."

Ralph smiled. "No, miss, he's a help, not a hindrance. He can clean up real well when he puts his mind to it. He's daft about the animals. Funny, really, seeing as he's from London and all. But I reckon he has farming blood in his background."

"I'm not sure about that, but if you don't mind him being out here, that's great. I've yet to sort out a place for him at school."

Kenny stood straighter, looking serious. "It's okay, Penny, if you can't find anything. Ralph can teach me lots of things."

Penny hid a grin. "Yes, Kenny, I'm sure he can, but I promised your mother that I wouldn't let your lessons suffer. I'm going to do my best to keep that promise." The young boy looked so disappointed, Penny had to add, "But I hear that with the number of evacuees in the village, the school has offered a half day of school to all pupils, so you can still work with Ralph when you are free."

"Oh, thanks, Penny, you're the best."

Penny took a step back just in time to avoid the child's dirty hands as he advanced towards her.

"It's okay, *mon petit*. You can hug me later when you have washed."

"Careful, boy. Miss Penny doesn't want to go into the village smelling like the cowshed."

Kenny took a fit of laughing. Penny went away delighted that at least one of the three children had fully settled into their new life.

The same could not be said for Kenny's sisters. While they, too, enjoyed roaming about the farm and meeting the animals, both of them were missing their parents badly. They had taken to wetting the bed, a fact that Penny only noticed when she caught eight-year-old Helen trying to wash out a sheet.

"Darling, what are you doing?"

"Nothing, miss." Helen went scarlet.

"Sweetie, don't worry. Nobody is going to get cross. Did you have an accident?"

"It was Mary. Please don't tell on her. She's only little."

Penny bent down to give Helen a hug. "Of course she is, and I'm sure she's missing your parents. I know I miss Gracie loads when I'm not in London."

The little girl sniffed, trying not to cry.

"Here, let me take those." Penny put the sheets to one side. "Now, why don't we change the bed. Then we can have a look through the attic to see what toys we can find for you to play with."

"Toys?"

"Yes, sweetie. At one time, there were children living in this house and I'm sure they have left some things in the attic. Let's go and have a look together and find out."

"Will there be spiders up there? I don't like them." Helen looked dubious about going exploring.

"I don't like them either, so why don't we hold hands – then we can protect each other."

Helen nodded and, hand in hand, they went off to find Mary, who was in the kitchen with Cook, eating some biscuits.

"Cook, can I please borrow Mary and a couple of those biscuits? We're off on an adventure."

Cook smiled. "An adventure, Miss Penny? Now, where might you be going?"

"Meme said that there might be some old

toys in the attic, so we're going to see if she's right. I think both girls deserve a treat after being so well behaved."

"That's a great idea, and when you are done, there will be a lovely meal waiting for them. Mary has been a great help and is an amazing cook."

Mary beamed in delight before taking Penny's hand. The young girls had great fun exploring the attics of the old house, routing out toys that generations of Hamiltons had used before them. Mary's favourite toy was a rocking horse that had been broken for years, but thankfully Ralph could repair it.

That night, Penny read both girls their bedtime story. "Now, darlings, if you need anything during the night, come and wake me up."

"Thank you, Miss Penny."

"Helen, why don't you and Mary just call me Penny? Calling me Miss all the time makes me feel like a teacher."

In response, the two girls gave her a big hug. "Good night, Penny," they chorused.

Penny stayed at the estate until she was satisfied the children were happy and settled. Kenny cycled off to school in the afternoons, leaving him time to do the milking and other chores in the morning. The two girls went to morning lessons, with one of the older servants walking them to and from the village. It gave the servants time to see what was available in the local shops and also a chance to exchange gossip with the village folk.

"I will miss you more than the children will, my dear."

"I think they will keep you busy, Meme." Penny bent down and kissed her grandmother on the cheek. "I love you. Thank you for doing this for me."

"No, Penny, thank you for being such a wonderful member of this family. Now, keep safe in London and don't let my daughter-in-law upset you too much."

CHAPTER 26
JANUARY 1940

"This war is so tiresome," Harriet exclaimed as she waltzed into Penny's bedroom, uninvited. "It's bad enough we have to follow the stupid blackout regulations and our men have to sign up but now food is going to be rationed. Mother said we won't have our English breakfast any more. How are we supposed to function?"

Penny tried to squash her temper by ignoring her cousin. She'd no idea how well off she was. To some families, a cooked meal once a day was a luxury. Penny said nothing but continued getting dressed.

"Where are you going at this ungodly hour?"

"I've things to do. I've volunteered with the Women's Voluntary Service, you may have heard of them, the WVS?"

Harriet didn't acknowledge her sarcastic remark. "Get fed up working with children, did you?" Harriet opened Penny's wardrobe, searching through her clothes, taking out the occasional dress to hold up against herself and discarding those she found lacking on the bed behind her.

Penny made a point of putting the dresses back in the wardrobe and closing the door. Why couldn't her cousin get lost? "The children were evacuated out to the countryside as you well know." Not all of them had gone and some had now come back, but she wasn't going to give her cousin any information she didn't need to.

Harriet was now standing at her dressing table, sniffing the various perfumes Penny had received as presents for Christmas. Penny gritted her teeth as her cousin helped herself.

Not that she minded sharing but Harriet behaved as if she owned everything.

"I read in the papers that most have come back now that the bombs didn't fall. Honestly, this government is just trying to strike fear into us. There's been no bombs or gas attacks. The troops have barely fought any battles. It's just such a phony war."

Penny had had enough. "Go away, Harriet, I'm not interested in listening to your senseless prattle. True, some children are back with their parents, but they would be safer if they had stayed in the country. If you spent one day with a refugee child from Europe, you would see just how real this war is."

Harriet sniffed. "You mean a Jewish child. That lot are always causing problems moaning about this, that and the other."

That was enough for Penny. She marched to her bedroom door. "Get out now before I do something I regret. Take your vile opinions and leave."

Harriet laughed, her eyes dancing with amusement. "Didn't take long to get under your skin. Why so sensitive, cousin dearest? Was your dear mama one of them? Is that where you got such dark hair and eyes? Those genes certainly didn't come from the Hamilton side of the family." Harriet patted her golden curls in place.

Seeing red, Penny wanted to pull those curls out one by one, but that wasn't going to help her case. She lived in hope Uncle John would realise she was mature enough to join up.

"Tell me, cousin darling," Penny began and, satisfied at seeing Harriet's eyes widen, she continued, "is your bad mood related to Peter's lack of proposal? Did you imagine you would be one of those debutantes who'd be married in your first season?"

It was well known Harriet had been walking out with Peter for months and yet he was no nearer to making a declaration.

"How dare you?" Harriet moved closer, her fingers curled into claws.

"Truth hurts, doesn't it?" Penny purposefully adopted a sweet, pitying tone and had the satisfaction of seeing her cousin turn scarlet. Thankfully, they heard Uncle John downstairs telling Perkins he was ready to leave if Miss Penelope would like a lift, or the encounter may just have ended in a brawl.

Penny smiled sweetly at her cousin, grabbed her coat and ran.

CHAPTER 27
APRIL 1940

"Come on, Penny, it'll have started if you don't hurry up." Gracie turned to the coat rack to grab her jacket. She'd read so much about this new film, she couldn't believe they were going to actually see it. Penny came racing down the backstairs, waving the tickets she'd gone back to her bedroom to collect.

Cook looked up from her recipe book. "Stop shouting, Gracie. Lord above, is there no way to get peace in this house?"

"Gracie's in love, Cook. Don't you know she's getting engaged on her next birthday? Unless Charlie changes his mind and finds someone else, of course." Penny winked at Cook so Gracie didn't react to her teasing.

Gracie gave the older woman a kiss on her cheek. "Sure you don't want to come see it? The newspapers are full of praise for Clark Gable and he's gorgeous. Vivien Leigh is good too."

"I read the papers, girl. Off you go and don't be late." Cook went back to muttering, writing something on her pad with her worn-down pencil.

Gracie said, "It's three and a half hours long. Thank goodness Penny went around earlier and got the tickets. I heard the queues go halfway around Leicester Square."

WHEN THEY ARRIVED at the cinema, they walked past the long queue, Penny ignoring the muttering voices while Gracie's face heated. She'd never sat in the dress circle before but Penny's uncle had insisted on treating them. He'd warned them not to tell his wife.

There wasn't a sound in the cinema as everyone was glued to the film. It didn't matter there was a war on or that their loved ones were off fighting; for a couple of hours they could disappear into a long-forgotten era.

"Look at her, she made the dress from the curtains. Imagine Lady Louise's face if I did that for you?" Gracie whispered, but shut up fast at the glare she got from the people surrounding them.

When they finally left the cinema, Gracie couldn't decide who she liked best: Rhett or Ashley.

"Don't be so predictable, Gracie. Rhett is the one everyone is supposed to like. He is what you say, a rake? Ashley, he knew what the war would do, he realised it from the very start and yet he still went to fight. That's a man."

Gracie took Penny's arm. "At least we'll never fall out over boyfriends. You can have Ashley and I'll settle for Rhett."

The two of them giggled as they walked

out onto the square. Suddenly Gracie stopped, not able to move.

"What's wrong?" Penny asked. "There's people behind us."

"Look, Penny, it's all different. None of the signs are lit up, it's all dark. All you can see in the sky are those blasted balloons."

Gracie stared at the large silhouettes hanging over London. She still didn't understand how balloons were supposed to protect them from bombs.

"Come on, let's get back to Cook and tell her all about the film. Maybe she'll be tempted to come with us next time."

They made their way carefully in the blackout, thankful for the white paint on the kerbs. The number of road accidents had increased astronomically with the blackout; some said the number of people killed on the roads was twice that of previous years.

THE NEWS on the wireless for the next few weeks made for depressing listening. It seemed that contrary to all opinion, the Nazis were pushing back the British and winning every battle. Penny was distraught as she listened to report after report of more areas of France falling to the invaders.

On entering the library and catching Penny in the act, Gracie urged her, "Penny, stop listening, it's not helping."

"I can't. Why aren't we fighting back? Why was my country so badly prepared?" Penny paced the floor.

Gracie sighed, making Penny feel guilty. "Sorry, Gracie, I know it's hard for you too."

Penny hadn't mentioned Gracie's birthday for fear of upsetting her. She knew she was dying for Charlie's proposal to be made official by way of a ring. But at the same time, Madame Bayard might be fighting for her life.

As if she read her thoughts, Gracie muttered, "Charlie and Stan don't have any leave.

I guess my birthday doesn't count for much when there's a war on."

Penny couldn't say or do anything to make her friend feel better, not when she was so miserable too.

CHAPTER 28
FRANCE, 27 MAY 1940

Charlie rubbed his eyes. He couldn't believe the vision of carnage below him. The beaches were littered with the smoking wreckage of abandoned trucks and other military equipment. On the horizon, he could see dark smoke billowing from the harbour and town behind it.

His chest tightened as he struggled to accept what he was seeing. There on the sand and in the water, in the middle of the hellish scene, were orderly lines of soldiers waiting patiently to get off the beaches. Some of those men must be waist deep in water.

Even as his mind wrestled to make sense

of the scene below him, he recognised that he couldn't do much to help. The RAF was heavily outnumbered. The Luftwaffe was everywhere and seemed set on preventing the soldiers from escaping. They were bombing not only the beaches but the ships, too.

He swore as he saw a hospital ship take a hit. Couldn't those swine see the red cross? Clenching his teeth, he squinted at the sky, desperately seeking an enemy plane. He badly needed to make a difference, even a small one to give the soldiers a chance. He rubbed his sweaty palms on his trouser leg before aiming his guns at the nearest Henkel. His aircraft shuddered with the bursts of fire, but he was more concerned with the effect on the enemy. He hollered as his opponent's engine started smoking, the plane pulling to the left. He wanted to watch it fall out of the sky but couldn't risk it. His fuel was dangerously low, so with great reluctance he announced to control that he was heading back to base.

It was too late. He didn't see the pilot that hit him, but his aircraft almost stalled. The controls were gone. He had to get out. His body froze; he knew he had to jump but his legs wouldn't move. The sweat ran down his forehead into his eyes, blinding him. He thought he saw Gracie crying. He shook. *Go now!*

Somehow he got outside, but only momentarily as the wind speed was so fast it blew him back into the aircraft. Time slowed. Everything moved in slow motion. This was his last chance. He climbed up and jumped again, this time clearing the aircraft.

He glided for a couple of seconds to make sure it was safe to release his chute. Thankfully, it opened on the pull of the cord. Blast, he was heading into the trees. He felt something fly past his cheek. Was it a bullet? Had he landed in the midst of the Germans? Just as his mind registered someone was firing at him, pain exploded in his right leg. He crashed into the top of a tree, falling down through the branches and landing awkwardly. He swore, before catching sight of the men running toward him. They were dressed like farmers. Relief flooded through him until he realised they must think him to be German. He called out, "*Je suis Anglais!*" over and over again.

The men held onto their guns, but stopped firing. They moved closer to the tree; Charlie saw they were older, around the age his father would have been. Their leader stepped forward and cut him loose from where his parachute had caught on some branches, then muttered something to the other men.

In heavily accented English, the leader spoke, "Sorry, *monsieur*, we thought you were German."

The other men grabbed the remains of his parachute and quickly buried it.

"Good job you can't shoot straight!" muttered Charlie, fingering Gracie's chain.

"We'll take you to the medic. There's a French squadron stationed locally."

Charlie couldn't put his full weight on his leg, relying on two of his rescuers for help to walk. He wished for a car but he might as well have wished for a plane to pluck him up and fly him home. The man who spoke English told him the Germans were stopping all vehicles. Charlie didn't want to be sent to a prisoner-of-war camp so put up with the pain.

It took over two hours to reach the French squadron; when they arrived, the camp was in chaos. Burning remains of planes dotted the fields. French soldiers were packing provisions into trucks.

His rescuers left him with the medics; he barely had time to thank them before they disappeared, worried for their families. Charlie grimaced as the medic washed his wound out with some iodine solution, leaving his leg a funny colour. He took the painkillers offered, being in the form of a bottle of wine.

The French medic shrugged. "You're lucky we have a bandage and splint to wrap it. Everything else has gone. The morphine, the disinfectant, all gone." The medic took a pack of cigarettes out of his pocket, offering one to Charlie, who accepted. The medic struck a match and lit both of them. Charlie's hands were shaking too much from the pain, or at least he hoped the medic thought it was pain. He was terrified.

"What's going on?" Charlie asked, indicating the trucks and men surrounding them.

"Our fight is over. We, how you say it, wave white flag and become prisoners."

"Surrender?" Charlie spat on the ground. "I'm going back to my unit."

"But how are you going to get there? You can hardly walk."

Charlie clawed his way to his feet, grabbing a stick as a crutch. He glared at the other man. "I'll crawl if I have to, but I'm not giving myself up. Why don't you come with me?"

The Frenchman sighed dejectedly. "I've to obey orders."

"I'm not subject to your orders. I'm going home." Charlie limped off down the road, but then stopped as he realised he hadn't any idea where he was going. He had a map, a silk one, but he didn't want to show that to the French.

"Wait, *monsieur.* I will help." The medic

took a last drag of his cigarette before crushing it under his foot. "I've family not far from here. My cousin owns a tiny boat. He'll take you. He has this mad idea that he's going to join the British army."

Charlie smiled a slow smile. "Thank you. I think it would have taken me too long to get home on my own."

"*Oui, monsieur.* My way is better?" The medic took a swig of wine before raising the bottle to Charlie.

"*Oui,*" laughed Charlie before clapping the Frenchman on the shoulder.

"GRACIE, WHERE ARE YOU?" Penny called out from the hallway.

"In the sitting room; what's wrong with you? Your aunt will hear you shouting." Gracie pulled Penny into the front room and closed the door.

"We have to go to Victoria station ... The trains, they're coming," Penny stuttered.

Gracie saw that her face was moist with sweat.

"Penny, calm down, take a breath. You're not making any sense."

"One of the doctors who comes to the orphanage, he said he was going to Victoria to help. He asked for volunteers. I know we're not nurses but I've done first aid training with the WVS, and we can make tea or coffee or hold cigarettes or…"

The drawing-room door opened, admitting Lady Louise followed closely behind by her husband. "Penelope, what is the meaning of this?" Lady Louise spoke shrilly. "Your hysterics have interrupted the whole house. Take a hold of yourself."

Uncle John moved closer to Penny, putting his hand under her elbow. "Louise, she looks as if she has had a bad shock. Get her a brandy. Sit down, Penny. Now calm down and tell us from the beginning."

Penny sat and took a few breaths before she spoke in a calmer voice, although it still trembled. Gracie saw her eyes were still wide with shock. What on earth had happened to her?

"Uncle John, the English are running away. They're leaving France in little and big boats and coming to Dover. From there, they are being sent by train to London." Gracie gasped but nobody seemed to hear her. They were all staring at Penny.

"There are huge casualties. Men are dying. They are looking for volunteers to be there to meet them." Penny jumped up and grabbed Gracie by the arm. "Come on, we have to go. Now."

Gracie caught a glimpse of Lady Louise drawing herself up to her full height, her tone haughty as ever. "Wait a minute. The British never run away. You've got a nerve…"

Sir John stood, taking control of the situation.

"Be quiet, Louise." His tone brooked no argument. Then he turned to the young girls, but addressed them in a calmer voice. "Gracie, would you mind going with Miss Penelope as you may just keep her out of trouble.

Perkins and I will drive you down there. Louise, perhaps you could round up some of your friends too. It's bound to be chaos."

"But John…"

"Not now, Louise. There isn't a minute to lose. Gracie, take some aprons from the store."

In less than fifteen minutes, they were on their way. The traffic wasn't heavy and Perkins drove as if there was someone chasing them. As soon as they arrived, Gracie looked around and saw it was organised chaos.

Penny grabbed Gracie by the arm, saying, "Over there! I can see some of the nurses I know from the orphanage…"

Gracie wondered whether Alice was among them, but she didn't get a chance to check. They ran over to the nurses and offered to help.

The trains arrived, one after the other, dislodging their human cargo.

Tea and coffee stations had been set up by the Women's Voluntary Service and others.

Each soldier was greeted with a hot drink, a cigarette, sandwich or a bun. Most were so hungry, they shoved the whole sandwich into their mouths.

Gracie couldn't believe her eyes; these men didn't look like real soldiers. She pictured her brother Frank, his uniform ironed with its perfect creases. These men looked like they had fought hand-to-hand combat before going for a swim. Their uniforms were torn and ragged, stained with sea water, but it was their eyes she couldn't bear seeing. All of them looked spooked, as if something totally beyond their comprehension had happened to them. She served tea after tea, losing sight of Penny, who'd offered her first aid skills to the nursing teams. She heard that the worst of the wounded had been taken off at earlier stations, but there were simply too many of them. The walking wounded wandered aimlessly around the station, their bandages looking blood-stained and grubby.

With tears in her eyes, Gracie sent up a silent prayer for Charlie and Stan – surely they would be safe as both were in the air force? Then she prayed for her brother Frank. He'd a wife and child to come home to. Just like these men, his family were waiting for him. She picked up another pot of tea and started pouring once more.

Gracie didn't want to believe the titbits of conversation she overhead. Who would? German guns had strafed the men as they waited on the beaches for boats to take them to the large ships trapped outside the harbour by low tide levels. Bombs destroying packed hospital ships, all those aboard either blown to smithereens or left to drown.

How could it have come to this?

One of the female volunteers lit a cig-arette, letting it hang out the side of her mouth as she poured yet another cup of tea. "If these are the best of the British army, does that mean Hitler and his henchmen are on the train after them?"

Gracie heard the question but couldn't answer.

"No, of course not. The British never run

from a fight. They won't let them over here. Not while one British man is still standing." Penny sounded exactly like her aunt, speaking with a cut-glass accent.

Open-mouthed, Gracie stared at Penny, who, catching her looking, sent her a wink before turning to light a cigarette for another soldier and give his friend a kiss on the cheek. As the man passed Gracie, he turned to his mate. "Almost worth it to get a kiss from that beauty."

The trains kept coming, Penny and Gracie working side by side with the other volunteers. Finally, the number of new arrivals slowed to a trickle and they were sent home to rest. Gracie longed to go and see her mam but she'd spent days away from her job. She and Penny made their way back to Belgrave Square where Cook took one look at them and ordered them to bed.

~

IT TOOK a couple of days for them to return to some semblance of normal. Penny spent more time with the WVS, her aunt having deemed it a suitable occupation given a number of her friends were involved in it, while Gracie was soon busy again, running back and forth for Cook. Penny was often at the orphanage, where despite their best efforts not all of the children had been evacuated, but her aunt just assumed the WVS was keeping her busy.

One afternoon, Penny walked home smiling at something a child had said to her. Then she saw the telegram boy cycling away from the house. Her heart in her throat, not caring if her aunt saw her, she ran to the servants' entrance.

The kitchen door was still open, and Gracie was standing there, holding a telegram in her hand.

"Gracie, what is it? You're as white as anything. Sit down. Your hands are trembling."

Gracie blinked, so she must have heard her though she didn't move. Penny put her bag on the counter, catching Cook's eye, but the older woman shrugged to show she didn't know anything. Penny dragged over one of the kitchen chairs and pushed Gracie into it, worried she might faint or something.

Penny tried again. "Gracie…"

Gracie looked up, her face whiter than the clouds in the summer sky, tears streaming down her cheeks. "It's Charlie. He's been shot down."

"Gracie, I'm so sorry." Penny clenched her hands into fists. "Do you want to go home?"

Gracie shook her head, her eyes going to the telegram as if re-reading it.

"Penny, he's not dead. He sent the telegram. He didn't say where it happened, but he's in England. He's in a hospital on the coast, doesn't say which one, but he says he'll be home soon. He wants me to meet him on Wednesday."

Flopping into the chair beside her, Penny stared at Gracie.

"It's true, he's alive." Gracie laughed

shakily. "I don't know why I'm crying. He's safe. I can see him next week."

Penny exchanged a glance with Cook, before she leaned forward to grip Gracie's hands. "It's the shock of knowing something worse could've happened. How badly was he injured?"

"He doesn't say, but it can't be that bad if he's being discharged at the weekend. Maybe he won't have to go back?" Gracie looked down, swallowing repeatedly. "I shouldn't think like that. It's selfish of me."

"Gracie, look at me." It took Gracie a few seconds to meet Penny's gaze. "It's not wrong to want to protect the man you love." Penny hesitated before continuing. "But I don't think Charlie would cope very well if he wasn't able to fly. He loves it so much."

"Yes, I know that. But it's just so dangerous. Every day we hear of pilots being killed or seriously wounded."

"Look at all the sailors being drowned on the convoys or those poor blokes left on the Dunkirk beaches. It's the war. It wouldn't matter what service Charlie was in, he'd still be in danger." Penny stood. "You need something for the shock. Cook, maybe you could make us all a pot of tea with some real sugar."

"Good job Charlie isn't here to see me now. I can't be very attractive with red swollen eyes and a tear-marked face."

Penny smiled, knowing her friend was embarrassed at losing control of herself. She pushed a loose blonde strand of hair behind Gracie's ear. "Charlie would love you if you arrived for your date wearing a paper bag over your head. He's going to love your short hair; you look so sophisticated. Don't dry those tears up too much. We need to convince Cook to part with her sugar ration and that will not be easy." Penny winked at Cook to show she was joking.

The woman snorted into a tissue before trying to smile. "It's more than sugar I'll need, young lady, if these telegrams keep arriving and scaring the life out of me."

CHAPTER 29
JUNE 1940

Charlie couldn't believe the attitude of Londoners to the defeat the British forces had suffered. They didn't seem to think the lads who had left London just over six months previously with their heads held high, confident of an early victory, had been sent running with their tails behind them.

The taxi driver who dropped him at Hyde Park had spoken of Dunkirk as if it was a miracle, not a massacre.

"They did well, our lads. Your lot weren't much good, though. Where were ye? My son was out there on that beach. He said he never saw one RAF plane the whole time."

"We did the best we could. Our planes didn't have the range we needed. We had orders not to…"

"Orders will always be the excuse, won't it? Still, my lad got home so I shouldn't be complaining. You look done in, to be fair."

"I was shot down and barely escaped myself." Charlie hated having to excuse himself. It wasn't his fault the RAF hadn't been able to help. If he shut his eyes, he could still see the boys, standing on the beach and in the water. The red water.

"Here you are, lad. Sorry about the outburst. Shouldn't be blaming anyone but Hitler. No charge. Off you go."

Relieved to reach the Maison Lyons, he sat down at an empty table near the window. Based on the conversation he heard from the surrounding tables, the taxi driver was not alone in his opinions, both on the miracle of the survivors and the usefulness of the RAF.

Some miracle. He sat straighter, trying to resist the urge to say something. He didn't begrudge the welcome those evacuated had received. After the hell they'd been through, they deserved any kindness that came their way. He wondered if they could sleep. Every time he shut his eyes, he saw the lines of soldiers waiting to board the ships just to watch their mates blown to kingdom come.

His hands shook as the matronly waitress brought over the tea he'd ordered. She leaned towards him, enveloping him with the smell of sweat and baking. "Are you feeling funny? You look rather pale."

"Fine, thanks," he replied shortly in the hope she'd leave him be.

"You look like you need a good sleep. I've heard about you pilots. You burn the candle at both ends. Think you're invincible, don't you?" She ignored his look of frustration. "On leave, are you? Do you have long?"

"A few days."

She wiped some non-existent crumbs from the table. "Waiting for your girl, are you? My lad is in the Territorials. He's still in France. Or at least we think he's." Patting

Charlie on his shoulder, she went to another table to take an order.

Looking out the window, Charlie spotted Gracie making her way to the coffee shop. His throat tightened as he gazed at her. She'd never looked so beautiful, with her golden hair cut short and just a touch of lipstick on her face. He couldn't wait to hold her, to feel her arms around him, hear her telling him she loved him.

The bell chimed as she pushed the door open, her bright eyes scanning the room until they met his. Her face lit up as she hurried over to his table.

"Charlie."

He stood, grimacing as he put his weight on his ankle. His wince of pain didn't go unnoticed.

"Are you all right? Can I get you anything?" Her voice sounded anxious.

"I'm fine, Gracie, stop fussing." He caught the wounded look his brittle tone caused. "Sorry, darling." He caught her hand between his. "Let me look at you. You grow more beautiful every time I see you. How are you?"

"I'm fine now I've seen you. I've been worried sick. Where did you get shot down? Were you in England?"

"Shush, one question at a time…"

He signalled for the waitress. When she arrived at their table, she said, "So, you're his girl. Got your work cut out for you there. I was just telling him he looks as if he needs his sleep. Carousing too hard, I dare say."

Gracie held out her hands as if she'd grab hold of the waitress. "Charlie's a hero. They shot him down and he was injured fighting for his country."

"Take it easy, ducks. I didn't mean no harm." The waitress turned to Charlie. "I'm sorry."

"Don't be, please. Gracie, my girlfriend, doesn't mean to be rude. She's been anxious about me. She's usually quite nice." He gave the waitress what he hoped was his most charming smile.

When the waitress left to get their order,

Gracie wouldn't meet his eyes. Once again, he took her hands in his, stroking them. "Stan warned me you spoke a lot with your hands; he said they flapped all over the place."

She glared at him, making him laugh.

"Gracie, I've missed you so much."

Her eyes smouldered as she returned his gaze. "I'm sorry. Mam says it's the Irish in me. Dad says I should have been born with red hair."

He leaned forward, pushing a strand of blonde hair out of her eyes. "I much prefer blondes!" he whispered. The air between them sizzled. He felt her legs trembling against his under the table. He fought the urge to kiss her right there in full view of the other patrons.

"Have you seen Stan? Mam was worried when he didn't come home on his last leave."

"Don't let on I told you but he went to see Alice instead. Said he'd to talk to her about something."

"Did he propose? Please say he did. Alice is perfect for him; she's more serious, but that's what he needs. Does he play jokes on the other pilots?" The waitress coughed discreetly, interrupting the moment. Gracie said, "I'm sorry for earlier. I didn't mean to be rude."

The waitress beamed. "That's all right, love. This war is taking its toll on us all. Now, enjoy your cakes. I slipped an extra one on the tray to help build his strength back up."

"I hope your boy returns soon," Charlie said, thankful the waitress had intervened when she did. He didn't want to be the one to tell Gracie the Stan she'd known had disappeared – replaced with a more serious, sombre version. Dunkirk had had an impact on all of them. He pushed those thoughts from his mind, not wanting to ruin his precious time with Gracie. He forced a smile as the waitress told him off.

"I do, too. Keep yourself safe, now. No more jumping out of those planes."

~

THEY LEFT LYONS, Charlie telling her he'd something to show her. Gracie didn't care where they went, so long as he was here and his arm was around her. They chatted about this and that until she realised they were standing near the Serpentine in Hyde Park.

"Gracie, I missed your birthday. We had some plans, if you remember."

She tried to look serious but failed miserably as the smile broke through. "Charlie, do you mean…?"

"Yes, darling. Unless you've changed your mind of course."

He picked her up and swung her around not caring about his ankle. She giggled, feeling more carefree than she had in months. She didn't care who saw her as she planted a kiss on his mouth.

He pulled away gently and went down on one knee, taking a small box out of his pocket. "Gracie Thompson, will you marry me?"

He opened the box to show a solitaire diamond ring, the stone glittering in the sunlight.

Tears flowed down her cheeks as she nodded her head. She couldn't speak.

"Is that a yes?" Charlie asked.

She held out her hand, holding it with her other one in a bid to stop it shaking. He placed the ring on her finger and she threw her arms around his neck. "I love you, Charlie Power, with all my heart."

He held her close as she cried, her tears a combination of happiness at the moment and relief he'd come through Dunkirk when so many hadn't.

"Let's go home and show your mother, shall we?"

"Can we go show Penny first? She'll be so excited, and it will give her something to think about. She's so worried about her friends in France." Immediately Gracie regretted mentioning the war as his eyes darkened with memories. "No, you're right, Mam and Dad should be the first to know. Lead on, Mr Power."

"Certainly, Mrs Power." He kissed her

again. "I like the sound of that. Love, honour and obey has a nice ring to it, doesn't it?"

She patted him playfully on the arm before staring at the ring once more. "Charlie, it's just perfect. Look at the way it shines."

CHAPTER 30

Penny stormed into the kitchen, her heels tramping across the freshly mopped tiles.

Gracie was about to protest at her work being ruined but then she saw Penny's pale face, the distressed look in her eyes. "What's wrong?" she asked.

"Uncle John just told me. Pétain has surrendered to the Germans. He has told the French people not to fight. How could he do that? He's supposed to be a war hero, and he just handed over my country to the Nazis." Tears glistened in Penny's eyes but whether they were from frustration or worry for her friends, Gracie wasn't sure.

"Sit down, Penny. I'll make you a strong black coffee from Cook's secret store. Just don't tell her. I know nothing about what's happening in France. Maybe he didn't have a choice?"

"Of course he'd a choice. He should have kept fighting." Penny paced back and forth. "Gracie, thank you, but I don't need coffee. I need to do something. Anything. Oh, poor Madame Bayard. She loved Pétain, but she won't enjoy living under the Germans. I have to go back. I can help."

"Go back? Don't be silly, Penny. You can't just get on a train and head to France. Even if it was possible, your uncle would never allow it."

Penny stamped her foot. "It's so unfair. Why did I have to be born a girl? If I'd been a boy, I could fight. I wouldn't have surrendered." Tears of frustration fell down her cheeks. "Why aren't they fighting back, Gracie? Don't they know what Hitler is capable of?"

"I don't know, Penny. Come on, drink this while it's hot."

Penny continued to pace the room. "I have to do something. There must be some way to help."

"When you have calmed down, why don't you go down to see Mam and the kids? They would love to see you. Kenny is driving Mam up the wall. All he can talk about is the farm. Every other evacuated child is thrilled to be home but not my little brother. Mam heard him telling his friends he wished the bombs would come so he could go back down to Suffolk." Gracie threw her hands in the air. "Have you heard anything like that? Seriously, you would be doing me a favour as I feel guilty for not going to see Mam more."

"Gracie, your mother understands that you want to spend as much time as possible with Charlie. Especially now you are engaged." Penny sipped her coffee. "That's a great idea. Are you sure your mother won't mind?"

"Course she won't, she'll be glad of the help."

N<small>ELL</small> T<small>HOMPSON</small> <small>GREETED</small> Penny warmly and invited her in. "I suppose you're here because you heard the children were back?"

Penny nodded. "How are they?"

"The girls are grand; they're out playing with their friends. Kenny is a different story; I sent him off to the shops, sick of him being under my feet all the time."

"Gracie mentioned he hadn't settled back in so well."

"Kenny is homesick for the country. He keeps talking about the animals and how much he enjoyed working with some man called Ralph."

Penny smiled. "Ralph is a pacifist working on the estate."

Nell pursed her lips, her eyes narrowing. "You mean a coward who won't fight?"

"I wouldn't call him that. He offered to

become a stretcher-bearer, but with his background in farming the government thought he was better placed working on the farm. He's a Quaker and their religion prohibits them from killing anyone, regardless of their nationality."

"I don't think I'll tell Gracie's dad much about this Ralph. I can't see him approving of young Kenny being around such a man."

"You haven't met him, Nell. If you do, you may just find you change your mind." Penny decided it was best to change the subject. "Have you heard from June and Molly recently?"

"Yes, they write to me regularly. June's expecting again, so she stayed put with her parents while Frank is away."

"Is there any word from him?"

Nell looked worried. "We get the odd letter, but it is always heavily censored. It's so frustrating not knowing where he is. And you can't find out anything by reading the papers." Nell looked down.

"What is it?"

"Well, I know we're not supposed to, but I sometimes listen to Lord Haw-Haw. What if he's telling the truth? What if it's only a matter of time before they march through England?"

"He's working for the Germans. Of course he's lying."

"But he sounds so…" Nell paused. "So convincing."

"Yes, he's good at his job, but believe me, he's just trying to wind us all up. He wants to lower our morale so we cave in to the Germans. When we win the war, they will hang him for treason."

"I've been stupid listening to that show."

Penny gripped Nell's hand. "You are a mother who is worried to death about her children, those serving and those too young to do so." Nell gave her a weak smile and Penny changed tack. "So, have you heard from Stan? Have he and Alice set the date yet, or do you think they will wait until the war is over?"

"Alice has her heart set on getting married. Can't blame her, really. She could get lodgings near him if they were married." Nell picked at the cloth she was holding. "Stan is dead against it. He says…" Nell's eyes welled with tears.

Concerned, Penny got up to fetch her a drink of water."I'm sorry. I didn't mean to upset you."

"You didn't, Penny. It's Stan. He's different. He was always the joker of the house, but now he never seems to smile. I worry about him." Nell looked up. "I'm being silly, aren't I? The war isn't anything to joke about."

Penny placed her hand on Nell's.

"The RAF didn't come out of Dunkirk very well. People seem to blame them for not being around. From what Charlie said, it wasn't their fault. They were hopelessly out-numbered. Charlie was a bit out of sorts, too, according to Gracie."

"I would be, too, if the people I'd gone to help had shot me." Nell stood up. "Will you stay for dinner, love?"

"No thanks, Nell. It's hard enough to feed a family these days. I'd best get back, or my aunt will have a search party out looking for me. Give the kids a kiss from me and tell them I'll see them soon."

"Thanks for coming to see us, Penny. Take care of yourself."

CHAPTER 31
LONDON, JULY 1940

Penny searched the house looking for her uncle. She needed his permission to join up and was determined today was the day she'd get it. She'd had enough of sitting around while girls her age were already in the services.

She found him sitting in the library, his newspaper folded on his lap. He didn't seem too busy. She walked in, saying, "Hello, Uncle John. Today was Bastille Day. I went to Whitehall, to the Cenotaph where the Free French Forces were gathered. General de Gaulle was there. He looked so impressive. He is much taller than I expected." Penny's eyes shone. "At least he hasn't given up on France. Not like Pétain."

Penny didn't want to think of the war hero who she felt had sold out France too quickly to the Nazis. Instead, she thought about the French men who had marched through the streets of London. All regiments were represented, from sailors with their red pom-poms on their caps, the blue-uniformed aircrew to the French tank crews.

"There were women marching too, Uncle John. They wore khaki uniforms and were marching close to the Free French soldiers. They looked like movie stars with their white gloves and steel helmets."

Penny looked at her uncle, who smiled back at her. Feeling brave, she put her thoughts into words.

"I wish I could invite some of these men back to the house for dinner. I would love to hear more of what's happening in France."

Her uncle shook his head sadly. "I would like to see your aunt's face if you were to do that. You know how she feels about foreigners. Best not, Penny."

Penny was about to argue until her uncle pointed out it wouldn't be fair on Cook. She couldn't be expected to entertain several surprise guests at a moment's notice. Penny paced up and down the library. There must be something she could do to help France. Those women marching today … maybe she could join their regiment.

"Is there something else, Penny?"

"Sorry, Uncle John, I was miles away. What did you say?"

"I asked you if there was something else you wanted to say. You will have a hole worn out in the carpet if you keep pacing like that."

Penny looked closer at her uncle. He looked older; the lines around his eyes were more pronounced. She thought he looked exhausted and worried. It wasn't the right time to ask his permission to join up – but when would be the right time?

"I was hoping you would agree to me joining the services. France is my country, and I can't bear to sit here doing nothing. I want to be like the women who marched today."

"Penny, we've been over this. You are too young. Your parents would expect me to look after you."

They wouldn't expect you to wrap me up in cotton wool. But at the look on his face, and the tone he used, she kept her opinion to herself.

"Sorry, Uncle John."

"Don't apologise, we are all feeling the pressure. I was listening to Mr Churchill. He made a special speech for Bastille Day."

"What did he say, Uncle John?"

"He's promised that France will be liberated."

Penny's spirits soared; that was the best news she'd heard in a while.

"When?"

"Patience, Penny. Nothing happens quickly in war. The Germans are much better prepared than we thought. We should have paid more attention to what they were doing."

"Why didn't anyone listen? All those people who ran away from the Nazis told us that Hitler was planning another war. They were ignored."

"Nobody wanted another war. It was easier to pretend or hope that Hitler would keep his promises."

"Well, that didn't work, did it? Now he's marching all over my home, killing my friends, and I'm stuck here doing nothing. It's not fair." Penny's head hurt as she pounded her fist on the table in frustration.

"War is never fair, young lady."

Her uncle's tone warned Penny not to say or do anything else. She looked at his face, waiting for a further reprimand for her behaviour. He was staring into the distance. He seemed to have forgotten she was there. She turned and ran out of the room, holding her stomach. One day, she'd fight with General de Gaulle and nobody was going to stop her.

∽

GRACIE SAT in the kitchen listening to the wireless with Cook and Mr Perkins. Penny sneaked in and took a seat without the butler commenting. He was too enthralled with the news coverage.

"The British fighters are coming in an absolutely steep dive. You can see the Germans' bombs leaving their machines, tumbling into the water below. Machine-gun fire lights up the sky. I can't see our Spitfires. There's one coming now, oh no, it's going down in flames."

Gracie moved and switched the wireless off, tears streaming down her face. Charles Gardner, the BBC reporter, could be talking about Charlie or Stan.

"Thompson, I was listening to that."

"You leave her be, Mr Perkins." Cook sniffed. "That poor lad was someone's son. The reporter should be ashamed of himself; the way he was talking you'd swear it was a horse race at some derby. Those brave boys are making the ultimate sacrifice to save our country; their death is not something to be described for our amusement."

Penny glanced at the butler, whom she thought pompous and old-fashioned. For once he seemed stuck for words. She wished she knew how to comfort Gracie but what could she say? The news wasn't good. The RAF didn't have enough planes or pilots. What had they been doing when Hitler was building up his Luftwaffe?

"Quite right, Cook, I let myself get carried away. But don't you worry none. Our boys know what they've got to do. We have the likes of young Charles and Stanley in the ranks. They'll do us proud. Why don't we have a nip of sherry and raise a glass to our boys in blue?"

Penny rushed to get the bottle Cook kept for emergencies as the woman seemed to be stuck to her chair. Before long, each of them had a glass in hand.

"To our boys, let them make us proud." Mr Perkins held up his glass.

"Cheers," the ladies responded.

CHAPTER 32
AUGUST 1940

"Charlie is at the door to see you." Cook didn't look directly at Gracie. She seemed intent on shining the cutlery she was drying up.

"Charlie? Really. How wonderful." Self-consciously, Gracie pulled at her hair before racing to the door.

As she opened it, he held out his arms. "Darling, come here."

"Charlie, Cook will see." Gracie looked up at Charlie, wondering what was going on. He also wasn't meeting her eyes. She shivered.

"What's wrong, Charlie?"

He moved towards her. She saw the pity

in his eyes and suddenly understood the meaning of the phrase "frozen with fear".

"It's Stan, isn't it?"

Charlie nodded.

Gracie bit her lip, clinging to her composure for dear life. "What happened?"

"I don't know for sure, darling. We flew a mission last Friday, and he didn't come back. I was due leave so I asked the CO could I come and tell you. He agreed but…" He hesitated before adding, "Your parents should have had a telegram by now."

Gracie slumped into Charlie's arms. "I should have known."

"Darling, how could you have? You don't know when we're flying."

"He's not dead, Charlie." Gracie shook her head. "My twin brother is not dead. I would have felt it if he were."

Charlie held her as she cried. When the storm had passed, he walked her back into the kitchen and explained to Cook what had happened. Cook made her a cup of tea laced with sugar.

"I've been keeping some back to make a cake," Cook whispered. "I'm so sorry to hear your news, Gracie."

"Stan is fine, Cook." Gracie dared Charlie to contradict her. "He'll walk through Mam's door in the next few days and prove this was a mistake. Just you wait."

She saw Cook look at Charlie, who shook his head in response to the unasked question. She ignored it.

"I must go and see Mam and Dad if that's okay, Cook?"

"Of course it is, lass. You take your time. I'll clear things with Mr Perkins and His Lordship."

Gracie went to give Cook a hug. "Please tell Penny what happened," she whispered in a voice choked with emotion.

"I will, love. Now look after yourself."

Charlie had a car waiting outside, and they drove down to Gracie's parents.

"Where did you get the car?"

"One of the lads lent it to me," Charlie answered, his eyes fixed on the road. "Gracie, darling, accept what happened. The men closest to him didn't see a chute."

"Never! I'm not giving up on Stan." Gracie wrung her hands together. "When we were little, I would know when he was in trouble. If he was dead, I would know in here." She hit her fist repeatedly against her chest.

They drove on in silence. Soon they reached her parents' house. As they pushed open the front door, Gracie squeezed Charlie's hand. She knew she'd to keep strong for her parents, but inside she just wanted to fall into bed, pull the covers over her head and pretend today hadn't happened.

Her parents had pulled the blinds, so the house was quite dark. She could see her mam sitting in her kitchen chair, her face a mask of grief, holding in her hand the dreaded telegram.

Gracie went over to kneel at her feet, rubbing her mam's hands together. She looked up to see her father's shoulders heaving. He wasn't making a sound.

"Shall I put the kettle on, Gracie?" Charlie asked.

"Charlie, did you see what happened to my boy?" Gracie's dad asked hoarsely. His eyes were red, raw amid his pale face.

"No, sir. We usually fly together, but that day I was babysitting a recruit. I mean, I was watching his back…" Charlie cleared his throat. "Stan was my friend and a fantastic pilot. I wasn't there when he needed me. I'm truly sorry for your loss. I feel dreadful."

"It's not your fault." Gracie's dad turned to look out the window. "It's those Germans."

Gracie took the yellow telegram out of her mother's hand. It had been crumpled up, but the words were clearly visible.

We regret to inform you that your son, Flying Officer Stanley Thompson, is missing, believed killed.

She couldn't read any more; her sight blurred. She gave her mam a quick hug before busying herself making tea.

"Has Alice been told yet, Dad?" she asked

her dad quietly. A howl of pain told her that her mam had heard her question.

"Yes, love. One of the neighbours kindly offered to go round and tell her. I should call to see her." He looked helplessly at his wife. "Maybe when your mam is a little better. I'm not much use dealing with female emotions."

"Dad, I don't believe Stan is dead."

"Gracie, not now," suggested Charlie.

Gracie threw her hands in the air, wanting to stamp her foot in frustration. "Yes, now. You didn't see his plane go down. He could've bailed out. Only last week he was showing me the compass in his shirt button. He could've landed in France."

"Gracie, darling, you're clinging to false hope. The lads would have told me if they had seen anything."

Gracie stayed quiet for a moment. The only sounds in the room were her mam's sobs and the clink of her dad's teaspoon as he stirred his tea incessantly.

"But nobody saw his plane go down, did they?"

Charlie shook his head.

"See." Gracie smiled. "Then there's hope. I bet Stan is holed up somewhere in France waiting for the resistance to get him out. Just you wait. We'll get another telegram soon. Or he could even walk through that door."

Gracie looked at Charlie, willing him to agree with her, but he was staring over at her mam. Gracie turned to see what he was looking at. Her mam was glaring at her.

"Can't you read, girl? It says it right there. Your brother isn't coming back and the sooner we get used to it, the better."

"I don't believe that, Mam." Gracie made a move towards her mother. "I can't believe he's dead."

"Well, try. We all have to face facts. That's what war is all about. People dying." Mrs Thompson turned to Charlie. "Thank you for coming to see us, Charlie. Now, please take Gracie home. I want to go and see Father Joyce about a service for my son."

"Mam…"

"Gracie, come on. Let's leave your parents alone." Charlie pulled Gracie to him. She clung to his arm, not believing her mother could behave like this.

"My sincere sympathy to you both, Mr and Mrs Thompson. Gracie and I'll leave now. We'll see you both again soon."

Gracie's mam didn't seem to register their leaving, but Gracie's dad walked behind them to the door.

At the door he put a hand on her shoulder. "Don't judge your mam too harshly, Gracie. It's her way of coping. She knows she can't afford to fall apart. Not when Frank is still out there somewhere and she has the little ones to think of, too. Charlie, look after my girl."

He closed the door behind them.

"Gracie, wait for me."

Gracie pulled away from Charlie. "I know you think I'm wrong, but I can't believe he's gone. Not Stan."

"I don't know what to believe, Gracie. All

I know is that he didn't come back." Charlie avoided her gaze.

"No, you know something more than you're telling me. What is it, Charlie? Did you see his plane burn up?" Gracie shivered despite the sunshine.

"No, darling. I never lie to you. But Stan was acting funny these last few days. He said something really weird. Something about it being lonely up there in the sky."

Gracie stared above Charlie's head at the blue summer sky. There wasn't a cloud in sight, and it looked so peaceful. *Where are you, Stan?*

"He kept talking about how many of our friends had died. It was as if he was…"

"As if he was what?"

"I don't know, Gracie. We never talk about our mates who don't come back. Every time you get up in the air, you know there's a chance you won't come back. Oh, I knew I shouldn't have said anything."

The tears ran unhindered down Gracie's face as the enormity of what had happened hit her. It wasn't just the news about Stan or her mother's reaction but the understanding that the man whom she loved dearly faced such danger every day.

"It's just so unfair, Charlie," she wailed into his shoulder. "Why did this blasted war have to start? When is it going to end?" She looked into his eyes. "Will we both be here when it does?"

She knew there was no answer to that question. All they could do was take each day and make the most of it. There was no point worrying about tomorrow.

CHAPTER 33
SEPTEMBER 1940

It had taken a few weeks for Gracie's mam to accept that her views and those of her daughter were different. Nell Thompson had arranged a service for her son in the belief he was dead. Gracie had claimed she'd to work that day but they both knew why she didn't go. Finally, they had called a truce and made a tacit agreement not to discuss it. At her next visit home, the atmosphere was less tense than it had been.

"There was another raid on the RAF bases last week. Do you think they will bomb London?" Gracie's mam asked her as she set the table for tea.

"I don't know, Mam, but I think you should send the kids back to Suffolk. They miss the farm and it would be a lot safer. You should go, too."

"I can't just leave your dad. How would he manage? If he's not working, he's volunteering. He can't look after himself. He needs someone to cook his dinner, wash his clothes…"

Gracie stirred the teapot. The tea ration didn't make strong tea; you ended up drinking hot coloured water. Yet another thing this blasted war had taken. She shook her head impatiently. "Mam, Dad's a grown man. I'm sure he'll be fine."

"No, Gracie, my place is by his side, but maybe you're right about the kids. I'll have a chat with your dad tonight when he gets back from work. What are you up to this evening?"

"Penny and I are going to see *Gone with the Wind*."

"Again? You must have seen that film a hundred times."

Gracie laughed. "Not quite, Mam. You should come with us."

"No thanks, love. My gallivanting days are over. You enjoy yourself. Say hello to Penny, too."

As THE GIRLS walked home after the film, Gracie said, "Penny, I think it gets better every time we watch it. I'm sorry Mam wouldn't come, but..." A wailing siren interrupted her.

Penny grabbed her arm. "We need to get to the shelter. Come on, Gracie."

"But Mam is at home alone with the kids. Dad is out. I need to get back to them."

"Your mother will expect you to head to the shelter. She'll have the kids out in the Anderson by now. Oh, my God, can you hear that?"

The ground started shaking; the girls could hear the familiar boom and crump sounds not far off. Penny cried, "Gracie, move. That sounds close."

Hand in hand, they ran out into the street, looking around for the nearest shelter. A police officer directed them. "As quick as you can, girls. This lot are keeping the fire-watchers busy."

Gracie paled. "Oh, no. Dad. He'll be busy rescuing people tonight."

"He'll be fine. Now, come on." Penny took her hand and pulled her along.

THE RAID LASTED HOURS. When the all-clear sounded, the girls walked out of the shelter, squinting in the sunlight.

The ground crunched as they walked over shards of glass. Burnt trees and scorched grass reminded them that nature was suffering, too. The air smelled of tree sap and dust.

"Gracie, look at that house. It looks like a knife cut it through the middle. I hope the family is okay." Penny shuddered. "Their bed is still there, but it looks like the wardrobe and other furniture were thrown out." She pointed to a smouldering pile across from the house. "Be careful, there's glass everywhere."

They passed people sitting around in huddles outside damaged homes. One lady sat on the ground cradling what looked like a pile of rags. Gracie moved towards her but was stopped by a policeman. "Leave her be, love. That's her baby. Or, at least, it was."

Gracie's stomach heaved as the implication of his words hit home. She looked at the lady, wondering how she'd ever deal with her loss.

Penny said, "Come on, Gracie, it will be quicker to go to my house. We can have a cup of coffee, change and then try to get to Lewisham."

"You go on, Penny, I've to get home. I need to check that they are all right."

"I'm not leaving you." Penny took Gracie's hand. "The buses may still be running. Let's walk until we find one."

Hand in hand, they walked. They

passed plenty of people, but instead of the
usual friendly London greeting, vacant
stares met them. The surrounding roads
were too badly damaged, but someone said
they could get a bus from Victoria. They
walked towards the station, but as they
grew closer, the scene was even worse.
There were firefighters everywhere, covered in black soot. Gangs of men, and some
women, were digging through rubble and
debris with their bare hands. In the middle
of the chaos was a van serving hot tea and
sandwiches.

Penny looked around anxiously. "Gracie,
can you get home? I think I should stay and
help."

"We'll both help."

"But what about your family?" said
Penny.

"I can't walk by and ignore all this. Mam
would expect me to help." Gracie put her
shoulders back and stood taller. There was no
way she was leaving Penny to work here
alone.

They went up to a harassed-looking ARP warden. "What can we do?"

The warden stared dubiously at them. "You girls should get off home. You look like you have been out all night."

"We have. We were in a shelter. We're on our way home, but we can't just walk on. I know first aid and Gracie can make the best tea in England."

"You're too young to be a nurse," he said dismissively.

"I know, but I've been working at an orphanage and took a first aid course last year. Please let us help." Just when Gracie expected to be told again to go home, she heard Penny say, "My uncle, Lord Hamilton, would expect me to."

The warden straightened visibly. "Yes, Your Ladyship, erm, I mean..."

"It's Penny. Now where should I go?"

Gracie gazed at her friend with admiration. She'd always known Penny had an inner strength but it was the first time she'd seen her use her status to achieve something.

The exhausted man pointed towards a group of people. "The ladies over there will tell you what to do." He turned to Gracie and smiled. "Come with me, I could do with a cuppa. I'm sure the ladies over at the tea wagon wouldn't say no to another pair of hands, love."

THEY STAYED at the scene for a couple of hours. Penny lost count of the number of injuries she encountered. Some victims had burns; others had been hit by falling rubble and had suffered broken bones. Wounds needed to be cleaned before being dressed. They sent those with broken bones to the hospital.

Penny asked, "Why don't we just send the kids to Great Ormond Street? I know they don't look after adults but they could go to the Middlesex."

The overworked doctor smiled wearily. "Haven't you heard? This is just one scene of many around London. The hospitals are over-crowded. They are only admitting the most serious cases. Nurses and other medical staff are treating people in the streets around them. It's chaos everywhere. And bound to get worse. They say the Germans will be back tonight."

It was nearly evening by the time the girls felt they had done enough to leave. Gracie was getting increasingly anxious about her own family. She felt guilty leaving but she needed to know whether they were safe. "Penny, you don't have to come with me. You could go home. I'm sure Lady Louise will be worried."

"Hardly. She probably doesn't know I'm missing. Meme is at the estate, so there's no-body to worry about me. I'm coming with you, and that's final."

IT DIDN'T TAKE LONG to get to Lewisham. Thankfully, Gracie's house was still standing.

Her mam was outside talking to a neighbour. Gracie shouted to get her attention and then ran into her outstretched arms. "Oh, Gracie darling, I was so worried. When you didn't come home, I thought I would never see you again. Penny, give us a hug, too."

"I'm sorry, Mam. The policeman made us take shelter. We left as soon as the all-clear sounded, but…"

"Come on inside. Your dad is still out but he sent a kid over earlier to tell us he was safe. He has to help clear up."

Gracie shuddered, thinking of the images her dad would deal with. "You should let your aunt know you're safe too, Penny."

"Where are the kids, Mam?"

"They are asleep. They were so scared last night. I should never have let them come back from Suffolk. They are going back as soon as we can organise it."

CHAPTER 34

LATE SEPTEMBER 1940

Gracie and Penny emerged from the attic, covered in dust and cobwebs. They dragged the boxes filled with paper down the stairs to the kitchen. Cook had a friend who'd come to collect them for the paper drive. The metal railings from the garden had been the first to go, followed by spare pots and pans to be turned into Spitfires.

Cook coughed as the girls arrived in her kitchen.

"Look at the state of the two of you. Never thought I'd see the day when Her Ladyship's granddaughter looked like a tyke from the streets."

The girls exchanged a glance; it hadn't been that long since Penny had turned up looking like a beggar following her flight from France, but they said nothing. The bombs were taking their toll on everyone but especially the elderly staff like Perkins and Cook.

"We have to clear the attic, Cook. You heard the ARP warden, he says they're a fire hazard."

"Don't like that man, too bossy for his blue britches. Having girls on the roof doing fire-watch duty. What's this country coming to?"

Penny hugged Cook, cutting off her tirade. "Why don't you sit down and rest your leg? I've to get off now. I promised the orphanage I would pass on any toys I found, and they will love the footballs. You can't find new ones anywhere with the rubber shortage."

"I think I'll do that, thank you, Miss Penny." Gracie waved Penny off, insisting Cook stay in her chair. The old woman needed a rest.

LATER THAT MORNING, Cook had recovered enough to make luncheon for Sir John.

"Can you please take this up to the conservatory where Sir John is waiting, Gracie?"

"Yes, Cook," she said, picking up the silver-edged tray.

"Don't drop it. That's milady's favourite tea set. It was a wedding present. Lord knows why she didn't take it with her to Suffolk."

Gracie looked at the old country roses tea set. The cups and saucers were so delicate, the red roses so vivid on the white background. The rims of the matching milk jug, sugar bowl and teapot were also edged in gold. Mam would love a set like this.

The butler opened the door to the conservatory when she got there, allowing Gracie to walk in and place the tray on the table.

"Would you like me to pour, Sir John?"

"No, thank you." Sir John looked up.

"Gracie, why are you bringing up the tea? Where is Agnes?"

"She left last week to work in a munitions factory, sir."

"Oh, yes, I forgot. What about you, Gracie? Do you plan on leaving us, too?"

"No, sir. My dad doesn't approve of women going into the services." Gracie sighed, thinking of all the notices posted everywhere exhorting women to join the forces, the WAAF, Wrens, the ATS or even the Land Army.

"I doubt he'll have much choice given the way things are going, but I'm glad your father thinks that way. We would be lost without you. Where's Penelope?"

"She went out for a little while." She hoped he didn't ask for more details.

He smiled in dismissal.

"Thank you, sir."

Just as Gracie reached the kitchen, the sirens wailed.

Cook looked up and said, "Blast those Germans. My soufflé will be ruined."

"Don't worry about that, Cook. We need to get into the cellar. Come on, now." Gracie held the older woman's hand. She knew Cook didn't like being in the cellar. She'd told Gracie years ago how the workhouse staff used to punish the children by locking them in a dark cabinet for hours at a time. This had left Cook fearful of the dark and enclosed spaces. She never used the Tube train and always sent one of the younger staff into the cellar if she needed something.

Gracie could sense her fear and sought to reassure her. "It will be all right, Cook. I won't leave you. Mr Perkins is coming down, too."

The house shuddered above them just as Mr Perkins joined them. "Sir John's gone to the office; he said he'd have enough time. But I don't…" Whatever the butler was about to say was drowned out as they heard an enormous crash. "That sounded a bit close," said Mr Perkins. They sat in the cellar for about an hour, Gracie's hand sore from Cook squeezing it, until finally, the all-clear sounded.

Gracie wanted to distract Cook as they made to go back upstairs. "Cook, any chance you could rustle up something to eat? I'm starved."

"Gracie Thompson! Now is not the time to be thinking of your stomach. We don't even know if we still have a roof over our heads yet." Cook's expression was affronted.

Gracie burst out laughing. "That's the Cook I know and love." She hugged the old woman to her.

"Oh, you," said Cook, but she returned the embrace. The butler pushed open the cellar door, resulting in a cloud of dust. They all started coughing, the dust-laden air making breathing difficult. Holding their aprons over their mouths, Cook and Gracie cautiously stepped into the house.

"What on earth…" said Gracie. Dust covered every surface in a thick layer.

"My kitchen. Oh, my poor kitchen,"

wailed Cook, a look of abject despair on her face.

"There's no real damage done, Cook. We'll have it sorted in no time." Gracie hoped she sounded more optimistic than she felt.

"Gracie, you come with me. We need to check the rest of the house," Mr Perkins said. "Cook, we'll be back shortly."

"No, I'm coming with you. I don't want to stay here alone," Cook said, gingerly stepping out with them into the rest of the house.

The three servants made their way cautiously up the stairs. The hall mirror was cracked but, thankfully, the glass hadn't splintered. They pushed the library door open. The dust was everywhere, covering the carpet so thickly you couldn't see the pattern but there didn't seem to be any structural damage.

"Oh, my goodness. Look."

Cook pointed towards the conservatory. The floor was covered in glass and broken roof tiles. A large piece of glass stuck out of a hole in the chair where Sir John had sat an hour or so previously.

"Thank God Sir John didn't stay in there," Gracie said as they moved towards it.

"Be careful, more glass could come down from what remains of the roof." Cook stood gazing into what was left of the conservatory.

Gracie followed Cook's stare and found her eyes drawn to the little china milk jug lying on its side, the white milk marking a trail through the brown dust.

"Her Ladyship's china. It's ruined," wailed Cook.

"Come on, Cook. Let's get back to the kitchen. I'll make you a strong cup of tea with plenty of sugar."

"But the rations…"

"Sod the rations. You have had a big shock and need it. Once we've had a hot drink, we can make a start on getting this place cleaned up. Mr Perkins, will you join us for some tea?" Gracie asked the butler. When he hesitated, she said, "Please, Mr Perkins. I know there's work to be done but it will be easier on a full stomach."

"No, thank you, Gracie. You take Cook

down to the kitchen and get started. I want to check on His Lordship. I won't be long."

"Thank goodness Lady Louise and Miss Harriet are visiting her parents down the country. She'd be very upset seeing this," Cook said as they left the ruined conservatory.

Gracie thought "upset" didn't quite describe how Louise would have reacted, but wisely kept the thought to herself.

As they crossed the hallway, the front door burst open and a dishevelled Penny ran in. "Gracie, where are you? Are you all right? Oh, my goodness…" Penny stopped, staring around her. "It's such a mess."

"We can clear the mess up. Where were you when it started? You hadn't left long. Are you all right?" asked Gracie, taking her friend's arm as they went down to the kitchen.

"I got to the orphanage. We took the children to the cellar and stayed there. It's so deep underground that we heard nothing. It was quite a shock to come out and see all the damage."

Penny looked around her. "The children will be sent away again, though. It's not safe here, not for the children. They have been through enough already."

"Have a cup of tea, Miss Penny."

"Thanks, Cook, I'm parched." Penny looked around her. "Where's Uncle John and Mr Perkins?"

"Sir John was having tea in the conservatory but left for his office just after the siren went. I guess he thought that the raiders wouldn't reach this side of London so quickly." Gracie took a sip of her tea. "Mr Perkins came into the cellar with us but wanted to check on your uncle once the all-clear sounded."

Once the tea had finished, Penny said she was going upstairs to get changed. She insisted she was going to help get the mess sorted.

Gracie convinced Cook to lie down for a little while. She was worried about the old lady, who had yet to recover her colouring. The last few nights' raids had taken their toll on her sleep, and today's close call had really shaken her.

Looking about her, Gracie wasn't sure where to start. There was so much to do. She was glad of Penny's help. It would take hours to get the house sorted.

It will probably be done just in time for tonight's raid. Gracie had to stop herself thinking like that. Being defeatist would not do anyone any good. They were still alive, weren't they?

CHAPTER 35

Later that same day, Gracie found Penny in the library. She watched her friend reading for a moment, and before she'd said anything, Penny looked up and spoke.

"Is your family okay?"

"Yes, thank God. Dad worked through for almost twenty-one hours. Oh, Penny, it's dreadful. There were over four hundred people killed and that number is expected to rise." Gracie paced the floor. "Almost two thousand were injured, many of them seriously. All in one night. And for what? Germany can't believe we're going to give in to them?"

"Nobody really knows what Hitler believes." Penny put the book down on the polished table.

"The more he bombs our homes and cities, the harder we'll fight. I, for one, am not sitting around any longer. I'm joining the WAAF. I don't care what Charlie or Dad has to say. I've to do something more useful than dress your aunt."

"I'm sure Aunt Louise can learn to dress herself, but what's this about Charlie? And what about your parents?"

"Dad won't be happy about it and Charlie will go mad when I tell him, but they won't have much choice, will they? The rumours are that conscription for women is coming soon. It stands to reason they will call up single women first. After all, they made us all register earlier this year."

"Will your dad not make you wait?"

"To be conscripted? I don't think so. Mam told me he lost thirteen of his friends the night of 7th September when the Abbey Road, ARP Cleansing and ambulance station in West

Ham took a direct hit. I can't see how he could stop me being useful now."

Gracie walked over and picked up the book Penny had been reading. She turned the pages.

Penny said thoughtfully, "What did you mean about Charlie going mad?"

Gracie walked over to the shelves to replace the book. "He doesn't agree with me joining up."

"He is probably worried you will get hurt or worse."

Gracie took a breath. "I could get killed here in London. I need to do something. I can't stand waiting around for the next raid." She looked at Penny. "You've read the newspapers. The government wants women to do their bit as well. Why shouldn't I be one of them?"

"Calm down, Gracie, I'm on your side. You know I'm desperate to join up too. I think it's wonderful. What will you be doing?"

"I'm not sure but the other day I spoke to

the recruiting officer about the Observer Corps just to find out more. I guess I would have to complete basic training first. I've always been fairly good with maths and the officer said that was important. You have to track enemy aircraft movements once they have come over Britain."

Penny frowned. "Isn't it a bit late if they are already over us? I thought the whole idea was to stop them coming near Britain."

"Well, of course they try, but they're not always successful. If they have people on the ground working out how many planes there are, what type, are they bombers or fighters or both and in what direction they are flying, then warnings can be sent around to the different RAF bases. The planes can be scrambled and directed to cut off the raiders." Gracie tidied up some newspapers that had been left on the table as she talked. "Of course, I don't know if they will accept me; they may want me to work on barrage balloons."

Penny burst out laughing at the idea of her

tiny friend trying to control the enormous balloons that floated in the sky. She smothered her giggles when she saw Gracie was not amused.

"Sorry, Gracie." Penny stood up. "You know I'm behind you all the way. Now I've to get dressed. Do you have time to dress my hair for me? Aunt Louise asked me to go to afternoon tea with the Gilberts. I've to find something suitable to wear."

Gracie looked at her friend's creased blouse and cream skirt covered in what looked like food splashes, evidence of Penny helping Cook again. "Lady Gilbert would send you around to the servants' entrance if you turn up like that. Go upstairs, I'll be up shortly. I just need to check something with Cook."

Penny ran upstairs, wishing she could join up with Gracie. Opening the bedroom door, she headed straight for the walnut wardrobe.

She rummaged through the clothes, hoping for inspiration.

"Have you found anything yet?" asked Gracie, coming into the bedroom.

"No. What about this?" Penny pulled out a pale green silk day dress.

"Are there going to be any men at this tea party?"

Penny shook her head. "I don't think so. Why?"

"If it is just ladies, this would be more appropriate." Gracie picked out a blue velvet dress. It had a modest bodice with a pleated skirt that fell just below the knees.

Penny pulled a face, but Gracie insisted.

"Look the part or you will only upset your aunt."

Penny got dressed, still thinking about Gracie's plans and her own fruitless campaign to be allowed to do the same. "I wish I could join up. I'd do anything, even work on those balloons you were talking about. Although, I'm not sure what they are for."

"Charlie says they stop the enemy from

flying low down and being able to drop bombs more accurately. The balloon gets in their way and forces the planes to fly at a higher altitude. The idea is that the higher they are forced to fly, the less accurate their bomb dumps will be. Charlie says our men can find them easier if they can't sink low into the clouds."

Penny tried to contain the giggles but couldn't any longer.

"You should listen to yourself. It's Charlie this and Charlie that. I think the reason you want to join the WAAF is so you can keep tabs on Charlie."

Gracie blushed. "Well, that was part of the reason, but don't you think that the girl in the air force blue uniform on the recruiting poster looks ever so smart? Although, of course, I want to be near Charlie, if I can."

"Pity they don't let women join the RAF or you could be in the same squadron."

Gracie threw a pillow at Penny, and it hit her squarely on the head, leaving a few loose feathers settling in her hair. "Now you're just being silly."

"I'll miss you so much when you go."

"Well, I have to pass the interview first so I'm not sure how long it will take. Don't worry, you will be busy. I thought you were volunteering at the hospital? That will help you make friends. You can always come over to my house to see me when I get leave. I'll write to you, too."

"Make sure you do. I want to know everything, so when my time comes I'll be so knowledgeable that they will accept me straight away. It is so exciting, isn't it?"

"Yes, it is."

"Are you scared?"

"Well, a little. But then, I'll think of you and all you have achieved since you arrived here, looking like something the cat dragged in."

Penny laughed and looked in the mirror. "I'm not sure that Aunt Louise would see much improvement if she could see me now."

"I don't know. She may think that feathers

in your hair is a new fashion trend. Why not add a few more?"

Gracie hit Penny with a pillow and she grabbed another from the bed, hitting her right back. Soon, the room was covered in loose feathers and the two girls were giggling uncontrollably on the bed.

The clock chimed on the landing, bringing an end to their fun.

"Oh, no, I'll be late. Quick, please, help me get ready. Aunt Louise will kill me."

"Stand still, Penny, and let me get the feathers out of your hair." Gracie looked her friend up and down. "Look in the mirror."

Penny gazed at her reflection. What a change between now and how she'd looked an hour or so ago. It should please Aunt Louise. How she wished she was going anywhere else than tea at Lady Gilbert's.

"Thanks, Gracie. Sorry about the mess."

"Don't worry, I'll have it sorted in no time. Now, you best get going."

THE NEXT MORNING, Gracie dressed carefully, determined that today was the day she signed up. Cook was used to her taking an hour or so to do the shopping due to rationing with the queues and everything. There was a recruitment office nearby. As she neared it, Gracie was relieved to see the women lining up outside seemed to be just like her. Breathing a sigh of relief – she'd expected them to be university graduates or ladies like Miss Harriet – she joined the queue.

"Why the WAAF, Miss Thompson?"

"My fiancé was shot down during Dunkirk, he flies Spitfires, he survived and is still flying. But my twin, Stan…" *Stay focused; they aren't going to take on a crybaby.* She swallowed before continuing, "My brother was shot down in August. I wanted to join up then but my parents, well, they were upset. But now with all the bombing, it doesn't sit right to stay in my job when I could be more useful. I mean I thought I could do my bit. I spoke to one of your recruiting officers and she mentioned she was looking for maths skills for the Observer Corp. I was good at maths at school, well, until I left at fourteen…" Gracie trailed off. She was making a proper mess of this but to her surprise the officer smiled.

"Don't look so nervous. You're joining up but we won't send you to fight the Germans. Not today anyway." The joke helped to break the ice. The uniformed woman took a note of Gracie's date of birth and checked her papers. "You will go through training to see which position you are most suitable for. You will have to sign the Official Secrets Act as well. Loose lips sink ships, you know."

"Thank you. When will I get my papers?" Gracie's heart thumped against her chest. This was it. She didn't think she'd be allowed to say she'd changed her mind now.

"Less than a month, I should think. As you said, things are heating up. Thank you for coming, Miss Thompson. Next."

Gracie left the recruitment centre and walked back to the house, totally forgetting the shopping. Once Cook saw the empty bags, her eyes widened, and then she saw the expression on Gracie's face. "You've done it, haven't you? You've joined up."

"Yes, Cook. I had to." Gracie held her hand out as if begging Cook to understand. "I can't sit back doing nothing. Not while Stan is out there missing somewhere and we're being hit with bombs every night. It's not right."

"It's not right young girls going off to war, that's the truth, my girl. What will your parents say?"

Gracie didn't meet her eyes. "I'm not sure."

"Well, best you go and find out."

"Now?"

"No time like the present." Cook's mouth was drawn in a thin white line, her disapproval made evident with her banging the pots on the table.

∾

IT TOOK ages to reach Lewisham with buses running late and being re-routed around unexploded bombs or large craters left in the ground. Gracie tried to keep her eyes on the road ahead. She hated seeing the remains of houses where families had once lived. The ones which looked like half had fallen down leaving the other side untouched were the worst.

She arrived home hoping to have a word with her mam first before they faced her dad together but it wasn't to be.

"Gracie, love, are you all right? What are you doing here?" Her mam's worried tone brought her dad downstairs, wearing his vest and trousers.

"What's wrong?"

"Nothing, Dad, Mam. Cook suggested I take advantage of the family being out and call down to see you."

"Gracie Thompson, I know a fib when I see one. Out with it. Are you in trouble?"

The heat rose in her cheeks as both her parents stared at her. "No, Mam. Of course not. Charlie respects me. I mean I wouldn't..." Too embarrassed to continue, she changed the subject. "But you're right. I've to tell you something."

Now she was facing her father, she didn't feel so brave. She opened her mouth to tell them but closed it again. She'd lost her voice, feeling as if she'd swallowed sand. She went to the kitchen to get a glass of water.

"Gracie, spit it out. You're scaring me." Her mam's worried tone broke through her fear.

"I've joined up. I've been thinking of doing it for ages, since Stan ... since he was shot down and then with all these bombs. I'll have..."

"You've done *what*?" her father roared at her, causing her mam to clutch his arm.

Gracie stood firm. "The government will introduce conscription for women soon, they said so on the news. I'm young, single and healthy. My country needs me. The posters say so and so does Pathé News when you go to the cinema." Blabbering away like a run-away train wasn't going to settle her father.

"Gracie, have you been to the recruiting office already?"

"Yes, Mam."

"Well that's it then. No point in us shouting or carrying on. You've signed your life away to the government for the duration."

Disappointment flooded Gracie. Her parents weren't proud but angry.

"Mam, Dad, can't you see? If I was a boy I would already be fighting. I have to do my bit. The sooner we beat the Germans, the quicker everyone comes home. Charlie, Frank…" *Maybe even Stan.* "Please be proud of me."

Her dad gave her a look and retreated back upstairs.

"Mam?"

"Don't mind your dad, love. He's been on duty for so long he doesn't know his own name. I'll talk to him. So the WAAF, then? They've nice uniforms, don't they?" Despite her words, her mam's eyes glittered with un-shed tears.

"I'm sorry, Mam, but I had to do it."

Her mam held out her arms and Gracie moved into her embrace. "I know you did, love, but that doesn't mean we have to like it. Never thought the day would come when I was sending my girl off to war. It was bad enough with the boys."

Gracie didn't stay long, not wanting to see her dad again. She took her time getting back to London. What would Charlie think? She was seeing him at the weekend. He'd be proud of her, wouldn't he?

CHAPTER 36

Thrilled to see Charlie waiting for her at the Marble Arch entrance to Hyde Park, Gracie ran into his outstretched arms. "I can't believe that our park looks like the Germans invaded with all the trenches and barbed wire. Not to mention the bomb damage around London."

"Never mind that. Give us a kiss, Gracie. It seems like ages since I held you."

She stood on her tiptoes, placing her lips on his. The kiss he gave her sent thrills down her spine. It took every ounce of willpower to break their embrace. Social conventions were still strict despite the war. Nice girls simply didn't get carried away in Hyde Park.

"I could kill my parents for not letting us get married." She kicked at a piece of grass.

"Gracie, maybe they are right? You know I love you, but I can't bear the thought of leaving you a widow."

She looked up so fast, she almost lost her balance.

"What? I thought you wanted to get married."

"I do, Gracie, but with me flying and…"

"You care more about your planes than you do me."

"Gracie, I love you and I love flying. While I wouldn't have wished for war, now I make a difference. Don't make me choose between you and flying, please."

Gracie knew she couldn't do that. She loved him and wanted whatever made him happy, even if that took him away from her for a while.

"You know I won't make you choose."

He put his arm around her waist. "Come on, let's go and see the ducks, if they're still there."

They walked arm in arm for a while.

"So, what have you been up to? How are things at the house?"

"Charlie, I've joined up. Women's Auxiliary Air Force." She looked up at him, expecting to see her joy reflected in his eyes. Instead, he moved slightly away from her, folding his arms across his chest.

"You, in the WAAF? What does your dad say about that, then?"

Gracie stayed silent, not wanting to relate her father's reaction as it still smarted.

"I knew it, he was horrified and for good reason. You know what they say about WAAFs?"

Irritated, she retorted, "No, what?"

"That they are officers' ground sheets." Charlie ducked out of the way just in time as Gracie moved to give him a playful poke in the ribs.

"Oh, you!" Gracie didn't fully understand what that meant, but she knew enough to understand that it wasn't flattering. "I don't care. He can't do anything. I've joined the WAAF and I want to work near your base. Nobody is going to keep us apart, not the RAF or anyone else, for…" She stopped talking, taking in Charlie's reaction. He wasn't looking at her but was shaking his head. "What's wrong? I thought you would be happy?"

Charlie was frowning, looking into the distance. "Happy that my fiancée is going to be miles away from her family, on a base surrounded by lots of strangers? Mainly single men. Why would you think that?"

"But, Charlie…" She scraped a hand through her hair.

"But nothing. I can guess why you have opted for the WAAF. You obviously want more excitement than I can give you." Cold eyes glared at her as he cracked his knuckles.

Gently, she reached out for his arm, but he brushed her off. "I thought it would please you. I'm finally going to be doing my bit to help win this war."

"If you want to be useful, why not work in a factory with the other women? Or volunteer at a children's hospital or nursery?" He towered over her. "Being ogled by young men is not my idea of working for the war effort."

"Of all the stupid, misguided arguments I've heard in my life, yours takes the biscuit, Charlie Power. How dare you accuse me of treating the service as some sort of match-making service? Until ten minutes ago, I'd no interest in any other man. I was happy with the one I was seeing. The one whose ring I wear on my finger." She stopped, realising that her shouting had attracted the attention of other people walking in the park. She glared at him. "I obviously don't know you as well as I thought I did. I'm going home."

She stormed off, leaving him to run to catch her.

"Oh, Gracie, darling, come here and give me a kiss. I love it when you get riled up. You go a lovely shade of pink."

She didn't have time to think of an answer as his lips met hers. They melted into each other's arms, and Gracie surrendered to the sensations that overcame her. Her anger cooled. She must have misunderstood him.

Something that felt this good couldn't be possible if he believed what he'd said.

All too soon, Charlie broke their embrace. "Let's continue our walk. We have put on enough of a spectacle for one day."

Gracie, flushed and disorientated, swallowed hard to regain her composure. She glanced around her. Relieved to see nobody staring at them, she looked at Charlie imploringly. "Charlie, we need to talk. About earlier…"

"Not now, Gracie. Let's just walk, hold hands and enjoy the sunshine. The war can wait for a couple of hours."

Gracie's chest tightened, the heaviness in her stomach making her feel ill. She couldn't believe that they had just had a massive fight. She'd never thought of him as the jealous type before. She looked at the man at her side, whom she loved so much. Perhaps she'd misunderstood. Charlie was obviously not prepared to discuss or resolve it. Although the sun shone high in the sky, she shivered.

CHAPTER 37

Sir John surprised her. "I believe we are losing you, Gracie. Penelope tells me you've joined up. She seems to think she should be going too."

"Yes, Sir. I mean, no, Sir." Flustered, Grace shut her mouth but Sir John smiled.

"You've worked hard during your time here and we are all very proud of you. We shall miss you of course but our country's need is greater. I assume your parents are very proud of you too. I believe you will receive your call-up papers shortly so why not leave at the end of this week? You will have things to sort out and I imagine your mother would welcome some time with you."

"Thank you, Sir John." She'd a sudden urge to hug him but that was totally inappropriate. He turned to Cook, who was sniffing into a tissue. "I know you will miss young Gracie, Cook. We'll try to replace her but it may be time for you and Mr Perkins to retire to Mother's estate. My wife may stay with her family and I can go to my club."

"What of Miss Penelope?" Cook asked.

Sir John looked at Gracie, curving his mouth into a half smile. "I think my niece will join up as soon as she can, don't you?"

Gracie was sad to leave the house, Cook and, of course, Penny but thrilled to have a few days to spend with her mam. Maybe it would be enough to get her dad speaking to her again.

ALL TOO SOON, it was time for her to leave home and head to the recruitment centre in

Kingsway. Gracie came downstairs feeling quite grown-up in the skirt and jumper her mam had made for her in honour of her leaving home.

"How are you feeling, lass?"

"Excited and nervous, I think. What if they don't like me? The recruiting man said that it was usually ladies from good homes they took." Her mother raised her eyebrows at that. "What if I'm not up to the job? What if they send me home?"

Her dad bristled. "Stop thinking like that. You passed the interview, didn't you? They wouldn't have accepted you if they thought you couldn't handle it. They will be glad to have you. What more could they want than a sensible young woman from a good, decent family? You don't have to make excuses for where you're from, young lady."

Gracie realised she'd offended her father. She gave her dad a quick kiss on the cheek.

"Sorry, Dad. It's just the nerves." She stole a quick look at him. "Dad. I know that you didn't want me to join up but I really needed to do something, especially after seeing all the destruction these last few months and … well, with Stan being … gone. I would really like your approval before I go."

Her mam spoke up. "Your dad knows that, love. It's a big step, leaving home, especially when we thought it would only happen when you got married. Who'd have thought that young girls would join the army?"

"Mam, it's the air force."

"Oh, whatever. What time do you have to be at Kingsway?"

"The letter said to be there at 10 a.m. sharp."

"Well, you'd best get going. You don't want to be late on your first day." Her mam's tears choked the words so that they came out as a whisper.

Gracie gave her mam a hug, then picked up her bag and headed out of the door.

"Gracie, wait."

Surprised by the rough tone of her father's voice, Gracie turned around.

"I might not agree with your actions, but I'm very proud of you." He took a deep breath. "Take care, love. We'll be here waiting when you get your first leave."

Gracie ran back to hug her father, who held his arms open. "Thank you, Dad. I love you." She wiped the tears away, straightening her shoulders before picking up her bag. "See you soon." She could feel her parents' eyes on her back as she walked away, but she didn't risk turning around. Her emotions threatened to overcome her, and she wasn't sure she could stop herself running home if she looked back.

WHEN SHE ARRIVED at the train station, she was relieved to find that there were lots of other girls looking as uncertain as she did milling around. She walked over to one girl who stood slightly aside from the group.

"Hi, I'm Gracie. I'm getting this train to my new posting. Are you on your own, too?"

"Mavis Adams, and yes, I am." The girl gave her a shy smile. "Thanks for coming over. They all seem to know at least two or three other people, don't they?"

"It probably just seems that way. They may have been at school together or come up on the same train or something like that. They may not all be at the same posting as we are. If they are, I'm sure they will include us at some point." Gracie hoped she looked as confident as she sounded.

"Well, tough on them if they don't. I didn't join up to make friends, did I?"

Gracie burst out laughing. "Well, I hope you will be my friend. I think you'll be a breath of fresh air."

Gracie saw another studious-looking girl nearby who also appeared a bit lost.

"Why don't we…" She and Mavis turned to one another and both started talking at once, then laughed.

"I'll ask her, shall I?" said Mavis as she headed over to the other girl. Gracie watched as the girl broke into a big smile.

She really is quite pretty when she smiles,

thought Gracie, as the other two came back to where she was standing.

Mavis said, "Gracie, this is Jessie."

"Pleased to meet you, Gracie. Shall we get on board and grab some seats? I don't fancy standing the whole way."

They were lucky to find some seats together and spent the long journey getting to know one another. They shared their sandwiches and stories as if they had known each other for decades as opposed to hours. It was a good job they got on, as endless delays due to damaged track or troop trains lengthened the journey considerably.

Gracie looked at her surroundings. "So, this is Bridgnorth. It seems tiny. Not sure we'll have much fun around here."

Mavis nudged Gracie, but it was too late. A distinguished-looking older woman in full uniform stood over them and stared at the girls.

"You're not here to have a good time. You're here to learn how to take orders and become useful to the war effort." Continuing in an icy tone, she said, "We only have six weeks. I hope that's enough time. Pick up your cases and follow me."

"Looks like our transport awaits," whispered Jessie, pointing at several lorries waiting for the train.

Soon they arrived at the training stations.

They were led into a hut with thirty-two beds in it.

"We have to share with other girls?" one of the other recruits said, sounding surprised.

"Guess so, unless they are going to sneak a few men in here," said Mavis.

"Mavis!" Jessie said, looking cross, while Gracie smothered a smile. Jessie continued, "Quick, pick those three. We don't want to be at opposite ends of the hut."

Gracie and Mavis did as Jessie said.

"I hope they don't expect us to sleep on these things. Haven't they heard of mattresses?" Gracie looked in horror at the iron-framed metal-spring beds covered with three hard squares. There were no sheets, just two rugs and one rather dubious-looking pillow.

"It's not the Ritz, is it?" Mavis commented as she opened her case.

"No, it's not, but it's home for the next six weeks, so we might as well make the best of it," said Jessie.

They weren't left alone long before being told to go to the ablution blocks.

"What the blazes is an ablution block?" whispered Mavis.

"I've no idea, but it doesn't sound too pleasant, does it?"

Gracie was relieved to see it was the military name for the toilets and washrooms. The facilities were fairly primitive, but they wisely kept any comments to themselves. The corporal didn't look like her mood had improved with the journey.

"Cheer up, we're heading for the cookhouse now. It can only get better." Jessie smiled.

Gracie wasn't as optimistic, but her stomach was growling.

CHAPTER 38
NOVEMBER 1940

Dear Penny,

I hope you're keeping well and staying in your aunt's good books. I know it is hard to do, but it will make life a lot easier.

I'm a little homesick. Just don't tell anyone. I've written to Mam and Dad and told them I was thrilled and having a whale of a time. They have enough to worry about without having to add me to their list.

The journey here was endless, what with all the delays and everything. I was lucky, though, as I met two girls on the train, Mavis and Jessie. Both are from London, so I can understand what they say. With some girls, you would think they came from a different country altogether with the way they speak. There are a real mix of people here, including a few who would get Miss Harriet's nod of approval.

Mavis worked in a shop before joining the WAAF and is determined to have a good time. She wants to be a driver for the officers. They should accept her, as so few of us can actually drive. Jessie is the daughter of a reverend, and this is her first time away from home. I don't think she had a proper job before, but she's really clever. She was supposed to go to university, but the war changed all that. She's as quiet as Mavis is noisy, but they get on really well. Jessie is determined to look after us, although we're all the same age. She says she misses her younger brothers and sisters, who I gather have all been sent to live with some aunt down in the country somewhere. I told her she was welcome to mind mine anytime we got back to London.

When we first arrived, we had to have an FFI parade – its proper name is free from in-

fection and it was just awful. We had to line up and then some orderlies looked over our hands very carefully before turning their attention to our heads. They were looking for nits. Thankfully, they didn't find any on me but they found some on the girl standing next to me. They sent her to the line where people were waiting to be decontaminated. Everyone could see those in the line and you should have seen their faces. Some girls were making fun of them, but Mavis soon put a stop to that. She reminded the bullies that anyone can get nits – you never know where you pick them up and that some may have come into close encounters with those pesky mites on the trains down here. That thought wiped the grins off their faces.

Next, we had to give our names and addresses before being fitted for our new uniform. Let me tell you that the model on those posters we looked at wasn't posted to our station. None of the uniforms fit properly. The powers that be hadn't reckoned on the fact that girls come in all different shapes and sizes. The uniform itself is pretty, being airman blue. We were each given a jacket and a skirt, but we have to wear steel-grey lisle stockings and black leather shoes. Mavis is quite small and a little on the cuddly side, whereas Jessie is tall and straight, yet they issued them exactly the same size. We had a merry laugh, though, and it was a great way to break the ice with the other girls. It is hard to take yourself seriously when you look like you're wearing a mix of your mother's and little sister's hand-me-downs.

The worst bit is the regulation dark blue bloomers, which had some girls in tears laughing. Some older women said they were genuine passion-killers, but I don't really know what they meant by that.

Luckily all those sewing lessons Mam made me take have come in useful. I made a few adjustments to my uniform so it fits nicely. I helped Mavis and Jessie adjust theirs, as well. With the cap on, we all look much smarter.

It was a bit weird folding up our civvies in

brown paper so that we could post them back to our family. I think that's when the reality dawned – we're here now and we won't be going home until it's all over. Of course, we'll get leave and such.

Most of the girls are nice. It is hard not to get to know people very well when you share the same eating, dressing and sleeping space. There's a little bickering – to be expected, really, seeing as we all live and work in such close quarters. I'm lucky, as I was used to sharing a room with my sisters, but some girls have only ever slept alone and they say the noise of twenty girls sleeping keeps them awake.

The language is hard to get used to. It seems the air force has its own way of speaking and we need to catch on quick. We got our irons today. That's what they call our knife, fork and spoon. We have to keep the same set for the duration and wash them in a communal tub after meals. I would love to see Cook's face if she saw what was floating in this wash bowl.

We don't sleep on mattresses, but on these horrid things they call biscuits. They are quite uncomfortable, but it is amazing what surface you can sleep on when you need to. Some "young ladies" amongst us said they were going to get their mamas to send down proper mattresses, but nothing seems to have come of that plan. It's freezing at night, but then we're in the middle of winter. Spring can't come fast enough.

Everyone is treated the same, regardless of whether their father is a lord or a landlord of the local pub. The powers that be don't really care, so long as the job gets done.

We're training pretty hard. Our corporal says that the fact we're women means that some air force crews believe we'll be no use to them. She's determined to change their minds and has us marching up and down all the time. We could march in our sleep if we weren't so tired.

Anyway, please write back to me care of the above address and tell me all the news from home. Say hello to Cook for me.

Take care of yourself,
Gracie

As she'd suspected, she, Mavis and Jessie became firm friends and enjoyed going out together. She wished Charlie was nearby. Although they seemed to have put the argument behind them, she still felt uneasy.

Jessie was lucky. Her fiancé, Pat, was a pilot stationed on base. The girls got into the habit of heading out with Pat and some of his male friends whenever they had some time off. Gracie wasn't interested in dating anyone, obviously, but she got on well with Pat's best friend, Steve. The pilot reminded her of her twin Stan, always ready with a joke to lighten the mood.

"How come the pilots are always going out? Shouldn't they rest between flights?" Gracie asked one morning as she and Jessie walked to the ops room. They were on the early shift.

"Pat says it's impossible to sleep when

they are on ops. So they go to the pub to blow off steam. A few drinks help them get some sort of sleep, otherwise they just close their eyes and see all the horrible things they have seen up there." Jessie gazed up at the sky. "Imagine seeing your friend get hit in his plane or worse, shot by some German as he's parachuting out. I can't believe some of the things we hear."

Gracie didn't want to talk about it.

"What? Why have you gone so pale?"

"You were on a break but we had a Canadian call in to say goodbye."

"No."

"Yes, Jessie. He gave us his call sign, Three-Two, and then asked us to give his love to his mother. He didn't come back."

Jessie shook her head. "That's not going to happen to my Pat or your Charlie. They will be all right; they have to be."

They walked on in silence. As they neared the ops room, they spotted some pilots coming back from the medical officer's room.

Jessie put her hand on Gracie's arm.

"Look at the state of them. Surely someone could've driven them back."

Gracie stared at the pilots' faces, thankful she didn't recognise any of them. Still, their condition shocked her. One had his arm in a sling; another could only walk with the help of his mates as he couldn't put his weight on his bandaged ankle. A third had a large bandage over his face, covering one eye.

"I wish there was something we could do to help them. Look at their hollowed-out eyes; they look like they haven't slept in an eternity." Gracie sent up a quick prayer Charlie was in a healthier condition than these guys.

"We can and will help them. First, I'm going to speak to the CO and let him know what I think of them having to walk back. Then when our shift is over, we can call on them and ask what we can do to help. Mavis and the other girls will help us too."

Eight hours later, they made good on their promise. Knocking on the door of the pilots' quarters but staying outside so they couldn't be put on a charge, the girls grinned at each other as the door opened. The pilot's eyes widened when he saw the group of WAAFs standing there. The girls pushed Jessie forward.

"Um, em, we saw you come back this morning and wondered if there was something we could do for you? Maybe you have some darning or need a collar turned or…" Jessie looked at the other girls as the pilot stayed silent.

"Cor blimey, what you lot doing 'ere?" The voice matched a face that looked all of fifteen years old. All red hair and freckles with a big cheeky grin. Gracie saw his arm was still in the sling. "Can you iron a shirt? I usually do it but as you see, I'm a bit tied up. Could still take ye all out for a drink after, though."

"We'll iron the shirt; you can rest." Mavis's retort wiped the grin from his face. Perhaps she noticed as she added, "When you've recovered, we'll go dancing."

"You're on." The boy, Gracie couldn't

think of him as a man, ran back into the quarters, returning with his shirt, which he passed to Mavis. The other pilots handed over shirts with missing buttons, a couple of pair of socks that needed darning and some other ironing.

"Could you perhaps sew this for me?" the pilot with the injured eye asked Gracie. "I would…"

"Course I can. Congratulations on your promotion."

He didn't meet her gaze with his good eye. "Thanks. Doesn't seem something to celebrate when it's due to all the lads getting lost over France, does it?"

Gracie's heart broke for these young men. Despite their injuries, they had to go back up there in a couple of days. No matter how long she was on the airbase, she couldn't get used to seeing a pilot one day and finding him gone the next. And that was with strangers. These guys were losing their friends.

"Don't think like that. Everyone needs a leader. The others look up to you; it's obvious how they behave around you. Will have this back to you tomorrow. Back on shift in an hour." Gracie sniffed before speaking louder. "Come on, ladies, the CO will have us in Jankers if we're late back on duty."

With promises of drinks and dances, they retreated back to their duties.

DURING THEIR DAYS OFF, they visited local villages or went on long walks. This was encouraged if only to get the girls away from the constant loss. They'd each become adept at listening with one headphone and using the other ear to count the lads back after an op. The crackling voices of the pilots rang out through the ops room but not as loud as the screams of those who were never coming home.

If they were not on duty in the evenings, they headed to local public houses or went to dances organised by the social committees.

There were plenty of male partners. Not

just other pilots, but also the ground crew and other staff stationed at the base. Someone once said the uniforms make a man. Gracie wasn't too sure of that, but they helped. There were many ordinary-looking blokes who looked like young gods on the airfield.

Mavis often went on dates, but never with the same guy. She was adamant that the time for serious romance was after the war was over. For now, she was solely interested in having a good time.

"I don't know how you do it, Mavis," Gracie commented when they were both alone in the hut getting ready to go to the pub.

"Do what? Curl my hair like this? It's easy. Here, I'll show you."

"No, silly. Go out with so many men. Don't you ever like one of them enough to see them again?"

"Stop trying to marry me off, Gracie. Serious relationships are yours and Jessie's scene, not mine." Mavis winked. "Now, do you want me to do your hair or not? I've mastered the victory roll. Let me show you."

Mavis pulled Gracie's blonde mass into the fashionable style, pinning it in place.

"See? Easy. Now, James gave me some lipstick last week. You can borrow it. The colour would work really well with your baby-blue eyes."

"James? I don't think I met him. Is he going tonight?"

Mavis grimaced. "Not unless he's coming as a ghost. He bought it the other day."

Gracie shivered and shook her head. "That's not nice, Mavis."

Mavis looked at Gracie stonily. "Maybe not, but that's the reality. Our boys are getting shot down in droves. It's pointless falling in love with them. You only end up hurt."

Gracie flinched at the hard tone Mavis used. "You can try to put the tough guy front on but it doesn't wash with me."

Mavis looked indignant.

"You're the first one to comfort anyone who gets bad news from home or gets a telegram. Look at how you handled poor Linda last week…"

"I wasn't being nice. Her constant crying was keeping me awake."

"Keep telling yourself that, but I know different." Gracie regarded her friend. "Was your boyfriend killed?" she asked softly.

The colour drained from Mavis's face. She swallowed hard before answering. "I've never had a serious relationship. Now, do me a favour and drop it. Let's go, we're going to be late. The pub closes at ten and I could do with a drink."

The tone of her friend's voice and the guarded look in her eyes told Gracie that now was not the time to pursue the subject. "Okay. I won't make you tell me, but if you want someone to listen, I'm here."

Mavis gave Gracie's hand a quick squeeze. "I know. Now can we go?"

CHAPTER 39

A couple of evenings later, Gracie returned to the hut after her shift to find Mavis there alone.

"Are you all right? I thought you were on duty with Jessie this evening." Gracie had started to feel concerned about Mavis, who hadn't seemed herself since their conversation the other night. Her friend didn't seem to be able to sleep. Her tossing and turning had woken Gracie the previous night.

Mavis said, "I was supposed to be, but two of the girls called in sick so I've to cover an eight-hour shift tomorrow instead. I'm going to get an early night."

"Do you want to talk? You don't seem yourself."

"I'm fine, thanks. Just tired. Stop fussing, you're driving me nuts." Mavis smiled but her eyes were suspiciously bright. "Good night, Gracie." Mavis pummelled her pillow before curling up as if she were going to sleep.

"Good night. Sleep well."

Gracie went out to clean her teeth. On her return, she watched Mavis for a bit before going over to sit on her friend's bed.

"Mavis, I'm worried about you. It's obvious something is wrong. Can you not tell me? I might be able to help."

"Nobody can help." Mavis stuck her head under the covers. "Leave me alone."

"You're not in trouble, are you?" asked Gracie warily.

Mavis shot up in the bed, almost tipping Gracie off. "What type of girl do you think I am?"

Gracie reached out for her friend's hand. She stroked it. "I think you're a wonderful person. So kind and thoughtful. But I know there's something wrong and I feel responsible. I upset you the other night when we were going out to the pub."

Mavis shook her head. "You didn't upset me, you were just speaking the truth. I know what the other girls say about me. They think I'm fast for dating so many men. But it's easier. You can't get attached to someone you don't know."

"Why are you so afraid of loving someone?"

Mavis screwed her eyes shut. Gracie felt her shiver.

"It's losing someone I'm afraid of. I can't face that again." Mavis held her breath, the tears glistening on her eyelashes.

"Oh, Mavis, come here." Gracie held her while she sobbed. Eventually the sobs subsided.

Mavis sniffed. "Sorry."

"What happened to you, Mavis?"

"You know I come from West Ham. One night, the sirens went. We all headed out to the shelter. It was the same one my aunt, uncle and their family always used. They said it was safer than sitting under the stairs at home. Mum wasn't convinced. She hated sharing with strangers. But the ARP warden insisted we leave our house. We didn't have the space for a shelter in the garden. It was one of the worst nights of bombing; they kept coming. The shelter was so noisy. People were crying or shouting at others to pull themselves together. Some woman started a sing-song, but it was hard to hear the singing over the noise. Mum was feeding the baby while telling Lizzie, my little sister, a story. Dad was doing his best to keep our spirits up but I could tell he was frightened too. His eyes…"

Mavis's gaze was focused on a spot over the other side of the room. She didn't appear to hear Gracie. "I don't remember what happened next. I must have lost consciousness. When I woke up, I couldn't hear anyone. It was so quiet. I called out, but no one answered. I tried to move, but something pinned me in. I was so thirsty. I felt something dripping on my shoulder. I thought it was water. I tried to turn my head to drink, but I couldn't. I tried so hard." Mavis rocked backwards and forwards gently as she spoke.

"At some point the ground stopped shaking. That meant the bombs had stopped. Eventually, I heard someone shouting. I tried to yell to tell them we were there, but the words wouldn't come. The wardens dug me out with their bare hands. They took me to the hospital. Being covered in blood, they thought I was badly hurt. There were so many people, some with horrific injuries. I had a sprained wrist, so they patched me up and sent me home." Mavis shuddered.

"It took me hours to get home. I walked most of the way. Finally, I arrived at our house. It was unharmed. The milk bottles were sitting on the doorstep." For the first time Mavis looked directly at Gracie. "That's when I knew. Mum would never have left the milk out."

"Oh, Mavis, I'm so sorry. I had no idea."

Gracie's mind flew to her parents and siblings. It was bad enough Stan was missing but to lose her whole family … She couldn't bear it, tears filling her eyes at the very thought. She moved closer to her friend, wanting to offer comfort but not sure how.

"They were all buried together. Dad, Mum, Lizzie, the baby, my aunt, uncle and two little cousins." Mavis clenched her fists. "What did any of them do to deserve that? Nothing. I joined up immediately after the funeral and here I'm."

"I don't know what to say." Gracie twisted her hands in her lap, wanting to give Mavis a hug but feeling if she did, Mavis may fall apart. The girl was so strong dealing with all of this on her own.

Mavis stiffened, taking a hanky to wipe the stray tears from her eyes. She caught Gracie's direct gaze. "There's nothing you can say. Now you might understand why I can't get involved with pilots. I can't put myself through all that pain again. I won't."

CHAPTER 40
DECEMBER 1940

The operations continued day and night. The girls lost track of the days, even the weeks as they worked hard and played harder. Rumour had it the pilots used aspirin to sleep, Benzedrine to wake up and a blast of pure oxygen to get rid of any lasting hangover.

As Gracie yawned coming off a late shift, she wondered if she could borrow some aspirin. The constant flights were taking a toll on everyone. Sleep when it did come was broken. In her dreams, Gracie heard the screams of those pilots whose planes were on fire. She prayed over and over that Charlie wouldn't be hurt like that.

"What's got you looking like you sucked a lemon?" Mavis asked, butting Gracie with her elbow.

"I was just thinking of our boys. Aren't they so brave, going up there again and again." Gracie hesitated; they made it a point not to talk about a rough night. "I can't get those screams out of my head."

"That was tough. To give him his credit, the officer did try to turn off the radio but it got stuck or something. That poor devil, he's probably better off dead."

Mavis fell silent too as they walked back to the Waafery. They reached the front and as Gracie turned to walk around to the back door, Mavis pushed her through the front.

"You're going to get us both in trouble. The front door is only for officers and NCOs. We'll be cleaning the lav with our tooth-brushes."

"Only if we get caught." Mavis grinned before running ahead to jump on her bed. "I could sleep for England but I know as soon as I hit the pillow I'll be wide awake." Mavis sat back up again. "What we need is a drink."

"Not tonight, Cinderella. We need sleep. We're going out tomorrow night, remember."

"I guess you're right. But I won't sleep a wink, you know."

Less than five minutes later, her friend was snoring. Gracie pulled the blanket over her before heading to the ablutions block. She couldn't go to bed without washing her teeth first, no matter how tired she was.

The next night, they were all sitting around in the pub laughing and joking when Gracie noticed that, instead of being at the centre of the fun, Steve was looking very serious.

Pat moved seats to sit beside her. "Gracie, listen, this isn't easy to ask but could you check on Steve? I've tried but he won't talk to me. You know how it is, us men can't be seen as lacking moral fibre." Although Pat said it in a jokey tone, the look in his eyes was serious. Gracie looked in Steve's direction before turning back to Pat.

"Are you calling Steve a coward?" she whispered, not wanting anyone to hear her.

"No!" His response earned them a look of concern from Jessie and the others.

"What do you mean then? That's the phrase the brass use when they tell a pilot to stand down."

"Steve's having a hard time. You know how he babysits the new guys. It's taking its toll. The losses and everything."

Gracie knew what Pat meant. They saw it every day in the ops room. Some of the new pilots didn't last longer than a few weeks and the replacements arriving at the base looked younger every time.

"I've tried talking to him but he tells me I'm seeing things that aren't there. I'm not, I know that look in his eyes. I've seen it in other pilots. They've given up believing they'll make it through."

Gracie's stomach churned. She liked Steve; he was a nice guy.

"What can I do?"

"He likes you. I know you have Charlie

but maybe you could just try to talk to him a little. He might open up. I've got Jessie but he's got no one."

Gracie nodded. "I'll try."

SHE FOLLOWED Steve to the bar when he went to order the next round, stopping him before he returned to the others.

She leaned on the bar next to him and gave him a friendly smile. "Pat asked me to check up on you. He says you're having a hard time."

"Me? I'm fine." But his smile didn't reach his eyes. She stared back at him. "Danny Newton didn't come back today." Steve took a large gulp of his drink.

Gracie bit her knuckle. She hated hearing about pilots being killed. She couldn't help but think of Charlie. "Oh, that's awful. I'm not sure I know him."

"He was one of the new batch that joined

the other day. He'd only been flying a few months and was so excited at going on the raid. He didn't have a chance."

"Did you see it happen?" she said.

"Right in front of me. It was a direct hit."

"Steve, I'm sorry."

"He was just a kid, Gracie. What the heck was he doing flying last night? He should have still been in school."

"I'm sure he wouldn't be flying if they didn't think him ready."

"You'd like to believe that, wouldn't you? But I'm not so sure. We're really short of pilots. Those training courses seem to get shorter by the day." He drained his drink and nodded to the barman for another.

"Nobody would blame you for being scared." She bit her lip, hoping she hadn't offended him.

"But that's just it. I don't feel scared. I feel nothing. My friends are dying, I'm killing other pilots and I can't feel a thing."

Gracie was worried by the way Steve's

hands shook as he tried to drink his beer. He put the glass back on the counter and clenched his hands by his side. He talked as if she wasn't there.

"The new ones are excited. That every time we go out on a raid someone doesn't make it back, doesn't seem to hit them for a while. Then you can almost watch the realisation hit that every time they take off, their chance of returning goes down. The odds are stacked against us, yet I've made it through. So far. Why?"

Gracie didn't know what to say. "You're a superb pilot…"

"Johnny, Tim, Peter and the others were excellent pilots. Peter was just about the finest pilot in the RAF, yet he bought it. Why not me? Every time I go up, I wonder, 'Is this it?'"

"Oh, Steve." She patted his hand but withdrew immediately when he tried to hold on to it.

"I just wish I could feel something. Scared, angry, anything. When I'm flying and someone buys it, I don't even react any more. Of course, I check for a chute, but that's automatic. It isn't because I care."

"What about when you're flying back from a raid? Do you not feel relieved?"

"No, just a sense that tomorrow it will start all over again. The call will come, we'll fly out and will I come back next time?"

Gracie rubbed his arm, but he didn't appear to notice.

"I have to fly. It's my duty. I'm a coward."

"You're not a coward, you daft thing. You and the other men are all incredibly brave. You should think about the good you're doing. You're helping to win this war."

"I don't think about the end of the war. It doesn't seem real."

"So, what do you think about when you're coming back?"

"I think about all the things I haven't done yet. The places I haven't seen. I've never even…" Steve stopped as his neck coloured. "Sorry, Gracie. I forgot who I was talking to."

She gave his hand a squeeze.

"Maybe you really need some time off. You're exhausted. You've flown several raids, and with the shortage of pilots it's even more of a strain than it should be."

"There's no way I'll get leave now. We're too short of pilots. I'm due leave soon. That's if I come back from the next raid or the one after that."

"That's no way to talk, Steve. You can't have that attitude going up in the air."

"Sorry, Gracie."

Gracie shook her head. "No, I'm sorry."

"Don't be. You shouldn't get involved with pilots."

"Typical RAF attitude. You think I'm falling for you." She tried to reduce the tension by joking. He smiled and responded in kind.

"Well, isn't every woman? Can you not see them queuing up, eyes wide with jealousy that I'm sitting here having a drink with you?"

Seeing as the only women in the pub were with their boyfriends, Gracie laughed.

"I do like you, though, Gracie."

"Don't, Steve." She turned, looking for the other girls. It was time to leave.

"I know you're in love with Charlie. He must be a terrific bloke."

"He is."

"Okay, but can we still be friends? You can find me a splendid girl to take out. Shouldn't be that difficult with these handsome good looks and glorious body."

Gracie burst out laughing. "You don't need any help. There are plenty of girls who would love to date a hero. Don't get all big-headed on me. There's something about the uniform. Come on, drink up. It's getting late and we all need to get back before we end up on a charge."

Steve walked her back to her barracks in silence. Gracie was thinking about Charlie. She wondered how he felt taking off night after night when so many of his friends never made it home. She knew it frightened him – you would be an idiot if you weren't terrified – but she also knew he didn't want to worry her by talking about it. She never asked him about it, taking the view that if he wanted to talk, he'd have said so. They had an unspoken pact to live every day as if it were their last.

Where was Charlie now? Was he safe or still over Germany?

"Thanks. Gracie. You're the best." Steve kissed her on the cheek before leaving.

"Take care, Steve."

FOR THE NEXT TWO WEEKS, Gracie anxiously counted back the planes after each raid Steve flew. Thankfully, he made it through and he sought Gracie out before heading home on leave. She was relieved that his face looked a little less strained.

"Take care, Steve, and try to get some rest."

He grinned. "Rest may not be at the top of my agenda."

Gracie rolled her eyes. "Well at least get

some sleep in between all the dates." She gave him a quick hug before heading back to her hut.

CHAPTER 41

Penny looked up from her latest letter to Gracie. She was struggling to find something to talk about.

Penny decided to come back to her letter when she was in the right mood, and went to find Cook to see if there was anything she could do for her.

Cook looked up as she came into the kitchen. "Hello there, Miss Penny. And how are you today?"

"I'm bored, if I'm honest. I can't face knitting another sock or sewing on another button. I was trying to write to Gracie, but

I've nothing to say. Do you have anything that you would like me to do?"

"Not really, miss. I've already done the shopping, although with rationing you could hardly call it that. How I'm expected to bake a decent cake with so little butter or lard is beyond me." The older woman looked thoughtfully at Penny. "Bert is out in the garden digging for victory, but I guess Her Ladyship would have a fit if you were to help him."

"Ah, but Aunt Louise isn't here. She's out visiting. Again! Thanks, Cook."

Penny headed out into the vast back garden. She was surprised to see how much work Bert had already completed.

"Hi, Bert. Cook said you might like some help."

"I'd love some, miss, but not from you. Thanks all the same. The mistress would fire me."

"She won't do that, Bert, and you know it. She knows she's expected to make this space produce food and she isn't going to dig it up herself, now is she?" Turning on the charm, she grinned at the old man. "I work on the farm when I go to Suffolk, so why can't I help you plant some vegetables?"

"All right, Miss Penny, you win. But please go inside and put on something more suitable than that dress."

"Thanks, Bert. I'll be back soon," she said as she raced indoors with a new lease of life.

PENNY SPENT an enjoyable few days helping the old gardener whenever her aunt was out of the house. She liked listening to his stories. He'd known her father and Sir John when they were little boys. He told her how her father had always been fond of animals. He always had a pet of some sort trailing around after him, from an injured bird to a wounded fox cub. Bert helped fill so many gaps in Penny's thirst for information about her family. He spoke highly of Meme, too, telling Penny her grandmother was just about the kindest lady he'd ever worked for.

"What about Aunt Louise?"

"I'll not dignify that question with a response."

Penny burst out laughing. "Sorry, Bert, that was mean. I was only teasing you."

Seeing his reaction, she changed the subject.

"Why is Cook collecting all the food waste in a separate container, Bert?"

"That's for the pigs, Miss Penny."

"Are we going to have pigs out here, too? I can't see Aunt Louise liking that idea."

Bert grinned. "No, miss. Cook has a friend in the local council. They are running a pig-rearing programme. Those that help feed the pigs will share in the meat when the pigs are old enough to be slaughtered. I think Her Ladyship will be glad of whatever Cook can do to improve the quality of what they set on the table, don't you?"

"Oh, I see. Can anyone join these schemes?"

"I think so, girl, but you would have to check with Cook." He smiled at Penny. "I'm sure Cook will let you have a few slices of bacon."

"I was thinking of Gracie's parents. Her mother has some hens, which she's using for eggs, although I guess she'll cook them, eventually. Bacon goes well with eggs."

"Aye, it does that. Now, we'd best get back to work. Standing around chatting all day will not get those potatoes sorted."

PENNY'S GARDENING experience came to an abrupt end when she met her aunt coming back into the house while covered in fertiliser.

Louise recoiled, looking her up and down distastefully. "Heavens, what's that smell? Penny, what have you done now?"

"Nothing, Aunt Louise. I was just helping Bert out in the garden."

"Go upstairs and change out of those

clothes at once. From now on, you will stay by my side, seeing as you simply cannot be trusted not to stay out of trouble."

As Penny wrote to Gracie later, her short-lived freedom had been fantastic. It had almost been worth the price of having to accompany her aunt on many fundraising and social outings. If her aunt thought she was going to spend the war sipping tea, she was in for a surprise. She was even more determined than ever to find something to do to help the war effort.

CHAPTER 42

JANUARY 1941

Gracie was fed up with all the talk of war being over soon. It was the uncertainty that was getting to everyone. That, and the January blues. Christmas had been a bit of a washout, as neither she nor Charlie had leave at the same time.

They couldn't see each other as often as before. It was difficult getting her leave and his to match. But she was sometimes grateful regulations kept them apart. She didn't think they could wait much longer. It was getting harder to stop at just kissing and cuddling. She wasn't sure what came next, but her mam had warned her never to let a man see her knickers. That was how babies came and there was no baby coming into her mam's house unless it's mother had a wedding ring on her finger. They had brought her up to be a respectable girl, and that was that. Charlie understood, and he was very good about it, but she knew he struggled with it, too.

It didn't help that she worried constantly about him. She'd lost count of the number of Charlie's fellow pilots who'd died already.

Gracie lay back on her bed, enjoying the silence of the hut. She was seldom alone, and it was nice to get some peace.

Her thoughts drifted back to Charlie. She could see a change in him when they were able to meet, and had noticed his letters weren't as frequent or as chatty as they'd once been. He wasn't as carefree as he once was. Sure, he still smiled, but the smile didn't light up his eyes like it used to. Instead, his eyes had an apprehensive and tired look about them. But then, he *was* tired. He'd been flying so much lately, and the strain was bound to take its toll.

The door to the hut banged as Jessie and Mavis came in, interrupting her thoughts.

"Oh, my feet," Mavis complained as she flung herself on her bed. "I thought working in a shop all day was hard work. If I could go back to that now, I would never complain again."

Gracie and Jessie laughed. They had heard endless stories about how much she'd hated working in the shop. Almost as much as she loved being in the WAAF.

Jessie said, "Why don't you have a bath? You can use some of my bath salts."

Mavis sat up, using her elbows to support her, frowning in Jessie's direction. "Jessie, why are you always so nice? Don't you ever get grumpy?"

Jessie's eyes sparkled. "I don't have any reason to be upset, do I? I'm marrying Pat and my two new best friends are going to be my bridesmaids. What more could I want?"

"An end to the war?" suggested Mavis.

"Well, that would be lovely." Jessie turned her attention to Gracie, who had stayed lying on her bed. "What's up with you, Gracie?"

She didn't get an answer as Mavis jumped in.

"She's missing Charlie. It's all right for you and Pat. At least you're stationed at the same base. Why doesn't Charlie put in for a transfer?" asked Mavis.

Gracie sighed. "He did, but they turned it down. I just wish we could've some time on our own. But when we go home, everyone wants to see us. Mam and Dad want us to visit and Charlie has to see his mother. We never seem to get time alone."

"Ha, hormones getting to you, love?"

Mavis's comment sent the heat flushing through Gracie's face. Jessie pinned Mavis to her bed with a look, reprimanding her in her best officer's tone.

"Mavis, don't embarrass Gracie. We don't all have your loose morals."

"Oh, come off it, Jessie. As if you and Pat haven't anticipated your wedding vows."

Jessie turned a pretty shade of pink, but

didn't answer. Mavis turned her attention to Gracie.

"Why go home on your next leave? Why not go somewhere, just the two of you?"

Gracie couldn't do that to her parents. She was a good girl. Yet, what if Charlie died before they got married? She'd never know what it was like to really love him. But her mam would kill her if she found out. Her thoughts jumbled up in her mind as Mavis kept talking.

"If you don't tell them when you have time off, your parents won't be expecting you, will they? Then you can have your wicked way with Charlie and come back here with a big smile on your face."

Gracie threw her pillow at Mavis to shut her up. Even though the girls were close friends, Gracie was mortified.

"Stop it, Mavis. You're embarrassing her." Jessie looked straight at Gracie. "Nobody can or should tell you how to live your life, but for what it's worth, my view is that life is too short not to make some time for yourself. Who knows what's going to happen in this blasted war, or how long it is going to last."

Gracie nodded in agreement, almost surprising herself in the process. She agreed with everything Jessie said.

Mavis laughed gleefully. "Wow, Jessie, you certainly don't sound like a preacher's daughter. In one sentence you have advised Gracie to lie, have relations with her intended, and cursed. You'd better be careful and not let your dad catch you acting like that."

"Oh, shut up, Mavis. One thing I've learned is that it is easier to ask forgiveness than to seek permission. Anyway, we each have to live our own life. Gracie will do what she thinks best."

Gracie found her voice at last. "Don't you think Charlie will think I'm fast if I suggest we go away together?"

Mavis and Jessie exchanged a look before bursting into giggles.

"Stop laughing at me, you two." Hurt, Gracie sat up straight on the bed.

"Sorry, Gracie. But honestly, we don't think Charlie will be anything other than thrilled," Jessie apologised.

Mavis added, "Come on, girl. If you're old enough to fight for your country, you can ask your fiancé out on a date."

A knock on their hut door interrupted them. "Thompson, section officer wants to see you. There's a telegram for you."

Gracie's hand flew to her mouth and she sagged against her bed. "Charlie. Oh, no, please don't let it be Charlie."

"Come on, Gracie, we'll go with you. Won't we, Mavis?" Jessie rushed to Gracie's side, helping her from the bed. It was as if her legs couldn't understand the instructions from her brain to stand up.

Mavis's eyes spat fire. "Yes, of course, and when I come back, I'm going to kill that orderly. Couldn't she have been more sensitive?" Mavis took one arm, Jessie the other, and between them they got Gracie to her feet.

With her friends on either side, she rushed

to the office. Her hand shook as she knocked on the door.

"Come in."

Gracie saluted her section officer, who was sitting behind her desk. "You wanted to see me, ma'am."

"Yes, Thompson. Stop looking so scared. Didn't Aircraftwoman Second Class Murphy tell you it was good news?"

"Good news, ma'am?" Gracie dug her nails into the tips of her fingers to prevent the blackness overtaking her.

The section commander stood up and walked around her desk. "Gracie, sit down, please. I'll have words with Murphy." She smiled at Gracie. "Your parents sent a telegram for you this morning. Here it is."

"My parents, ma'am?" Gracie couldn't stop herself from repeating things. Her hand shook so much she let the telegram fall.

The section commander bent down to pick it up. "I think I should read it to you."

Tears stinging her eyes, Gracie nodded.

"*Stan alive. Got a message from Red Cross today. He's a POW. Letter to follow.*"

Gracie slumped forward, the tears flowing down her cheeks. Her commanding officer handed her a hanky.

"I take it Stan is your young man?"

"No, ma'am, he's my twin brother. They shot him down over France in July. The RAF advised my parents he was missing, believed killed." Gracie smiled at her boss. "Thank you, ma'am."

"I'm very glad that it was good news. It is much easier to deal with things when one knows the facts. Don't you think?"

Gracie couldn't help thinking that the commander wasn't talking about Stan, but she didn't want to pry.

"Yes, ma'am."

"Off you go now, Thompson. I'm sure your two friends are waiting anxiously outside."

"Yes, ma'am. Thank you, ma'am." Gracie saluted and left the office to find Mavis and Jessie pacing up and down outside.

Grinning like a madwoman, she flung herself at them. "He's alive."

They both hugged her, with Jess saying, "Oh, that's wonderful, Gracie. Now, do you need more of a sign to plan your weekend away with him?"

"Stan's alive. It wasn't Charlie." Gracie burst out laughing at the confusion on her friends' faces. "Stan's my twin brother. They shot him down over France. It was too painful to talk about him. He's a POW. He's alive." With a whoop of joy, Gracie jumped into the air.

The sound of a throat being cleared noisily behind her brought her back to her senses. She looked up into the eyes of the wing commander.

"Sorry, sir. Didn't see you there, sir."

"At ease, Leading Aircraftwoman. It's not every day we get good news, but perhaps you'd best take your celebrations elsewhere."

"Yes, sir. Thank you, sir." The three friends saluted smartly before marching off quickly to their hut.

CHAPTER 43

Gracie wrote to Charlie telling him about Stan and also asking if he'd like to spend their next leave alone. She was thrilled when he agreed, suggesting a hotel that was far enough away to reduce the risk of meeting anyone they knew.

Her mam and dad didn't even know Charlie was on leave. She told them she was going to spend that leave with a girlfriend. She felt guilty lying to her parents, but they would never have let her spend the weekend alone with her boyfriend and that was exactly what she wanted. They could stop them getting married, but they couldn't stop them being together. Gracie was determined to show Charlie just how much she loved him.

The girls in her hut knew that she was going to spend the weekend with her boyfriend, although they didn't know it was her first time. They would have teased her mercilessly. Only Jessie knew the truth. She'd reassured Gracie that Charlie wouldn't think anything less of her and had even insisted on lending her a beautiful pink silk nightgown.

She looked at it lying at the top of her case and her cheeks grew pink at the thought of Charlie seeing her in the nightdress. She couldn't imagine lying next to him in bed. She wasn't completely sure of what was going to happen between them, but from listening to some conversations the other girls had, she had an idea. She didn't really want to think about it, though. She couldn't imagine her mam and dad doing something like that, and told herself that the girls had been winding her up.

She hoped that Charlie was happy about this weekend. She knew that he was prepared to wait until they were married but that he, too, was impatient to be with her. They loved each other deeply, and, she reminded herself, if her parents had been agreeable, they would have been married by now.

CHARLIE HAD SAID he'd meet her at the White Horse hotel – a rather grand name for a village pub. She waited outside as it wasn't considered nice for a lady to be seen inside a public house, particularly in the middle of the day. Charlie must have been held up travelling, as he was very late. Rather than stand outside the pub, she walked back to the station to meet him at the train.

Thankfully, she didn't have to wait too long. Charlie was surprised, but thrilled, to find her waiting for him. "Sorry I'm late, darling. It is so good to see you." He kissed her on the cheek before taking her arm and walking down the road.

"You're very quiet. Are you okay? Are

you sure about this? It isn't too late to ask for separate rooms, you know." He took her gently in his arms and kissed her.

"I'm okay," she said, looking into the face of the man she adored. "But won't they check the ration cards and see we aren't married?"

"No, darling. One reason I picked this hotel was the fact that a lot of couples like us stay here. The owners are sympathetic to wartime romances."

She wasn't too sure she liked their love affair being described as a wartime romance. This was the real thing, wasn't it? She looked at Charlie, but he was looking ahead.

They walked into the reception area and it thrilled Gracie to hear Charlie introduce her as Mrs Power. The girl behind the desk barely glanced at them or their ration books.

"Will you want supper in your room?"

"No, that won't be necessary. We'll eat in the main dining room," Charlie answered.

"It's room six at the end of the corridor, second floor."

They went upstairs, and Gracie gasped

when Charlie grabbed her and carried her over the threshold.

"In my mind this is our honeymoon, even if we have yet to make it to the church. I love you, Gracie Thompson."

Inside the beautiful room was the biggest bed she'd ever seen. It was covered in a pretty patchwork quilt that must have taken someone years to make. She put her overnight bag in the bottom of the mahogany wardrobe and turned to look at Charlie. After all this time, she wasn't sure she was ready to take this next step.

Charlie must have sensed her mood as he suggested going for a walk around the park. Gracie jumped at the chance to get some fresh air, and hand in hand they went.

Charlie put his arm around her as they chatted about the recent events at their respective bases. Rain started to fall, and they scurried to the shelter of some trees. Charlie kissed Gracie so passionately it took her breath away.

"I love you so much."

"I love you, too, Charlie."

Their kisses grew deeper and more demanding. Now she was certain that they were doing the right thing. As the rain didn't show any sign of subsiding, they ran back to their hotel. Laughing, they stumbled into their room and Gracie was thankful that the fire was lit and the room warm.

"We must get out of these wet clothes or we'll both catch our death."

"Here, let me." Charlie gently pulled Gracie towards him and started undressing her.

WHEN SHE WOKE, he was watching her. She was so happy, although her body hurt slightly. She stretched out like a cat, almost giving in to the urge to purr. Instead, she smiled at him, but when he didn't respond in kind, her heart lurched.

"Charlie?"

"Shhh, don't speak. Just let me hold you

and look at you. I love you so much. I never want this night to end. I can't bear the thought of not being with you for weeks and weeks."

She knew then that he dreaded leaving as much as she did. She'd have given anything to spend the rest of the war tucked up safely together, but that was not to be. They had a duty to their families and their country. But they didn't have to go back just yet.

She moved her body suggestively against his, kissing his neck and behind his ear.

"Are you trying to seduce me, Miss Thompson?" he said, looking directly into her eyes.

She nodded before pulling him down into a passionate kiss. For now, he was hers and she wasn't sharing him with anyone. War or no war.

THEIR TWO DAYS FLEW BY, and when it was time to head back to their respective bases, Gracie fought hard not to let the tears fall.

"Gracie, darling, please don't cry. We'll see each other again very soon and I'll write to you as often as I can."

"I just wish this war was over, or at least that you were on the same base."

He hugged her, saying, "I'm going to go and see your dad on my next leave. Maybe I can persuade him to let us get married. There's no sign of the war being over soon." He kissed her again. "If we were married, you could give up the WAAF and find quarters near my base. We could see each other as much as possible."

She ignored the fact he assumed she'd give up her job without a murmur. She'd a more important question to ask.

"Charlie, do you think less of me for suggesting this weekend?" Gracie looked at him, suddenly feeling shy.

He put a finger under her chin, forcing her to meet his gaze. "I love you, and nothing and nobody is going to ever change that. I'm so glad that we spent the last few days together."

"Me too. I love you even more than I did

before." She kissed him on the lips, despite being in the middle of a station platform. He was her man, and she didn't give a hoot who knew.

Gracie's train was the first to arrive. Charlie hugged her fiercely before helping her to find a seat. "See you soon, my darling. Take care."

Then he was gone.

GRACIE RETURNED to the base feeling very low. Thankfully, her hut was empty except for Jessie, who appeared to be having a nap but woke as Gracie put her case on the bed.

"You okay?" Jessie asked, rubbing her eyes as she sat up in bed.

"Sort of. I know I shouldn't grumble, but I hated leaving him. It will be ages before I see him again."

"Chin up, lovely. You don't know that. He may bag another weekend's leave shortly. So, did you have a good time?"

"Oh, Jessie, it was wonderful." Gracie could feel the blush creeping up her cheeks.

Jessie gave her a quick hug. "Yes, it is, isn't it? We're so lucky, Gracie. I know the war is awful and we wouldn't wish it on anyone, but without it, I wouldn't have met Pat and you might not have met Charlie. We have found two fantastic men who love us as much as we love them. Others aren't so lucky."

They were both thinking of Mavis, who still hadn't changed her mind about going steady with one man. Gracie didn't know if Mavis had told Jessie why. She hadn't said anything, as it wasn't her secret to tell. Anyway, Mavis wasn't the only WAAF whose views on romance were so casual.

"Come on." Jessie jumped out of bed. "Let's go and see if there's any hot cocoa left. That will cheer both of us up."

Gracie frowned. "Why do you need cheering up? Has something happened?"

"No, nothing serious. I just put a run in my last pair of stockings and I hate having to paint my legs with gravy."

Gracie burst out laughing. She knew Jessie was exaggerating, as she wasn't one to take such silly things seriously. She was lucky she'd such good friends, and they had come courtesy of the war, as well.

CHAPTER 44
FEBRUARY 1941

"Come on, Gracie. The dance will be over if we don't get a move on."

"I'm coming. Where's Jessie?"

"She's gone ahead with Pat and Steve. We thought you'd want to avoid walking with Steve."

"Thanks, Mavis." Gracie gave her friend a grateful smile. "Steve is a lovely bloke, but he's asked me out so often now, it is becoming embarrassing."

"I wish he'd ask me out. He's very cute!" Mavis looked wistful.

Gracie laughed. "You think any man in uniform is cute."

"Guilty. Now, come on, there's an entire room of uniformed men just waiting to get their hands on us."

"Mavis!"

The two girls ran giggling towards their bikes and cycled off down the road towards the village.

When they got to the hall, Jessie called them over to a table where she, Pat, Steve and the others were sitting. As they approached, Gracie was relieved to see that Steve had asked a girl out to dance. Maybe he was getting the message.

No sooner had she sat down than a French pilot asked her to dance. He introduced himself as Stefan and seemed very charming. She danced a few dances with him, finding him easy to talk to, although he was a little full of himself. She put that down to language differences. His English was good, but it wasn't perfect.

After the third dance she said, "Stefan, I would like to go back to my friends now."

"Okay, but why don't I buy you a drink first? All that dancing is making me thirsty."

"A lemonade would be lovely, thank you."

Her friends were all on the dance floor, so she sat alone at the table until Stefan returned with their drinks.

"Thanks." She took a sip of the drink and grimaced. It tasted different. He saw her looking at it.

"Sorry. Don't you like it? The man at the bar said they had to find another supplier. I can go up and get you something else. A cider, perhaps?"

"No, this lemonade is fine. I don't drink. My fiancé wouldn't like it." That wasn't really true, but she didn't want Stefan getting any ideas. "He's a pilot, too." Gracie wished so badly that Charlie was here.

Stefan glanced around him. Gracie laughed. "No, he's not here. I wish he was, but my bad luck meant they posted me to a different base to his."

Another pilot greeted Stefan. As they

spoke, Steve came up to Gracie, giving Stefan a look. "Want to dance, Gracie?"

"No thanks, Steve." She answered curtly, but surely he knew how she felt by now.

"Listen Gracie, that guy you're with…"

"Not now, Steve." She turned her back on him. Was he jealous? She smiled as Stefan finished talking to his mate. He turned back to her as they were left alone again.

"My wife is not here either. I miss her, so perhaps we can keep each other company. You can tell me about your pilot and I can talk about my wife and children. And we can dance."

Gracie felt more comfortable now she knew he wasn't looking for anything other than a chat. It just went to show that men got lonely, too, even the daredevil pilots. She smiled at Stefan as he took her hand and led her to the dance floor once more.

≈

GRACIE TRIED TO SIT UP, but the room swam around her. *My head.* She felt dizzy and sick and had a feeling of dread in her stomach. She couldn't remember anything. How had she got home from the dance? She realised that she wasn't wearing her uniform but couldn't remember getting undressed. She glanced around her but the other beds were empty. Where were the other girls?

She tried to get up again, but it was no use. The second her head left the pillow, her stomach started churning.

The door to the hut clanged; Gracie groaned aloud as Mavis came in.

"You're awake then, love? How do you feel? Awful, I'm sure. I could kill that bloke." Mavis put her hand on Gracie's forehead. It felt lovely and cool.

Gracie tried to sit up but her head hurt too much. "What guy?"

"Don't tell me you don't remember what happened last night at the dance?"

Gracie tried to shake her head, but it

ached. She tried to move other parts of her body, but everything seemed to be tender.

Her stomach churned. "Oh, I think I'm going to be sick."

"Lie down and try to stay still. You have a hangover, and you've had a rough night."

"A hangover? Don't be daft. You know I don't drink." But even as she said that out loud, she knew it wasn't lemonade.

"Well, you did last night, and you had quite a bit. Do you not remember anything? We thought you were joking about never having touched alcohol before, although I guess now we know you were telling the truth."

"I remember going into the dance with you and it being very busy. We saw Jessie, Pat and his friends and at some point, some foreign pilots came over to join us all. I re-member one. His name was Stefan or some-thing like that. He seemed nice." Gracie tried to look at Mavis, but the light hurt her eyes. She closed them and lay back on the bed. "I remember dancing with him and think he bought me a drink. It tasted funny, but I was thirsty after all the dancing and I finished it quickly. Then I started feeling odd." Gracie tried to sit up. "Steve tried to tell me something about him, but I figured he was just jealous. Stefan was really kind."

"Sure he was. He offered to take you outside to get some air, didn't he?"

"I don't know. I just remember feeling really ill and looking for you and Jessie, but I couldn't see you. Stefan said he'd take me to find you. He'd seen you over the other side of the hall."

"What a rat!"

Gracie looked at Mavis in shock. "Mavis, I didn't go outside with him. You know I'm not that type of girl."

"Oh, but you did. We didn't notice you were missing at first, but then when we couldn't find you inside, someone said they had seen you leaving with a young blond officer. Steve and I went outside and initially thought the person had been mistaken, as there was no sign of you."

Gracie frowned. "Steve? Why was he looking for me?"

"He was worried. He didn't like you dancing with the pilot. I thought he was jealous too. In fact, I teased him about it."

"Oh, Mavis."

"Don't you 'oh Mavis' me. You have bigger things to worry about than me teasing Steve."

"It turns out he heard that your new friend Stefan had a bit of a reputation. He tried to warn you earlier in the evening, but you wouldn't listen."

"I just thought he was trying to ask me out again. You know he keeps doing it although he knows I love Charlie. Oh, God, Charlie. What will he think of me? Please tell me what happened next. I can't remember a thing." A tear slid down Gracie's cheek and she angrily swiped it away.

"Steve and I were about to go back inside, but then we heard a girl screaming. We didn't know it was you, at first. You really have a set of lungs on you, but that's a good thing. God only knows what would have happened if you didn't."

"I was screaming?" Gracie's feeling of dread increased. She still couldn't remember what had happened, but her instinct told her she didn't really want to know.

"Look, lovey, what happened isn't your fault. The pilot thought his luck was in and when you protested, he decided he wouldn't take no for an answer. He gave you a slap and you lost consciousness. For a minute, we thought we were too late."

"No, he didn't." Gracie wrung her hands. "He couldn't have. I wouldn't do that," she whispered.

"Gracie you were out cold. You couldn't have done anything. Steve had to carry you. I ran to get Jessie and Pat."

Gracie cried. Mavis gently put her arms around her. "That dirty snake was quite rough with you, so you look a bit of a sight."

"Does everyone know what happened?"

"No, of course not. You know how gossip spreads on this base. Steve carried you back here, but Pat stayed behind to see to your attacker. He gave the guy a good hiding. He won't be going near another girl for a while, that's for sure. I stayed with you, and Jessie went for ma'am."

"Oh, no." Gracie put her head in her hands. "Is she going to send me home?"

"No, she was amazing. I know we all think she's a bit of a cold fish, but when it comes down to it, she really cares about us. She thanked the boys, but told us all that as far as she was concerned, she never saw any men in our hut. Stupid regulations mean that Steve could face charges if anyone knew he'd been here, even if he was being your knight in shining armour."

"Oh, don't call him that, please."

"Well, he was, and you will have to thank him. You can't ignore him after all of this."

Gracie knew she'd have to say something, but she preferred not to think about that at the moment.

"Will he or Pat get into trouble?" Gracie asked.

"No. Well, not unless the guy talks, but I'm guessing he'll keep quiet. Pat told him that he'd finish him if he ever came near any of us again. Here, now, sip this. It will make you feel a bit better."

Gracie took the cold water and sipped carefully. Her stomach started protesting.

"Ma'am said she'll talk to you when you're ready to see what you want to do about everything. But in the meantime, she told me and Jessie to put you to bed and to take turns staying up with you in case you needed anything."

"Oh, Mavis, I feel so stupid. I thought he was a nice guy. He seemed so lonely, being so far away from his family and everything. He told me all about his wife and child who are stuck in France and how worried he was about them with the Germans and everything."

"The problem with you, my girl, is that you're too good a listener and you think everyone is lovely. They aren't. The Nazis aren't the only baddies in this war. We have some real snakes on our side, as well. Now, let's see what we can do about your face."

Gracie stared into the mirror, looking at the swollen face reflected back at her.

"Oh, God, what would Charlie say if he saw me now?"

"I'm sure he'd find Stefan and finish what Pat started. Now, come on. We have to come up with a reason you look like you do before the other girls come back. We told them you were sick, but that doesn't explain your face. Say you walked into something in the blackout."

CHAPTER 45

FEBRUARY 1941

Gracie left the ops room and went back to their hut with a heavy heart.

Mavis was there and greeted her cheerfully. "What are you doing looking so glum? The sun's out and your shift is finished." Mavis was smiling at her, but her smile died as she caught the colour of her friend's face. "Okay, so what's up with you?"

Gracie sat on her bed and covered her face in her hands.

"Come on, Gracie, this isn't like you. What's the matter? You have me worried now. Is it Charlie? Has something happened to him?"

"No, it's not Charlie."

"Well, who then?"

"It's Pat. He's gone."

Mavis paled, "Pat? How do you know? Where is Jessie? Does she know yet?"

Gracie shook her head. "Steve sent in a radio report during the night. It was too busy to leave earlier, so many planes … The CO asked me to find Jessie, what with the wedding and all. We're to take Jessie to her office."

Mavis stood and paced the floor. "Curse this war anyway. Is there no hope?"

"No, it was a direct hit, and nobody saw any parachutes. Mavis, how can we face her? We'll break her heart. They were so much in love." Tears streamed down her face.

Mavis handed her a hanky. "Come on, chin up. She needs us. I'm coming with you. Just give me a sec to throw on some clothes. I'll be put on a charge if I venture out like this."

Hearing the catch in Mavis's voice, Gracie knew her friend was trying hard not to let her emotions break through. She went over to her, holding her around the waist from the back. Mavis turned, sobbing into Gracie's shoulder.

When the sobs subsided to an occasional shudder, Mavis raised her tear-stained face. "It's so unfair. They were so much in love."

"Nothing's fair. Pat was such a lovely man." She gave Mavis one last hug. "Wash your face first. We need to be strong for Jessie."

Gracie was grateful Mavis was coming with her. They went looking for their friend and eventually found her in the canteen, talking about the upcoming wedding.

"Of course, we'll be in uniform. Mummy isn't too happy as she'd visions of me being married in white, but as I told her, I don't care what I wear as long as we can finally get married."

Gracie took a deep breath before moving towards the group where Jessie was sitting.

"Hi, Gracie. Oh, are you all right? You don't look too well. In fact, you and Mavis both look a bit pale…" Jessie looked at her friends, from one face to another. She stood up.

"Oh, God, it's Pat, isn't it?"

"Jessie, the CO wants to see you in her office…" Gracie avoided her friend's eyes, not wanting to see her pain.

"No," Jessie screamed, and then fainted. Gracie and Mavis managing to catch her before she hit the floor. Gently they propped her up into the sitting position. Mavis sent somebody for some strong tea and asked someone else to find their boss.

Jessie gradually recovered consciousness and began rambling. "It can't be. Last night was his last mission. He was being transferred to Norfolk as an instructor. He wouldn't be flying. You're wrong. You're wrong…" She looked at Gracie. "Please be wrong. Gracie, tell me it's not true."

"Oh, Jessie, I wish I could." Gracie rubbed her friend's hands between her own, trying to warm them up.

Jessie kept talking. "It's too soon to know.

He only took off a few hours ago. Maybe they bailed out. He could be a prisoner of war by now. Couldn't he?"

"No, love, he's not a POW. Steve saw his plane get hit." Gracie put her arm around Jessie's shoulders. "He didn't have a chance; it was all over so quickly. He wouldn't have suffered." Gracie didn't know whether this was true but she didn't care. She was prepared to say anything that could make Jessie feel a little less devastated.

"I can't live without him, I won't live without him." Jessie dissolved into tears as her friends gathered round her.

"Come on, Jessie, we have to see the CO and then we'll get you back to the hut. The doctor can give you something to help you sleep."

"I don't want to sleep. I want him, do you hear me? I want my darling Pat. Oh, Gracie, someone has to ring Mummy and tell her. She'll have to call…"

"Don't worry about that," Mavis spoke

up. "I'll look after it for you. Now please, Jessie, come with us."

THEIR COMMANDING OFFICER gave Jessie a week of compassionate leave, but the girls weren't sure that she'd come back at all. She'd looked so forlorn standing at the station on her way home to break the news that instead of a wedding, they would have a service to memorialise Pat's death. They couldn't even have a proper funeral.

Leaving the station after seeing her off, Gracie and Mavis walked, arm in arm, back to the base.

Mavis confided, "I know that some girls think that I'm fast, getting involved with lots of different men. But I couldn't face what Jessie is going through. I just couldn't."

"Yes, you could, Mavis. You will find someone special and discover that love doesn't come with a timer attached. You can't help who you fall for. At least Jessie knew Pat loved her and they shared some very special times together."

"Well, thinking of that won't keep her warm at night, will it?"

Gracie shrugged, knowing her friend thought she was right. But she wasn't. Gracie was sure Jessie felt the same as she did. It was better to have known genuine love and lost it than never to have had that feeling.

"Come on. Let's get back. It's freezing out here."

PENNY READ Gracie's letter again. Poor Jessie.

"*Au diable cette fichue guerre!*"

Hugo gave a wry smile. "Now, little cousin, don't let Mother hear you cursing. She definitely wouldn't think that language was ladylike."

"Stop laughing at me, Hugo. Gracie's written to tell me her friend just lost her fiancé in a raid. It was his last one, too. They were going to make him a flying instructor."

"That's a bad show. Poor bloke."

"I feel so useless doing nothing when Gracie and her friends are all working so hard," she said.

"I would hardly call volunteering all hours with the WVS and at the hospital doing nothing. You'd be at the children's home too if they hadn't closed that for the duration and evacuated them to the country."

Penny glared at her cousin.

"Hugo, how do you know about me volunteering at the hospital? It's supposed to be secret. Please don't tell your mother. She'll only stop me from going again. It was bad enough the last time and it took me ages to convince her I would go socialising instead."

"Calm down, Penny. I will not tell on you. Truth be known, I thought what you did with those Kindertransport kids was admirable. All those snotty-nosed kids. Better you than me."

"Oh, you should have met the children and listened to their stories. They were just horrifying. I know that they have evacuated English kids, but at least they are in the same country. Some of our children don't remember where they came from, never mind what their parents look like."

"Our children?" he said, raising an eyebrow.

"You're laughing at me again." Penny glared at her cousin.

"I'm sorry. I shouldn't be teasing you."

She glanced at him under her eyelashes, relieved to see he did appear to be genuinely sorry.

"Anyway, I came to find you to tell you I'm heading down to the estate for the weekend and wondered if you wanted me to take anything down to the brats – sorry, kids."

"Oh, that would be wonderful. I'll see Mrs Thompson today and ask her. She's bound to have some letters or cards she wants them to have." Penny glanced over at her cousin. "Underneath it all you're rather soft, aren't you?"

"Me? You have to be joking. Given what

people have been saying about me, I need to do something to improve my reputation."

Penny eyed Hugo's suit. Why wasn't he in uniform? He must have an important desk job somewhere. He didn't spend a lot of time in the house but maybe he had his own place in London. Somewhere to escape from Aunt Louise and her hints about getting married and carrying on the Hamilton name. She wanted to ask him about the Nazis but something stopped her.

"Well, whatever your reason, I'm grateful."

CHAPTER 46

Their leave had been cancelled so many times, she'd given up counting. Charlie had promised he'd be able to see her this month. She'd been looking forward to it until his letter arrived.

Gracie waved the paper in the air. "Mavis, it's so unfair. Charlie can't get leave to come to the dance."

"Well, there's a war on, you know, darling. Why don't you ask Mr Churchill to put everything on hold to allow you time to see your man?"

Gracie threw a towel at her friend.

"Thanks for the sympathy."

"I'm sorry, Gracie. I'm feeling a bit down in the dumps today. Don't mind me. I'm sure Charlie will make it up to you. The guy is besotted."

"Maybe. It's hard to keep the romance going when we never get to see each other. I'm sure there are plenty of WAAFs down on his base that could help keep him amused."

It was Mavis's turn to throw the towel back.

"Don't be daft, girl. Vivien Leigh herself could walk onto that base and Charlie wouldn't notice. He only has eyes for one woman, and that's you."

Feeling ashamed, Gracie sat up straighter.

"We all need this dance, don't we? The last few weeks have been miserable. I need a kick in the pants. Poor Jessie. Here's me complaining I never get to see Charlie, but at least he's alive. For now."

"Don't beat yourself up. We're all allowed to let this war get to us sometimes. Just don't make a habit of it."

THEY ARRIVED at the dance to find the lads from Pat's squadron had kept a table and chairs for them. Pat's absence was so marked, Gracie could almost feel his presence. She felt someone looking at her. Glancing up, her eyes met Steve's. She blushed, feeling the heat spreading up from her neck to her hairline. She swallowed hard to try to moisten her dry mouth. What must he think of her? She'd have to thank him for protecting her from Stefan.

"How are you doing, Gracie? You look miles away."

"Fine. Thanks, Steve. How are you? I heard about your promotion. Congratulations."

"Thanks, but then they didn't have too much choice. All the good men like Pat are getting killed. Have you heard from Jessie?"

"Yes. She's back from leave, but they transferred her to another base. She couldn't bear to return here. For once, the powers that be had a heart and let her be stationed nearer to her home."

"Pat would be thankful for that. He was mad about Jessie. They made a great couple."

Steve looked closely at Gracie. When the others were distracted, he leaned closer to her and whispered, "Are you sure you're okay?"

"Yes, I'm fine, thanks to you and Pat."

"Did you hear Stefan bought it?"

Gracie shuddered. She didn't even want to hear that man's name again. She shook her head.

"I suppose some people would say he had coming."

"Oh, don't say that, Steve. What he did was awful, but nobody deserves to die. Not at his age. His poor family."

"What family? From what I heard, they were all killed at the start of the war."

"Maybe that's what made him how he was. Listen, I'm really grateful for what you did that night. You know, carrying me to bed and everything…"

"Well, this is cosy, isn't it?

Gracie spun around to see Charlie glowering at Steve. "Charlie!"

"Perhaps you might want to tell me what you were doing taking my fiancée to bed."

"Charlie, shush. Other people will hear," Gracie begged him as she tried to take his arm. But he shook her off.

"Oh, worried about your reputation, are you? Don't suppose you were thinking about that when you were in his arms. You are a disgrace."

Gracie paled.

"Don't speak to Gracie like that," Steve said furiously.

"Oh, Steve, please don't get involved," begged Gracie.

"No, please, Steve. Pray continue. Why don't you come outside and you can explain to me how I should speak to my fiancée?" Charlie thrust his face so close to Steve's, their noses were almost touching. Gracie saw his hands clenched into fists.

"I'm not coming outside, although I would love to belt you for what you have implied about Gracie. She's one in a million and doesn't deserve to be treated like this." Steve gave Charlie another dirty look before saying, "Why don't you give her a chance to explain?"

Gracie pulled at Charlie's jacket but he shrugged her off.

"You think I'm stupid and naïve? I don't see my girl for weeks and walk into this dance hoping to surprise her, maybe even cheer her up. Instead of being upset, I find her cosying up to another guy and thanking him for taking her to bed. I don't need an explanation for that. Well, mate, you can have her. I never want to see her again."

After his outburst, Charlie stormed out of the dance. But before he left, he cast a glance over his shoulder. The look of devastation and hurt on his face cut Gracie to the quick. He looked exhausted, stressed and thinner than when he'd held her in his arms. She hurried after him.

"Charlie, wait."

Charlie stopped. It took him a few seconds before he turned. His eyes were hard as flint as he looked at her coldly.

"Mother was right about you all along. Goodbye, Gracie."

He couldn't believe it. She hadn't done what he thought she had. She tried to match his pace but the ground was mucky and her tight uniform skirt hindered her. She hiked it up and ran after him.

"No, Charlie, you don't understand. It wasn't like that, I swear." He seemed to hesitate – she saw from the look on his face he was fighting his emotions. Anger and hurt. When Charlie didn't say anything, she continued, "Steve didn't take me to bed in that way, Charlie."

He held out a hand, stopping her. "Are you kidding me? What other way is there for a man to take a girl to bed?"

"He carried me because I couldn't walk, I was out cold. There was a guy, and he put alcohol in my drink and…"

The colour drained from his face, and he blinked rapidly. "Oh, this just gets better and better. While I was out there risking my life night after night, you were going out with anyone who asked. Drinking and getting drunk. I don't know you anymore. You're not the girl I fell in love with. Why don't you go back to your current beau? We're finished."

"Oh, Charlie, no. Please, you don't understand."

Gracie couldn't believe this was happening. She looked pleadingly at Charlie, but he wouldn't look her in the eyes.

"You're right, I don't understand. Now, leave me alone. You're making a show of both of us."

Charlie stalked off, leaving Gracie staring after him.

"I love you, Charlie," she sobbed, falling onto her knees in the middle of the road.

He must have heard her but he didn't turn around.

Mavis appeared with Gracie's coat and wrapped it around her. "Get up, Gracie, love. Let's get you out of here. You're shivering."

"But Charlie … he's gone. I need to tell him … to explain … to…"

"You can write to Charlie. Let him cool off first. You know what men are like. Their pride gets hurt and then they say and do things they don't mean." Mavis tried but failed to pull Gracie up from the road.

"Oh, I think he meant it, all right. You don't know Charlie. He's a man of his word." Gracie's voice conveyed her sense of panic mixed with disbelief.

"Charlie doesn't know the full situation. Look at it from his point of view. He's not the only one who thinks there's something between you and Steve," Mavis said coldly.

Gracie mutely shook her head, looking up at Mavis in disbelief.

"Yes, I know there isn't, but Charlie doesn't. He was probably tired after the journey and everything." Mavis pulled at Gracie again. "Get up now, love. Everyone's looking."

Gracie allowed Mavis to drag her to her feet and help her on with her coat. "You love him and he loves you. He must do or he wouldn't have got so upset. Write to him and all will be well."

Gracie wasn't sure if Mavis believed what she was saying or whether she just thought it was what Gracie wanted to hear. But she needed to hope everything would be all right. Otherwise, her life wasn't worth living. She loved Charlie too much to lose him.

BUT IT WASN'T ALL RIGHT. Gracie wrote letter after letter, but they all went unanswered. She lost a lot of weight and her friends grew concerned about her.

Steve caught up with her one day in the canteen.

"Gracie, I heard that you and Charlie haven't made up yet. I'm so sorry."

Gracie couldn't look up, too embarrassed to be discussing this with him. She was still mortified at what Charlie had said in front of him. "Don't be. You did nothing wrong."

Gracie moved away from him, but he followed her.

"Maybe I should write to him and explain. You know, man to man."

No, that would make things worse. Why can't he leave it alone? "Thanks, Steve, but please don't. He wouldn't believe I hadn't asked you. Now, please don't seek me out again. The last thing I need is for Charlie to hear gossip about us," she begged him as she moved away.

"All right, Gracie, if that's what you want. But I'll always be here for you. You know how I feel about you."

She turned to look back and smiled wanly at him. "Look after yourself, pilot."

Gracie meandered back to her hut, feeling Steve's eyes on her. She felt bad for hurting him, but he wasn't the one she loved. There would never be anyone for her but Charlie.

CHAPTER 47
LONDON, MARCH 1941

Gracie was looking at Penny admiringly. "You look amazing. That dress is just perfect. Miss Harriet is going to have kittens when she sees you. Although you'd best put a smile on your face or you risk turning the food sour. This should be the most exciting night of your life. Do you know that there are rumours even the Duke of Kent goes there wearing his RAF uniform?" said Gracie.

Penny tried faking a smile. She'd missed her friend, who had come to visit her on leave. She hoped Nell Thompson would insist on her daughter eating and sleeping. Gracie looked shattered and was far too thin. She didn't laugh so quickly, either, as she used to before she left.

Penny knew about Gracie's argument with Charlie and the reasons behind it. She thought Charlie deserved a good slap for thinking Gracie would be unfaithful.

She turned from the mirror and took a step towards Gracie. "Gracie, I'm so sorry that you've heard nothing back from Charlie. He'll calm down. He loves you." She took her friend's hand in hers.

Gracie removed her hand. "He might have once, Penny, but I'm not so sure he does now. Why won't he answer my letters? He should have given me a chance to explain."

Penny stood up and gave her friend a hug. "Yes, he should and he will. His pride's hurt but he'll come round. When you get back from leave, there may even be a letter waiting for you."

Gracie smiled wanly. "I hope so. I miss him and, with the RAF flying so much, I worry about him too." Gracie picked up the brush to work on Penny's hair. "Now, enough talk about my worries. Who are you going dancing with?"

"Harriet and Peter."

Gracie stopped brushing Penny's hair and looked at her friend in the mirror. "You're going with those two?"

Penny smiled sadly. "It's not like I've much choice. Eligible young men haven't been beating down my aunt's front door to ask me out. In fact, forget eligible. No man has ever asked me out."

"Is that what has you so glum tonight? I thought you'd be glad your aunt is letting you go to Café de Paris."

Penny stood up and looked at her reflection in the long mirror on the wardrobe door. The emerald evening dress, a gift from her uncle, flattered her figure and set off her dark hair and eyes.

She patted her head nervously. "Gracie, are you sure my hair looks all right?"

"I can't believe you copied me and got it all chopped off. It's liberating, isn't it? So much easier to manage. It suits you, makes you look older."

"Aunt Louise turned scarlet when she saw me. You would think I'd told her I was joining the chorus line in the West End. She's such a snob." The laughter fell away as Penny sighed. "Look at me, laughing when London has been through so much. The bombings and everything. Even now, Uncle John won't let me join up."

"Looking like that, you will do a lot for the morale of the troops."

The girls looked at each other and laughed. Penny had missed Gracie so much. On impulse, she gave her friend a hug, not caring her dress could get creased.

"Come on, girl, snap out of it. Put a big smile on your face. As Mam says, you need to count your blessings. You have a warm and safe home while many people are facing starvation or worse. You're young and healthy, and you could get to dance with the prince. I've to go now. Mam wants me home early in case there's another raid. Go and have some fun," said Gracie.

Penny gave Gracie another quick hug, knowing what a big effort her friend was making not to give in to her tears. "I wish you were going, too, but I know that you would only go if Charlie was taking you. He'll come round. You'll see. Thank you so much for coming to see me on my birthday. Enjoy the rest of your leave. Don't forget to write and tell me all the news when you get back to base."

The room seemed so empty once Gracie had left. Penny wished her friend was going to the café. Harriet would have been quite upset, though.

She knew it was unusual in London society for the niece of a lord to have a maid as a best friend. But one thing about the war was that attitudes were changing. There were society girls in most of the services. Some were even working in factories, though her aunt insisted that was a rumour.

Her thoughts were interrupted by a knock on the bedroom door.

"Taxi is here, miss."

"Thank you," Penny said, taking one last glance in the mirror before making her way downstairs.

Harriet and Peter were already in the taxi but her uncle was waiting for her at the bottom of the staircase.

"You look amazing, Penny darling." He kissed her on both cheeks and wished her a happy birthday. "I got you something small. I hope you like them."

He handed her a jewellery box. A pair of diamond drop earrings glittered as she opened the lid.

Tears pricked her eyes. "They are beautiful," she whispered, struggling to maintain her composure. "Thank you, but you have given me so much already."

"Nonsense. If my brother had brought you

and your mother back here, you would have had plenty of nice things over the years. Meme wanted you to have something special. She helped me pick them out from the family collection." Her uncle smiled down at her while she put the earrings on.

"Now, my dear, your chariot awaits." He bowed formally, causing her to laugh. "That's better. Can't have tears or a long face on your birthday."

He held the door of the taxi open to allow her to move inside. Closing the door behind her, he waved them off with a smile. Penny stared out the window, taking in the sights. They travelled past Hyde Park Corner on their route towards Coventry Street. There were loads of people around, including lots of young men and women in uniform. She saw some couples walking arm in arm and couldn't help wishing she'd an actual date for this evening.

The wail of the air-raid siren started just as they left Piccadilly Circus.

"We should stop and find a shelter, shouldn't we?" she said reluctantly.

Harriet snorted with laughter.

"You only live once, Penelope dear." Peter smirked at her. "Let yourself go a little and enjoy whatever time we have left."

CHAPTER 48
LEWISHAM, LONDON

It didn't take too long for Gracie to get back to her parents' house in Lewisham. She opened the front door, calling out, "Mam, I'm home."

"Hi, love. Come into the back room. There's tea in the pot. How was Penny?" Nell Thompson smiled at her eldest daughter.

"She looked amazing, Mam. She got her hair cut after a row with her aunt. I thought it would look horrible, but if anything she looks even more beautiful. Her uncle bought her a gorgeous dress."

"Who's going with her? Could you not

have gone? It would do you good to dance the night away," Nell said.

Gracie turned away from the obvious concern in her mother's eyes. "I've no interest in dancing." *Not without Charlie.* Gracie stirred the tea. "Penny is going with Harriet and her boyfriend, some guy called Peter. She's sad she doesn't have an actual date, but then maybe she's better off. If she doesn't fall in love, her heart can't break." Gracie couldn't stop the tears from falling. "Oh, Mam, what if I never see Charlie again?"

Nell took her daughter in her arms and gave her a big cuddle. "Charlie Power needs time to get over his pride, that's all. He'll come round. Just you wait and see."

"That's what Penny says," said Gracie.

"He will. Believe me, when I next see him, I'll give him a piece of my mind for doubting you. You haven't given another man a second look since you met young Charlie. Any fool can see how much you love him."

The fierce look on her mam's face made Gracie laugh despite feeling so low. Her mam's temper riled up if she thought anyone was being disloyal or unfair to her family. Charlie was in for it when her mam next saw him. There was no doubt about that.

She glanced at the mantelpiece where Stan's photo took pride of place. What was her twin doing now? Were the Germans treating him properly? At least as a POW he wasn't flying night after night seeing his mates crash and burn around him. Maybe it was a blessing he'd been captured.

The sirens started wailing. "Not again. Don't those ruddy Germans ever get a night off?" muttered Nell as she gathered her ration book and other valuables to her and headed off to their shelter.

"Where's Dad, Mam?" Gracie asked, following behind her mother to the dugout, as they called the Anderson shelter. She said a silent prayer that God would keep her family, Penny and Charlie safe tonight.

"He went up to the warden's post early. I think he wanted to have a cup of tea with his mates before they headed out on duty again tonight. They need to recruit more volunteers."

"Why are people not coming forward?" Gracie asked.

"Your dad and the others are working four to six hours every night on top of their day jobs. Some people say that they couldn't manage without sleep." Nell pursed her lips. "Not that there's much chance of some shut-eye with that racket up above."

Gracie listened to the drone of the planes and whistles of the bombs.

"That one sounded a bit close," Nell said as the house in front of the shelter shook.

"Does Dad sleep at the post, then?" Gracie asked, trying to shake some dust out of her hair.

Nell started laughing.

"What's so funny, Mam?"

"Your dad said the lads will take turns having a kip on an old mattress they put under the stairs. They have to be ready in case there's a big raid. That means keeping their torch and whistle handy and sleeping with their tin hats on." Nell dissolved into a fit of giggles so contagious that soon Gracie was laughing, too. The sound of bombs dropping and machine guns rattling faded into the background.

CHAPTER 49

The Café de Paris was everything Penny had imagined it to be, and much more. She wanted to pinch herself to make sure she wasn't dreaming. She glided down the long, steep staircase, holding Peter's arm. She didn't want to trip and make a spectacle of herself. She could see why people said this was the safest place during an air raid; the stairs went on forever. It was weird to think that they were going so far underground, but then you wouldn't have guessed it from the surroundings.

Finally, they entered the actual café. It was smaller than Penny had imagined it to be, but it was everything else she'd dreamed about. No wonder the Prince of Wales liked coming here. The ladies were all gorgeous. Despite the relatively early hour of 9.15 p.m., the café was busy. Her stomach turned with excitement as Peter escorted her towards the gallery. They climbed a couple of steps up to their table in the gallery overlooking the dancefloor.

As Peter held her chair so she could sit down, he asked, "Would the birthday girl like some champagne?" His hands grazed her shoulders, causing goosebumps. She could tell Harriet was glaring at her but didn't meet her eye to confirm it. Leaving one hand on her shoulder, Peter used the other to raise his glass to Penny and wish her a wonderful birthday. To her dismay, he leaned in for a kiss. She'd to bend her head to prevent his lips from contacting her skin.

"Oh, look, Harriet, there's Lady Bailton with her two daughters. They're waving over at you." Penny pointed into the crowd, dis-tracting Harriet from what had happened.

"Peter, thank you for the birthday wishes. Please go and mingle with Harriet. I'm quite happy to sit here, taking in the atmosphere."

"Penny's right. Let's go and say hello," Harriet said.

She hadn't realised she'd been holding her breath until Peter removed his arm and took Harriet's hand. Honestly, what did Harriet see in him?

She looked towards where the band was setting up. She could hardly believe that she'd soon see "Snakehips" Johnson in real life. She'd spent countless evenings listening to his music on the BBC. Her aunt disapproved, saying that swing was common. Thankfully, her uncle liked to listen to the show and often invited Penny to sit with him.

As she watched the glamorous couples below, she couldn't help thinking how nice it would be to have a proper date. He'd be in uniform, perhaps a fighter pilot or maybe a sailor. She didn't mind what he looked like so long as he was brave, strong and fun to be

with. The return of Harriet and Peter interrupted her fantasy.

"Oh, poor Penny, sitting here all alone on
her birthday." Harriet smirked.

She didn't let her cousin's snide remarks
upset her.

"Oh, look, Harriet, he's here." Penny
stared in wonder at the twenty-six-year-old
whose voice had stolen her heart. The music
started and the floor filled up with young military officers and their gorgeous companions.
Peter had wandered off, leaving Harriet and
Penny sitting alone at the table. Penny was
glad that Harriet wasn't interested in chatting,
as it meant she could sit back and take in all
that was happening around her. The band
hadn't been playing long when Penny recognised her favourite tune, "Oh Johnny, Oh
Johnny, Oh!". But she only heard a couple of
seconds before there was a tremendous bang
and darkness descended.

AFTER WHAT SEEMED LIKE HOURS, but was probably only minutes, the realisation that a bomb had hit them registered. The blue haze was gradually lifting, and Penny watched in horror as music sheets fell like confetti on the carnage below. Moments ago, uniformed officers had been whirling their partners around the dancefloor. Now, they were frantically looking for them using torches, cigarette lighters or matches. The bomb had blown out all but one light. The dust and smoke weren't helping the level of panic.

Penny became aware that a woman was screaming hysterically. Before she could think twice, she reacted.

Slap! The Honourable Harriet Hamilton stared at her, a shocked expression on her face. Penny couldn't blame her. Her hand stung from the blow, but at least Harriet had stopped shrieking. She never would have dreamt of raising her hand to her cousin before, but the noise level in the café was deafening enough without her screaming.

Harriet clutched her face. "You've probably left a bruise. If you have, I'll make your life even more miserable than it is already. I knew Peter shouldn't have agreed to Father's request to bring you here for your birthday. You have no idea how to behave in public," Harriet snarled, still holding her cheek.

"Oh, do shut up, Harriet, and look around you."

Instinctively, Penny moved towards the wreckage to help the survivors.

"Penny, wait. Where are you going? Don't leave me here alone. Where is Peter? Typical, he's never around when you…" Harriet stopped mid-sentence as she noticed a tear and stains on her dress. "Oh, my beautiful new dress," she wailed.

Penny ignored her as she stared in horror at the scene developing on the dancefloor below her. She'd thought that the men running around bending over the injured were there to help. But instead of feeling for a heartbeat, they were helping themselves to the victims' wallets and valuables. She felt sick. And now her cousin was more concerned about a stupid dress than those lying dead and dying around them.

"A bomb has just dropped on top of us and, as usual, all you care about is yourself. Pull yourself together and stop whining. Some people are badly hurt."

Harriet, clutching her stained dress, looked around. "The management said it was safe to be here. Just wait until I tell Father. He'll have words with Mr Poulsen."

Penny regretted being so harsh. She realised Harriet was suffering from shock. She grabbed her cousin's hand, hoping she didn't start screaming again. "Come on, we have to see if we can help."

"What do you mean, help? What can we do? We need to wait here until Peter rescues us. I'm sure that he'll be back any minute." For a second, she was the haughty, spoiled, self-assured girl Penny knew so well. But then she stopped talking, and her composure faltered. "Aren't you?" Harriet's lip trembled.

Penny looked at her grimly. Now wasn't the time to tell her that her beloved Peter had probably already left. As far as Penny could see, he loved wearing his army officer's uniform, but only to impress the ladies. It appeared he'd no intention of fighting for his country. He was happy for his father to arrange a cushy office job at the War Office.

Penny knew Harriet wouldn't help anyone but herself. She had to get her cousin to safety before she could look to help the injured survivors. She forced herself to adopt a more cajoling tone. "Harriet, I don't know what has happened to Peter, but I know that we need to get you out of here." Penny looked around. "We aren't injured, but there are dozens who are and some even worse. Our friends were on that dancefloor. They have probably gone somewhere safer, so let's go and find them."

She hoped she sounded more confident than she felt. Chaos surrounded them. She looked once more at the scene below. The initial screaming had stopped, replaced by low moans and desperate cries for help. It was unbelievable. One minute the band had been playing to a packed dancefloor, and now there was a big hole where the musicians had been standing.

Holding hands, the girls moved as quickly as they could towards the exit. Someone else doing the same said people were gathering in the Mapleton Hotel across the street.

"Come on, Harriet. We'll go to the Mapleton. It's where Peter will look for you." Penny dragged her for-once speechless cousin behind her. All around them, wide-eyed staff members were trying their best to help the less fortunate. Ladies in full evening dress struggled to hurry. Many were suffering more injuries as they tried to escape the debris descending around them.

One casualty caught Penny's attention. It took her a few seconds to recognise her as the girl who'd been much admired at Harriet's coming-out ball. The girl had worn a flattering coral-coloured dress.

She'd easily been the most beautiful debutante there, never mind the bravest. After all, not everyone would have had the guts not to wear white. But look at the state of the poor girl now. Blood was gushing down her face from a jagged cut just above her left eye. She was trying to stand up, while her friend was trying equally hard to get her to sit still, obviously afraid the lady was seriously injured. As Penelope watched, another lady tore strips off her own dress to stop the blood flow.

At that moment, Penny realised that she couldn't just walk away. She might not be a nurse, but she had her first aid qualification, and she was young and strong. She could help the injured get out or maybe comfort a patient while they waited for a doctor to arrive. But first she'd get Harriet to safety; her aunt would expect her to do that.

CHAPTER 50

The air-raid wardens shouted at them to leave. "Hurry, now. Move as quickly as you can. The Germans haven't left yet. They'll be back with more bombs."

"You try rushing in a long dress," Harriet said. "My shoes were made for dancing, not walking on scorching pavements. Wait until you see my blisters."

Penny caught the look the warden sent in their direction. Her ears turned red, not from the heat but from embarrassment at her cousin's remarks. Harriet was a spoilt brat. Penny grabbed her cousin's arm rather roughly and pulled her through the door of the Mapleton.

She stood still, not believing her eyes at the scene in front of them. Harriet gasped with horror, grasping Penny's arm tightly. They had been surrounded by walking wounded, but the more seriously injured were lying in the hotel's lobby, waiting for ambulances to arrive.

"Oh, my God, Penny, look at that girl. Her face will never be the same. How will she go out in society now?"

Penny crossed herself. "Shut up, Harriet. She isn't deaf. I'm sure she's more worried about staying alive than what she looks like." Penny glanced at the wounded; there were sufficient people helping them but what about the people they'd left behind in the café? She recognised some of the faces from those who looked unhurt, if a little shocked. "There are plenty of our friends here. You can stay with them. I'm going back to the café."

Most of the ladies were struck silent with terror, but not her cousin. Harriet seemed to have come through her ordeal relatively un-scathed, not that she'd admit that for a second.

"I absolutely forbid you to leave me here alone."

Harriet was using the voice she reserved for speaking to her servants. Despite this, Penny was beyond listening to her cousin.

"Look around you. You know almost everyone here, so you are hardly alone. I'm going back in there and if you had an ounce of concern for anyone other than yourself, you would come with me. We must be able to do something."

Penny left Harriet still lamenting the state of her new dress and headed back towards the carnage of the café. Inside, people were still moaning, but it was much quieter than before. Penny sighed with relief at first; then she re-alised that this could only mean that the most badly injured had since died or lost con-sciousness.

She headed towards a group of girls who had once been wearing pretty dresses and striking hairstyles. They were now dressed in rags and covered in glass and other debris. The lucky ones had only sustained superficial cuts and grazes on their once-stunning faces. As she moved forwards, Penny tripped over something. She looked down at the floor, confused to see so many shoes were strewn around. For a moment, she couldn't grasp why people would have left their shoes behind, but the truth gradually dawned on her. The dead and seriously injured didn't need shoes.

As she got nearer, she saw an RAF officer break open a bottle of champagne.

What a callous idiot. But rather than drinking the alcohol, he poured it on an injured woman's arm, seeming to use it to clean the wounds. Penny immediately felt awful for thinking badly about someone trying his best to help. With no running water, what else was he supposed to use? Just as she was about to offer her help, he looked up and caught her standing there, staring at the blood flowing out of his patient's arm.

"Oh, thank goodness." He looked up briefly. "David Andrews. I would shake hands, but as you can see, I need some help." His gaze lowered to her full evening gown. "I thought maybe you were with the Red Cross. You're not hurt, are you?"

"No. I came back to help," stammered Penny, her attention glued to the blood gushing from the wound.

"Help? Are you a nurse or Red Cross? Are the ambulances here yet?" Without waiting for an answer, he said, "Hold this."

Barely looking up, he handed Penny what looked like a bandage. Her hands were shaking so badly that she let it fall. He swore as the napkin hit the floor. He grabbed Penny's trembling hand and pressed it down against the arm of the young lady lying on the floor beside him. "Press tightly, and for God's sake, don't let go."

The woman didn't appear to be alive, but as Penny's hand pressed against the cool skin, she felt a flicker of movement. She averted her eyes as he tore open the girl's dress, exposing more of her legs than was decent. Seeing Penny's reaction, he said, "I take it from your blushes you aren't a nurse. Would you rather I obeyed social convention or tried to save her life?"

Penny's cheeks flushed with colour, and instinctively she moved her hand away.

"Don't be an idiot. She'll bleed out if you don't keep that pressed down tightly."

He poured champagne into a napkin before using the cloth to bathe a nasty-looking cut on the girl's right thigh. The light glinted off the large shard of glass protruding from the centre of the bloody mess.

"I've to get that glass out of there and stop the blood or we'll lose her. It is going to hurt and she may regain conscious, so do you think you can hold her still?"

Penny looked into his eyes and nodded. She gripped the girl's shoulders. He worked quietly and efficiently, all the time making soothing noises. Penny didn't know if they were for her benefit or his unconscious patient. Just as he'd anticipated, the girl briefly regained consciousness but quickly passed out again. The pain must be horrific.

He removed the glass just as the ambulance crew arrived and took over.

With so many injured and a shortage of ambulance crews, they had to work hard to help those who had survived the initial bombing. David told Penny to keep talking to the patients to prevent them going to sleep. Penny spoke softly in French to a young, conscious, yet badly wounded de Gaulle officer.

After some time, the air-raid wardens ordered them to leave. As they made their way to the exit, broken glass crunched under their feet. He handed her his jacket.

"You're shivering."

Penny didn't feel cold, but she was fighting the urge to cry and she couldn't stop her body from shaking. She knew that the people she'd helped, hadn't been complaining, so she was not about to start. Instead, she tried to make conversation.

"You're a brilliant doctor."

He gave her a shy smile. "I'm not a doctor. Well, not yet. I was studying medicine when the war started. You were great in there. If you plan on becoming a nurse, I'll give you a character reference."

Penny shrugged her shoulders. "I'm not sure what I want to do, yet. My aunt isn't keen on my joining the services or becoming a nurse."

"Why not? We need qualified nursing staff. Given how the war is progressing, the demand is only going to increase."

Penny mimicked her aunt's voice. "Have a nurse in the family? Penelope, dear, do try to stop highlighting your vulgar upbringing, especially in the drawing room."

David laughed. "Well, for what it's worth, I think you would make an exceptional nurse. But I can understand how your aunt's objections could cause a problem. Now, please let me escort you back to your party, as I need to check up on my friends."

"Please go, I'll be fine. I can easily find my cousin on my own. In fact, I think I can hear her over there." Penny pointed to a corner of the room where a girl was complaining rather loudly.

"You mean you're related to Harriet?"

"Oh, you know her?"

"Yes. We go way back. Now, I'll take you up on your kind offer and make my departure. Thank you for all your help, Miss Penelope."

Her stomach lurched when he smiled down at her. He'd remembered her name. He had such lovely, kind, blue eyes. *They almost match his uniform*, Penny thought dreamily, before pulling herself together. How could she be thinking about his eyes when people were dying tonight? Penny felt a deep sense of shame at thinking such frivolous thoughts when so many families would never see their loved ones again.

When she arrived home she sent a message to Gracie to tell her she was safe. The next day she heard that Gracie's family had also survived the latest raid. Gracie was on her way back to her base. Penny hoped that some good news was waiting for her best friend.

CHAPTER 51

A few days after the bombing, Penny's aunt called her to the drawing room. As she walked in, she was taken aback to see David standing there dressed as before in his grey-blue Royal Air Force uniform. Officers' uniforms fitted better than those worn by ordinary soldiers, yet another sign of the comforts having money offered. She tried to focus on what her aunt was saying.

"Penelope, you didn't tell me you knew David. He went to school with Hugo, so we have known him and his family for years. He called to check that you and Harriet were all right after the tragedy the other night. When I think of what my poor darling daughter went through…" Louise lifted her hand dramatically to her mouth. "This awful war … just when you think things can't get any worse, a bomb lands on your family."

David moved forward to lead her aunt to sit on the couch. "Try not to upset yourself. It's all over now, thank goodness."

He winked at Penny, causing her to cough into her handkerchief to stifle the giggle that threatened to erupt. She wished she was wearing something more flattering than the simple rayon day dress she'd put on that morning. She'd been up in the attic, hoping to find some toys and old clothes to take to the shelters for the bombed out children. Thankfully, she'd thought to remove the turban she'd been wearing around her head. Her aunt would have killed her had she seen her dressed in what she considered servants' clothes. She hoped she wasn't covered in dust, or worse, and didn't have any cobwebs in her hair.

Louise simpered, "You always had lovely manners, David. Please call me Louise."

Penny could swear her aunt was flirting with him.

"Lady – sorry – Louise, would Harriet and Penelope grace me with their company for a walk around Hyde Park? I know I should have called in advance. I've to be back by 6 p.m., so it would only be a short stroll. Please say yes, as it is such a beautiful day."

"Oh, but Harriet isn't here. She works now as a secretary in her father's office. After work, she's going visiting with Peter. You know Peter Redway, Earl of Arundel? His father is the Duke of—"

"Oh, what a pity I missed Harriet." Penny smiled as David smoothly interrupted what was likely to be a litany on Peter's family tree. "Please tell her I was asking for her. So, it would appear that your niece is free this afternoon. Please say I can take her out for a short stroll around the gardens?"

"Well, I don't see why not..." her aunt said. "Penelope, change into something smarter. You never know who you may meet taking the air. David will have a drink with me while you dress."

Penny ran before her aunt could change her mind. She changed and returned just as David finished his coffee. "Thank you for your hospitality, Lady … I mean, Louise. I'll call to see you again soon. Good day."

David and Penny walked across Hyde Park in silence for a while, enjoying the sunshine and sounds around them. The smell of cut grass made a pleasant change to the stench and dust coming from the rubble on the streets after the raids. In the distance they could hear the sounds of traffic but for now, there was a little peace.

The park was swarming with people. You could almost forget there was a war on if you ignored the fact most men and a few women were in uniform and there were few children running about in the sunshine. That and the sandbags scattered around the monuments, the victory gardens ploughed and sown with vegetables.

David turned towards Penny as they walked. "I'm sorry that I didn't give you warning that I was going to call. I bumped into Peter earlier and he mentioned he was taking Harriet out. I thought it would be a great chance for us to continue our chat from the other night."

Penny's heart leapt, realising he'd meant to see her alone. She raised her eyes, meeting his, but had to look away.

"So, how are you feeling? Have you got over the shock yet?" His voice was so low, she'd to move closer to hear him. She tried to get a hold of her emotions and fell back on humour.

"Do you mean the shock of finding that Peter rescued the entire female clientele on his own?"

She was glad when he laughed. They headed towards the Serpentine.

"I wish they hadn't closed the pool for the duration," Penny said. "I loved coming up here with Gracie on a hot summer's day."

"Your aunt let you go swimming?"

Penny didn't return his look. "We didn't tell her."

David smiled, a look of admiration in his eyes. "I think you are quite the rebel, Miss Hamilton."

Penny sighed. "My aunt has so many rules, I find it hard not to break a few of them. It's all above board. They have separate areas for women to change into their bathing costumes. Queen Caroline dreamed up the idea of an ornamental lake in Hyde Park back in 1730. She wasn't totally against the idea of people going swimming in it."

David chuckled. "I don't think she'd have meant men and women swimming together, now, do you?" He glanced over at her. "Anyway, where did you learn to speak French so well?"

"I'm French, so it comes naturally." She looked at him frowning and laughed at his confusion. "I was born in France. My mother was the daughter of the farmer who found my father gravely wounded after a battle. He'd sustained a head injury, and at first he didn't know who he was." Penny stopped talking, as she didn't want to bore him.

"What happened? How did he regain his memory?"

"My mother nursed him back to health, and by the time his memory fully returned, the war was over. He fell in love with my mother, and they stayed living in France. He knew his brother, or perhaps more likely his brother's wife, would never accept a farm girl as his wife, so it was easier not to come back."

"So war has certain advantages," he said.

Penny stared up at him. Was he laughing at her or had she misunderstood? "Pardon?"

"It sounds like a genuine love story. You know, your father meeting your mother like that. Most of our class marry those their families pick out for them. It is rarely, if ever, a love match." David looked pensive.

"Well, that will not happen to me. I'll marry a man I love or not get married at all. Oops." Penny pulled at the pleats in her skirt, embarrassed at having been so honest. "Sorry.

Getting married to someone just because their family is in Burke's Landed Gentry is just so cold. You have to live with that person, not their ancestors. It makes me mad."

David looked over the top of her head. "Sometimes life isn't that simple."

For a second Penny thought they might not be talking about people in general but something more personal, but she dismissed the notion. They had only met once.

"Well, it should be. They are hardly going to force us into arranged marriages. After all, this is England." She looked at him, willing him to agree.

"Oh, to be young," he said.

"Are you laughing at me? You aren't that much older than me, are you?" Penny looked at him carefully.

"I'm twenty-three, going on ninety. Anyway, enough about me. Are your parents still in France?"

Penny shook her head. "Papa never fully recovered from his wounds and died young. Mama died some time later. She wanted me to come and live with my aunt and uncle. I've been here since. I intended going home as soon as I was old enough, but then the war came."

"I'm sorry about your parents." David pulled at his collar. "Have you not thought of joining up?"

"I can't, as I'm still underage and my uncle won't give his permission. Ironically, he doesn't want me mixing with the working classes! I wish they had introduced conscription for women from age nineteen and not twenty. Then I wouldn't have to wait another year. I feel so useless, especially after last weekend. I do some work with the Red Cross now my services are no longer needed at the Society of Friends Orphanage. Most of the kids were evacuated, so I only call in now and again. I've joined the Women's Voluntary Service. Lady Reading convinced Aunt Louise that I would be useful."

"Well, aren't you?"

"I feel I could be of more use than making cups of tea and sandwiches. Although, it can be fun. One woman is teaching me how to drive, only don't tell my uncle. He doesn't think women belong behind the wheel of a car."

"So why the rush to do something different?" asked David.

"I don't know. The women at the WVS are lovely and everything, but they are all so, well … old. I wanted to join the WAAF when Gracie left ages ago, but I wasn't allowed."

He looked confused. "Who is Gracie? I've never heard Harriet mention a sister."

Penny burst out laughing. "Harriet barely knows Gracie's name, although she has worked at the house since she was about fourteen. My aunt employed Gracie as a maid. Meme, my grandmother, knew I was lonely. She encouraged me and Gracie to spend time together." She didn't mention Gracie saving her life. He might think her stupid to have run away.

"It sounds like your grandmother is ahead of her time. There aren't many who would encourage such an unlikely friendship."

"I think Meme knew that having grown up on a farm, I would be more at home with Gracie and her kind than with the gentry my aunt worships. I consider her my equal, and my best friend. I miss her."

David laughed. "I can't argue with those sentiments. Maybe when this war is over, people will realise that, underneath it all, we're all the same."

"I hope so." She bit her lip, her stomach feeling like she'd swallowed a lump of lead. She stared into the distance. "I hope there's something left of my country when the war is over. I want to go home." Her voice trembled as she fought the tears back.

She was beyond grateful when instead of commenting on her distress, he made a joke. "And leave Harriet and her esteemed boyfriend? I can't imagine why?"

Penny smiled weakly but couldn't speak. They walked on in silence, but it was companionable rather than uncomfortable. Penny wondered what France would look like after the battles taking place there, if London looked this bad. Everywhere she looked, there was evidence of the damage inflicted on the buildings that surrounded the park. Yet against that backdrop, the flowers and trees in Hyde Park seemed to be blooming in spite of the war.

Penny picked a flower from a bush, taking off one petal at a time as she had done as a child. "I wish Uncle John would reconsider. He seems to think that the forces are dangerous. Doesn't last weekend prove that nobody is safe?" asked Penny.

"Have you considered becoming a translator? Language skills like yours are in short supply and are just as useful in the war effort. Perhaps your guardians may take kindlier to you working for the government," David suggested.

"I hadn't thought of working in an office. It doesn't seem like really helping, if you know what I mean. I want to be more involved than just sitting behind a desk."

David stopped walking, a look of consideration on his face. "I think you underestimate how useful you could be. There's a genuine need for people who speak fluent French in the RAF. Our boys should know some basic words to help them get back home if they have to bail out. Perhaps you could start work translating and then see what opportunities come along." David glanced at his watch and his brow furrowed. "But we must get back, or your aunt will think I've kidnapped you."

They walked back to Belgrave Square. Penny wished he'd take her hand. She invited him for tea, but he declined, saying he'd another appointment. He smiled, gave her a quick kiss on the cheek, and then he was gone.

CHAPTER 52

Penny shut the door behind her and headed straight up to her room. She didn't want to talk to anyone. She slipped off her shoes and lay down on her bed, staring at the ceiling. An hour passed before a noise on the landing outside made her grab a book. The door opened.

"So what have you been up to, then?"

Penny groaned as her cousin came into the bedroom. "What do you want, Harriet? I'm busy."

Penny saw her cousin's pointed look at the book she was reading and realised she was holding it upside down. She put it down on the pillow beside her. She watched Harriet walk across the deep, red carpet and look out the window before turning back to look at her. Penny didn't like the smug look on her cousin's face.

"Mother tells me you went out with David Andrews today. What was that all about?"

Penny sat up, hoping that by moving, her cousin wouldn't spot her reaction to the question. "We just went for a walk. It's hardly news of the century."

"Mm, so touchy. Do you have a soft spot for David?" Harriet fingered the quilt lying across the bed. "He is rather dreamy, I suppose, if you like the tall, blue-eyed Englishman look. Do you?"

"Don't be stupid, Harriet. He called to see both of us. To check that we were okay after the other night."

"Yes, I know that's what he told Mother, but something tells me there was more to this walk than you are letting on, my dear cousin."

Penny walked over to the bedroom door and held it open. "Go away, Harriet, and take your dirty mind with you. David and I went for a walk in broad daylight through Hyde Park. If you hadn't been out with Peter, you could've come, too. There was nothing more to it."

Harriet moved towards the door. "Ah, but you wanted there to be, didn't you? I can see by your face you are quite smitten by the rather dashing Mr Andrews. I wonder if the feeling is mutual. Although you aren't his usual type."

"What do you mean by his usual type?"

"Oh, nothing. Don't mind me. By the way, Mother said to remind you we are dressing for dinner this evening. She has invited some important people over and doesn't want you showing us up." She looked Penny up and down as if inspecting goods on a stall. "If you need help choosing what to wear, just call me. Mother doesn't want anyone letting the side down."

Penny wanted to slap the smirk off Harriet's face.

"I thought you were going out with Peter this evening. Did he get cold feet? Again?"

Penny smiled as Harriet slammed the door on her way out. She returned to her bed, picking up her book, but it was useless as she couldn't concentrate.

David Andrews. What a lovely name. She lay back on the pillow, replaying their walk, the way he smiled and laughed. He was gorgeous. Her eyes grew heavier. It was a late dinner this evening, so she'd time for a nap. She didn't fight too hard and sleep soon took over.

As it happened, an air raid cancelled dinner. The raid didn't last too long, but by the time the all-clear sounded it was after midnight.

CHAPTER 53

Weeks passed and there was still no word from Charlie. Gracie had written so many times. Penny had suggested in a letter recently that she try to get some leave to visit Charlie, but Gracie couldn't bear the thought of him treating her so disdainfully again. The silence was bad enough, but the look in his eyes that last night had been unbearable.

She still went out with Mavis occasionally, but it wasn't the same as when Jessie had been there, too. Jessie was still grieving for Pat – her occasional letters suggested that she felt her life was over, too.

Mavis came running up to Gracie one day.

"There you are. I've been looking for you everywhere. Some pilots from Charlie's base have just landed. Their plane was hit, so they didn't want to risk flying any further. You need to speak to them."

Mavis wouldn't look at her. "What is it? Is Charlie with them? Is he still refusing to see me?"

Mavis's expression was solemn. "Gracie, you need to prepare yourself. It's not good news."

Gracie grabbed her friend's hand. "Is he dead?"

"They don't know. He was hit in the same attack. His plane went down."

"Did they see a chute? Did he bail out? Where was he when it happened? Was he over England?" Gracie fired the questions at Mavis, who shook her head repeatedly.

"I don't know, Gracie. That's why you need to speak to the pilots. Come on, they've gone to the canteen to get something hot to eat."

Gracie felt like she was someone else.

One minute she was in the hangar talking to Mavis, the next she was standing in front of the pilots. She didn't recognise any of them personally but they looked just as exhausted as Steve and the others.

"Hi, I'm Gracie. My fiancé is with your group – Charlie Power?"

The reaction showed they knew him. Nobody would meet her eyes. She pressed her hand against her stomach, hoping it would stop the churning. "Did you see anything? Please tell me he was okay," Gracie begged, her voice trembling with unshed tears.

"Sorry, miss, we can't. He ditched in the sea. It doesn't look good. We didn't see a chute but then we had been hit ourselves, so we were concentrating on getting back home."

Mavis came back with a hot drink for Gracie. "I told Cookie you've had a shock. Drink up."

Gracie nearly choked as she took a sip; it had been heavily laced with Scotch. This couldn't be happening. Suddenly, she needed to be by herself.

"Thank you very much for letting me know. I hope that your plane is fixed soon so you can get back to your friends. Mavis, I need a walk." Her friend stood and started for the door. "No, please don't come with me. I'm sure these boys would like some company."

Gracie walked away, although her legs felt like she was moving through mud. She couldn't believe that Charlie was dead. She'd know – Stan's accident had proved that. She trusted her instincts. Her heart would have told her. He had to be alive. He just had to be.

But then the little voice in her head started talking. *You're responsible. You broke his heart. How would you know if he was still alive or not? It's not like he cared about you. Maybe he didn't want to make it out of the plane.*

～

FOR MANY NIGHTS Gracie's dreams were full of Charlie trapped in his burning plane, unable to release his harness as the flames engulfed him. Charlie in the cockpit fighting for his life. Charlie, Charlie, Charlie.

Her nightmares meant not only was she not sleeping, but neither were the girls sharing her hut. They begged her to take leave but she didn't want to go home. Home to the memories of the life she'd had with Charlie. She volunteered for every task she could, hoping that being exhausted would mean she didn't wake the others up. She didn't care about herself; nothing mattered now.

She looked for a telegram every day, but nothing arrived. Mavis and the other girls felt that she wasn't accepting the facts, but she didn't dare. She couldn't go on living if Charlie was dead, so she'd no option but to believe he was alive. Somewhere.

CHAPTER 54

BRITISH CHANNEL, OFF THE COAST OF ENGLAND

Our Father, hallowed be thy name, Our Father, hallowed be thy name.

Charlie repeated the only words he knew from the Lord's Prayer. He'd never been a churchgoing man, but he was desperate. The pain was incredible, like nothing he'd ever experienced before.

He was cold, too, but he didn't start swimming. He vaguely remembered someone telling him that you had to conserve body heat if you wanted to survive. It was better to allow the vest to keep you afloat than it was to try swimming. It used up too much energy. Floating on the top of the water didn't seem to help, though. It seemed to make him colder. The water helped relieve the pain. Slightly. He just wanted to sleep. To close his eyes and forget about the cold, the pain and…

No, he mustn't fall asleep. He forced himself to keep talking. He started praying again or at least repeating that one line. He wished he'd paid more attention in Sunday school. He begged God for help.

CHARLIE HAD BEEN in the sea for about an hour before a rescue craft picked him up. They had almost killed him by going over him in the water, causing a cracked skull. He was lucky. He wouldn't have lasted much longer.

They transferred him to a hospital in East Grinstead with skills and experience in treating burns.

A nurse came to cut off the remains of his uniform. He was shaking so much, he wondered how she didn't cut him.

"Don't worry, pet. It's the shock. Your body has been through the mill and back again. Dr McIndoe can work wonders. He's had plenty of practice."

Charlie detected a note of sadness in her voice. It made him angry. He didn't want anyone's pity.

"Can I get anything for you, Flight Lieutenant Power?"

"No," he whispered. "Thank you, Nurse."

"Perhaps you would like me to help you write a letter to your girl. I'm sure she's frantic with worry."

"No, thanks. I don't have a girl. Not anymore."

"I don't believe that for a second. I've yet to meet a pilot who hasn't got a girl. Most of them have problems sticking to just one."

Charlie knew that the nurse was trying to cheer him up, but he wished she'd just go away. He desperately wanted Gracie, but she wasn't his girl. Not now. Not ever.

~

"Oh, you have woken up, young man."

Charlie heard the kindly voice, but it took a few moments for his eyes to focus on the face.

"You're one of the lucky ones."

Charlie pulled a face at that comment, causing the doctor to continue.

"Landing in the sea saved your life, young man. We have learned that brine baths help the skin heal. We shall have to take a piece from your rear to cover a little of your arm, but otherwise your skin should grow back nicely on its own."

Charlie cleared his throat. It was still difficult to speak.

"The smoke from the fire damaged your vocal cords, but we don't believe it's permanent. I would suggest you don't take up singing soon, though." The doctor smiled.

"Will I still look the same? You know, when you're finished?"

"Not exactly the same as you used to, old chap, but you'll look better than you do now."

"Thanks, Doctor," Charlie mumbled, turning his head into his pillow.

"Now see here, Power. Help us help you. Don't give up. Now why don't you let Nurse write to your girl and ask her to visit?"

"There's no girl. Thank you, Doctor, but I'm tired and would like to get some sleep."

CHAPTER 55

Gracie booked a long-distance call to the hospital in East Grinstead. She still couldn't believe that Charlie had been admitted some weeks previously and no one had told her. Just wait until she got her hands on him and his mother. She'd kill them herself.

The nurse who answered told her, "I'm sorry, Miss Thompson, but Flight Lieutenant Power doesn't wish to speak to you."

"What do you mean, he doesn't want to speak to me? I'm his fiancée. I thought he was dead and have only just found out that he's alive. I've to see him."

"I'm sorry, miss, but we cannot give permission for a non-relative to see a patient."

"A non-relative? I'm his fiancée, for God's sake."

"I'm sorry, miss. Goodbye."

Gracie held tight to the telephone receiver, staring at it in her hands. The conversation had been so short, she didn't even have to wait for the pips to go. She couldn't believe it. After all he'd been through, he still didn't want to see her. He was a stubborn fool. There was nothing that was going to keep her away from her man now that she knew where he was.

She headed back to her hut to pack some things and then went to the office to see her superior officer.

She stood to attention, waiting for the officer to acknowledge her by telling her to stand at ease.

"Ma'am, I wish to request some leave. Please." Gracie held her hands tight by her side; now was not the time to let them do the talking for her.

The officer barely glanced up from the paperwork covering her desk. She looked just like the rest of them, lines of fatigue around her eyes, her skin pale as if she'd been inside too long. A small wave of guilt hit Gracie but she pushed it away. Charlie was all that mattered. For now.

"Not now, Thompson. You know we're short-staffed as so many have gone down with this wretched flu."

Her muscles tightened as determination overrode the guilt her superior's words induced.

"I know, ma'am, and I wouldn't normally ask, but they have found Charlie."

"Charlie?" The officer looked up.

Gracie kicked herself. How would the woman know Charlie? "Sorry, ma'am. Flight Lieutenant Power. He is my fiancé and I thought he was dead. His plane crashed, you see, and his mates didn't see any parachute. So I..." She trailed off as she glimpsed something like amusement in the woman's eyes at her babbling.

"And now he has turned up right as rain, has he?"

Gracie pinched the palm of her hand with her nails, to keep her voice steady. Now was not the time for dramatics.

"Well, yes and no, ma'am. He has turned up, but he's in hospital in East Grinstead. I don't know the extent of his injuries, but he's alive and I want to see him. I've leave due. I've not taken it due to the outbreak but this is important. Please, ma'am, it would only take four days. I can leave really early in the morning and be back on night duty on Thursday night. Please say yes, ma'am."

The officer put her pen on the desk, leaning back in her chair. She folded her arms across her chest. "Does Flight Lieutenant Power know you're coming?"

"Erm, no, ma'am." Gracie didn't want to look at the officer; she wasn't used to lying and it was too embarrassing to explain. But she'd underestimated the woman.

"What is it, Thompson, I can see you are hiding something from me. Now, out with it."

Gracie sighed. Maybe if she told the truth, or at least part of it, she'd get her leave. "Well, you see, ma'am, he has said he doesn't want to see me but I know that isn't true. The nurse must be mistaken. We wanted to get married before the war started, only my parents wouldn't let us. They said that marriages in haste at the start of the war wouldn't last." Gracie bit her tongue. She didn't like lying but couldn't bring herself to tell the officer they weren't married as Charlie thought she'd been unfaithful with Steve. "Now we aren't married and he says he won't see me and I have to know what's going on, ma'am, I just have to."

"Okay. Calm down, Thompson. Don't want you getting yourself in a state, now do we?" She scratched the side of her neck, obviously considering the matter. "I doubt you will be much good to us until you see him for yourself. Your commitment to the service, not taking leave and filling in for missing colleagues, hasn't gone unnoticed."

Gracie's heart fluttered; she was going to say yes.

"You can have the time off but be back here on time for night duty on Thursday night or I'll put you on a charge personally."

"Thank you, ma'am." Gracie wasn't sure how she managed to sound so calm. She wanted to throw herself at the officer and hug her.

The officer stood and moved to the other side of her desk, holding Gracie's gaze. "Gracie, you must prepare yourself for the worst. We have all heard stories of the horrendous injuries that our men endure when their plane crashes. If he has been taken to East Grinstead he may well be badly burnt. It sounds like your pilot may be trying to protect you and spare you some hurt."

Gracie's eyes filled despite her best intentions.

"Yes, ma'am, but he's wrong. It hurts me more not to see him or to think he doesn't want to see me than seeing him burned. Obviously, I don't want him to be wounded, but if we had got married, we would be together for better or worse. In my heart, I'm married to Charlie, I mean Flight Lieutenant Power, and I'm going to be by his side regardless of how he feels. I'm a grown woman and I don't need protecting."

The officer nodded her approval.

"I'm not sure that the young pilot knows quite what he has let himself in for. I only hope that he's smart and grateful for your love. He is a lucky man to be alive and you're very lucky to know where your man is. My fiancé has been missing in action since Dunkirk. I refuse to believe he's dead, but his family are certain we would have heard by now if he was a prisoner of war. I can't bear the thought of losing him and refuse to accept that he's gone. I would know in here if anything had happened to him." She rested her hand over her heart. "Take care, Gracie, and let your young man know exactly what he means to you."

Gracie wanted to say something about the

woman's loss, but the officer had already turned to retake her seat.

"Thank you, ma'am. I will."

"Go now, you don't have a minute to lose. You will have to pack."

"I did that already." Gracie clapped her hand over her mouth. Why had she admitted that?

The officer raised an eyebrow, but didn't comment. Gracie saluted, walked to the door and, once she'd closed it behind her, she ran to her room. She collected her bag, said goodbye to her friends and was down at the station within an hour of meeting her superior. She'd not risk missing the train, not when the timetables were all messed up as it was.

CHAPTER 56

Charlie must be horribly injured; that was the only reason she could think of for him refusing to see her. She knew if she'd been injured she'd want Charlie and nobody else. She tried putting herself in his shoes, but knew that no matter what, she'd never have avoided seeing him. The journey seemed to go on forever.

Finally, she arrived at the hospital and asked to be taken to see Charlie.

"Wait here one moment, miss. The doctor wants a word first."

Gracie was pacing the corridor when the doctor arrived.

"Miss Thompson?"

"Yes, Doctor. Now, please don't tell me I can't see Charlie as I've no intention of leaving your hospital until I do."

"I wouldn't dream of it, miss."

"Oh." Gracie's cheeks burned as she realised she'd been rude to this man who was only trying to help her. "I'm sorry, it's just I've been so worried."

"I wanted a word to prepare you before you see Charles – sorry, Charlie." The doctor rubbed the back of his neck as if he didn't know how to warn her.

"Doctor, I'm stationed on an airbase. I've seen some … casualties. I'm stronger than I look." Gracie took a deep breath, immediately regretting it as the antiseptic hospital smell filled her nostrils.

"As you know, he has been badly wounded, but it isn't his wounds that concern me. Well, not the physical ones, anyway. You see, he has refused to interact with the other men on the ward. He speaks, but only when spoken to and usually never more than a word or two. I believe he's suffering from mental fatigue and, quite frankly, I'm not sure how to reach him. I was hoping that you could help us."

"Me, help you? But I thought you wouldn't let me see him."

"No, Miss Thompson. That wasn't my choice. It was his."

"Oh." She realised with disappointment that she'd almost convinced herself the people at the hospital had stopped it from happening.

"To be frank, I'm not sure how successful you will be. We thought his mother might have been able to convince him but, sadly, that wasn't the case."

"His mother? Charlie's mam has been to see him?"

"Oh, did you not know? I just assumed that she'd have told you, given your engagement..." The doctor shuffled from one foot to the other. He wouldn't look her in the eyes, but seemed transfixed by a space just above her head. He was obviously uncomfortable.

"No, Doctor, Mrs Power doesn't approve of me and never agreed with our engagement. She wanted Charlie to marry her friend's daughter. As he doesn't want to see me, maybe she thinks that opportunity still exists."

"I don't think so, Miss Thompson. It would seem that Mrs Power doesn't believe that anyone would want Charlie. She was quite vocal on that subject."

"What do you mean, nobody would want Charlie? She's his mam, for goodness' sake. Maybe it was just the shock of him being alive? How many times has she been here?"

It was the doctor's turn to look embarrassed. "I don't like to speak ill of people but … well, she has only seen him the once, back when he first arrived here. I'm afraid the visit didn't go too well."

Gracie felt she should defend Charlie's mother. "I'm afraid she lost her husband in the last war. Charlie is her only son – she was obviously distraught."

The doctor didn't seem to agree. "I'm not sure you understood me. We're used to dealing with devastated relatives, especially wives and mothers. This was, well to be frank, Miss Thompson, I'm not sure what did the most damage, the physical wounds inflicted by the enemy or the emotional damage he's since suffered at the hands of his mother."

Gracie bristled. "What did that old bat say?"

He blinked at her reaction.

"Well, she seemed to think that she'd already done her bit for the war effort. She more or less blamed Charlie for the situation he finds himself in. She said something about his father being the same and then she left. In a hurry. We haven't seen her since and I don't believe that her son has heard from her, either."

"Why, the self-centred old cow," Gracie fumed. "Excuse me, Doctor, but I can't believe what I'm hearing. Charlie told me that his mam didn't want him joining up, but to treat him like that. I could kill her."

"I would prefer you directed your energy towards Charlie. He needs you."

"Sorry. Of course, Doctor. Just tell me what you need me to do."

"I need you to reach him and convince him that the treatment we propose is worth giving a go. There are no guarantees, but we're fairly confident that we can improve both the appearance and utility of his hand. We have done all we can for his facial burns and I believe that his looks will improve considerably over the next few months."

"Facial burns?" Gracie swayed.

"I'm so sorry. I forget that you haven't yet seen him. Yes, I gather it took some time before he could get out of the plane. He was lucky to land in the sea. The salt water helped a lot. If he'd landed anywhere else, I doubt he'd have survived."

"You have already operated?"

"Yes we have, and with some success. But

he won't let us work on his hand. He says that I should use my time to help those that matter!"

"He is quite a stubborn man, my fiancé, but I'll see what I can do."

"Thank you, my dear. Now let me take you to him."

CHAPTER 57

They walked down the hospital corridor, Gracie conscious of the noise her shoes were making as the doctor glided along on his rubber heels. The smell of disinfectant clung to everything. They walked by wards, each bed surrounded by a curtain. In some, she saw men lying around in hospital blues chatting to each other. They were all so young. A couple looked at her but some stared past her as if reliving the horrors they'd escaped. Nurses walked past in starched white uniforms, nodding at the doctor. The butterflies in her stomach expanded rapidly with every step she took. When would they reach Charlie? What would he say? *Please don't let him still be angry.*

The doctor stopped at a ward. "Ready?" he asked. Gracie, having lost the ability to speak, nodded. The doctor gave her an encouraging smile before walking into the eight-bedded ward.

They stopped at the last bed, the one near the windows. Gracie stared at the bandage-covered man in the bed. She held her handbag tighter, her knuckles turning white with the effort not to cry out in distress. She forced herself not to flinch at the extent of the burns, particularly on the left side of his face. He looked so vulnerable lying there, his red face in stark contrast to the pristine white sheets.

"Good morning, Power. You have a visitor today, a charming young lady called Gracie."

"Tell her I won't see her. Not now, never."

She flinched at his words, his voice totally different from her Charlie's. It sounded like he'd smoked eighty cigarettes in the last hour. But not just that, there was bitterness there too. After the exhausting trip, the sleepless nights, as well as the hours spent on duty due to being short-staffed, Gracie's patience snapped.

"You can tell me yourself, Charlie Power. I never believed for a second that you were a shirker."

His voice rose to match hers. "Me, a shirker? What are you talking about?"

"That you would leave me to face the world alone? To bring up your child on my own. I've to deal with the gossips: ma'am at my unit, and what about my parents? And then there's your mother. You're a coward, and make no mistake about it."

"A coward, I'm not. Wait, what did you say? A baby? What? You can't be…"

"So, you're calling me a liar?"

"Are you really?" whispered Charlie.

"Yes, I am and don't you go saying that it's not yours. It is bad enough that the father of my baby is a conceited prig, without him turning into a callous snake who denies his own child."

"But…"

"But what? What excuse are you going to come up with now? I'll tell you one thing, Charlie Power, you will not hear the end of this. If you think I'm going to let you wallow there in self-pity while I bring our child up on my own, you have another think coming."

Behind her someone started clapping, then the entire room followed suit.

"Hey, grumpy. Need a lesson or two in the birds and the bees, do you?" shouted one of the bedbound patients.

Gracie turned her sternest face to the man who had shouted at her. "That's enough of that type of talk, thank you very much. If you don't mind, this is a private conversation."

"Don't mind at all, love. It's better than the usual entertainment we get down here."

It was only then that Gracie realised that in her anger, she hadn't given a thought to the other patients on the ward or to the nurses and doctors attending them. Her cheeks flamed, and to make it worse there was a male orderly coming straight towards her. She decided her best defence was a good offence. "Now, don't you go telling me I can't be here because I'm not going anywhere." Gracie stood facing the orderly with her hands on her hips.

"Miss, I wouldn't dream of telling you to go anywhere. I'm here to applaud you. Charlie Power, you're a lucky son of a gun and if you don't grab your chance to wed this woman now, you will have to fight off a crowd of us with Dr Stevens at the top of the line."

He turned back to Gracie. "I was simply going to suggest that you two might want to continue this conversation somewhere more private."

"Well, I would but he said he wouldn't see or speak to me so I'd no choice but to speak to him out here on the ward."

The orderly winked at Gracie before saying, "Well, I'm guessing he didn't want to see you as he fears you won't love him now that you've seen him. He must think you're rather vain and would prefer to be seen with a more pleasant-looking fellow."

"Who are you calling vain? My Gracie isn't like that. She's the best girl in the world," Charlie protested.

"Well, if you think that why did you refuse to see me?" demanded Gracie.

Charlie looked away. "You know why. I had my reasons."

"What reasons? If you're talking about the dance, you don't know the real story. You never gave me a chance to explain. So, why can't you get dressed now so we can go somewhere and talk? Properly. You can tell me why this ring on my finger means nothing. Why you don't love me."

"I love you. I've always loved you. But it isn't that simple."

"Yes, Charlie, it is. Now, get dressed and I'll wait for you outside in the grounds. Just don't run out on me."

"Gracie, I've a broken leg. I can't run anywhere, even if I wanted to."

"Oh, I didn't realise. Do you need a hand to put some clothes on?"

"I thought it was taking his clothes off you were interested in," shouted one patient.

Gracie's face flamed, but before she could say anything Charlie spoke up.

"Make another crack like that, mate, and the doctors will replace your head, never mind your fingers."

"Keep your hair on, lad, what's left of it. I was only having a laugh."

"I don't find it funny when it is my fiancée that's the butt of your jokes."

"You have decided you're going to marry her after all, then?"

Gracie turned on her heel and walked out of the ward, holding her head high as if their comments hadn't embarrassed her. What had she been thinking of? If her mam knew, she'd kill her.

She paced up and down the terrace until, finally, she saw Charlie coming. The same male orderly who had congratulated her earlier was pushing his wheelchair. She went to greet them, thanked the orderly, but told him she could push the chair. He left. She pushed

Charlie towards a table overlooking the gardens where they could sit and talk in private.

Charlie didn't respond when Gracie parked the chair at the table and refused to look at her.

Gracie said, "Charlie, I deserve better than this. I haven't got all day. My train leaves in an hour." She decided to put him under pressure. She didn't want him to push her away again.

Charlie remained silent, his face set in a stubborn mask.

The sound of piano music wafted behind them.

"Is that a nurse?" she asked, thinking it might be best to pretend they were just having a chat.

"No, it's one of our lads. He used to play in one of those dance bands. He's trying to get his speed up again, but it's difficult using his toes instead of his fingers."

"You mean he's playing that with his feet?"

"No, he's playing with his hands, but the

doctors had to use some of his toes to grow fingers." He sounded less bitter, if anything a little amused. But then his next words changed the tone. "You would be amazed at all the different bits and pieces they use to put us back together."

An uncomfortable silence grew between them.

"Charlie, please talk to me."

"What, about him?"

"Who?"

"That guy I saw you with at the dance. You know, the one who…"

"That guy's name is Steve Menton, and if you had hung around long enough, you would have been able to thank him for saving your fiancée. Some pilot put alcohol in my lemonade, you know I don't drink, and tried to take advantage of me, but thankfully Steve and Pat were there to save me. There is and was nothing between me and Steve. We're just friends. I love you, Charlie Power. I thought you loved me, too."

"Oh, Gracie, I love you, I've always loved you, but I can't marry you."

"Why? Have you married someone else? Did a nurse jump on you and force you into a church?"

"No, of course not. Stop being silly."

"You have a nerve, telling me off."

"Gracie, you don't understand…"

Gracie finally exploded. The tension that had been building up ever since she'd discovered he was alive bubbled over.

"You're right, I don't understand," she shouted. "There has been no one else for me since we first met in that cinema all those years ago, and I thought you felt the same way. You're going to have to explain it to me in very simple terms, so there are no misunderstandings. I'm not leaving here until everything is clear."

When Charlie stayed silent, she continued but lowered her voice. "You really hurt me, you know. You should have had more faith in me, in us."

He wouldn't look at her, the right-hand

side of his face turning as red as the burnt part. He kept swallowing. She waited for him to answer. Would he? She was starting to lose patience when he sighed deeply before saying, "Yes, I know, and I'm sorry. I was so jealous when I saw that guy talking to you. It's obvious that he has feelings for you."

"Steve's feelings are nothing to do with me. I've never led him on. He knows that there's only one man for me, YOU!"

His eyes burned with anger for a second but it was gone just as fast as it arrived, replaced by guilt.

"But, Gracie, I didn't know that. I just saw the way he looked at you, and then when I heard what you were talking about, I…"

"You put two and two together and came up with ten. How could you? After everything we have been to each other?"

CHAPTER 58

"Gracie, I'm sorry. I don't know what got into me. Everything was going wrong. All my friends were dying, I couldn't get to see you and when I finally got there, he was by your side. I was overcome with jealousy. I did realise I was wrong and that you wouldn't behave like that. I was going to come and see you to apologise and try to make it up…"

He stared at her, begging her to understand, but he knew it was a lot for her to take in.

"Why didn't you?" asked Gracie.

So there was hope for him. His heart swelled; he thought it was going to beat right out of his chest. He smiled before saying, "I got on the wrong side of a German!" He took a deep breath. It was now or never. He had to make her see she meant the world to him.

"It was my own stupid fault. I wasn't paying attention and let him get behind me. You never let the enemy get behind you. But I was lucky. I bailed and landed in the sea. Some fishermen picked me up and here I am."

"I don't understand. If you'd realised that you were wrong about us, why did you not let me know you were all right? Why did you tell the staff you didn't want to see me?"

She was glaring at him. Although she'd every right to be angry, he needed her to be more understanding. He tried again.

"That had nothing to do with you or that dance." He saw her raise her eyebrows. She didn't believe him. He jabbered, "You know that I've a tough time with my mother. Well, she feels that my father burdened her when he came back from the war. He died of his wounds, but it wasn't for some time after the war. He was gassed and was never the same again. He used to have awful nightmares, not just when he was asleep. He often took a funny turn during the day, sometimes in front of the neighbours. They were very nice about it, but Mother was ashamed. I know it was hard for her. She thinks she did her best, but he died knowing that she wished he'd never come home."

Gracie's deep intake of breath showed she was as shocked as he expected her to be. "No, Charlie, she couldn't have meant that."

"Yes, she did. Not everyone is like you or your family, Gracie."

"But why did she marry him if she didn't love him?" she said.

"Well, that's the thing. She says she loved him and that they were very happy before he went off to war. So, that got me thinking that with me like this, you would end up hating me and wishing I'd died rather than being a burden on you…"

He stopped to draw a breath, but before he could continue she began to berate him.

"Charlie Power, of all the things you could say to me. Not only did you let yourself down thinking like that, but you let me down, too. You aren't and never will be a burden on me. You aren't even that badly injured."

Charlie would have raised his eyebrow at that if he had one. He said nothing as she was in full stride.

"Seriously, Charlie, I know you're burned and it must have hurt a lot. It probably still does, but you're not the worst off. There are men in this hospital who've lost limbs, who've lost their sight. They're not feeling sorry for themselves."

He saw Gracie was having difficulty keeping her voice down. He tried a softer tone to get her to understand, or at least to stop shouting.

"I don't feel sorry for myself – I feel sorry for us. I can't be the husband I should have been. How am I going to provide for my family with my hand like this?"

He ripped off the bandage.

He heard her gasp of breath as she saw

the extent of the damage. He wouldn't have blamed her if she'd looked away. Not many people wanted to see a hand burned to the bone. She didn't avert her gaze but reached out to touch him, hesitantly, as if afraid she'd hurt him. After a moment or two, she looked up at his face. He saw the pity in her eyes before it was quickly replaced by anger.

"You still have your left hand and you will just have to learn how to do things one-handed. Jessie would give anything for Pat to come back, one hand or no hand. But he can't. He's dead. You're still alive."

Instinctively, Charlie ducked slightly. Gracie looked like she was going to hit him. Wisely, he decided not to say anything but to let her speak.

"I don't want to hurt you, but I only want you. I don't care about having fancy things and all that. It means nothing if I don't have you to share it with. I can work and support both of us until you're fully recovered, and then I'm sure that there are things you can do.

That doctor seems to think he can help, but said you wouldn't let him."

"You can't work. Well, not for long. Aren't you forgetting about the baby?"

"Oh, that." She looked sheepish. She picked a flower and studied it closely.

"What do you mean, 'Oh, that'?" He tried but failed to keep his tone patient.

"I'm not pregnant, Charlie. Not yet, anyway. I only said that to shock you and get your attention."

He looked at her, shocked to the core. His Gracie didn't tell lies. Or did she?

"Don't look at me like that. I was desperate to see you and you wouldn't let me into the ward, so I had to think of something. I couldn't think of anything better. It worked, didn't it? Anyway, if I'd been pregnant after our weekend together, I should be the size of a whale by now. Get the doctor to check your powers of observation." She clamped her hands over her mouth as if she regretted the harsh words – no matter how true.

Charlie was dazed and totally confused.

He also felt sad at the loss of the baby. His baby. The baby that never existed. His silence must have worried Gracie as she kept talking.

"I want your baby, Charlie, but not now. We're going to get married as soon as we can. Perhaps there's a priest here who will do it. I'm sure we can get a special licence."

Was she trying to kill him? First a baby, then no baby, and now she was talking about getting married. Today?

"Get married? Now? In a hospital? But, what about your parents? And my mother."

"Yes, now. What do you want to wait for? I nearly lost you once, and I'll not let that happen again. I don't give a hoot about what your mother thinks and I know that Mam and Dad will understand. They don't need big gestures to show their love, and neither do we. We just need to be together, and we can't do that unless they marry us. Of course, I wish Penny, Jessie and Mavis could be here, but they will understand."

Charlie put his good arm around her and

gently kissed her. "Can you stop talking, just for a few seconds?"

"All right … but only if you do that again," she said.

"With pleasure." Once again, he kissed her.

They separated reluctantly. He tried to get out of his chair to get down on one knee, but the cast got in the way.

"What are you trying to do? Kill yourself?" she said.

"No, darling, I'm trying to ask you to marry me again. Properly, but it seems this cast of mine won't play ball."

Gracie threw her arms around his neck, nearly knocking him and the wheelchair over. He settled her on his lap, not caring that she was hurting his leg.

They kissed and cuddled for a while.

"You have lost a lot of weight, Gracie. Were you ill?"

"Desperately." She glanced shyly at him under her lashes. "I was dying from a lack of love."

"Never that, my darling. I never stopped loving you." He kissed her again.

"So, how long will you have to stay here at the hospital?" she asked.

"Well, I don't really know. The doctor wanted to do some more work, but I kept putting him off. I wasn't sure whether it was worth it."

"Of course it is. Anything that can help is worth trying, isn't it?"

Charlie paused, not sure whether he should tell her.

"What is it? What are you not telling me?" she asked, shivering.

"He said that if they can repair my hand enough I might fly again." His heart flipped at the look of naked fear in her eyes.

She looked away. "But you wouldn't want to do that, would you?" She looked back into his eyes. "That's a stupid question, as I can see you would. Honestly, haven't you done enough?"

"You haven't been up there. It is an amazing feeling. Don't get me wrong, I don't like killing other people and I never want to go on a bombing raid, but flying is a wonderful experience. It is so peaceful and…"

"Yes, it looks like it." Gracie was angry again. "I give up. I'll never understand that side of you. You're keeping both feet on the ground and that's an order."

"Yes, ma'am." He gave in for now, hoping that in time she'd change her mind. "On one condition."

"Name it." She grinned.

"Can you kiss me again and tell me all about these babies we're going to have?"

"With pleasure." They kissed and talked for a long time, all the time holding each other, never wanting to let go.

CHAPTER 59

Gracie pushed Charlie's chair back to the hospital to find out who they needed to speak to about getting married. A special licence took a little time to organise, although Dr McIndoe managed to pull some strings and the papers arrived within a few hours.

Gracie stayed in the nurse's quarters the first night, and the next morning one of them very kindly lent her a dress as she'd nothing suitable. The same nurse was her bridesmaid, and the doctor who had applauded her that first day was the best man.

The registrar agreed to marry them in the grounds of the hospital to allow the other, less mobile patients to attend. Dr McIndoe and his staff donated beer and other alcoholic drinks. The hospital kitchens cooked a wedding breakfast including luxuries unheard of in wartime London, such as baked ham, boiled eggs and a real wedding cake.

Gracie smiled all day, moving amongst the patients and making sure they all felt part of her special day. She listened to their jokes and told some of her own. A couple of patients appeared to be finding the day difficult, and she was quick to reassure them that love would find a way to make them heal. When one man told her his wife had left him because losing his leg meant he wouldn't be able to dance, she'd suggested that he take dancing lessons when his false leg was attached. "Show her what she's missing. You never know, she may come back to you, although there's many a wonderful girl out there who wouldn't have left you."

Every so often her eyes sought those of her husband. *Her husband.* Just saying the words made her shiver. She was so happy, and although she enjoyed the day, she couldn't wait until they were alone later.

Nobody would part them again.

She told Charlie to pinch her a couple of times to make sure she wasn't dreaming. He kissed her instead. When dusk came, they were surprised but pleased to be offered a private room in the hospital.

"Can't have it for more than one night, but I guess that it is better than nothing," said the kindly doctor.

"Thank you so much for everything." Gracie kissed the man on his cheek.

"No, thank you, my dear. If only all the wives and girlfriends were as brave as you are. I've lost count of the number that run screaming for the hills once they see the reality of the injuries aircrew receive."

"Really?" Gracie was surprised.

"Not everyone is as brave as you are, Mrs Power. Or, if you will forgive me, as stubborn."

"Shh, don't let my husband hear you

saying that. He may want a divorce." She
laughed.

"I won't. She's stubborn, but that's
nothing compared to her temper." Charlie
touched her face. "If they sent Gracie in one
of her tempers into Hitler's lair, he'd come
out begging for peace."

"Oh, you." Gracie pretended to be upset,
but inside she was spinning with happiness.
His wife. Mrs Gracie Power.

They were so enthralled with each other,
the doctor had to cough to get their attention.

"I hope you both will be happy together."

"We will, sir. You can bet on it." Gracie
answered. For both of them.

CHAPTER 60
LONDON

Penny put down the letter she'd received from Gracie, welling up with joy at hearing that Charlie was alive and her friend had got her happy ending.

She wished she'd been at the wedding, but she completely understood why they had gone ahead. With this war, nobody knew what tomorrow would bring. "Live for today" was the motto most people had taken to heart.

She read through the rest of Gracie's letter, shocked to hear of the extent of Charlie's injuries. Gracie hoped that the surgeon could restore some movement to his hand. He'd also try to repair the damage done to his face.

Penny ran down to the kitchen to tell Cook about the wedding.

"Oh, poor Gracie. Her mam must be so upset at missing her daughter's big day. You'd think they could've waited for her parents to get down to East Grinstead," muttered Cook, shaking her head.

"Come on, Cook, you know the powers that be have said we shouldn't travel. I think it's wonderful they are finally married after everything Gracie and Charlie have been through."

"Yes, Miss Penny, it is, but they will have a tough life ahead of them. It sounds like his injuries may stop him finding work. I wonder what they will live on."

"Cook, that's enough of that talk. You should be dancing around the kitchen. Gracie got to have her happy-ever-after ending. Charlie is alive." Penny whirled about the kitchen, making Cook laugh.

"Okay, Miss Penny, you win. Now, what should I give them as a wedding present?

With the war on, it's not like I can go into a shop and just buy anything I fancy."

"You're determined to be miserable today. I'm sure they would love some of those tins you have stored away. Maybe some tea or sugar, perhaps? I'm going to go see Gracie's mum later. I can take your present over. See you later, Cook."

She left Cook wiping what looked like a tear from her eye. She decided Cook might be more of a romantic than she let on.

PENNY HADN'T TOLD her family she was going to visit Gracie's mother. She also intended stopping by the orphanage to check on the few children who were still in residence. Despite trying to enter the house quietly, her aunt called for her as soon as she stepped into the hall.

"Penelope, is that you? Come in here, please."

"Coming, Aunt Louise." Penny threw a desperate glance into the mirror hanging in the hall. Impatiently, she pushed at the loose strands of black hair. Her hair was growing long again, but was at a difficult-to-manage stage. Holding her breath, she walked into the library.

"Yes, Aunt Louise?" Penny looked towards her aunt perched on the sofa opposite the window, a book on the table beside her. It amused her, the way Louise tried to give off the impression she was in the library to read. She couldn't read a comic strip. Then Penny spotted a man standing at the window. He looked familiar. *Oh, no.*

"Hello, David." Penny wished she'd taken more care of her appearance. Her aunt clearly thought so, too.

Louise frowned. "Look at the state of you. What have you been doing? There wasn't a raid today, was there?"

"No, Aunt Louise. I'm sorry. I came home to get changed, but then you called me in here." She looked at her aunt's angry face. "Erm, I was playing."

"Playing?" Her aunt looked confused. "With whom?"

"I called in to the shelter to see the children. There aren't many left now, what with them being evacuated, and…"

"Oh, that's enough, Penny. I'm sure David doesn't want to hear all about those wretched children of yours."

David met Penny's gaze and winked before turning his attention to her aunt.

"Louise, I would love a cup of tea. Do you think that would be possible?" he said.

"But of course, David. I don't know where my manners are today. I should have rung for tea when you arrived."

"I'll get it." Penny was desperate to leave the room.

"Penelope, sit down. I'm sure Cook or Perkins can manage a tea tray between them."

"But, Aunt Louise, they're exhausted. With all the raids lately, they haven't been getting much sleep, and now that all the other servants have…"

"Penelope." Her aunt used what Penny called her servants' voice.

"Yes, Aunt Louise. Sorry." Penny sat down, looking helplessly at David. He seemed intent on staring out the window at the garden.

"I see you have been digging for victory, Louise. How wonderful."

"Why thank you, David. We all have to do our bit, you know. The queen turned her rose gardens over to growing onions, did you know that?"

Penny glared at her aunt, who was preening up at David. *Do our bit.* What rubbish. Maybe she should tell David how much grief she gave poor old Bert for digging up her rose bushes. Not to mention how annoyed she was when she found out Penny had been helping him.

Penny sighed. She'd learnt to pick her battles with her aunt.

She occupied herself by opening the door for Cook, taking the tray as soon as she could. She smiled apologetically at the elderly woman. She looked so old and exhausted.

"At last. Penelope, please serve."

"Yes, Aunt Louise." Penny served, all the time wondering how much longer the war would have to last before her aunt woke up to the changing times.

"How did you get on with the job application, Penny?" asked David, smiling at her.

His smile set her heart racing. "Fine, thank you. I start next month."

"The War Office must be quite desperate," said Louise.

Despite the warmth of the sun's rays coming through the window, the atmosphere in the room was chilly.

When neither David nor Penny commented, her aunt sighed. "I guess that there aren't many people around who can speak both French and English fluently."

David put his cup down and walked over to the window. Once out of her aunt's line of vision, he winked at Penny. "You have done a wonderful job, Louise. Anyone interviewing

Penny would know she comes from a family with position."

He had her aunt eating from his hand.

"Thank you, David." Her china cup clinked off the saucer in her hand. "People don't realise how hard it was to turn a country girl into a lady. Although by the look of my niece today, one would find it hard to believe she was a member of the gentry."

"Nonsense, my dear Louise. It's quite the fashion now for young ladies to do something for the war effort. Didn't you hear that Princess Elizabeth has supposedly told the queen that she wants to join up when she finishes school?"

Louise looked horrified. "Surely the queen won't allow that? The princess could mix with anyone."

"The queen was all for it. She didn't leave the castle when asked to. She wants her family to experience what everyone else has to, and that includes the bombing raids. Speaking of which, I must press on. It's such a beautiful day and we all know what that means."

Penny nodded, but her aunt looked blankly at them both. Penny explained. "The bombers could be back tonight. There won't be any cloud cover to protect us." Penny turned to David. "Let me see you to the door."

"Louise, always a pleasure. Thank you for tea. I'll see you again soon."

David followed Penny out of the room. "Don't take too much notice of your aunt. She's a frightful snob, but underneath I don't think she means any harm."

Penny snorted, causing him to laugh. "Sorry. That wasn't ladylike."

"Good luck with the new job, Penny. Look after yourself."

"You too, David."

He leaned forward to kiss her on the cheek. Closing the door behind him, she was grateful for the support of the wood at her back. Her legs were wobbling as she touched her cheek where his lips had been.

EPILOGUE
EAST GRINSTEAD

Gracie looked at the sleeping form beside her. She still couldn't quite believe they were married. Despite her earlier protestations about wanting to do her bit for the war, she'd realised her place was by her husband's side. She'd given the service one hundred per cent when a member but Charlie needed her now.

She didn't regret resigning from the WAAF and transferring her services to the hospital. Dr McIndoe had helped smooth over any rough feathers her actions could have caused. She was thankful her CO had been understanding. The hospital needed volunteers so she was still doing war work, but her desire to serve her country was outweighed by her need to support Charlie.

Gracie's feet hurt. Matron had assigned her to another ward so she wasn't nursing Charlie, but she got to see him every day.

The work was hard; everything had to be spick and span. She spent the day making beds, feeding patients, warming bedpans and emptying them when used. Her past training working in the big house came in useful. She already understood the need for cleanliness. The risk of infection to any patient was dangerous, but particularly those treated for burns. She particularly hated having to wash the bandages by hand. They would be sterilised afterwards. The smell of burnt flesh got into her nostrils and no amount of fresh air removed it.

Thankfully, she didn't have to dress the wounds. Only properly qualified nurses did that, but she helped with the saline baths. Seeing the wounds other pilots had suffered helped her put Charlie's injuries into perspective. Yes, he'd suffered facial burns and his poor hand would never fully recover, but some men had lost their entire face. Others had to have arms or legs amputated, leaving them crippled for life. Charlie had been so lucky, really.

She loved the little hospital. It had grown in size since Dr McIndoe had worked there, but it kept a college hospital atmosphere. The demand for treatment facilities for burned aircrew increased. She was lucky to get lodgings in the town nearby.

"Hello, darling, how are you feeling today?" she asked Charlie after gently kissing his forehead. She sighed as she got to rest her feet on the chair by the bed. She worried about how Charlie was going to react following his first operation on his hand. She didn't want to think about his dream of returning to flying but she knew he hoped not to be crippled for life.

Dr McIndoe had performed the surgery and the bandages were due to come off the following day. Matron had arranged for Gracie to be present when this happened.

"Gracie, is that you?" asked Charlie groggily.

"Of course it's me. There aren't any other nurses who kiss you, are there?" Gracie joked.

"Oh, don't make me laugh, Gracie, it hurts."

Gracie took Charlie's good hand in hers and stroked it. "Go back to sleep, my darling."

"Will you read to me, Gracie, please? It helps to dull the pain."

Gracie picked up a copy of *Great Expectations* and started reading from where she'd left off last time. When Charlie was asleep, she went around to each of the men in the other beds in the room. She refilled water bottles, fetched pints of beer and fixed pillows, making sure she spent a little time with each patient. Dr McIndoe encouraged all hospital staff to treat the men as ordinarily as possible.

Unlike other hospitals, the men wore their

own clothes or their uniforms. They didn't have to wear the convalescent blues usually worn by injured air personnel. The patients could come and go as they pleased. He encouraged the men to go out in public to the nearby town of East Grinstead. The townspeople, used to seeing Dr McIndoe's guinea pigs, didn't stare. This gave the men a chance to recover from the psychological impact of their wounds.

She lost count of the number of times the men had confided to her that their girlfriends had broken things off once they saw them. Gracie could have cheerfully put those selfish, vain women up against a wall and shot them. After all they had been through, the aircrews deserved better.

As she cycled back to her digs, she prayed that the results of Charlie's latest operation would be good. The doctor had promised that Charlie could soon live in lodgings with Gracie. He'd go back to the hospital as and when needed. They could finally start their married life together properly. She sighed at the thought of waking up next to her husband every day. Her husband.

SHE PARKED her bicycle at the side of the small bungalow and walked into the house. The smell of boiled cabbage greeted her just as it did every day. Things were heavily rationed, but her landlady could learn a few tricks from Cook. Still, it was little enough to moan about, given what was happening elsewhere in the world. Stan would probably dive into a plate of boiled cabbage if he'd the chance. Mam had copied his postcards word for word in her letters to Gracie.

"There you are. Post came this morning. It's from your mum."

"Thank you, Mrs Brown." The secret service should snap up her landlady; she missed nothing. Gracie took the letter up to her room to read in privacy. If she took the letter into the back room, Mrs Brown would want to know every word.

Sighing with relief as she removed her shoes, she lay on the bed, ripping the envelope open.

DEAR GRACIE,

I never thought I'd have to write a letter like this. I wish I could visit in person but you know that's not allowed. There's no easy way to say this, darling, but Penny is in hospital. She's gravely ill. I know you have your own worries with Charlie (I hope his treatment is going well). but I had to tell you.

GRACIE RUBBED the tears from her eyes as the words danced across the page.

PENNY WAS INJURED in a bomb attack. She'd have been fine but two young girls were trapped under the rubble of their home and ...

well, you know what Penny is like. The building collapsed and she was buried alive. They got her out and she's in the hospital. That's all I know for now. The story has been in the London papers but I'm not sure if you've already heard.

Find a phone and ring the house as soon as you can. Cook will know the most up-to-date news.

Be safe, my darling girl. If I got my hands on Hitler, I'd murder him myself. Slowly.

All my love,
Mam

GRACIE RUSHED to put her shoes on her feet, grabbed her purse and ran down the stairs. Ignoring Mrs Brown's call, she ran out the door and down the street to the nearest payphone. Picking up the receiver, she prayed she'd get a line. The telephone rang and rang but there was no answer. She put the receiver back in place. *Darn it, Penny, why didn't you stay out of it?* But then that wasn't her friend's nature.

She stared out to sea, wishing she could walk on the beach but that was forbidden. Even if she dared to break the rules, the barriers prevented her. She gave it fifteen minutes before she tried the number again.

"Hamilton residence."

Never had she been so glad to hear Perkins' voice. The line wasn't very clear. She sensed he was struggling to hear her. She shouted into the receiver.

"Mr Perkins, it's me, Gracie. Please tell me about Penny. Is she…" She couldn't make herself say the word "dead".

"Miss Penelope remains in the hospital. I've told you people before. We have no comment."

"No, no, Mr Perkins. Wait, it's me. Gracie."

"What did you say? Wait, Thompson, is that you?"

"Yes, it's me. How is Penny?"

"She's lucky to be alive." *Beep beep beep.* Gracie fought the urge to scream. She'd been cut off.

But Penny was alive. For now.

I HOPE you enjoyed the story of Gracie and her friends. Find out what happens to Penny and the girls in the next book, Penny's Secret Mission.

ACKNOWLEDGMENTS

This book wouldn't have been possible without the help of so many people. Thanks to Shaela for my fantastic covers. Shaela is a gifted artist who makes my characters come to life.

My two Victorias - I have an amazing editor - Vicky and a wonderful proofreader, Vicki. But sometimes errors slip through. I am very grateful to the ladies from my readers group who give me feedback on every book. They support my work by sharing online. Please join my Facebook group for readers of Historical fiction. Come join us for games, prizes, exclusive content, and first looks at my latest releases. Rachel's readers group

Last, but by no means least, huge thanks and love to my husband and my three children. And Gracie, our dog.

ALSO BY RACHEL WESSON

WWII Irish Stand Alone

Stolen from her Mother

Orphans of Hope House

Home for unloved Orphans (Orphans of Hope House 1)

Baby on the Doorstep (Orphans of Hope House 2)

Hearts at War (WWII)

When's Mummy Coming

Revenge for my Father (coming Summer 2022)

Hearts on the Rails

Orphan Train Escape

Orphan Train Trials

Orphan Train Christmas

Orphan Train Tragedy

Orphan Train Strike

Orphan Train Disaster

Trail of Hearts - Oregon Trail Series

Oregon Bound (book 1)

Oregon Dreams (book 2)

Oregon Destiny (book 3)

Oregon Discovery (book 4)

Oregon Disaster (book 5)

12 Days of Christmas - co -authored series.

The Maid - book 8

Clover Springs Mail Order Brides

Katie (Book 1)

Mary (Book 2)

Sorcha (Book 3)

Emer (Book 4)

Laura (Book 5)

Ellen (Book 6)

Thanksgiving in Clover Springs (book 7)

Christmas in Clover Springs (book8)

Erin (Book 9)

Eleanor (book 10)

Cathy (book 11)

Mrs. Grey

Clover Springs East

New York Bound (book 1)

New York Storm (book 2)

New York Hope (book 3)

Printed in Great Britain
by Amazon